"I want...to... love my husband."

Berry spaced the words to give them emphasis, to be sure he understood.

"Then love him." Simon's voice was light as if he was laughing inside. "There's no law that says you can't."

"I want to be sure that he loves me," she said stubbornly.

He laughed so uninhibitedly that she drew back.

"The first thing you've got to learn about men in this country is that they can woo a woman with soft words if that's what she wants to hear. Never believe soft words, Berry. Pay a mind to what a man does."

"I like soft words," she said angrily.

He laughed and she wanted to hit him. She balled her fist and prepared to swing. Before she could move he was kissing her again with a violence that stunned her. She couldn't tell if he was kissing her or trying to hurt her. After an instant his lips softened and her resistance vanished.

They drew apart slowly. "You may like soft words but you like hard kisses better," he said with a deep chuckle...

Later Berry's mind was boiling with emotions. One thought stood out above all the others. *She would make him love her and she would make him say it!*

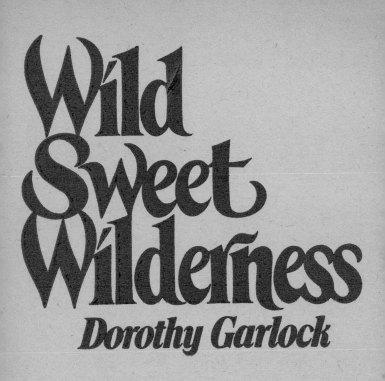

Wild Sweet Wilderness

Dorothy Garlock

POPULAR LIBRARY

An Imprint of Warner Books, Inc.

A Warner Communications Company

POPULAR LIBRARY EDITION

Popular Library books are published by
Warner Books, Inc.
666 Fifth Avenue
New York, N.Y. 10103

A Warner Communications Company

Printed in the United States of America

First Printing: May, 1985

10 9 8 7 6 5 4 3 2 1

This book is for
Mark Lemon
For all the reasons he knows—

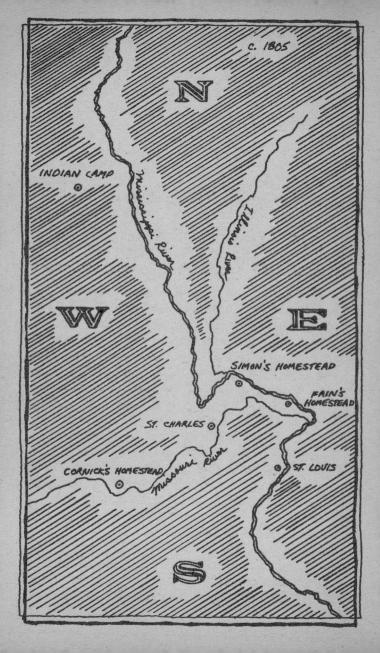

Chapter One

The trail had been long, endlessly winding through a tunnel of leafy trees that reached enormous heights. The train of wagons, carts, and men on horseback, with women and children trudging beside the wagons, came out of the forest and stopped on the ridge overlooking the river. Eyes fastened with fascination on the gap in the forest beyond the wide Mississippi, through which flowed the muddy Missouri River. Every man, woman, and child on the wagon train had heard about the expedition led by Captains Meriwether Lewis and William Clark, which had set out in the spring of 1804, just a year ago, to explore the vast continent west of the Mississippi. The company of thirty-two men had descended the Missouri in a flotilla and nothing had been heard from them yet.

Berry Rose Warfield leaned on the back of the weary oxen that pulled the light wagon and glanced over her shoulder to see if Rachel was awake. Her eyes softened tenderly as they rested for a moment on the sleeping face, before she turned to rap the ox smartly on the rump with a stick and put the beast into motion to follow the wagon driven by the Negro man her father had purchased before leaving home.

Somewhere beyond the frontier settlement of Saint Louis, through thick forest stretching dark and silent, would be her future home. She and Rachel had been reluctant to leave the snug cabin in Ohio. They had argued and pleaded with Berry's father and cajoled to no avail. Asa Warfield had been determined to join the caravan of families going west to the country beyond the great river. He had been fired up by the promise of five hundred acres of good forest land that abounded in game and was rich enough to grow a tobacco crop. It was time for Asa to move on because his whoring and drinking had earned him the contempt of all his neighbors. He had unleashed his explosive temper once too often and was no longer welcome to spend his evenings in the local tavern.

Berry slowed her steps and let the wagon catch up with her so she could look once again at the pale face of the light-haired woman lying on the feather bed. Rachel was flushed with heat and her hands cradled her large, protruding stomach. This was her third pregnancy since Asa had brought her home to the Ohio cabin after buying her bond from the tavern owner. He had told his eight-year-old daughter, Berry, that he had married the girl and insisted that she call her "Ma" although there was less than eight years' difference in their ages. Love had grown between the two, and now, ten years later, they were as close as sisters.

"How do you feel?"

Pale and pretty, with light blond hair that framed a face dominated by haunted blue eyes, Rachel lay unmoving. She had been ill throughout most of the journey. "Better." She smiled at Berry with affection.

"Mr. Benson wants to push on until we get to the place where we'll be ferried across the river before we stop for the night. He thinks we can get there before dark." Berry spoke quietly, but the sparkle of excitement shone in her gray-green eyes.

"Glory! Won't it be grand to be put once again?"

Berry wiped the sweat from her face with the end of her apron and laughed with delight. "When we're put, we'll have to live in the wagons until we get a cabin built."

"At least we won't be moving," Rachel said with a grimace.

Berry's eyes searched Rachel's face anxiously for signs of pain. "We'll make camp soon and you can get out and walk a spell. That ought to make your back feel better. You're not going to lose this little 'un like you did the other two," she said with determination.

Rachel watched the slim girl move up to the ox and give the beast a friendly pat on the back. Berry grows more beautiful every day, she thought. I couldn't love her more if she was my own. How long will it be before Asa works out a scheme to sell her to the highest bidder? He'll separate us if he can. I know he will! I'll kill him first! Her heart beat wildly at the thought of Berry's being subjected to the brutality Rachel had suffered at Asa's hands.

Since Berry had grown to womanhood their roles

had changed. She now protected Rachel. Asa no longer dared to cuff her or throw her down behind the curtain and satisfy himself on her body as he once had done. Long ago she had moved into the loft to sleep beside Berry, and Asa spent more and more of his time at the tavern. Rachel was pregnant now because he had caught her in the cabin alone and forced her to submit to him. She had been sick at heart when she discovered she was going to have his child. Now she was resigned to it. Within her was a little life. If it lived, she would love it.

Fortunately, Berry had inherited none of her father's personal characteristics, except for his midnight-black hair. And although she wore hers braided and swirled in a coronet on top of her head, she couldn't conceal its rich luster. It sparkled in the sunlight as if embedded with a thousand stars. Small wisps of curls broke free and framed a face of high sculptured cheekbones, a complexion like alabaster, and a full, soft mouth that was quick to smile. Her gray-green eyes gazed frankly and inquiringly from beneath curving dark brows, but it wasn't her facial beauty and long supple body that made her striking. It was her bearing. He head rode on her slim neck proudly, as if she were a princess. She was slender to the point of appearing fragile, but the set of her chin, the candor in her dark-lashed eyes, and her carriage all combined to show strength of character.

Rachel watched the slim body that was undeniably shapely beneath the worn dress. Berry is totally unaware of the eyes that follow her, she thought with a stab of fear. Asa is plotting something. I've seen him watching her, him and that crowd of no-

goods he rides with. I'll not let him ruin her life.
I'll not!

The wagon train reached the outskirts of Cahokia and their camping area at dusk. The town was one of the three old French towns that George Rogers Clark and his frontier militia had wrested from the English back in 1778. The English had inherited the towns after the French and Indian wars and used them as a base for Indian raids south into Kentucky. Now, Cahokia was used as a trading center and a ferrying port for settlers crossing the Mississippi to Saint Louis, the gateway to the West.

The slave, Israel, unhitched and hobbled the team and came back for the ox. Berry helped Rachel to get down from the wagon, then began to build a cookfire. The bugs and mosquitoes swarmed about her face and she waved them away impatiently. A welcome gust of wind from the river whipped a curl across her temple and billowed her skirts, giving momentary relief from the insects.

With slow patience Berry squatted beside the stones left by a previous camper and arranged dry leaves as tinder. On top of this she spread rotted, crumbly pulp from the center of an old, weathered log. She took a scant handful of gunpowder from a leather bag, closed the neck carefully against the damp air, then squatted down and poured the gunpowder over the rotted pulp, being careful to leave a trail. She took a flint from her pocket and struck expertly, igniting the powder. The blaze raced across to the leaves and punk. The fire caught. Berry hunched her shoulders and nursed the tiny blaze, feeding it handfuls of leaves, then twigs. Smoke billowed up and she squinted her eyes against it. Soon she heard the crackling of the burning twigs. When the blaze was steady she laid larger pieces of wood over them, building them into a pyramid so there was room for a draft underneath.

While Rachel sliced cold cornmeal mush to fry, Berry fried the last of the venison that Mr. Benson, the organizer and leader of the train, had given them from his kill the day before.

"Have you seen Asa since nooning?" Rachel stood aside so Berry could pour fat from the skillet onto a flatiron grill.

"No. But he'll show up for his vittles. He's riding ahead with those two men who joined up when we crossed the Kaskaskia."

"I don't like their looks."

"They look like something the hogs threw up. Pa says they're trappers. He's swallowed whatever they've been telling him hook, line and sinker. They've got some hair-brained deal cooked up to get Pa's money. I'm not doubtin' that!"

Rachel's eyes wandered around the camp. She felt a shiver of dread. The wagons were scattered, each family taking advantage of the safe campsite to have a little privacy.

"Don't go far from the wagon tonight, Berry," Rachel murmured as she bent over to place the slabs of mush on the griddle.

"I already thought of that."

The big black man approached with arms filled with dead branches for the fire. He bowed his head several times before he spoke. "Ah got the wood, missy." The shaggy head turned from side to side, as if in silent warning.

The man's face was so black that when he spoke, Berry could see only the whites of his eyes and the gleam of his teeth and none of his facial expression. For some time now she had been convinced that he was smarter than he let on to be. He seldom spoke, did the work of two men, and gave Asa little cause to reprimand him.

Asa was more than glad to leave the care of the wagons and the teams in the hands of the women and the slave and ride ahead of the train on his sorrel mare.

"Thank you, Israel. I understand what you're telling me." She smiled, and his broad face split in a wide grin. "Are you hungry?"

"Yass'm."

"There'll be plenty put back for you."

The slave beamed. "Yass'm. Ah put the hog fat on the wheels." He backed away still bobbing his head up and down.

Rachel, chuckling softly, got down on her knees beside the fire. "Don't it beat all? When Asa brought him home, I didn't think he had a brain in his head."

"Haven't you ever looked into his eyes?"

"His eyes? I've had no reason to."

"He's not as stupid as he lets Pa believe. I think he hides his feelings behind that blank face." Berry turned the meat with a long-handled fork. "Wouldn't it be terrible to be a slave, Rachel?"

Rachel put her hand on Berry's shoulder so she could get to her feet. "What do you think we are, honey? All my life I've been at the beck and call of someone who paid someone else for me. All your life you've had to do for Asa and to put up with his meanness. Women are slaves so they can have a roof over their heads and food to eat."

Berry rocked back on her heels. "It won't always be like this. I'm not goin' to walk around on eggs for the rest of my life. And . . . if Asa touches us again . . . I'll brain him!"

Rachel set the tin plates on the box beside the fire. "He's comin'," she murmured. "He's got three men with him. I hope he don't expect us to feed them all."

"He will, but I'm gettin' Israel's out first." Berry grabbed a plate and piled it high with meat and fried mush. "Throw a cloth on it, Rachel, and set it aside."

Asa Warfield was a short, thickset man with coal-black hair and a clean-shaven face. Years of heavy drinking had bloated a face that had once been handsome; now it was constantly flushed and perspiring. Asa never worked when there was any other way to get what he wanted, and it was evident by the smile on his face as he walked proudly up to the fire that he was working on a scheme that would put money in his pocket.

"Howdy, daughter, Rachel," he said with honey-eyed exaggeration. "I brought company fer supper."

"I've cooked just enough for us," Berry said impatiently.

Asa's anger flared. "Then cook more, girl. What's the matter with ya? Where's your manners?"

Berry looked across the fire. Two of the men were the trappers her pa had been riding with for the last few days. They stood grinning at her. They were dressed in buckskins and wore knee-high fringed moccasins. One was picking his teeth with the blade of a long, thin knife; the other, an older man with a bushy beard and rotted teeth, leered at her openly. The third man stood apart from the others with his face in the shadows. He too was dressed in buckskins, but instead of the fur cap he wore a brimmed, flat-crowned hat pulled low over his eyes. Berry gave the three men a scornful look, picked up the plate of food, and went to the end of the wagon, out of sight of those who stood beside the fire.

Her eyes searched the darkness for the black man and found him squatting beside a large oak. She waved and pointed to the plate of food she had put on the tailgate of the wagon. Then she dug into the food box for the salt pork and another loaf of cornmeal mush.

Rachel dished up the food. Asa swaggered forward and took the plates from her hand and passed them to the men. She could tell by his smell that he'd been at the whiskey jug. Apprehension caused her to move with guarded calm as she sidled away from him.

The men hunkered down at the edge of the circle of light with their plates. One of them began telling Asa a tall tale about a happening on the river. When he finished, he laughed and elbowed one of the other men, who made a crude remark and grinned inanely across the campfire at the women. Rachel was filled with a growing uneasiness.

Angry because she and Rachel would have to eat salt pork instead of the venison steaks, Berry slapped the meat into the skillet and moved it over the blaze. She lifted the lid of the iron teakettle, dropped tea leaves into the boiling water, and set it on the edge of the fire to steep.

"They've been passin' the jug," Rachel murmured.

"They won't pester you," Berry promised. "Sit down on the box and stay by the fire."

"It's not me I'm worried about."

"Hand me the plates and don't look at them."

Berry was forking the long strips of greasy meat out of the skillet when one of the men left the group and came to the fire.

"That thar tea done yet, girlie?" The man smelled like a wet goat, and Berry turned her head away, repulsed.

She lifted the kettle. He held a tin cup in his hand and moved close. He rubbed his knee against her leg. Berry backed off and turned to the side; he followed her movement, keeping his leg against hers, and blew his foul breath in her face. Her stomach churned and her body went icy cold, then hot. Seething with rage and indignation, Berry retreated a second time. He followed, pressing closer. Her control snapped. She tilted the kettle toward his cup, then with a jerk of her wrist she moved it. Hot liquid flowed out onto his hand.

"Ye . . . ooo!"

The cup fell to the ground and simultaneously his arm lashed out and struck her across the breast. She staggered back and flung the kettle from her. It hit the ground and the boiling water splashed into the fire, causing a hissing sound. Berry struggled to regain her balance and keep from falling. By the time she had done so, the man, roaring with anger and pain, was reaching for her. "Ya bitch! Ya goddamn bitch! Ya burnt me!"

Berry jerked a long, thin blade from her apron pocket and held it in front of her. Her small body tensed with determination. She'd suffered her last indignity at the hands of trash!

"You touch me, you mangy, flea-bitten polecat, and I'll cut your liver out and feed it to the buzzards!"

"What's this? What's this?" Asa yelled from behind her.

The trapper made a grab for her and Berry lashed out with the knife. He jumped back, shouting curses. "The goddamn bitch ruint my hand on purpose!" he yelled.

Asa lashed out and grabbed Berry's arm and jerked it up behind her. "What the hell's wrong with ya, gal? You're due a whippin'." He tried to pry the knife from her hand, but she held on to it stubbornly.

Rachel jumped up and hit Asa on the arms with her fists. "Leave her alone! She's got to protect herself if you won't do it."

"Get away from me, woman!" Asa roared. "You've shamed me!" He was so angry that his voice cracked. He shoved Rachel aside and she stumbled against the wagon.

Berry twisted away, the knife still in her hand, and ran to Rachel. She stood in front of her, her hand curled around the shaft of the knife, the tip pointed at her pa. All caution left her. Anger, resentment, and disappointment in her father boiled up inside her, and hostility flowed out in angry, unguarded words.

"Don't talk to me about shame," she shouted. "You've shamed me all my life, and my mother before me! What kind of man are you to let this worthless riffraff come in here and rub up against me? And... don't you hurt Rachel. If you do, you'd better not sleep in this camp, or I'll cut you! I swear it!"

Stunned by her outburst, Asa stood with his mouth open. His face turned an even darker red as he realized the import of his daughter's words and that other men had heard them.

"Hush up!" he roared. "Don't you be tellin' me what you'll do, you ungrateful little split-tail! You belong to me till I pass you to another man. You'll do as I say... both of ya! I'll do with ya what I want, by gawd!"

"We're not slaves, or animals!" Berry hissed. "You'll not treat us as such. We've put up with your meanness and cuffing for the last time." She drew a deep breath, and her next words came out loud and clear so they could be heard by all. "And we don't have to put up with the trash you haul in, neither! So get 'em outta here!"

Asa couldn't believe Berry was saying this to him. Humiliated almost beyond endurance, he lifted his fist to strike her. She didn't flinch or back down. The blade flashed out in front of her and Asa's fist paused in mid-air. The snicker behind him caused him to spin on his heel.

"I ain't heared of no man 'round here what couldn't handle his womenfolk." It was the bushy-faced man who spoke. "Thought ya said they'd come docile-like, Mr. Warfield." He spit into the fire.

Fear circled Berry's heart. What was he talking about? She blurted her thoughts: "What's he talkin' about?"

Asa turned to her with a look of pure hatred. "You'll find out, missy. You'll be sorry for shamin' me like you done."

"I gotta get me some bear grease on my hand, George. Mr. Warfield'll have to get his women in line afore we can get down to real talkin'.'"

"They ain't goin' to get away with it," Asa promised. "Israel," he shouted. The slave appeared like a shadow at the end of the wagon. "Fill my jugs with Kaintuck' for my friends. Be fast about it or I'll lay a whip to your back!" Asa turned his back and Berry allowed the hand holding the knife to drop to her side. "I'm right sorry my women raised up a ruckus." He tried to put some dignity into his voice when he spoke. "I ain't had a firm hand on 'em. I jist been too busy what with gettin' things sold and bein' on the trail and all. They'll be whopped back in line soon's I get settled."

"What they's needin' is ridin'." The crude remark came from the man with the burned hand, and Berry felt another surge of anger toward her father when he allowed the remark to pass. She heard Rachel gasp when Asa chuckled.

He picked up the two jugs Israel had set on the ground beside him and followed the trappers out of the circle of light. "You comin', Witcher?" he said to the third man, who stood motionless in the shadows. The man murmured something. Asa shrugged and disappeared in the darkness.

Berry looked across the fire at the man in the flat-crowned hat. He was holding his plate in his hand, his head tilted to one side as if he was listening. There was something about the way he stood, motionless but alert, that told her he could spring with the quickness of a cat and that their ordeal wasn't over. This was the first time she had really looked at him. All she could see now was the outline of broad shoulders and slim hips . . . and the hat.

Israel began to feed small twigs and branches into the fire. They caught and burned, the blaze building to light the area. The man stood quietly. It seemed to Berry that he didn't move a muscle until the fire was blazing and the light reached out to him. Then he walked past Israel as if he weren't there and placed his empty plate on the box beside the fire. He continued walking until he stood before the two women.

Berry moved in front of Rachel once again and waved the knife. "Stay back!" She met his gaze with her direct, black-fringed eyes, lifted her chin an inch higher, and thrust out her jaw.

"Thank you for the supper. It was hard to turn down the invite after being on the trail for days." He lifted his hand to the brim of his hat and turned to leave.

"Mister!" It was the polite gesture that caused Berry to speak. He paused and turned, but kept his distance. She looked at him closely. He was extremely tall, but whiplash thin. She'd noticed when he had walked toward them that his movements were so smooth he could have carried a cup of water on his head without spilling a drop. He looked a cut above the other two. His buckskins were soiled but not ragged, and he didn't stink, which was in his favor. He stood with his back to the fire; she couldn't see his eyes clearly, but she knew they were honed in on her. "What're you and them other two varmints hatchin' up with my pa?"

The expression on his face was one of quiet sobriety. He didn't speak, and the silence between them was disturbing. Berry watched him apprehensively.

"I never set eyes on your pa until a couple of hours ago. I've come up from Kaintuck' with a load of trade goods. I'm a trader and a guide. Your pa figured to do some trading with me and invited me to supper."

Berry continued to stare into his face. *He's not going to stare me down.* The thought made her lift her chin even higher, and she gazed at him with cold dignity. "That tradin' wouldn't have anything to do with me and Rachel?"

He looked at her for a long moment before he spoke. "I don't trade in human flesh, be it women or slaves." His words came out cool and clipped.

"Then why're you hangin' out with *them?*"

His mouth tightened and the creases in his cheeks deepened to severity. "I don't have to explain my actions to you, ma'am. But I'll tell you this. I don't hang out with the likes of Linc Smith and George Caffery. They're what you said, varmints. They're known up and down the river as thieving, lying, murdering scalpers, and your pa would be smart to steer clear of them."

Rachel's hand was on Berry's shoulder, her protruding abdomen pressed into the younger girl's back. In the stillness that followed the man's words,

Berry was conscious of the movement of life in Rachel's body and heard Rachel's sharp intake of breath.

"Go. We've not eaten supper, in case you ain't noticed." Her green eyes became glacial as they bored into his.

He hesitated while his eyes searched the camp. "Will the black be any help if you have trouble before your pa comes back?"

"Our trouble will be *after* he comes. But we don't need no help. I've got this knife and a musket, 'n' I can use both of them."

He smiled as if he didn't want to but was forced. "Glad to hear it." He put his hand to the brim of his hat and walked away.

"Oh, Berry! What've we done? Asa'll be crazy mad," Rachel said in a horrified whisper.

Berry watched the trader until he disappeared in the darkness. She put the knife into her pocket and closed her eyes for an instant. "What's done is done. We cain't keep on knucklin' under to him. The first thing we know he'll have me sold off. He keeps a-sayin' it's time for me to take a man. He'd see that he got somethin' for it, that's certain!" she said bitterly. "As long as we're together, we can stand up to him." Suddenly she laughed. It was total and unexpected.

Rachel stood transfixed. "It's not a laughing matter." Her eyes filled with tears. "Asa's got to do somethin' to save his face."

"Let him try! He won't do nothin' if I can help it." She laughed again. "We shoulda stood up to him long ago, Rachel." She tried to sound confident for Rachel's sake. "I'm not goin' to fret about it now. I'm hungry."

They sat on the box beside the campfire and picked at the fried mush. Berry left the fat meat in the skillet for Israel. He brought more fuel for the fire and piled it on. She suspected it was his way of trying to protect them by keeping the camp lit up. The slave moved like a cowering dog, but it was a comfort to have him there.

"The trader appeared decent." Rachel was holding on to Berry's shoulder again, and Berry knew she was hurting.

"I dunno about that. He was a mite better'n the others. Did you see the knife he wore in his boot 'n' that rifle he never let outta his reach? I'd bet he'd be a bugger in a fight."

"He was clean. I'm sick to death of dirt and stink."

Tiredness in Rachel's voice prompted Berry to say, "Why don't ya go to the wagon. I'll clean up this mess." She attacked the plates in a large wooden bowl. "I'll put the kettle on and we'll have a cup of tea. There'll be warm water left for a good wash."

Israel sidled up to the fire, bobbing his head up and down. The habit irritated Berry and she wished he wouldn't do it, but she didn't know how to tell him.

"Mistah, over there, tol' me ta give this ta y'all." He held a cloth bag out at arm's length and jerked his head toward the edge of the woods.

Berry's eyes found the trader standing in the shadows. His rifle was cradled in his arms and he still wore the brimmed hat. She took the bag from Israel's hand and untied the string at the top. It was a bag of raisins. She'd had them only one other time in her life. She looked back at the man and nodded her thanks. He tipped his hat and disappeared even as she watched him.

"Rachel! He's give us raisins! Now why in the world would he do that?"

"I . . . don't know." Her voice lightened. "But I'm glad he did."

"Don't go, Israel," Berry called. "Hold out your hand. We'll all have a treat tonight." She went to him. He stood trembling with his hands behind him, as if he were in shock. "Hold out your hand," she urged. He obeyed, and she placed a handful of the raisins in it. A smile split his face.

"Yass'm, yass'm, yass'm." He kept repeating the words as he backed away.

Berry's laugh rang out. It was a joyful, happy sound that broke the stillness of the night. "You're goin' to back into a tree if ya don't watch out, Israel."

"Don't tease him, honey. You've shocked him enough for one night." Rachel was smiling.

Berry handed her the bag. "Take them to the wagon. I'll bring the water. If we're lucky, Pa'll stay away all night."

Simon Witcher watched the girl accept the gift, then moved back into deeper shadows. He rested the butt of his rifle on the toe of his moccasin, used it to steady himself as he lounged against the trunk of a large tree. The color of his buckskins and the deep tan of his face made it almost impossible to see him in spite of his six-foot-four-inch height.

"Simon didn't really know why he stood there and watched the women, unless it was the musical sound of the girl's happy laughter as she called out to the slave. The sound had given him a surge of pleasure and his eyes were drawn to her.

Asa Warfield had come to Witcher's wagons and introduced himself. He'd said he was traveling with his wife and daughter to land he'd filed on west of the river. He was interested in the trade goods Simon had freighted from Louisville. After a half-hour of conversation he'd invited Simon to supper. The temptation to eat women's cooking had spurred him to accept. However, he had immediately regretted his hasty decision when they were joined by Linc Smith and George Caffery, as unsavory a pair as roamed the river.

Now a worried frown creased Simon's brow. He would have been forced to step in if the girl hadn't stood up to Linc and her pa. What the hell! He scowled, disgusted with his thoughts. The pregnant woman was the man's wife, the girl his daughter. He had no business butting into a man's problems with his family.

He stood there until the campfire burned down. The slave came to add more fuel to the fire, then melted into the darkness of dense growth beyond the wagons. Simon went back to where the freight wagons were parked for the night. He paused and made a soft whistling sound before he showed himself.

Two men materialized out of the darkness. "York'll take first watch," one said. "Though ain't likely ta have no trouble." He eased himself down on the ground and leaned against the wheel. His companion went to the second wagon, threw out a bedroll, and stretched out on it. "Seems to be a train of

farmers a-waitin' to cross." Simon took out a blanket
and crawled under the wagon. He placed his hat
and his gun on it and lay down. The big man by
the wheel was still talking. "It's a wonder they got
this fer," he said, snorting. "They ain't got no more
know-how than a Injun with his head cut off. That
land o'er thar'll give 'em a hard welcome."

Simon chuckled. "It's so. It's the same with most
that cross." He was silent for a while, then said,
"Fain, do you remember that pair that come in with
a barge full of goods a year back and said the freighter
had fell overboard and drowned? They said they'd
salvaged the goods."

"Yup. I remember 'em. Nobody believed it, but
there wasn't nothin' they could do."

"They're in camp. Took up with an Ohio farmer.
I heard 'em talkin' about setting up a tavern with
him."

"Farmer'd better watch his step. Them'd knife
their own granny for a gold piece." Fain had the
soft, slurry voice of a Virginian.

"Farmer's got a couple women with 'em. I hate
to see 'em get tangled with that pair."

Fain didn't answer. The men who lived in the
woods did not speak when there was no answer
required.

Simon closed his eyes, but sleep didn't come.
The picture of a face floated before his mind's eye,
a face framed with dark curls. A poignant loneliness
possessed him for the first time in a long while. Far
away, the sound of an owl echoed in the stillness.
Simon was as filled with unrest as was the owl. His
thoughts raced. For a moment he speculated on
how it would be to have a woman in his cabin, a

woman who waited for his return, a woman who whispered words of love in his ear. He turned restlessly.

Orphaned at the age of nine, Simon had been apprenticed out to work with a family named Pollard. They had been Scottish-Irish with six children of their own, but they had a lot of land to tend and a mill. The judge who had sent Simon there decreed that he work for his keep, and he was to be provided with proper food and care in return for his work. At age sixteen he was to be given a horse and a gun. His leaving had disappointed Mrs. Pollard, who had come to look on the boy as her own. In spite of that, Simon had left Pennsylvania and headed west. He had spent time in Virginia, then had come through the Cumberland Gap into Kentucky and Tennessee. He had learned the trading business, learned to fight, learned to judge men. He had filed on land and built a building to house his trade goods.

Now, ten years later, he was grateful for the time he had spent with the Pollards and grateful for the book learning they had given him along with their own children. Mr. Pollard had been a teacher and a scholar. Many times Simon had listened in awe to the man speak French, Spanish, and German. He'd been fascinated by the French language and had learned a smattering. It was useful to him in this area so full of Frenchmen.

Fain rolled up in a blanket and was soon snoring softly, but Simon's mind refused to let him rest. Two unprotected women, especially as pretty as the Warfield women, would be a big temptation to men like Linc Smith and George Caffery. The girl was spunky. She had set Linc to dancing with that hot water on his hand. That was all the more reason why Linc would be set to go back. The fact that one of them was big with child wouldn't matter in the least. And if the farmer got drunk enough...

Simon rolled out from under the wagon. He put on his hat so that York would know who he was, picked up his rifle, and, as silently as a shadow, moved between the trees toward the other side of the camp.

Chapter Two

The raisins are grand-tastin'." Berry dug her fingers into the sack and popped a few more in her mouth. "I could eat them all, but I reckon it would be hoggish."

They sat on the feather tick, a blanket around their shoulders. A bit of wick floated in a bowl of oil and gave off a faint light. Berry liked it when she and Rachel were alone inside the tarp-covered wagon with the front and back flaps secured for the night. It was homey and private. They had washed in the warm water and put on their nightdresses before treating themselves to the trader's gift.

"The raisins are good, but so was the wash," Rachel confessed. "I'm tired of eatin' dust." She took the precious wire pins out of her hair, placed them in a small box, and picked up the hairbrush. When she shook her head, the long coil fell and spread, making her look like a child.

"I'm hopin' we get a place near a clear running stream. We can bathe in it, put our wash pots on the bank, and have scrub water without havin' to tote it far." There was a wistful quality to Berry's voice.

"Asa's got wilder and wilder on this trip," Rachel said with a worried frown. "He might not farm. He might try to turn his hand to somethin' else."

"I'm afraid of it. I don't—" She broke off in mid-sentence and held her finger to her lips in silent warning. The campfire was still ablaze, and a shadow had passed between it and the wagon. "Keep talkin'," Berry mouthed silently, and gently set the bag of raisins in Rachel's lap.

Rachel's eyes grew large and frightened, but she cleared her throat and began to murmur words about their home in Ohio. Berry injected a word occasionally, all the while inching toward the back of the wagon. She heard the rasp of cloth or leather as it scraped wood, and saw the movement of the tarp as it was gently prodded from the outside. She motioned for Rachel to hand her the musket they kept loaded. Rachel reached for it and laid it on the feather tick within her reach.

Berry got to her knees, then to her feet. The movement at the end of the wagon was more obvious now as a knife sawed at the rope that secured the flap. Her foot nudged the tin chamber pot they kept for Rachel to use during the night. Berry had used it herself this evening, being reluctant to leave the wagon, and it was half-full.

A devilish grin tilted Berry's lips as the idea struck. She quietly removed the lid and lifted the pot by the bail. She raised it until she could grasp it with both hands.

Rachel talked on in low tones while they waited.

Sure that his presence had gone unnoticed, the man sawed at the ropes. Within minutes Berry saw the canvas go slack. She tensed for the moment the flap would be thrown back.

If she was surprised at all, it was by the way the whole end of the wagon opened up. *Blop!* The tarp fell, and Linc Smith stood scarcely three feet from her with a leering, drunken grin on his face. As he reached for her, Berry threw the chamber pot, contents and all. She saw it splash in his face before the pot struck him. She grabbed the musket.

"Ahhh...ahhh...!" Linc yelled and stumbled back. At that same instant a club came down on his head with a thud. His body went limp and he fell face forward in the dirt.

Israel, with both hands holding the club, rolled white-socketed eyes toward the astonished women.

"Israel! You coldcocked him!"

The slave began to tremble so violently that the thick stick of wood slipped from his fingers. The enormity of what he'd done paralyzed him with fear.

Berry saw his fear, and knowing he could be whipped to death for his action she said quickly, "Did he see you?"

"Naw...naw..."

"Good!" Suddenly she began to laugh. Peals of laughter rang out as she looked on the drenched form lying in the dirt. It was a tinkling, musical sound that reached the man in the brimmed hat, who stood in the shadows. He was fascinated by the sound and couldn't keep his own lips from twitching into a broad smile.

"Good heavens!" Rachel leaned over the tailgate and stared at the man sprawled on the ground.

Berry put down the musket, bunched her night-dress in her hand and jumped down from the wagon. "Don't worry, Israel. Nobody will know you did it," she said between fits of giggles. "What're we goin' to do with him?" She wrinkled her nose. "Phew! He'd scare a hain't in a thicket!"

"Yass'm . . . ah . . . yass'm." Israel was clearly terrified, and her mention of a ghost didn't help.

"Stop worryin'," Berry said gently. "I'll say I did it. And . . . thanks. Thunderation! You were takin' a chance."

Rachel was first to see the trader approach. She only had time to gasp, "Berry!"

"I'll say I did it." The voice was quiet and drawling, but just the sound of it caused Berry's heart to leap with fear. She whirled like a cat ready to fight. A soft chuckle came from the trader. "I was about to step in, but it appears like y'all don't need no help." He backed away a step. "Phew!" Rumbles of laughter came from his chest, and in spite of herself Berry's face relaxed into a grin.

She had no idea of the picture she made standing there in her white nightdress. Masses of black curly hair floated around her white face and gasps of laughter came from her soft mouth. She put her hand to it to stifle the giggles. Later, she was to wonder why she had been so sure he meant them no harm.

Simon circled the man on the ground and leaned his rifle against the end of the wagon. "Israel," he said to the slave. Then, "Israel?" He shook the man's arm to rouse him out of his fear and to get his attention. "Get on back to your sleepin' place. The fewer tracks you make around here, the better. I'll drag him off in the woods. If there's any questions asked, I'll say I bashed his head for botherin' the women."

"Lawsey me!" Israel stared at him in awe, then ran off.

"Phew!" Simon said again when he grasped the man by the collar. He dragged him into the underbrush a good distance from the wagon, and as he returned he swept the tracks away with a branch.

"Did we kill him?" Berry asked, then added, "I don't care if we did or not. I was goin' to shoot him anyway."

"It'd take more'n that to kill the bastard," Simon said, grunting. "But he might wish it had. He's full of whiskey, 'n' that bash on the head won't help."

"Why'd you come back?" Berry peered up into his face. "And why do you wear that hat so a body can't see your face?"

He laughed shortly. "You're just full of questions, aren't you?"

"How're you goin' to find out anythin' if you don't ask?"

"I had a hunch they'd get your pa drunk and come back."

"The other'n will come lookin' for him." Her eyes scanned the darkness beyond him.

Simon saw her anxious look, and the wish to bash more heads jerked at his mind. "He'll not come tonight. He and your pa are sleepin' it off on a pile of hides down by the river. But that'n," he jerked his head toward the spot where he'd left Linc, "he's goin' to be madder than a skunk with a twisted tail." He took a length of rawhide from under his shirt and started tying it to the wagon flap.

"I reckon he will. It was decent of you not to tell on Israel. They'd kill him. If they didn't, Pa'd whip him somethin' awful. He's not as dumb as he lets on," she added in the slave's defense.

"Get in the wagon and I'll tie the flap down and poke the end of the strap inside. When you want out in the morning, pull the strap and the knot will come untied."

Berry skirted the wet spot in the dirt and picked up the chamber pot. She couldn't suppress another bout of giggles. A bubble of laughter escaped her lips when she looked at Rachel's solemn face. "I know I'm makin' a fool of myself laughin'... but he looked so... funny!"

As she continued to laugh, she was such a pleasure to look at—all warm, sparkling, and pretty beyond belief. With an effort, Simon pulled his attention back to the tarp. He slit the canvas with a long, thin-bladed knife and laced it with the rawhide. Out of the corner of his eye he saw the blond woman reach for the chamber pot and whisk it out of sight. He almost chuckled. White women had notions that never occurred to Indian women.

Berry stepped up on the box to crawl over the tailgate and back into the wagon. Simon put his hands on her waist and lifted her lightly. She didn't protest, and he had a sudden notion to enfold her warmth in his arms and kiss her. Sternly he put such thoughts from his mind. She was soft and warm and so small it seemed he could snap her in two. But he knew she was tougher than she looked and that she had spunk. She'll need it, he thought with a fierce spurt of anger at her pa. He wondered if the man knew there were a hundred men on the river who would kill to get their hands on these women.

"Thank you, Mister . . . ?"

"Witcher. Simon Witcher."

"Do you live in Saint Louis? Will we see you again?" Berry asked boldly.

"More'n likely." Simon hesitated before he pulled down the flap. "I got a place up on the Missouri."

"That's a long way."

"It's no piece at all in this country. Where's your pa's land?"

"Across the river. He don't tell us much."

There was a small silence while he looked at the women and they at him. "I'll be at the ferry," he said, and let the flap drop between them. "Don't forget about pullin' the strap." He poked the end of the rawhide inside the wagon.

"Thanks," Berry called softly. "And thanks for the raisins, too."

"My pleasure." The masculine drawl was muffled as it came through the canvas.

Berry stood waiting expectantly, but he said no more. She turned to look down at Rachel, who sat with her back against the trunk. The women looked at each other for a moment and then Berry sank down onto the mattress. "Well, I never! Law, he's a strange one!"

"We don't have to worry about Asa tonight," Rachel said with relief.

"He's gonna be madder than a rained-on hen in the morning."

"I hope he's too sick to pay us no never mind." Her eyes twinkled. She showed a side to Berry that she never allowed to surface with anyone else. She loved the dark-haired girl. There had been no love in her life until Asa took her home to the thin, sad-eyed little girl. They had been a comfort to each other through the years. Berry had been all that made Rachel's life worth living.

"Rachel." Berry hesitated. "I never asked you, but somehow I knew that Pa didn't wed you. Did he?"

Rachel looked at her steadily and slowly shook her head. "He bought me for a horse and a hundred pounds of shot. It was either go with him or stay at the tavern and be a whore."

"But . . . why'd you stay with us after you growed up? He was mean to you! I hated him for it."

"Where would I have gone? Who would want Asa Warfield's leavings? Besides, I had you. You're the only person I ever loved and who loved me." Rachel looked down at her fingers pleating the material of her nightdress. "I wish this babe wasn't his. It could take on his meanness."

"It won't if we start it off right," Berry promised. "I didn't take on his meanness. My ma was sweet and gentle like you and she taught me book learning and she said, 'If you think of yourself as somebody, other folks will too.' I've thought about that a lot." Berry blew out the small light and lay down. "It isn't fair, is it, Rachel?" she said in the darkness. "It isn't fair that 'cause we're women we got to go along and do as a man says. I wish we could strike out on our own. We could clear us a place to live, or go downriver to a town and do some kind of work to earn our keep. It just isn't fair," she said again. "A woman has to have a man to stand between her 'n the mangy polecats what only wants her for fornication!"

"I remember way back being with a man and a woman who loved each other. They touched and kissed and laughed. I remember she'd run and he'd grab her and kiss her, and she'd laugh. It's so far back I can't remember who they were. I used to dream I'd find a man who touched me gentlelike and laughed a lot." Rachel's voice trailed away sadly. "Asa ruint me for that."

"You're not ruint!" Berry reached over and squeezed her hand. "I've got me a feelin' that somethin' good is waitin' for us across the river in that wild, sweet wilderness." Berry's laugh was a little shaky. She squeezed Rachel's hand again to reassure her as well as herself, then lay quietly, as her thoughts returned to the man in the brimmed hat.

"Where's Asa this morning?" The leader of the wagon train sat on his buckskin horse and spoke curtly.

"I dunno, Mr. Benson. But we're ready to go. We won't hold you up. Pa'll show up before we load on the ferry." Berry stood beside the ox and Rachel sat on the wagon seat.

"Well, I dunno if I'll let ya cross if'n he don't show up."

"He was drunk. He's sleepin' it off down by the river," Berry said carelessly.

Mr. Benson scowled and put his heels to his horse. Berry swatted the ox on the rump with a switch and it followed.

It was daylight when they moved out. Berry and

the ox took the lead, and Israel, driving the stubborn mules hitched to the heavy wagon, brought up the rear. Berry was glad to be leaving the campsite. She and Rachel had worried constantly that Linc and his partner would come back to the camp with Asa. It was an unusually warm morning for the end of May. The mist rose from the river as the air was stirred by a light breeze. The sun, coming up over the horizon, glowed on the white canvas tops of the wagons that lined the slope to the river. Berry's eyes searched for her father among the group of straggling immigrants, but she didn't see him or the trappers he'd been drinking with. She took off her bonnet and fanned her face. If Asa didn't show up, she didn't know what they'd use to pay the ferryman when it came their turn to cross.

The sun had reached a quarter of its way across the sky when Mr. Benson rode up to the wagon. "You're next. Move right on down and onto the boat." He didn't look at her and wheeled his horse to leave.

"Mr. Benson!" Berry had an uneasy feeling in the pit of her stomach. "Pa hasn't showed up and we don't have money to pay. We'd best stay here and wait for him."

"Your fare's paid. C'mon," he said curtly. He rode away, and Berry had no choice but to follow.

There were more wagons and horses on the flatland beside the river. Mr. Benson waved her on, urged her to hurry, and she had no time to look for Asa. The bargemen had tied the flatboat to the landing. Two of them stepped forward and grasped the ox by the horns, and although it bawled and resisted, they urged it onto the gently bobbing craft. Berry moved back and held on to the wagon frame as she took her first tentative steps onto the wet planks. The men dragged the balking ox to the front, looped a rope around each of its horns, and tied them securely to a brace. Another man stood ready with a hammer to coldcock the beast if it became frightened and tried to bolt.

Berry could tell by the commotion behind that the men were having difficulty getting the mules aboard. She knew Israel would be useless unless he was told what to do, so she edged her way to the rear of the wagon. To her surprise, she saw the trader. She recognized him by his flat-crowned hat; he was leading Asa's saddlehorse on board and instructing Israel on how to hold it. Two rivermen stood beside the mules and more men lashed the wagon to the deck. This done, crates of goods were stacked beneath the wagons.

It was scary but fascinating to Berry. She returned to the front of the wagon, wanting to share the excitement with Rachel. Rachel was not enjoying the experience in the least. Her knuckles were white where she gripped the seat, and her face was gray with fright.

"Rachel?" Berry started to climb up on the wheel. "Don't be scared, Rachel. They've poled this boat across a hundred times. They know what they're doin'."

"Hold on, little gal."

The drawl came from behind her. When Berry turned, her eyes were level with a broad chest covered with a leather shirt that fitted like a glove. Her eyes traveled up and up to a weathered face and bronze hair that swept back from a wide forehead and hung to shoulders that seemed a yard wide. The giant had twinkling blue eyes, and a stub of a pipe was in his mouth. He was the biggest man she'd ever seen, but rawboned big, without an extra ounce of flesh on his body.

"Who're you?"

"Fain. I'm goin' to give ya a hand and see ya get across." He looked up at Rachel. "Ya gotta come down off that seat, ma'am. It's a mite safer for ya to sit on the raft. I'll get ya an oilskin ta sit on."

"No! No..." Rachel shook her head. She looked as if she would be sick.

"We can't have ya sittin' up there," the man said firmly. He reached for her. "I won't let ya fall. I'm goin' to hold on to ya. Ya can count on it."

Rachel's eyes swung to Berry. "He won't, Rachel." Berry laughed. "From the looks of him, he could lift that ox down from there."

"Thanky, purty little gal." The man's laugh was a soft, rolling chuckle.

It could have been what changed Rachel's mind. She leaned over and put her hands on his shoulders. He grasped her beneath the arms, carefully lifted her over the wheel, and set her gently on the floor of the raft. She swayed, lowered her chin to her chest, and refused to let him go. "Oh...oh..."

"It's all right to be scared. Only a fool ain't scared some," the giant murmured to the top of Rachel's head. "Spread the cloth on the floor, little 'un, so she can sit." Berry spread the cloth and the man eased Rachel down. "Sit right down, ma'am. When we get goin' I'll be right by ya. Don't you worry none. I can swim like a beaver for all the size of me."

Berry sat down beside Rachel facing the back of the raft. She saw Simon Witcher standing beside Israel and her pa's sorrel mare. Why hadn't he come to speak to them?

"Why're you helping us?" she asked the big man.

"Wal, now, a man'd hafta be daft to not help purty womenfolk." He smiled broadly, holding the pipe stem in his teeth.

"Did Mr. Witcher tell you to help us?"

"Not just like that. We knowed ya needed help, and being the fine gentlemen that we are, we jist naturallike pitched right in." His clean-shaven face was alive with amusement. He was like a big friendly bear.

Berry's laugh floated out over the water like the song of a bird. Totally unaware that every male eye turned to look at her, she smiled happily into the twinkling eyes that smiled back. She liked this man. Liked him a lot. In all her life she'd not met a man she was more comfortable with, or one who in just a few short minutes had put her so at ease that she trusted him completely. She glanced at Rachel and found that she too was looking at him, and some of the strain had left her face.

Although he squatted beside them they still had to look up to see his face. He took the pipe from his mouth, knocked the ashes out on the floor of the boat, then put it in a pouch that hung on his shirt. "Don't ya move. I'll be back." He stood up. For such a big man he moved lightly.

"Fain. Mr. Fain . . ."

"Fain MacCartney, ma'am."

"My pa was drunk and didn't come back to camp last night. Ah...we're wonderin' where he could be."

"He ain't dead. Simon hauled him off and throwed him under our freight wagon. Them river rats he was with musta dosed up his whiskey. Your man's back thar with your slave, ma'am," he said to Rachel. "He ain't gonna be wakin' up fer a spell."

"He's not her man!" The words burst from Berry in bitter anger. "He's my pa, sorry as he is. That's all he is!"

"Berry!" Rachel's face turned crimson and she turned it away from the man's searching look, so penetrating, yet filled with understanding, that she couldn't meet his eyes.

"Berry? Is that your name?" Fain said easily, turning the attention from Rachel. "Strawberry or Raspberry? Maybe Chokeberry, huh?"

Berry caught her lower lip between her teeth as she did sometimes when she was trying not to laugh. The damp river air had turned all the loose hair floating around her face into tight curls. Her gray-green eyes sparkled with mischief. Fain thought he'd never seen a prettier, more alive woman in all his thirty-five years. The other one was a beauty too, but sad, and scared like a little doe caught in a trap. He had a sudden urge to throw the girl's pa in the river once they got halfway across.

Fain cursed silently to himself and moved down the raft to where Simon was helping lash the wheels of the heavy wagon in place. "Are ya goin' over?"

"No need, if you will. The other boat is coming back. We can load it."

"Wal, I ain't goin' ta be mis-put 'bout that. Them's

might purty women. That little 'un is about as purty as a covey of quail."

Simon looked at his friend with eyes so dark blue that they appeared black. "That's the trouble," he said simply. "Every horny bastard within miles will be after her like flies on a pile of fresh cow dung." He shrugged. "But it won't be no concern of mine once her pa sobers up."

Fain swore under his breath. Simon continued with his work. "Consarn it all! The little 'un said her pa wasn't the other'n's man. She blurted it right out, angrylike. What's that bastard up to?"

"I reckon he figures to start up a tavern and put them in it as a draw."

"They'd draw, ain't no doubt about that. Do you reckon they're that kind?"

Simon chuckled. "If they're not, the black-haired one'll fight him ever' step of the way. She's got spunk she hasn't used yet. The other'n has had the fight taken outta her."

"Shitfire!" Fain uttered the word and moved back toward the women.

"Watch the boy with the mare," Simon called, and jumped off the raft as the bargemen untied the ropes so it could drift free.

There were eight men with long poles on each side of the flatboat. They let the craft drift out until the current caught it and the front shifted slightly to the south. Then they worked in unison, poling to the distant point that seemed to be a good way south of where they had embarked.

Berry was surprised at how easily the craft rode in the water. She'd expected it to bob up and down like a cork. Instead, it rode the current so smoothly that scarcely any water lapped up on the planks.

Fain hunkered down beside them. "This is a good time to cross. The snows up north has melted and run down and there's not been much rain." He filled his pipe from his leather pouch and stuck it between his teeth. "Consarn it! What'd I do that for? I ain't got no fire."

Berry laughed and Rachel smiled shyly.

"Are you a trader like Mr. Witcher?" Berry asked after a brief silence.

"Naw. I'm not a trader. I make a trip or two a year with him. We got land that joins. We got cabins on it. Had to so we could get title, but Simon stays down at my place most of the time. Good man. The best."

"We hope Pa's place is by a clear stream. We thought..."

"Oh... oh!" The end of the raft suddenly swung with the current and Rachel grabbed Fain's arm.

"It's all right. That's not nothin'. Just a little fast water." He spoke calmly.

"I can't help it. I'm so afraid."

"Ya'll have to learn to swim. Then ya'll not be scared." Rachel suddenly realized she was holding his arm. She let go and looked away, embarrassed. Fain stood. "I'd best take a look and see how the boy's doin'. Sit tight. It's goin' to be smooth now."

"Why'd you tell him Asa's not my man?" Rachel whispered as soon as he'd left them. "What's he goin' to think? From the looks of me, he knows I've been with a man!" Her eyes were filled with anguish.

"I told him that so he wouldn't think you was tied to Asa. If you get a chance, you can go anytime you want to and Asa can't stop you. You paid out your bond a long time ago."

Rachel looked at her in horrified silence. When she spoke, her voice trembled. "I'm not goin' anywhere. I'd not go off and leave you! You . . . and . . ."

"If we get a chance we'll both go. Maybe there's a place in Saint Louis where we can work." Berry's mouth took on a stubborn look and her eyes narrowed angrily. "He's not goin' to knock us around anymore, Rachel. If he hits us again, I might kill him. I don't want to do it, so it'd be better if we could get away from him."

"There's nothing we can do in this wild place. I won't be no good to you at all for another month. And if this babe comes out right, it's got to be took care of." Tears came to Rachel's eyes, as they had so easily since her pregnancy had begun. "It'd be better if you wasn't hampered with me. I don't do nothin' but hold you down."

"Don't you ever say that again, Rachel Warfield!"

"Ain't Warfield. It's Tompkins."

"Tompkins?" Berry said with wonder in her voice. "Just think of all the years I've known you and I didn't know your name was Tompkins."

"There wasn't no reason to tell you." Rachel leaned over her lap and wiped her eyes on the hem of her dress.

"Look. We're about to the other side. It doesn't look much different, as far as I can tell. Of course, I know back of those trees there's nothing but more trees." Berry laughed lightly and lifted her chin to the cool breeze blowing off the water.

Fain returned and hunkered down beside them. "We'll be tying up soon. When we do, y'all get back up in the wagon and outta the way. A bunch a rowdys'll swarm on and lead the teams off. Ya just have to sit tight."

"Are you leavin' us?" It was Rachel who asked.

Fain's face creased in a smile. "I'll help the boy with the mare. I'll see ya strung out with your train. Don't worry none."

The front of the raft hit the heavy timbers of the dock with a jolt. As soon as the raft stopped rocking, Fain reached down and lifted Rachel to her feet. "Do ya want to stand for a minute after sittin' for so long?"

Both Berry and Rachel looked at him with astonishment. They'd never had a man treat them with such gentle attentiveness. Their eyes were drawn to his face. A rosy blush covered Rachel's cheeks.

Berry was used to filling the void when Rachel was speechless. "It'd help. The trip's been hard on her."

Fain ignored Rachel's embarrassment. "I'd 'spect so. Stand here 'n' hold to the wheel till the blood gets a-goin'. I'll look and see what the boy's doin'."

Fain came back dragging a heavy crate. He placed it beside the wheel, scooped Rachel up in his arms, and, as lightly as a dancer, stepped up on the box and set her down on the wagon seat. "Thar ya are, ma'am." He looked at Berry. "Your turn, little 'un." Before she could open her mouth she was high in his arms. He swung her easily up onto the seat.

"That was like bein' on a swing," she said, laughing. "Thank you."

"It was the most pleasurable thin' I've done in a

coon's age," he admitted with a low chuckle. He stepped away and pulled back the crate.

The men swarmed over the boat as Fain had said they would. Rachel and Berry watched from the wagon seat. The ox was untied and led off the boat and up a short ramp to level ground. Berry jumped off the wagon and went to lead the beast up the trail where she could see members of their party waiting.

Rachel cringed when she saw the leering looks of the boatmen as they gazed at Berry walking beside the ox, her young body swaying gracefully, her hair shining in the bright sunlight. Rachel's heart contracted painfully. They were in a wild, rough land among wilder and rougher men than they had ever known.

Chapter Three

The settlement of Saint Louis was larger than it had appeared when Berry viewed it from across the river. It was situated on ground not much higher than the river and protected from flood by a natural bank of limestone. Behind the town, to the west, on a forty-foot bluff, was a small stockade with several circular towers and a stone breastwork. It had been built as a defense against the Indians but now was used only occasionally by the soldiers.

There was one main road through the center of the town. It was rutted, dusty, and now filled with wagons, carts, dogs, and excited children; emigrants from Ohio seeking new homes. Weary farm women followed behind the wagons to urge a cow along or to hit at a village dog that ran out to nip at their heels.

The street ran parallel to the river and was lined on both sides with shops and dwellings. Other tracks led off toward the bluffs. The houses on these roads were of various sizes; some made of log and stone, some built cabin-fashion, all one-storied. They looked, Berry thought, permanent, solid, and grand.

Black-suited merchants and clerks with suspenders and sleeves rolled to the elbow came out to watch the caravan of settlers pass. They stood on porches or plank walkways built from the lumber of wrecked keelboats. Dark-skinned bargemen lingered in front of taverns and watched the young girl walking beside the ox. Several called out to her and some guffawed loudly when a dog ran out and nipped at her heels. She turned the switch on the cur, and it yelped and slunk off between the buildings.

Berry wished, desperately, that she was sitting on the wagon seat with a nice sunbonnet on her head. She would have liked to look her fill at the stores that lined the street and at the people who watched them pass. Instead, she kept her eyes straight ahead as if she weren't tired, dirty, and embarrassed to be stared at. Saint Louis was the largest town she'd ever seen. Mr. Benson had told her there were almost eight hundred people living there, but even so she was not prepared for its size; it was so much larger than she had expected.

Simon and Fain came out of a stone building on the edge of town and watched the caravan pass. Simon's eyes, shaded by his flat-brimmed hat, focused immediately on the girl. She walked as proudly as if she were promenading along a fine boardwalk. The dust raised by the wagons ahead swirled around her, settled on her shiny black hair, and clung to her damp skin. Her chin was tilted with determination not to be intimidated by the stares of the curious. She was the most incredibly lovely creature Simon had ever seen.

Fain watched his friend's face. Simon's eyes were narrowed, the dark brows lowered and drawn together. He stood as if turned to stone. He was plainly a man with things on his mind and not in a talkative mood. When Fain turned his steady blue gaze back to the wagons, he was surprised to see the wagon seat now vacant. His own brows beetled in question as the wagon passed. Then he saw a pale face topped with straw-blond hair peeking out of the puckered end of the wagon. Rachel seemed to be looking at him, but when he smiled and waved, she didn't return the greeting and swiftly moved out of sight.

"Light says Linc and George crossed the river a ways down and came up through the woods. I expect they'd planned to kill the farmer and make off with the women. Linc got coldcocked and I stole the farmer away from them. That put the kibosh on their scheme for a time, but they won't give up." Simon spoke with his head turned away from Fain, his eyes still following the girl. "I'd bet my right arm they'll show up at the wagon grounds tonight."

Fain looked at him and followed his gaze. "That ain't no bet at all." He shook his head. "Them are two fine-lookin' women 'n' 'bout as seemly as they come. It's a pity." He shook his head again and walked back into the building.

Simon stood for a moment longer, then turned to follow Fain. He was met in the doorway by the young French and Indian scout who worked for him now and then. The slim, quick-moving man was called Light. His real name was Lightbody. No one knew much about him or where he had come from. He came and went when the mood struck him. Always quiet and somber, he could move through the forest swiftly and silently. It was said he could almost trail a sparrow in flight. He was slow to rile; but when he was angry, he was a streak of chain lightning. Some people thought him part crazy and most steered clear of him. Simon had come to know him through a friend, a Virginian named Jefferson Merrick, who had a homestead on the Missouri several miles beyond the village of Saint Charles. Simon had a deep respect for the scout and would trust him with his life.

"Did Ernest pay you, Light?"

"No need."

"It's here when you want it."

"I'll be goin' upriver for Jeff soon. You want I take a message?"

"Then you've decided not to go with Pike?"

"Zebulon Pike is a fool. I'll not go north in winter. Waters freeze up, travel is hard."

"He's sent word he wants to see me. I'll head out in the morning. Tell Jeff to stop by Fain's if he comes this way."

Light nodded his dark head, stepped off the porch, and disappeared around the corner of the building.

Simon went inside.

The warehouse fronted the main street and backed to the river. Doors on both ends were open, letting in the only light. Simon and Fain stood idly surveying the stacks of goods that had been brought in from the wagons. Most of the stock in the warehouse had come up the Mississippi from New Orleans, but once a year he or his men took the heavy wagons over the trail to Louisville and traded pelts for tobacco, gunpowder, shot, salt, and other necessities. On his last trip to New Orleans he'd brought up barrels of coffee beans, bolts of cloth, pearl buttons, sewing thread, milled white flour, sugar, and spices. These were expensive goods and he still had most of what he had bought. He'd not make that mistake again. Most people in the sprawling, new, raw town got along on cornmeal, molasses, and tea, and spun their own cloth and made their own buttons from the shells that lined the riverbank.

Simon sold mainly to the merchants who ran the mercantile stores up and down the street and to the few stores in Saint Charles. They in turn sold the goods for whatever they could get out of it, sometimes at a large profit. He also bought and sold pelts, trading Indians tobacco for beaver, muskrat, shaved deerskins, and roots.

Simon found it a satisfying way of life. Some would say that he was a very rich man. He didn't think about it in those terms. He enjoyed transporting the goods to this small spot of civilization in the wilderness, but he didn't like anything about the dickering with merchants over the prices or keeping the books. He left all that up to Ernest Wenst, a solid German emigrant he'd befriended a few years back. Ernest and his helper, a freed black man by the name of Lardy, ran that end of the business.

Simon's great interest was the piece of land he owned upriver. He was happiest when he was there, with the forest on three sides of him and the river in front. At present he had only a small cabin on the land, but it was his dream to build a fine solid house on the bluff overlooking the river, clear some of the land for planting, and raise fine horses.

He had been toying with the idea of signing up with Zebulon Pike's expedition up the Mississippi to seek its source. Simon was glad now that he'd passed up the opportunity to go with explorers Lewis and Clark. By staying on his land for another year, he had obtained a clear title.

Simon liked the strong-willed, hard-driving Pike, even if Light did think him a fool, and had visited with him at his port of Kaskaskia several times. He still had a few weeks to decide if he wanted to put off building his house for another year and go adventuring. Somehow, the thought wasn't as exciting to him as it had been before he had left for Louisville. Maybe he was tired of traveling.

Simon often wondered why he hadn't turned the business over to Ernest and washed his hands of it. When he had first started trading he was motivated by the need for money. Now, he reasoned, he had a need to be busy, to have a reason to come to town, to see people. It was hard to admit to himself that he was lonely. The desire to have someone of his own had been bearing down on him of late. His life seemed strangely empty when compared to that of Ernest, who went home each evening to a wife and children.

Simon shook his head to rid himself of the notion and picked up a bale of furs and tossed them up to Lardy, who was stacking them to make space for the new stock. Work, he thought. Work so you can get that girl out of your mind. Even the hard work didn't stop his thoughts. Berry was the only woman he'd met whom he hadn't forgotten about a moment after he'd left her. Perhaps when they finished here, he and Fain would slip through the woods and see what was going on up at the wagon ground. She was too rare a girl to be ruined by the likes of Linc Smith.

The sun had gone down behind the foliage in the west, a fog had appeared low over the river, and the trees had faded into an indistinct mass of purple shade when curses from the wagon told Berry her father had awakened from his drunken stupor.

The wagons were spread out and parked at random in the large meadow. Everyone was tired, but excited that they were so near their journey's end. Tomorrow some would go north to the Missouri and some would take up land to the south. Berry and Rachel had no idea what Asa would do. He never discussed his plans with them.

From her place beside the cookfire where she was frying strips of meat and cooking corn pone, Berry watched the end of the wagon. Rachel sat quietly beside her, a look of resignation on her tired face. They'd been through this many times before and knew Asa would be as cross as a bull with a crooked horn when he awoke.

Setting her jaw and steeling herself for the unpleasantness that was about to come, Berry got slowly to her feet and placed a reassuring hand on Rachel's shoulder. She felt her tremble.

"Just stay out of his way," she murmured. "Why don't you crawl into the back of the wagon and lay down?"

"No. I'll not leave you to face him by yourself."

Asa came out of the wagon roaring curses. "Ya goddamn black bastard! What'd you take my money sack off for?" Israel was giving the wagon wheels their nightly greasing. Asa's fist lashed out and knocked him off his feet.

"Naw, suh! Naw, suh! Ah never..."

"Leave him be!" Berry shouted. "He hasn't touched your money. The trader dumped you in the wagon and took enough to pay the ferryman."

Asa looked at her with blurry-eyed astonishment. "We done crossed?"

"We crossed today." A sneer twisted Berry's lips and her look revealed her contempt. "A lot of help we got from you."

Asa's head throbbed. His anger and misery were aggravated by his daughter's haughty, independent attitude. "Shut your face! I ain't a-havin' no sass outta ya!" He hitched up his trousers and ran his fingers through his thinning hair. "Somethin' ain't right. I ain't never slept the day away afore."

"You never had your whiskey dosed before."

"Dosed? Who done it?"

"That trash you took up with done it. Sleep with dogs and you can expect to get up with fleas!" she quoted sarcastically. She turned her back on him and moved the teakettle closer to the blaze. A heavy hand on her shoulder spun her around.

"You done it!"

"If I'd-a done it I'd-a poisoned the lot of you. The river trash didn't sleep the day away. They didn't dose up their whiskey, just yours. And ... get your hands off me!" Hatred for this man who had made her life so miserable burned deep. It blazed from her eyes.

"It's 'bout time you showed some respect for your pa. I always put clothes on your back and filled your belly. Now you're gonna earn your keep. I got me some plans for ya, missy. You 'n' that scrawny bitch is gonna make me rich."

"You can forget any plans you have for us. We'll not be a part of anythin' you hatch up with those no-goods. Where's this land you was braggin' about?"

"I ain't a-breakin' my back on no homestead when I c'n get rich right here. I'm startin' me a tavern. Ain't none here that's got nothin' but used-up old hags in 'em. You 'n' her, soon's she gets that brat outta her belly, is gonna be my ace in the hole. Rivermen'll swarm in like flies jist to touch ya."

Berry heard the groan that came from Rachel and rage started deep inside her. It rose in tremendous waves until she was quivering from the force of it. "I knew you was rotten, but I didn't know you was so low down you'd do this! We won't do it!" Berry stuck out her jaw and placed her fists on her hips. "We won't do it," she shouted again. "You don't have no hold on us. I'm grown up now and Rachel's not wed to you. We'll not work in a tavern like common sluts!"

"You'll do as I say!" Asa roared. "I ain't havin' no more sass like ya done last night. I aim to strip the hide off ya!" His hand lashed out and grabbed her arm. Before she could brace herself, he jerked her toward the wagon and reached under the seat for the strap.

"No! Asa... no!" Rachel tried to wedge herself between them. "Don't, Asa... please..."

"Get out of the way, Rachel," Berry said calmly. "He'll hurt you."

"You're goddamn right! I ain't havin' no snotty, sassy talk from no slut!" His voice was laced with icy rage. He pushed Rachel and she fell to her knees.

While his attention was on Rachel, Berry jerked away from him. She ran to the end of the wagon and grabbed the gun. When she turned, she was holding the musket in both hands and it was pointed at Asa. "If you use that strap I'll blow a hole in ya big enough to drag this wagon through!"

Asa looked from Berry to Rachel on the ground. His lips parted in a snarl and his nostrils quivered with rage. He lifted the strap to bring it down on Rachel's back.

The dark, slim figure sprang into Berry's line of vision as if it dropped from the sky. A knife shot through the air with the speed of an arrow. It passed through Asa's leather shirt at the top of his shoulder and pinned him to the wagon box. The attacker's head was thrown back, and his lips were parted in a snarl like that of an animal. Buckskin clothes hugged his frame like a second skin. Berry would have been sure he was an Indian if not for the black hair tied, club-style, at the nape of his neck. In two seconds he was in front of Asa, a two-edged blade in his hand. He crouched ready to spring.

"Wh...what...?" Asa was stunned, then a frightened look appeared on his face.

"Beat woman and I keel you!"

"Who...What? Who're you?"

The man reached for his knife and jerked it loose, freeing Asa's shirt. Asa cringed and grabbed his shoulder. Blood seeped between his fingers from the cut made when the knife had grazed his skin. The stranger slipped one knife into his boot, the other into his belt. Ignoring Asa, he knelt beside Rachel.

"*Madame?*" His voice was hushed, almost reverent. "Did he hurt you?" His eyes examined her boldly.

Rachel was unable to speak. She shook her head.

"I help you. Please . . . ?" The gentle voice again.

"Thank you," she whispered.

He lifted her to her feet and held on to her until he was sure she was steady, then released her and turned back to Asa. He snatched the strap from Asa's hand and tossed it into the campfire.

"You got no right to do that!" A surge of courage stirred in Asa. He grabbed for the strap to pull it from the fire.

The knife appeared in the man's hand again. He kicked the strap farther into the blaze. "I watch. Next time I keel you." He didn't have Asa's bulk, but there was something in the way he moved and in his face that caused Asa to step back. "I watch," he said again and spun on his heel. He walked with light, quick steps into the woods.

A stunned silence followed. Berry exchanged a quick glance with Rachel. The man had not even glanced at her, but Berry knew that he had known she was there holding the gun. She still held it pointed at Asa. She lowered it, but watched him. She had no idea what he would do.

He turned his verbal abuse on Rachel. "Ya done took up with a breed! I oughtta've left ya where I found ya." He clenched his fist as if to strike her, then glanced in the direction where the man had disappeared into the woods. Fear of the knife was all that kept his hands at his sides.

"I never saw him before," Rachel said stoutly.

"You lie!" he said with a snarl and walked away. "Bring my vittles," he snapped at Israel as he passed him.

Berry went to the campfire. Rachel sat back down on the box, and Berry laid the musket in her lap. She dished up a plate of food and poured strong tea into a tin cup. She handed the meal to Israel, who was trembling.

"Leave it by him and come back here," she murmured.

"Who was he?" Rachel shivered. "He'd-a killed Asa."

"I was goin' to, Rachel. I swear it. It scares me to think I'd've killed my own pa. I don't know why I didn't shoot. That man just sprang out of nowhere, and somehow I knew that he was goin' to help us." She looked over her shoulder and noticed that Israel had left the food and sidled away. "I wonder why that man was watchin' us."

"His eyes were sad when he looked at me," Rachel said softly. "He looked Indian, but he spoke French."

"Well, I never! People poppin' in and out of this camp like jackrabbits." Berry put a piece of corn pone on a plate, handed it to Rachel, took one for herself, and sat down. "I'm not hungry, but I guess I'd better eat." She saw that Rachel was picking at her food. "You'd better eat too, Rachel. Eat what you want. I'll give the rest to Israel."

"What are we goin' to do? I remember how it was in the tavern, the pawin'... pinchin'."

"I don't know... yet." Berry looked beyond their camp to the cheery campfires of the other settlers. Children played happily, and women stirred the contents of steaming cook pots and called out to their men. One family nearby had made a home spot for the night. Soon the campfire would die down and the children would be put to bed. The man and his wife would snuggle into the blanket beneath the wagon and whisper about the happenings of the day. With a sad, haunted look of lost dreams and pitiful resignation, Berry said again, "I don't know."

"You mean everything to me, Berry," Rachel said suddenly, quietly. "I don't know what would've happened to me if not for you. I guess I've got to thank Asa for that. He's mean, sometimes worse than a rattler, but I don't want you to kill him."

The tip of Berry's tongue came out and moistened her dry lips. She was more upset over the fact that she'd almost shot her pa than she wanted to admit. "I don't want to. It'd bear down hard on me for the rest of my life. But he's not goin' to whip us again!" There was an iron-willed determination in her voice.

Rachel and Berry ate their meal and sipped at the hot tea. Lost in their thoughts, both women had forgotten about Israel until he came out of the woods, where he had taken Asa's food. His eyes were rolling with fear and his full-lipped mouth opened and closed, but no words came out.

"What's the matter, Israel?" Berry set her cup down on the ground and squinted up at him.

"They's . . . come, missy!"

"Who?" Berry asked, but she knew who, and icy dread closed around her heart.

"Them . . ." The slave gestured with a trembling hand.

Berry glanced beneath her pa's wagon. She could

see the shadows of two pairs of legs beside Asa's. She strained her ears but could hear only a murmur of voices. She took the musket from Rachel's lap, placed it on the box between them, and covered it with her skirt. She jerked her head toward the woods and Israel hurried away.

"Oh, Berry! Sometimes I think the workhouse or a brothel would be better than living like this. At least we'd know what to expect."

"Don't talk like that!" Berry hid her own fear behind curtness. "If I shoot one of 'em, the other one'll think twice before he comes at us. And ... maybe that woodsman is still watching." She reached down and put more fuel on the campfire. It blazed immediately and lit up the area.

The three men moved out from behind the wagon and stood in full view. They talked for a minute, then Linc Smith came cautiously toward the women. He had scraped the whiskers off his face and the cloth shirt he wore was clean. There was a silly, guilty grin on his face. He stopped several yards away, then moved closer, hesitantly.

"Howdy ... ah, ma'am." His small, close-set eyes never left Berry's face. She glared at him and watched his every move. When she didn't answer, he shifted from one foot to the other. "I ... was wrong ta scare ya like I done. I was drunk," he blurted, and grinned, as if that were all the excuse he needed. A venomous flash lighted Berry's eyes, and she swallowed the curses she wanted to scream at him. Linc snatched the fur cap off his head, as if he had suddenly remembered it, and glanced over his shoulder to where George and Asa stood at the front of the wagon.

It suddenly occurred to Berry that it was possible he didn't remember her throwing the chamber pot on him and being hit on the head. He had been so drunk that all he remembered was coming to the wagon. She could see that her silence was more effective than all the words she could hurl at him, so she remained quiet.

"Ah . . . your pa said ya could walk out wid me." He said the words with difficulty and stood expectantly.

At first Berry wasn't sure she had heard correctly. When the words finally penetrated her senses, she actually felt like laughing. So she did. She laughed long and loud in contemptuous snorts that even Linc Smith recognized as ridicule. His mouth clamped shut and his nostrils flared in anger.

"I'd rather walk out with a scalded cat!" she hissed.

"You're turnin' me down?" There was a different quality to his voice. All his muscles seemed to tighten and he thrust his head forward.

"Are you deaf as well as stupid?"

Linc came up on the balls of his feet and his hands clenched and unclenched. Never before had he humbled himself before a woman. He'd even washed himself, scraped off his whiskers, stolen a clean shirt. The wench was throwing his invite back in his face. Who in hell was she but a scrawny bitch? He glanced back at the farmer and saw that George was pushing him forward. He'd goddamned well better do somethin' and quick, or he'd wring the bitch's neck.

Asa sauntered up to stand beside Linc, and Berry's hand found the barrel of the musket where it lay on the box covered by her skirt.

"She ain't goin'," Linc said stupidly, as if Asa weren't aware of what had been said.

Asa hitched up his trousers. "Ya go on out wid him." He tried to put some authority in his voice. "I done give my word he could court ya."

"Court me?" Berry's voice squeaked with astonishment. "Court *me!*" she repeated with so much revulsion and surprise that she was hardly able to speak. Surprise gave way to anger. It welled inside of her until she thought she would burst from the force of it. "I'd rather die than have that belly-crawlin', yellow-backed, shit-eatin' buzzard court me!"

"Hush your mouth!" Asa shouted. "It's time ya took a man."

"You call that a *man!*" Berry spit toward Linc. "He looks more like a flap-jaw, warty toad! If you'd scraped the river bottom you wouldn't-a got more scum!" She jerked out the musket and pointed it at them, gripped in both hands. "Get 'em outta here or I'll kill... somebody!"

There was silence. The men stood as if nailed to the spot. Then George and Linc, acting in unison, sidestepped, leaving Asa standing alone. They moved to surround the women. Berry's heartbeat accelerated with fear and the hands holding the heavy gun trembled. Her eyes swung from one man to the other.

Suddenly both men stopped and sauntered back toward Asa, their eyes darting behind her. Berry knew someone else had come into the camp, but she didn't dare take her eyes from the men in front of her. She heard Rachel's long intake of breath and the slow release just as the buckskin-clad figure in the brimmed hat walked past her to stand beside the campfire. Fain stopped beside Rachel.

"Evenin'," Fain said. He stood with feet spread. He had a musket thrust in the belt at his waist, and a knife hung in a scabbard at his side.

Asa's eyes swung to Simon and back to Fain. "Who're you?"

"I come to collect my thanky for gettin' ya 'cross the river."

"Ya got it," Asa said begrudgingly. "Much obliged."

"How's your head, Smith?" When Simon spoke, Berry took her eyes off the men in front of her long enough to glance at him. He looked the same as last night. He had a musket in his belt and a long rifle in his hand. He was holding it by the barrel.

Linc seemed surprised for a moment. "Ya done it? Why'd ya bash my head?" Anger made him lose his caution and he took a step forward before he caught himself.

"'Cause it needed bashin' then, just as it needs it now."

Fear gripped Linc. The trader was goading him. He'd like nothing better than to kill him so that he could have the woman. Witcher was a man who didn't know the meaning of the word *quit*. He not only was rich, he was deadly in a fight. Linc never fought in the open if there was an easier, safer way of getting what he wanted. He had the girl's pa on his side. He could afford to back down this time.

"Let's go, George." He turned his back to walk away. "Ya comin', Warfield?" When Asa hesitated, he snapped, "Is the deal on or not?"

"It's on. I ain't sure if I oughtta leave the women."

Berry stared at her father with utter loathing, hating him with every ounce of her strength. Her hate forced the words out of her mouth. "Go! It'd be the happiest day of my life if I never set eyes on you again!"

"Watch your tongue, gal! I'm your pa."

"Much to my shame!"

Rachel's hand gripped Berry's arm. She leaned close and whispered, "Shhhh..."

Berry was instantly sorry she'd let her hate carry her away and embarrass Rachel in front of the trader and his friend. She clamped her mouth shut and looked down at the musket.

Asa followed George and Linc down the trail toward the river and the taverns that lined its muddy bank.

"That gal's got too much piss 'n' vinegar fer my notion," George muttered as soon as they were out of hearing distance.

"I'll tame 'er, by gawd! I'll take the fight outta 'er," Linc bragged.

"Leave 'er be," Asa said. "I'll bring 'er 'round. They ain't never stood again' me fer long."

"They ain't comin' docile, like ya said." There was bitter accusation in Linc's voice. "That'n needs ta be screwed, by gawd! Them keelboat men'd give a good bit ta get under 'er skirts."

A spark of decency, long suppressed, surfaced in Asa. "Hold on. I ain't agreed to my gal bein' no whore. The other'n can do the whorin'. Ya asked ta court my gal, 'n' she turned ya down. Let it set a spell. She'll come around."

"Humph!" Linc snorted. "She ain't gonna come

'round less'n you whap 'er butt. Whatta ya think them other'ns are hangin' 'round fer? They c'n smell a bitch in heat same as us. I ain't waitin' 'n' takin' Witcher's leavin's. Ya get 'er in line or the deal's off."

Asa walked in silence. His greedy mind was working fast. Linc had planted a seed that was growing by leaps and bounds. It might suit even more if Berry took to the trader. He had a whole building full of trade goods, and hadn't he and that big feller helped get them across the river? Maybe he was the one who had dosed the whiskey, what with his wanting to get next to the gal. Linc and George said their whiskey had been dosed too. It must've been the trader, Asa decided. He almost chuckled out loud. There's no means a man won't go to ta get him a spot o' tail! he thought.

"Whatta ya know 'bout Witcher?" he asked with as much indifference in his voice as his inner excitement would allow. "Who buys his goods?"

"Stores. Here 'n' upriver in Saint Charles," George answered.

"He got land?"

"Upriver a piece. Ya thinkin' a tyin' in with 'em?"

"It's a thought." Won't do no harm ta let 'em think I got other irons in the fire, Asa thought slyly.

"He ain't wantin' no tavern," Linc said.

"He might. I'm a-thinkin' I got somethin' he wants."

Linc's head swiveled slowly to look at Asa. The beady eyes hardened and his chest swelled with wounded pride. Ya bastard, he swore silently. Ya gawddamned bastard!

* * *

It was midnight. The tavern was noisy with the loud voices of drunken rivermen. Asa sat on a bench beside Linc and George and matched them drink for drink. His blurry eyes could scarcely focus on the tavern wench who carried the jug slung over her shoulder as she made the rounds to fill the tin cups and to collect the coins. He wasn't too drunk, however, to slip his hand beneath her skirt and pinch her bottom. She squealed and danced away from him.

He'd have the wench, he decided. He'd not had a woman, except for a drunken Indian gal, since he'd left Ohio. But first he would go outside and let water. He was about to burst. He lurched to the door, pushing his way through the crowd.

George looked at Linc and nodded. Linc sauntered carelessly toward the door, then darted out into the darkness. Minutes later he was back and the tavern wench was filling his cup with whiskey. He pulled her down on his lap and plunged his hand into the neck of her dress. She giggled, and wiggled on the hardness that pressed against her thigh.

"Thar's a settler out thar with his throat split open." A slurry voice made the announcement. "It was enough to make 'im wet his britches!" he said, snickering. He slouched against the plank that served as a bar.

There was an instant of quiet, then the voices rose again, as if the news was of no concern. Linc played with the woman on his lap and a satisfied look settled on George's face. The farmer ain't oughtta've said nothin' 'bout tyin' in with the trader, he thought. He glanced with admiration at his partner and watched him as he ran his hand up under the woman's skirt.

Linc and George stayed in the tavern until someone came and took away the body.

Chapter Four

I'm hankerin' fer a spot of tea." Fain was the first to speak after the men had left the camp.

"Help yourself." Berry laid the musket on the box. "I'll get a cup."

"I can use this'n if Miss Rachel's done with it." He poured from the teakettle into Rachel's cup, then sank back down on his haunches.

A long quiet settled on them. Simon leaned on his rifle, Fain sipped his tea, and Rachel tried to pull out her apron so that it didn't fit so snugly across her swollen stomach.

Berry stooped to dish up the food in the skillet beside the cookfire. She heaped the plate. "I'll fix some supper if you can wait for it. This is for Israel." She stood and waited for one of them to speak.

"We already et, ma'am, but thanky," Fain said.

Berry nodded and carried the plate to the wagon and set it on the tailgate. She knew Israel wouldn't come to the fire to get it. She returned and sat down on the box again.

"There was a man here tonight," Rachel said. She looked at Fain and he swiveled on his heels to face her. "He was here in the camp almost before we knew it. He looked Indian, but he talked French."

"Was his hair clubbed, slight build, 'n' moved fast 'n' sure?" Rachel nodded. Fain glanced at Simon and back at Rachel. "It was a scout called Light. He works for Simon some."

"We wasn't scared of him." Rachel glanced at Berry's set face. She's worried I'll tell that Asa was going to whip us with the strap, she thought, and wished she hadn't mentioned the man.

"Some folk think Light's kinda crazy." Fain threw the dregs of his tea into the fire. "He's part French and part Indian. His ma was killed by the French, his pa by the Indians. His young Indian wife and baby murdered by rivermen. Light kinda turned in on hisself. He's a quiet one, but he'd fight his way outta a sack of wildcats. He's the best woodsman, tracker, and knife man I ever knowed. He's got no fear and no doubt 'bout killin' if it's what's got to be done. But he's gentlelike with womenfolk."

Berry shivered. "Poor man. Is he a friend of yours?"

"I guess you'd call it that," Fain said thoughtfully. "Me 'n' Simon 'n' a couple fellers up on the Missouri is 'bout the only ones he has any truck with. If he come in 'n' showed hisself, he had a powerful reason. He's not much on mixin' with folks." Fain waited, but Rachel offered no more information.

Berry glanced at Simon and away. He hadn't spoken a word, but she could feel his eyes on her from time to time. A muffled cry from Rachel startled her and she turned quickly. Rachel was leaning back, holding her leg out in front of her. She'd been having muscle spasms for the last few weeks, and the only thing that gave her relief from the terrible pain was to walk. Berry forgot the men. She jumped up, straddled the leg Rachel had thrust out in front of her, put her hands beneath her arms, and tried to lift her.

"I can't..." Rachel gasped. "Oh...oh..."

"You've got to!" Berry tried to lift her again.

Large hands crowded her away. "Let me." Fain's great strength lifted Rachel easily to her feet. "Rub the muscles," he instructed. Berry fell to her knees, slipped her hands beneath Rachel's skirt, and rubbed the knotted muscles in her calf until they softened enough for Rachel to place her foot on the ground. "I'll walk her." Fain's forearm fit beneath Rachel's arm and his hand grasped her arm. She leaned heavily on him and took a painful step. Berry watched helplessly, grateful for the big man's help. They walked back and forth within the circle of light.

"When's she due?" Simon asked. He was still standing in the same spot, still leaning on his rifle.

Berry's face turned brick red. Men weren't supposed to mention such things! "Anytime," she snapped.

"I thought as much. She should move around more."

Pride prevented Berry from telling him that Rachel didn't ride in the wagon all the time because she wanted to. She would have preferred to walk some of the time, but her footgear wasn't stout enough. "You seem to know so much. How many younguns do you have?"

"None. No wife." He almost smiled.

"That don't mean..." Her voice lapsed and her eyes traveled past him. "Where's he goin' with her?" She could just barely see the glimmer of Rachel's dress as she and Fain walked into the darkness. She took a step after them, then turned and picked up the musket. Simon grasped her arm.

"Nothing will happen as long as she's with Fain."

"I trust no man!" Berry jerked her arm free.

"You trusted me...last night." This time he did smile. The spreading of his lips rearranged the features of his face pleasantly. He's handsome, Berry thought with an unexplainable little flutter in her stomach. Not pretty handsome, but not hard to look at. The warmth where his hand had held her arm was still there. He continued to grin at her. "What do you think he'll do? Throw her to the ground and have his way?"

"Ain't that what you men think a doin' all the time?" She could have bitten her tongue for saying the bold words. Color came up her neck and flooded her face for the second time. His low, rumbling laugh did nothing to ease her discomfort.

"When they're looking at a pretty woman, they do. Have you looked in a looking glass lately?"

"I've got no lookin' glass," she snapped, and moved back from him so that she could see his face without having to tilt her head so far back. The musket hung heavily against her thigh. She looked at it to keep from looking at him, then raised her chin and stuck out her jaw. She walked away from him.

At the end of the wagon she took several deep breaths and wondered why her pulse was hammering so wildly. She put the musket in the corner of the wagon within easy reach and stood for a minute with her hands gripping the tailgate. When she turned he was there; she almost rubbed against him. She swallowed a startled cry.

Simon leaned his rifle against the end of the wagon and placed a hand on each side of her. Her back was against the rough boards. She was caged by his arms and tall, hard body. She could scarcely breathe for the excitement that crowded her lungs. Later she was to wonder why she hadn't struggled and why she'd said something so stupid.

"I hate that hat!"

"Why? It's a good hat."

"Humph!"

"What does that mean?"

"Means I still don't like it."

"It keeps the sun off."

"Sun's not out now. You hidin' a bald spot?"

He laughed, and a puff of warm breath fanned her face. He smelled of leather, tobacco, and something tangy, like spice. "Take it off, if you're bound to find out," he invited softly.

She hesitated, then looked up at him with an impish grin tilting her lips. It seemed to her that she reached a long way up to grasp the hat brim. The hat was jammed tightly on his head and she had to tug to remove it. Thick, straight black hair grew back from a high forehead and fell down over his ears. He looked younger without the hat, almost boyish. A bubble of laughter came up and out of her mouth. It was soft and musical.

Simon's eyes devoured her face. "Satisfied?" My

God, she was pretty! More than pretty, he thought. She's spunky, and smart, too. Soft and sparkling as the morning sun.

"Well! You're not onion-slick on top. That's a fact!" She laughed again, a soft trilling sound.

"I like to here you laugh."

She held his hat in both hands. She felt it was some kind of barrier between them. Her face sobered. "I've not had much to laugh about lately."

"Why was your pa going to let a man like Linc Smith court you?"

She bristled with indignation. "I got somethin' to say about that! I'd not let that bush-bottomed, stinkin' buzzard bait court me!"

He waited a long time to speak. An eternity went by while his eyes held hers captive. Finally he said quietly, "I'll court you."

Berry felt herself go ice cold. The next instant she was burning hot, as a flash of anger raced through her body. Stunned, and then angered by his matter-of-fact proposal, she jammed his hat against his chest and pushed. "Don't do me no favors!"

"What're you riled about?" There was a puzzled frown on his face and he gazed at the flawless beauty of hers. Her flashing green eyes were lit with the fire of hostility. Goddamn, she was lovely! His heart began to beat with a new rhythm. He felt desire tighten his buckskins. He'd not admitted to himself that he'd had a hunger to be near her, to touch her, since he'd first seen her across the campfire. Her rejection spurred him to say, "Would you rather be courted by Linc Smith?"

Now she struggled. "I'd not take either of you if you was the only ones in the world walkin' on two legs! I'll not take just anything throwed out to me 'cause my pa's got no more gumption than a drunk hoot owl!" Her breath came in heated spasms. "I aim to do my own choosin'... if I choose at all!"

"I'm not likin' to be put in the same sack as Linc Smith." His mouth tensed and his eyes stared coolly down at her. There was a tight alertness about him now, something primitive and menacing. He was angry and didn't try to hide it.

"I never said you was the same cut," she hissed.

"Then why're you all riled up like a cornered cat 'cause I said I'd court you?"

"It was the way you said it! Like I was some sort of a low-down. Like... you was doin' a favor for a nobody! I'm just as much a somebody as you are, Mr. Simon Witcher, trader 'n' guide, even if I do have holes in my dress 'n' in my shoes. It ain't all on the outside that counts. It's here, on the inside." She struck her chest with her fist. "Here, I'm just as much of a somebody as you are, or any fancy woman with gold hairpins in her hair! Ya hear?" Angry tears filled her eyes and she refused to blink them away. "Now... let me go or I'll poke my knife in you!"

"I never meant it that way. I've not been around women enough to know how to talk to 'em. Course you're a somebody. You're like findin' a pretty pelt among a bunch of mangy hides." His voice was low and caressing. He reached for a curl at the side of her neck and wound it about his finger. "I can't see you wantin' to work in your pa's tavern, neither."

"Do you think I'm dosey?" she sputtered. "I'm not working in no tavern! We haven't figured out yet what we're gonna do if Pa won't take up land.

We're hopin' he'll get over this crazy notion of a tavern." Simon continued to hold the curl between his fingers. No man had ever touched her hair before and it was causing a confused, mixed-up feeling inside her.

Simon's eyes roamed her face. Strange feelings stirred in him. Had he been too long without a woman? This one was a beauty. She was a picture of flagrant outrage, her beauty highlighted by the high color in her cheeks and the sparkle of tears in her eyes. He wanted more than anything to kiss her. Just to kiss her and hold her, not to bed her. She was too rare a woman to use and discard. What would she do? Would she stab him with the knife she had in her pocket? He didn't want to risk frightening her by taking the knife, so he asked her.

"Will you stab me if I kiss you?"

To his surprise, she laughed. "Why do you want to?"

"Because you're so . . . pretty."

"I might not like it. I've not been kissed by a man."

"I'd like to be first." The shimmer in her eyes and the smile on her soft mouth made him feel shaky inside.

"What do I do?"

"First, we get rid of this hat." He took it from her and hung it over the barrel of his gun.

Berry's heart fluttered, and she drew the tip of her tongue across dry lips. The boldness of her actions, the sheer wonder of it, sent a thrill of excitement through her. Her hands lay palms down against the buckskin shirt that covered his chest.

She could feel the steady thump of his heart beneath her hand. Slowly, haltingly, he drew her hands up to his shoulders so that he could pull her close to him. The moment crackled with tension. The hands on her back pulled her against him. At first she was rigid, unyielding. It seemed indecent for her breasts to be touching his chest.

His nose nuzzled into the hair above her ear. "I'll not force you," he whispered.

Berry felt her heart pounding like that of a scared rabbit. She was frightened, yet it was so pleasant to be close to him. He had a scent like spices and fresh pine needles. Her hands moved higher and her fingers came in contact with silky hair that hung to the back of his shirt. She breathed deeply and leaned against him. They stood for a moment, suspended in time, before he turned his head and lightly touched her lips with his. It was over in an instant and his cheek was pressed to hers. She was disappointed.

"Did you like it?"

The whisper tickled her ear. She laughed. "I don't know. Is that all there is to it?"

"Maybe we should try it again." He liked the feel of this small girl in his arms. God! He'd never felt like this before. Not even with the women in that fancy brothel in New Orleans. He wanted to hold this lovely lass, cherish her, see that no harm came to her.

"If you want to." The whisper barely reached his ears.

The arms that enclosed her tightened, and she was conscious of the heavy pounding of a man's heart against hers for the first time. He lowered his head and pressed his lips to hers, held them there for an instant, then kissed her.

Berry had no time to think about what she was doing. She tightened her arms about his neck and offered her lips again. This time their breaths mingled for an instant before he covered her mouth with his. There was no haste in this kiss. It was slow, sensuous, languid. He took his time deliberately and she offered herself willingly. Berry could feel the hard bones and muscles of his body thrusting against the softness of hers through her cotton dress. There was nothing threatening about the arms that held her. She felt protected, sheltered, intimately cocooned in his embrace. Forces stronger than she compelled her arms to tighten about him and her mouth to part beneath his.

Mesmerized by his kiss, her thoughts fled, and feelings took over. Although his lips were soft and gentle, they entrapped hers with a fiery heat. There was a sweet taste to his mouth that was extremely pleasant, and his cheeks were rough against her face. Her fingers moved into the hair at the back of his neck as the bittersweet ache of passion was awakened in her.

Berry was only vaguely aware that his hand had traveled down her back to her hips and that she was pulled tightly to him. She clung, unaware of his restraint, unaware of the tremor in his arms. She felt as well as heard the raspy sound that came from his throat when he lifted his head.

Hoarse, ragged breathing accompanied the thunderous beat of his heart as he realized he had lifted her off the ground and that her arms were locked about his neck. He lowered her to her feet and looked down into eyes smiling into his.

"I liked it! It was much nicer than I imagined it would be." Her fingers stroked his lips. "I never thought a man's lips would be so gentle, or his mouth taste . . . sweet." She laughed softly, happily. "I feel strange, light and giddy. Is it always like this?"

"God Almighty!"

"Does that mean you didn't like it?"

He watched her face. There was no coyness or pretense about her. Her thoughts and feelings were uttered honestly as they came to her. He wanted more than anything in the world to grab her up in his arms and carry her into the woods to a soft ferny place and make love to her. Only her trusting acceptance of him prevented it. "I liked it," he whispered in her ear. "I liked it . . . too much!"

Her arms slid down from around his neck and she stepped back against the wagon. "I always thought I'd hate a man a-pawin' me." She shook her head in disbelief. "It wasn't like I thought it'd be at all. I thought it'd be hurtful and shameful. Rachel cried for days after . . ." She broke off and looked away from the piercing eyes that studied her face. "She said that she remembered a man and a woman who loved each other. They touched and they laughed a lot. They even ran and played together!" She looked up at him with wide, clear eyes. "I'm goin' to wait till I find a man like that, one who'll laugh 'n' play 'n' want to be with me more than anything."

Simon was silent for the duration of a few heartbeats. He didn't know what to say. He pushed a dark curl back from her forehead. "You'll find him," he promised. They stood quietly, listening to the night sounds. A squirrel chattered in the branches above their heads and an owl sent his lonely cry to the wide sky.

Berry shivered and reached into the wagon for her shawl. When she looked back at Simon he had put on his hat. Somehow with the hat on his head he seemed to be a different person. She walked away from him toward the fire. Her eyes searched for Rachel, and she felt a little tug of unease when she didn't see her.

When Simon joined her he held out his hand. Two small wrapped packages lay in his palm. Her eyes questioned his. "Take it. It's for you and Miss Rachel." She reached for the gift, shyly. "It's a sweet from New Orleans. I got a fondness for 'em." He smiled.

In the light from the campfire she could see the smile lines around his eyes and the creases on both sides of his mouth. She'd never be able to look at him again without thinking about his mouth pressing against hers. She put one of the packages in her pocket and carefully unwrapped the other. The sweet was round, softly brittle, and dark brown. She bit off a small piece and held it in her mouth. As it began to dissolve she raised laughing eyes to Simon's.

"It's what I tasted when we ... kissed!"

His smile broadened. The dark eyes that roamed her face were full of amusement. "I ate one on my way over here," he confessed. "They're made out of sugar and rum."

"It's good. I've not had anything like it before."

She took another small bite, then rewrapped the confection and slipped it into her pocket. She swiveled her head to look in the direction Rachel and Fain had taken when they walked away from the camp.

"Don't worry about her," Simon said. "Fain'd die before he'd let any harm come to her."

"It's just that we've always stayed together," she said haltingly.

"They'll be back soon. She needs the walkin'." He wanted to say something to take the worried look from her face. "Sit down and tell me about her . . . and you, and the place you come from."

He was easy to talk to. Soon Berry was telling him how it had been before Rachel had come to the farm, and how it had been afterward. She told him all the good things and carefully avoided telling him the bad. She laughed when she told him about the pet fawn, the chickens, and the big rooster that ruled the barnyard.

He watched her and listened and hoped Fain would take a long time coming back.

Rachel would sooner have died than cry out when the spasm knotted her leg muscles. The pain was almost as hurtful as the calling attention to herself. She still wasn't sure how much Simon and Fain had heard of what had occurred before they showed themselves in camp. Somehow, she saw a solution for Berry with one of these men—that is, if he didn't already have a wife. Long ago she had given up any hope of being happy with a good man of her own.

Fain lifted her off the box and Rachel pressed her

foot to the ground. She leaned heavily on Fain's arm and they began to walk.

"I had me one of 'em once," Fain said with a short laugh. "It hurt like holy hell! Simon 'n' me'd got caught down on the Big Muddy by a bunch-a Osage warriors. Seems like a white man had stole off with one-a their women 'n' not left the price of a rifle 'n' a bag of salt. Our powder was damp, so we had ta run for it." Fain chuckled again. "I ain't much for runnin' like Simon is. We run for 'bout five miles 'n' it started to rain. Wheee... it rained! After 'nother five miles I didn't care if the bastards caught up or not. I sit me down on a stump 'n' said I ain't goin' 'nother step. We found us a cave 'n' crawled in and built us a fire. In the night my legs knotted up somethin' awful. I stomped 'round in that cave all night and cussed them Indians."

Rachel knew he was talking to put her at ease and was grateful for it. "Did you steal the woman?" She wished the words back the instant they left her mouth because she didn't really want to know.

"Naw. She'd taken a shine to Simon 'n' followed us. We had ta ditch 'er, 'n' thought we'd covered our trail. Them Osages ain't no slouches when it comes to trackin', by gawd. They found us." He peered down into her face. "Leg better?"

"Yes, it's better. We can go back now."

"Don't ya want to walk a spell? Ain't it good for a birthin' if ya move 'bout a bit?"

It was only the matter-of-fact way he mentioned her condition that kept Rachel from swooning with mortification. "Yes, but... sometimes the walkin' is rough."

"It ain't rough here. We c'n walk a spell if'n ya c'n put up with the company."

"The company's fine. If you're sure you want to."

Fain chuckled, then stopped and knocked the ashes out of his pipe and put it in the bag that hung from his belt. "I sure do want to. It ain't but once in a hundred moons I get ta walk out with a purty, young woman."

"Don't!" They were in the darkness. Rachel stopped and would have pulled away her arm, but he refused to let it go.

"Don't what?"

"Don't talk like that. I ain't young, ain't pretty!" She wanted to cry. "Berry's young and pretty. Do you like her?"

He put his hand beneath her other elbow and turned her to face him. "The little gal is sightly. Spunky, too," he admitted.

"Do you have a wife?" The words came out in a whisper. Her head was bowed until her chin almost touched her chest.

"I had one once, back in Virginia. It was long ago."

"Berry'd make a good wife for a man who'd be good to her. She'd work hard and make a home place for him to come to."

"Are ya tryin' to match me up with the little 'un?" She couldn't look at him. "What about you? Was you a good wife to your man?" He lifted her chin and saw the glimmer of tears in her eyes. "I hadn't oughtta've said that," he said gently. "Ya was took, warn't ya?" She nodded. His big hand moved to the nape of her neck and he pressed her head to his chest. They stood there for several long minutes before Fain said, "I reckon we'd better get on." He slipped his arm beneath hers again; this time, his hand slid over her waist and grasped hers.

Rachel was agonizingly aware of the man at her side during the long silence that followed. With his hand holding hers, her arm firmly clamped to his side, he matched his steps to hers. They came out of the trees on a bluff that overlooked the river. The moon was lost momentarily behind a wandering cloud, an owl hooted, and the faint sound of a child crying reached them. She had never felt so safe or so peaceful as she did with this big, gentle man. A rush of regret washed over her and she began to tremble. A tear slowly trickled down her cheek. Her lower lip quivered. She summoned all her determination to speak, but her voice came out thin and weak.

"Fain . . ." She hesitated still. "If Berry don't get a man soon, her pa'll sell her off to some no-good that'll break her spirit and her . . . heart." She felt like a small child looking up at him.

"He'd do that?" He lifted a finger and wiped a tear from her cheek. "You're a good lass," he murmured and slipped an arm around her to hold her to his side. "Don't tremble so. We c'n sit a spell afore we go back. It's a purty sight, the moon on the water."

"Will Mr. Witcher go off and leave Berry alone?" She moved with him to a downed tree trunk. She was tired and her heart was beating twice its normal rate.

"I'm a-thinkin' he won't." His eyes searched her face in the wavering light of the moon. "We shoulda brought ya a wrap. It's a bit chilly by the river. If'n it won't scare ya none, I c'n put my arm 'round ya. It'll help some."

The moonlight fell gently on her face, molding it. She had a wistfulness about her. He liked the way she looked and talked. She had a lilt in her voice like Berry's. She was a woman, yet she was a girl, too. She was nice and tall and held herself proudly. Fain decided there was a lot about this woman that suited him.

For the rest of her life Rachel was to remember this night. She was consumed with a variety of emotions: contentment, because she felt so safe snuggling at his side; happy, because she'd never known such a gentle man; and excited, because what she was experiencing was so strange.

"How long have ya been with the Warfields?" he asked quietly.

"A long time. I was fifteen and now I'm twenty-six."

Rachel found herself telling him about being apprenticed out to families to work for her care. She didn't remember her parents but had been told they had died of the black sickness. She had lived with three different families before her bond had been sold to a tavern owner. She had come into womanhood there. The man had been good to her in a way. When Asa had offered a horse and a hundred pounds of shot for her, he had insisted that Asa wed her. Asa had promised they would go to the preacher, but they never had. He had taken her home to a lonely, sad-eyed little girl and to a filthy cabin.

"Berry needed me even more than I needed her,"

she said, remembering. "I'd never had anyone of my own before. She was someone to love, to take care of and to teach woman things to. I taught her to cook and to clean, to weave and to sew. She taught me to cipher and to read, things her own ma had taught her. And . . . she loved me. . . ." Her voice trailed away and they sat in silence. Then, as if compelled to finish the story, she said, "Asa wasn't so bad, at first. He didn't bother me . . . much. Later, he got mean, and I stayed in the loft with Berry. Sometimes it was kind of like he was scared of her," she finished with wonder in her voice.

"But the bastard forced ya!"

"Yes. When I knew I was going to have his baby, at first I wanted to die. I hated it, 'cause it might take on his meanness. Then I thought it might be sweet and pretty like Berry and I loved it and wanted it to live." Rachel leaned against his strength and burrowed her cold hands between his warm body and hers.

A peculiar emotion moved through Fain. There was something about this woman that touched a spot in his heart that he thought had been closed off since Elizabeth had died. Occasionally during the last fourteen years he'd enjoyed the company of women without feeling any more for them than the desire to bed them. He'd moved through this untamed wilderness responsible for no one but himself. Now settlers were moving in. It was rumored that the territory would soon be part of the United States. He'd have to decide soon if he wanted to settle among scores of people or move on west. He wasn't as young as Simon. He liked a warm cabin in the winter when the river froze over and snow filled the trails. He'd like a warm, sweet woman in it, too. One who talked and laughed, someone to listen when he talked.

An emptiness flowed through him. Memory stirred, painfully, uncertainly. His time with Elizabeth hovered, half-imagined, half-remembered. But it was enough to imbue his heart with a terrible loneliness and hurt. She'd been tall and thin, like this woman, and she'd died having a stillborn child, just as this woman could die.

He looked down at Rachel with a haunted look in his hooded eyes. He didn't want the pain of loving and losing another woman.

"If'n you're rested, we c'n go back."

Chapter Five

Asa Warfield lay dead.

His body lay wrapped in a blanket, his booted feet protruding from the end, in the shade of the wagon while the bury box was being readied. The Ohio settlers, out of respect for Berry and Rachel, had delayed their departure to assist with the burial. Mr. Benson and another man were building the box. Israel had gone to dig the grave.

Rachel and Berry sat beside the body and received the condolences of their neighbors. They had been in a state of shock since the stranger had come to the wagon grounds driving a cart with Asa's body bouncing in the back. Luckily he was identified by one of the men and rolled in the blanket before the women saw him. Since that time there had been a continuous parade of people coming to the wagon to offer sympathy, to bring food and to talk in hushed tones, their tongues clicking sadly.

By mid-morning the chatter was getting on Berry's nerves. She knew they were well meaning, wanting to do the "decent thing," but also eager to get the burying over so they could go on to the land awaiting them. With all the commotion there was no time for her to rest and consider what she and Rachel would do now. She began to wish the time away. The hours passed slowly, and finally it was time to put Asa in the ground.

Berry and Rachel walked behind the men carrying the rough plank coffin. The burial ground was a short distance through the woods. They stepped over downed tree trunks and skirted brush that caught at their skirts and whipped them around so that a good bit of ankle showed. It was of no concern to Berry. Her mind was on other things. They'll all be watchin', expectin' me to weep, she thought. But I won't. I'm sorry he died, truly sorry. But not more'n I'd be for anyone else. They can think I'm unfeelin' if they want to, but I'll not pretend grief I don't feel.

Rachel clung to Berry's arm. To the watchful women, her "condition" was the perfect excuse for her dry eyes. It would be harmful for her to indulge in the usual weeping of a newly widowed woman. Her eyes were lowered, the lids deep and heavily fringed. There was no color in her cheeks, but her lips were soft and red. "Fever," one woman whispered to another.

A parson had come up from the village. He was a long, black scarecrow of a man with a flowing white beard. He stood beside the grave, a large book in his hand. Mr. Benson, blustery but well meaning, stood beside him. The members of the wagon train gathered around. They arranged their ruddy faces to fit the solemn moment. Some of the women even managed to squeeze a few tears from their eyes.

The parson's hushed voice began the service. "We're laying to rest a beloved husband and father..."

Berry's chest tightened. The words beat at her mind. I'm a hypocrite, she thought, to stand here and let him say those words. He was not a husband, not a beloved father. She began to tremble and stiffened her body against it.

"This man whom Death has called to his reward in the great beyond..." The parson's bloodless face was grave as his voice droned on.

Berry's mind wandered. I wonder if we have to pay him for this? Where is Israel? Does Simon know Pa is dead? Who killed him? Was it the man called Light, or Linc, or George? Rachel's hardly said a word. Is she feeling sick and won't tell me? Was Simon serious when he offered to court me? I'll talk to Rachel about it. She'll know. Damn him! Why'd I let him kiss me? He'll think I'm a loose woman!

Berry came back to the present with a start. The people were singing "Rock of Ages," and the men were shoveling dirt in on the box. Rachel tugged at her arm and they turned away. She thanked the parson, thanked Mr. Benson, thanked the men filling the grave.

Back at the wagons, Berry took off her sunbonnet. A frisky breeze from the river loosened a lock of hair and whipped it across her temple. She had reached to tuck it back with her fingers when Mr. Benson and Mr. Hollis appeared.

Mr. Hollis was a widower with five children rang-ing in age from a toddler to a boy old enough to drive a wagon. His wife had died during the preparation for the trip west. He was a small man with a hawk nose and thin hair on top. His pants bagged in back and his wooden-soled boots looked many sizes too large for his feet.

Mr. Benson cleared his throat noisily. "Is Mrs. Warfield a-holdin' up?"

"Rachel's holdin' up fine. She's restin' in the wagon."

"It's what she should be doin'." He shifted his feet restlessly and looked away from her and back.

"Mr. Benson? Do you know where the land is that my pa filed on?"

"I don't know, miss. He never rightly said if'n he filed on any. If he did, he'd have a map in his pack 'n' it'd be marked." He paused, glanced at the man beside him, then said hurriedly, "Mr. Hollis here offered ta take ya along with him. He's needin' a woman, 'n' ya need a man ta stand by ya."

Somehow the words were not a surprise to Berry. She'd known almost from the first and had steeled herself to be civil. Now the eyes she turned on the man who fidgeted beside the wagonmaster were as cold as ice. Mealymouthed bastard, can't even do his own askin'! she thought. "Are you askin' for me or my stepmother, Mr. Hollis?" she asked with haughty dignity.

"Why... you, Miss Berry," he squeaked.

"And Mrs. Warfield?"

"She'd be... welcome...." He looked down at his feet.

"What about our slave, our two wagons, and our stock?"

"Well... I reckon you'd bring 'em with ya." There was a new note of eagerness in his voice.

"That's *so* kind of you, Mr. Hollis!" Her voice was heavy with sarcasm, her face red with anger. The farmer smiled victoriously. He'd heard her words but not the meaning behind them. However, the smile left his face when Berry let loose with a torrent of angry words. "You lily-livered, belly-crawlin' worm! My pa ain't cold yet 'n' you come here offerin' to take us in! You saw a chance to get your hands on two wagons, two mules, an ox, and three sets of hands to work for ya while you ride, nice 'n' easy, on Pa's mare!" Her nostrils flared and angry lights flashed in her green eyes. She continued through tight lips, "You worked one woman to death a-havin' your kids and a-plowin' your fields. Ya ain't no man to stay by a woman! Behind 'er is where you'd stand!" Berry had to stop and catch her breath.

"Now... see here..."

"You see here, ya vulture! Get the hell outta my camp!" She was so angry she was almost sick. "I ain't takin' no man such as the likes of you. You come 'round here again, ya struttin' rooster, 'n' I'll ... get my knife 'n' make a hen outta you!"

The man's mouth hung open. He stood in shock until the wagonmaster nudged him, then he turned on his heel and scampered away.

"Ya ain't oughtta talked like that," Mr. Benson said curtly as if he were talking to an unruly child. "There ain't no other man on this train without a woman."

Berry's eyes swung to him. "I don't give a... damn! I'll not take a scrawny, grabby little weasel like him! How could you think I would? It woulda been just dandy for *him*. He'd been set up good with me 'n' Rachel takin' care of his younguns and Israel to do his work. What woulda been in it for us? Rachel and me aren't goin' to jump out of the fryin' pan and into the fire!"

"Wal, what're ya goin' to do then?" He jerked the words out impatiently. "We can't wait on ya. It's gettin' on, 'n' crops has gotta be put in."

Berry took a deep breath to calm herself. "We don't know yet if we have land to go to. We haven't had time to talk."

The wagonmaster took his hat off and wiped his brow with his sleeve. "Women can't take up a tract o' land," he said with heavy disgust in his voice.

"Why not?"

"Wal, 'cause..."

"I'll go to a land man 'n' find out."

"We're leavin' in a hour's time, miss," he said sternly.

"Then go! We can't tag along if we don't know where we're goin'," she said stubbornly.

Indecision was written on the man's face. He rubbed his whiskers while he pondered. When he spoke, it was as if a great burden had been placed on his shoulders. "I reckon I c'n take ya in. It'll be a bunch, what with my woman's ma 'n' sister, 'n' our younguns." He scratched his head with work-worn, knurled fingers. "I just can't bring myself ta leave ya behind."

Berry's mind was made up in a flash. "We're not goin', Mr. Benson. We're figurin' on stayin' here, gettin' us a place 'n' startin' us a business."

"It ain't fittin'!" he stammered. "Your pa'd..."

"You don't know what my pa would think fittin'. He liked his drink. He never did a day's work if he could get me 'n' Rachel to do it. Him bein' dead don't change that!"

"By the Lord Henry, gal!"

"Goodbye, Mr. Benson. Thanks for helpin' to bury Pa."

"A hour, miss," he said sternly. "If'n ya want to come, pull in behind." He stalked off.

Berry watched him leave. Law! What had she done? She'd thrown his help back in his face. Well, it couldn't be helped now. She wouldn't take that Hollis for her man and they wouldn't follow along behind Benson and his family. She stepped up on the box and climbed into the wagon. Rachel lay on the pallet, her eyes open, staring. Berry unbuttoned her good dress and pulled it off over her head. She folded it carefully and put it in the trunk.

"Did ya ever think it'd come to this, Rachel?" she asked tiredly. "Pa's gone. I didn't think I felt sad, but I guess I do, in a way. I just wish he'd been a better man."

Rachel lay on her side, her arm folded beneath her head. She had been unusually quiet since learning that Asa was dead. "Asa should've stayed in Ohio. He didn't last very long out here where men are meaner 'n' wilder than him. I wonder who killed him."

"Somebody that wanted his money. He had money from the farm. If he was carryin' it, it's gone now." Berry slipped her everyday brown linsey dress over her head and tied her apron in place. "Did you hear what I told Mr. Benson?"

Rachel nodded. "And what you told Mr. Hollis,

too." She smiled, showing small, perfect teeth. The smile took years from her face.

"That mule's ass! Just the thought of havin' that short-brained lout touchin' me gives me the shivers!" Berry poked stray hair up into her braid with angry, short jabs of her fingers. "He stood there, eyes bulgin' and his mouth hangin' open like a fish about to take bait, all the time a-thinkin' he'd get his hands on Israel and these wagons."

"That's not all he was wantin' to get his hands on." Rachel laughed softly, then her face sobered. "For the first time in our lives we don't have somebody tellin' us what to do. I've been thinkin' about it since we heard about Asa." She pushed herself up from the pallet and painfully stretched her legs out in front of her. "Where's the guns, Berry? We've got a musket and Asa had a rifle and two more muskets. I'll clean 'em and load 'em. If any of that river trash comes around here with notions on their mind, we'll be waitin' for them."

Berry watched her while she talked. The woebegone look was gone from her face and her voice held a positive ring. "With three muskets and a rifle, we'd have four shots. It'd be enough to cause 'em to think a minute."

Rachel got to her feet. "Help me down, honey. Then you go through Asa's things and find the papers on Israel. We can't let those be stole away from us, or somebody'd come in 'n' take him away from us."

"That's right! I hadn't thought of that." Berry got out of the wagon, then guided Rachel's foot to the box so she could get down. There was a world of difference between the Rachel of today and the

Rachel who had cowered behind her yesterday. Instead of feeling resentment, Berry felt a surge of pity for the man who had so wasted his life and so dominated them that they were actually happier now that he was gone.

Berry and Rachel stood by their wagon and watched the train of settlers from Ohio move past them and down the trail to Saint Louis, where they would spread out and head for their new homes. The women called out to them and waved. Mr. Hollis drove by them without a glance in their direction. Mr. Benson paused. Berry shook her head. She could see his lips move as he swore. She couldn't curb an insolent grin. He cracked the whip over the backs of his mules and didn't look back.

When the dust had cleared, theirs were the only two wagons left in the long, flat meadow. Berry's throat clogged with wonder. So much had happened. She and Rachel were alone in a hard, unwelcome wilderness. Whatever was to happen to them now, there was no turning back.

Berry found herself thinking about Simon and gave herself a mental shake. She had to work to keep her thoughts from straying to him. Somehow she had expected him to come when he heard her pa was dead. If he'd been serious about courting her he'd have come. He knew the train was moving out today. But maybe he thought Asa would stay here and start a tavern. In a secret little compartment of her mind she admitted to herself that Simon was the reason she hadn't searched Asa's trunk for a land map. If she'd found one and the land was near Mr. Benson's land, they'd not have had an excuse to stay behind.

The best thing about their new situation, she decided, was the change in Rachel. Just twenty-four hours ago she had been a quiet, brooding woman whose spirit appeared completely broken. Now it seemed as if the dark depression that had gripped her had been washed away. She spoke in a gentle but positive way, and occasionally she laughed. Her eyes had lost their dull, passive look and were now bright with interest and excitement.

"Berry, are you sorry we didn't go with them?"

"No!" Berry brought her attention back to the present. "They didn't really care about us. They cared about our wagons 'n' that good plow tied to the side. And . . . the stock. They only saw us 'n' Israel as hands to work for them, not as people who had dreams 'n' wanted to be happy."

"They're gone. Let's forget them and plan on what we're goin' to do." Rachel sat down on the box at the end of the wagon. "Get Israel. We need to know if we can depend on him or if he'll run off the first chance he gets now that there's not a man to watch him."

"Do you think Fain and Simon will come to see about us?"

"I don't know, honey. We can't depend on it. They may have gone upriver by now." Rachel didn't want Berry to know that she too had nurtured that hope. "I know that musket is heavy to carry around, but keep it with you. Now if you'll get Israel we can find out if he's stickin' with us. Although I doubt he'd tell us if he wasn't. I saw him walkin' out to where he tethered the mules."

Berry returned with the slave. She took the musket from the belt of her apron and sat down. The heavy gun rubbed against her breast and she wondered how Simon and Fain could move about so easily with guns tucked in their belts. "Sit down, Israel. I'll break my neck lookin' up at ya."

The black man sank to the ground at their feet.

"Do you know how to shoot a gun?" Berry asked.

"No, ma'am. Ah never..."

"Can ya load one?"

"Yass'm."

"That'll help. I know you're good at bashin' in heads." Berry smiled into the big man's eyes and was rewarded with an awareness in his and then a broad smile. "Are you goin' to stay with us or run off the first chance ya get?" The question took the smile off his face.

"Naw, missy..."

"I didn't think you would, but I had to ask. From now on we've got to look out for each other. Do ya understand? You'll eat the same food we eat, you'll sleep in the wagon when it rains 'n' other times if ya want to. Take what clothes Pa had that ya can wear, and Israel... you'll never feel the whip on your back again."

"Lawsey me!"

He looked at her in wonder, a slow, warm smile spreading across his face.

"Rachel has your papers. If you stay 'n' help us now, someday you'll be free."

"Lawsey me, missy. I dunno free!" The broad shoulders sagged and the Negro hung his head.

"We won't think about it now. Bring the stock in close so some thief can't make off with them. And gather in enough firewood to light up this camp tonight. I'm thinkin' that river trash knows Pa's gone 'n' they'll come callin'. We can't depend on anyone to help us. We got to help ourselves."

"Yass'm. Yass'm, ah do dat, 'n' ah'll fill up the barrel wid water, too. Yass'm." He got to his feet. "Yass'm." He bobbed his head up and down.

Berry looked directly into his eyes, something she's always been told not to do. White folks were not to look into a slave's eyes any more than they'd look into the eyes of a dog or a mule. "I knew I could depend on you."

It seemed to Berry that Israel walked taller and prouder when he left them. She turned to see Rachel's eyes following him. "I told you he wasn't as dumb as he let on," she bragged. "Treat a man like a dumb beast 'n' he'll act like one. Treat him human 'n' he'll act human."

Rachel's eyes were filled with love and admiration. "You know a lot of things you never told me before."

Berry looked away, hugging her secret thoughts. *I've not told you the most important of all: Simon kissed me 'n' I'll never be the same again. My eyes are lookin' for him all the time. I want him to want me, not because I'm a woman and can ease the ache most men take a woman for. I want it to be like you said ... him wanting to touch me, laugh with me, play with me. ...* Aloud she said brightly, "Well, that's done. Let's go see what Pa had in the trunk."

Asa had filed on land! Berry found the contract and the crude map in the bottom of the trunk along with a small bag of coins. She and Rachel hugged each other.

"We'll go there and homestead. We won't say nothin' about Pa bein' killed. We'll live in the wagons until we can get a cabin built. How many coins, Rachel?"

Rachel finished counting before she answered. "Not more than twenty." Disappointed, she put the coins back in the bag.

"That's not very many for all the supplies we'll need. Maybe we can barter the mare," Berry said hopefully. Then, "How're we goin' to find this place?" She unfolded the map and turned it sideways. "This must be the river." Her finger traced a line. "This says Saint Louis and the marked-off spot is west and north of that. It's not on a river and it don't look like it's on a creek. How'll we find it?" she said again.

"We'll have to ask someone. We should've looked for the map before Mr. Benson left."

"I'm glad we didn't. He'd've not wanted us to homestead. He said women couldn't take up land."

"It'll be hard," Rachel said with a sigh.

"Not any harder than what we've been used to," Berry answered stubbornly. "Do you think Fain, or ... Simon would take us there?"

"They might ... if we ever see them again."

As evening approached, Berry cast anxious eyes around the clearing. Israel had carried in enough dead wood to keep a fire going all night. The mules, the ox, and the sorrel mare were tethered behind the wagons. She and Rachel each carried one of the muskets. The other musket, the rifle, the powder, and shot were under a cloth near the cookfire.

Berry unwrapped the sweet Simon had given her and took a small bite. She wrapped the rest and put it back in her pocket. Her hand caressed the paper lovingly. She had been careful to take only a small nibble now and then, and to hold it in her mouth so the treat would last longer. All day she had tried to keep him out of her mind. Now, the sweet in her mouth reminded her of his.

"We'll hitch up the team and go into town tomorrow," Rachel said, breaking into her thoughts. "We'll ask at one of the stores where we can find Fain or Mr. Witcher."

They ate a hasty meal and put away the cook things. As darkness approached, both women began to doubt the wisdom of their actions, but neither voiced her anxiety to the other. Rachel's face was drawn with worry. The ache in her back had intensified as the day wore on. She sank down on the box and leaned back against the wagon wheel. There was very little possibility of help coming from the half-breed scout or from Fain or Simon. If the men had heard of their plight and were concerned for them, they would have been here by now.

This place seems a million miles from the farm in Ohio, Rachel thought. There's no law in this land. The decent people in the town have no reason to think about the happenings at the wagon grounds where settlers come and go with regularity.

Rachel was as sure as sin that before the night was over, Asa's friends would pay them a visit. She'd seen the lust in Linc's eyes when he looked at Berry. She tried to reason out the best thing to do. They had to separate, she decided. The more she thought about it, the more sure she was that it was the right thing to do. She told Berry her plan and Berry agreed.

"You get in the wagon and rest, Rachel. I'll take

that old, dark quilt 'n' get out there in the dark so I can watch."

"I thought you could get in the other wagon."

"No. It's best if they think we're both in the same wagon like the other night. You take the rifle and one of the muskets. I'll take the other two." She helped Rachel into the wagon and then brought the guns to her. "Doesn't it seem strange that Pa would have three muskets?"

"He won 'em at cards, more'n likely."

Berry selected a spot among some leafy brush that grew around a giant oak. She spread the quilt, sat down on the edge of it, and pulled the rest over her lap. From this point she could see both the front and the back of Rachel's wagon and the stock tethered behind and to the side of it. She rested her back against the tree and took the sweet from her pocket. The treat was almost gone. She wanted to hold on to it a little longer, so she returned it to her pocket without taking a nibble.

Berry was tense and nervous and suddenly very tired. Her eyes searched the darkness for a sight of Israel. After he had brought the stock in and carried in a supply of fuel for the fire he had disappeared. As far as she knew, he hadn't returned to get his supper. She was acutely disappointed in him. Somehow she had been sure he wouldn't run off and leave them alone. She hoped Rachel hadn't noticed his absence. There was no need for her to worry until they were sure he wasn't coming back.

In all his life Israel had never felt important or needed until now. Suddenly he had been pushed into a new role—that of protector to the white women who had been kind to him, who had made his life bearable. He was ready to lay his life down for them, but what good would that do? His worthless life was nothing. He had to find someone to help them. His mind had worked at the problem all day. Who would listen to a slave? The thought came to him that another slave would listen. He had seen a black man standing beside a stone building when they had come through town. He would find him and ask him what to do.

When darkness settled, Israel slipped out of camp and ran through the woods toward the town. The thought of what the white men would do to the missy overcame the terror of being alone in the wilderness and the uncertainty of what he would do when he reached town. On the outskirts of the town he hunkered down to get his breath and try to figure out the best way to reach the building at the end of the street. There was no doubt in his mind that if he was caught out alone he'd be stolen away and resold in one of the towns down the river.

At this hour the street was dark and deserted. All the activity was around the saloons on the riverfront. Israel had no idea of how to find the man he'd seen the day before. He decided to make his way to the rear of the building, hide, and wait. His heart pounding with fear and excitement, he darted across the rutted road and slid behind the long row of buildings. He ran their length in short spurts, pausing to listen and to pick out his next stop. Finally he came to the stone building and squatted down between two barrels to rest.

"Oh, lawsey, lawsey..." he groaned. He picked

a few cockleburrs out of his feet and wished with all his heart that he were back at the wagon grounds with the missy.

When a huge hand grabbed the back of his neck and he felt the prick of a knife in his back, Israel's legs straightened out of their own accord and he shot up from his squatting position beside the barrels. Fear ran tingling down his spine and chilled his heart.

"What yo' sneakin' 'round here fo'?"

"Ah...ah..." A heavy hand spun him around. Terror clogged his throat.

"Talk, boy. You a runaway?"

"Naw...naw..."

"Ain't you that slave come a-drivin' them mules up ta the grounds yesterday?"

"Yassuh." Some of the fright left Israel when he saw the big black man was the man he was looking for. "Mistah Asa's dead. All them folk gone, 'n' a riverman's comin' ta get little missy." The words poured out of him in a rush.

"What you talkin' 'bout, boy?"

Israel tried to calm himself and explain the situation. He talked in short gasps. When he had finished, he asked about the white man with the pipe and the white man who wore the broad-brimmed hat.

"Mistah Simon done gone upriver, 'n' Mistah Fain gone home."

"Oh, lawsey...oh, po' missy..." Israel groaned.

"Hush up yo' moanin'," Lardy said sharply. "Moanin' don' help your missy. You go 'n' catch up to Mistah Fain. You go back, hide yo'self 'n' watch. If'n the riverman come, sneak up behind 'im 'n' bash his head. Don' get yo'self caught. White man'll split your gullet." He put the edge of his hand to his throat. "Go on. Git outta this town now."

The run back through the woods to the camp was not as frightening to Israel. He was buoyant with self-worth. He had done what he had set out to do. He'd gotten help for missy. When he reached the wagon grounds he hunkered down to watch before showing himself. The campfire had burned low. There was almost no light. He waited until he was sure there was no one around, then he slipped between the wagons and heaped some dead branches on the fire, waited until it blazed brightly, then slipped into the darkness again.

Berry became alert when she saw the figure at the campfire. She lifted the musket, then almost sobbed with relief when she recognized Israel's lanky figure. He hadn't run off after all! She leaned her head back against the tree trunk and watched him fade into the darkness. It was a comfort to know he was there.

Her bottom began to ache. She shifted her position. She was sitting on the knurled roots of the tree. The quilt was hot and scratchy, but it concealed her so well she didn't dare throw it off. She sat motionless, her body aching, and wondered why she'd ever thought the forest was a silent place.

The wind came up and stirred the top of the tree. It crackled and popped as if protesting the disturbance. An owl hooted and was answered by another a long way away. A pack rat scurried in the leaves, then hurried off on some nocturnal hunt. A nightbird whistled and Berry lifted her head to listen.

Didn't Indians signal each other by using such sounds? She tensed, waiting for an answering whistle or the sound of a footfall. None came and she settled back with relief.

She relaxed and let her mind wander to Simon. She went over in her mind each and every word they had exchanged. She wished, now, that she hadn't gotten so angry when he'd said he would court her. But... dammit! Why'd he have to say it like that? she thought. He'd said she was pretty. That was the reason why he wanted to kiss her. Her face began to burn over the thoughts that danced in her mind; thoughts of how he had felt against the front of her when his hand went down to her hips, cupped them, and pulled her against him. When he finished kissing her he had been breathing hard, too. Breathing as hard as if he'd been running a long way. Come to think about it, *she'd* never been so out of air in her whole life!

The hours passed slowly. When the birds left the treetops Berry was sure it was close to dawn. She was also certain that between the hardness of the ground, the ache in her back, and listening to the sounds of the forest, she would never go to sleep. But she was more tired than she knew. Her head began to nod... she jerked awake... nodded ... came awake, and finally she closed her eyes to rest them for a moment, and fell asleep.

Chapter Six

Whatever it was that woke Berry, she thanked God for it later. Her eyes flew open to see a motionless figure crouched before her. Suddenly it moved and a hand clamped hard over her mouth. She was caught by surprise and got only a glimpse of hard, bright eyes staring out of a bushy face. She could not cry out because of the hand. Fear rushed into her heart. Her reaction was purely instinctive and she was only barely conscious of what she was doing until she heard the deafening roar of the musket. Somehow she had managed to tilt the gun, where it lay in her lap beneath the quilt, and pull the trigger.

The hand left her mouth as the man was flung back. She heard the shot, smelled the smoke, and stared in mute fascination at the blossom of blood that spouted on her assailant's chest. He was jerked upright, then twisted crazily, reeled, and fell over backward, still twitching.

Berry's fingers dug into the rough bark of the

tree and she pulled herself to her feet. She was dazed, realizing only that dawn had come. The quilt lay in a heap around her feet. She dropped the still-smoking musket and reached frantically for the second gun. As she straightened, a second shot blasted the stillness. She screamed inwardly; in her shocked terror she was unable to make a sound. Then, as if out of a nightmare, an odd-looking figure in buckskin pants and a dirty, white cloth shirt raced toward her. Linc Smith! He was bareheaded, his hair stood out around his head like porcupine quills, and his teeth were bared like those of an attacking animal.

"George!" Then: "Ya bitch! Ya killed 'im!"

Everything beyond the powerful body hurtling toward her became blurred and indistinct. Berry could scarcely draw a breath into her lungs. Then she remembered that she was holding the second pistol. As if in a dream, she felt her arms lift the gun and her fingers tighten and pull. The sound roared in her ears; she closed her eyes against it as she was pushed back against the tree trunk by the force of the explosion.

Linc screamed. Berry looked with horror as he grabbed the side of his face. Blood seeped between his fingers and spilled down onto his cloth shirt in a crimson flood. He reeled and turned into the woods without another sound.

"Rachel!" The frantic cry came hoarsely from her throat. Her feet felt as if they weighed a hundred pounds each as she ran toward the wagon. "Rachel!" She stumbled against the body of a man lying crumbled, face down in the dirt. The frightened mules were straining against the ropes that held them, and the mare nickered and danced at the end of her tether.

Berry jumped up on the box and crawled into the open end of the wagon. Rachel was on the floor, trying to pull herself up into a sitting position. Smoke from the fired gun stung Berry's nostrils. She fell to her knees beside the other woman and threw her arms around her. "Are ya hurt? Are ya hurt?" She helped her to sit up and lean against the side of the wagon. "Did...they get in the..."

"Did I kill him?" Rachel looked at her with dazed, wide eyes. "Is he dead?"

"He's dead! Oh... Rachel...!"

"The rifle knocked me down. Get the musket...."

Berry grabbed the musket, crawled to the end of the wagon, and looked out. Her mind still hadn't accepted what had happened. Israel was trying to calm the mare. Her eyes swept the camp and then she gazed into the woods as far as she could see.

She called out to Israel, "Are they gone?"

"Yass'm." He had no time to say more; the dancing mare claimed all his attention. Finally he untied the rope and led her to the front of the wagon.

Berry returned to Rachel. "I killed George 'n' I shot Linc in the face! Oh, Rachel! It was awful!"

"Who is it... out there?" Rachel sat on the floor, her legs sprattled and her hands cupped beneath her abdomen.

"I don't know. I'll go see, and I've got to get the guns I left by the tree. Are you sure you're all right?"

"I'm fit for the shape of me. Let's leave this place! Tell Israel to hitch up. We can go down to the town." Moving carefully and awkwardly, Rachel eased her bloated body over onto the feather tick. Her face completely drained of color, she looked at Berry pleadingly.

Berry crawled to her, her heart hammering with fear. "Is it the baby? Is it coming?"

"I don't think so. I'll be all right if I can rest here for a minute. Load the guns. We can talk later."

Berry put the musket beside Rachel and loaded the rifle. The look of pain on Rachel's face filled her heart with dread. Carrying the rifle by the barrel, she climbed out of the wagon, looked around cautiously, then walked over and peered down at the man Rachel had shot. He wasn't anyone she had ever seen before, but from his dress he looked to be a riverman.

Morning light was flickering through the forest. With the rifle pointed in front of her, her finger on the trigger, Berry carefully skirted George's body and grabbed up the two muskets and the quilt. Afraid to turn her back on the woods, she backed away, while her eyes searched for movement among the trees. Back at the wagon, she threw the quilt inside and quickly loaded the guns. She thrust one into the waistband of her apron and placed the other and the rifle within easy reach in the back of the wagon. Rachel lay with her eyes closed and Berry thought she was asleep, until she spoke.

"I can't help you, honey. I wish ... I could...."

"Don't worry! There's nothin' you can do. We're goin' to hitch up and get out of here. Israel!"

"Missy..." Israel had untied the mules and moved them into position to be harnessed. He had the gear slung over his shoulder. His long arm and pointing finger directed her gaze to a humped bundle in the grass. "Him was gonna take the mules, but ah bash 'is head. The mules kick 'im."

"Is he dead?"

"Yass'm."

"There was four of them? Oh, Israel, you done good! If he's dead it's his own doin'! Hitch up as fast as you can so we can get away from here. There was one of 'em I didn't kill. He ran off in the woods 'n' he might be comin' back." A chill rippled along her spine as she realized what would have happened to her and Rachel if they hadn't armed themselves.

They were ready to leave in record time. Berry tied the mare on behind the big wagon, then moved up beside the ox and switched it lightly on the rump. As the ox pulled the wagon out of the meadow, past the bodies of the men they had killed during the early dawn, a hatred of men, of the river, and of the town began to burn in Berry. Since they had crossed the river, life had been an ugly dream. A small part of her mind argued against this. The few intimate moments she had shared with Simon were the exception. But, she realized now, she had blown the importance of all that out of proportion. He would have come to them if he had been as interested in her as she had hoped he was.

Berry strode along beside the ox, one hand on its halter, the other on the musket tucked in her belt. It was heavy and uncomfortable to carry, but it was a comfort to know it was there. She let her hand wander down into her pocket where the paper-wrapped bit of sweet Simon had given her remained. She brought it out and, without looking at it, crushed it in her fist and threw it into the grass alongside the trail. She would not be won over with a few treats and a kiss or two. He was more like Linc than he appeared to be, she thought angrily. He wanted the same thing, but he went about getting it differently.

Somewhere off in the trees behind the dense foliage, a blue jay squawked, a wren in the trees overhead scolded, and a squirrel scrambled away as the creaking wagons approached. The sun came up over the trees beyond the river and struck Berry in the face. She could see nothing of the town. She squinted against the glare and listened to the sound of hooves striking the hard-packed trail and to the jingle of the harnesses.

Berry debated what to do as they neared the crossroads in the trail. They could turn south and go down through the town's main thoroughfare and endure the stares of the locals as they poked one another with their elbows and snickered at the poor eastern deadbeats, or they could take the trail north in the direction of the land her pa had filed on. Except that Rachel's baby was due. . . . In Saint Louis there was no place for them to stay but at the wagon grounds, and they couldn't settle down *there*. More than likely they would have to handle the birthing alone anyway. But, Law! If anything happened to Rachel . . .

She knew she had no right to make the decision alone, so she pulled the ox to a halt and climbed up into the wagon.

Rachel raised her head. "Is something wrong? Why're we stopping?"

"How are ya feelin'?"

"Better," she said and smiled.

Berry was to remember, later, that Rachel always said "better" when she was asked the question.

"We've got to decide if we want to go into town or turn north 'n' try 'n' find the land Pa filed on. If we go on we may run into some settlers who'll show us the way."

"We can't go back," Rachel said with her calm reasoning. "It's best if we get as far from here as we can. We can't be sure the people in town will help us after they find out what we did."

"But what about you? We'll need help when you...?"

"We'll manage like we did before. Let's go on."

"Linc'll look for us. I shot him, 'n' he'll come for me."

"He won't be in any shape to look for us for a day or two. We can be far away by then."

Berry leaned over and kissed Rachel's cheek. "You sure you feel like goin' on?"

"Stop worryin' about me. Just keep on movin' north." Rachel carefully controlled her face to show none of the pain she was feeling.

"I'll try to keep the wagon out of the ruts so it won't jar you," Berry promised.

As soon as Berry left her, Rachel groaned and wondered how she could get through the day.

"We're goin' on, Israel," Berry called. "We'll stop for a early nooning 'n' I'll fix us a meal."

"Yass'm, missy."

By the middle of the morning Berry's feet hurt and she was so tired she wished she were able to handle the mules so she could ride part of the time. Sometimes she rode in the wagon pulled by the ox, but to keep the beast to the side of the trail and away from the deep ruts she had to walk beside it. As she stumbled along, there was a trembling in her bones and her head echoed with long, dull throbs. She tried to estimate how many hours had passed since she'd had a peaceful night's sleep, then put it out of her mind as other thoughts crowded in.

How glad she was now that she'd not taken Simon's offer to court her seriously. Damn, damn him! Damn Fain, too. Surely in a place the size of Saint Louis word had spread that her pa had been killed. If those men had cared what happened to them they would have come, or at least sent the half-breed scout. Berry straightened her back and stuck out her jaw stubbornly. She would find the land Asa had filed on. It was theirs now. They'd build a cabin with Israel's help, and raise a garden. She'd teach Israel to shoot so that he could hunt meat. They'd make a place for themselves without help from anyone.

Shortly before noon she spotted a rabbit huddled beneath the brush that lined the trail. She took the musket from her belt and held it with both hands while she sighted down the barrel and pulled the trigger. The rabbit jumped and fell. She had hit it, but it wasn't dead. She ran back and held the mules while Israel ran it down and killed and skinned it.

At noon they pulled to the side of the trail and Berry quickly built a cookfire and started the rabbit roasting on a spit. Israel watered the stock and loosened the harnesses so they could lower their heads and nip at the grass beside the trail. Berry reloaded her pistol, all the time watching behind and ahead of them. Her eyes burned and she had to hold them wide to keep them open.

Rachel was sitting with her back against the trunk when Berry went to the end of the wagon. "Do you want to get out for a while?"

"I think I'll stay here if you don't need me. I could use a spot of tea."

Berry turned away. She couldn't help thinking she'd never seen Rachel's face so drawn or her lips so bloodless. She forgot her own discomfort. She poured tea for herself and Israel, then took the teakettle and a cup and set them in the wagon near Rachel. As soon as the meat was done they would move on. They could eat it while they were moving.

The air was warm and scented with the blossoms of flowering trees and vines. Berry was unconcerned with the fact that it was a glorious summer day and the breeze lifted her hair and cooled her neck. She was so tired that she had let down her guard and seldom glanced behind them. She had to concentrate on putting one foot before the other so that they could reach a spot where they could camp for the night. It had to be a place where they could defend themselves again if necessary. They were out here alone and had not seen another human being, not even on the river the few times the trail curved and they had seen it.

An hour had passed since they had stopped for nooning. More than anything Berry yearned for a cool drink of water. She decided to put it off until they reached the next hilltop. Israel's shout jerked her out of her lethargy.

"Missy!"

Berry stepped away from the ox and looked back. Fear took her breath away. A rider was coming up fast. She squinted her eyes, but all she could see was the running horse, its rider bending over its neck. She ran to the end of the moving wagon and reached for the rifle.

"What is it?" Rachel asked anxiously and started to crawl to the end of the mattress.

"Rider comin'. Stay where you are!" It was all Berry had time to say. In another minute the rider would be on them. She almost fell beneath the hooves of the mules Israel had speeded up to get close to the other wagon. She glanced back, then ran ahead to catch up with the ox and pull it to a halt.

She could hear the pounding of the hooves and the labored breathing of the horse by the time the wagon stopped. She turned and pointed the rifle at the rider. Black hair was blown back from a wild, angry face. Simon glared down at her. Why hadn't the fool worn his hat so she would have known who it was? The crazy thought flashed through her mind as he pulled the lathered horse to a halt.

"Where the hell are you going?" he yelled.

Angry because he was angry, and angry because she was so relieved, Berry shouted, "None of your damned business!"

"Stop pointing that rifle at me—it might go off!" He swung down from the horse.

"Nobody invited you to get down!" She followed his movements with the end of the rifle barrel.

Simon reached behind his saddle for his hat, snatched it from beneath a strap, and pushed out the crown. He slapped it on his head.

"Berry!" Rachel called from inside the wagon.

"It's that . . . trader. He ain't stayin'." The eyes she turned on Simon were as green as a stormy sea. "We don't need nothin' from you. Get on your horse 'n' get!"

He walked straight toward her, grasped the rifle barrel, and pushed it upward. "Have your lost your mind? What in hell do you mean striking out alone? Why didn't you stay in town? Why didn't you send for me when your pa was killed?"

"You got as many questions as a dog's got fleas!" Berry said comtemptuously. "You get this straight, Mr. Trader, I'm never going back to that town! Never! My pa filed on land and Rachel and me are going to live on it. We don't need nothin' from you!"

"Berry . . ." Rachel had crawled to the end of the wagon.

"It's all right, Rachel," Berry called, but she kept her eye on Simon. "Mr. Witcher's just passin' by. We'll be goin' on as soon as we give the team a little rest."

"I'm not passing by, goddammit! I've been on that river all night and got down to Saint Louis to find you gone. If you'd had the gumption you were born with, you'd've let me know your pa was dead before I took off upriver. Hell . . . women got no more brains than a speckled hen!"

"We got enough brains to take care of ourselves. If you went up to that wagon ground you'd've seen *that!* You . . . mule's ass! Nobody asked you to come here and . . . stop us!" It was beginning to be too much for Berry. Her lips trembled, and she looked away from him, not wanting him to see the tears in her eyes. She left the rifle dangling in his hand and went quickly to stand beside the ox.

"Mr. Witcher..." Rachel called.

Simon was looking at the bedraggled figure with the slumped, tired shoulders. Her hair, damp from sweat, had broken loose from its braid and curled on her neck. He turned his attention to the woman who called out to him.

"Ma'am," he said and stepped nearer.

"We need your help, Mr. Witcher," Rachel said carefully. Her eyes were full of tears and she drew her lips between her teeth to hold them steady.

Simon's eyes traveled past her face to the mattress where she had been lying and saw spots of blood. He looked back into her pleading eyes. "Is it your... time?" He spoke as softly as he could.

"The pain isn't regular yet. But it won't be long."

"Go on back and lay down."

Simon screwed his hat down tighter on his head and picked up his horse's reins. He had gone upriver early yesterday morning to see Zebulon Pike. Light had sent word to him by a French fur trapper who was headed upstream that the Ohio farmer was dead and that he was leaving on an important mission for Jefferson Merrick. Simon knew that Fain would stay in town no longer than necessary, so he had paddled most of the night and part of the morning to get back to Saint Louis. After he'd gotten his horse at the livery, he'd ridden up to the wagon ground. There he had seen three dead bodies within a fifty-foot radius of where the wagons had been; the only man he had recognized was George Caffery. Tracks showed that an ox-drawn wagon and one pulled by mules with a horse tied on behind had made a hasty departure. There had been no sign of Linc Smith, and Simon had naturally assumed he was with the wagons. Pain had knifed through him at the thought.

He came up behind Berry now where she leaned on the patient ox. "What happened to Linc Smith?"

"I shot 'em in the face 'n' he run off in the woods."

"Did he hurt you or Rachel?"

"No. We didn't give 'em a chance. The rifle knocked Rachel down when she fired it. She says it didn't hurt her. What do you care anyway?" She lifted her head and turned it slowly. "You've held us up long enough." She gave the ox a resounding slap on the rump.

Simon jerked on the harness before the animal could move. "Get in the wagon. You're so tired you're about to drop."

"I've a mind to do no such..."

"Hush up, and mind me! Linc could be on your trail right now. He won't come alone, he'll bring a bunch of river rats with him. Besides that, we've got to get Rachel somewhere, and quick. The nearest and best place is Fain's."

"What do you mean?"

"She's spotting blood. Don't that mean her time is near? If you wasn't so bull-headed you'd've seen it."

Berry's arm lashed out to strike him. He caught her wrist in mid-air. "I'd never do anything to hurt Rachel! I was doin' the... best I could." Her voice dripped hurt and desperation. Sobs began to constrict her throat and her words came out jerkily. She had no control over the tears that blinded her.

She covered her face with her hands and turned her head away. Her pride kept the racking sobs locked inside her.

"I know you did. And you done good." His voice was close to her ear. "Get in the wagon and sleep awhile. You're worn out."

"No. We got to go on."

"I'll lead the ox. Get in the wagon. We're wasting time." Simon didn't wait for her to answer. He swung her up in his arms, carried her to the back of the wagon, and set her down inside. "Make her lay down and get some sleep, ma'am," he said to Rachel. "She's so tired she's not showing good sense."

He left them and Berry crawled to the feather tick and sank down beside Rachel. Her head ached with a dull, persistent throb and her heart was a heavy lump in her breast. She buried her head in her arms and began to shake as reaction set in. Rachel's hand moved up and down her back in a soothing motion.

"Get some sleep, honey. We're in good hands. Mr. Witcher knows what to do."

"But... I hate him!" she said, sobbing.

Rachel was quiet for a long while. "Even if you do hate him, we've got to accept his help. Go to sleep. You'll feel better when you wake up."

Simon told Israel to keep up, then tied a lead rope to the halter on the ox and mounted his horse. He was more worried about Rachel than he was about Linc catching up to them. He didn't know anything about birthing, but he knew enough to know things were not natural and right with the woman.

A grimness settled on his expression. He'd kissed a fair number of women in his day, most of them in New Orleans—dance-hall girls and high-class whores who were experts at pleasing a man in a variety of sexual ways—but none of them had stirred him as much as this beautiful little Ohio farm girl, with her musical laughter and innocent curiosity. She was the only woman he'd ever met who was completely unaware of the effect her beauty had on a man. From the very first he'd felt a strange urge to protect her, to keep this harsh wilderness from crushing her bubbly spirit.

Simon had always known that someday he wanted a wife and a family to take care of. When he thought about it, it was always something for the future, not now. He still felt that way. He wasn't going to be stampeded into taking over the care of these women. For too long now he had planned to go upriver with Zebulon Pike. He couldn't very well tie himself to a woman and then go off and leave her. It would be a dangerous journey, one that might very well claim his life, but the adventure would be well worth the risk.

Simon hadn't believed that Asa Warfield would be stupid enough to try to start a tavern on the waterfront. He had fully expected Asa to pull out of Saint Louis with the emigrant train and settle on land as hundreds of other settlers had done. That would have made it easy to find the girl if, after a time, he decided she was the one he wanted. That fool Warfield, by getting himself killed, had ruined Simon's plan. Whom did he know who would take the women in and look after them? There were any number of unwed men in the territory who would jump at the chance. The thought didn't settle pleasantly in his mind.

He watched the trail and selected it with care. This close to the river there were only rocky hills, and the comparatively level part of the trail was sandy. He halted the ox at the top of a hill and waited for the mules pulling the heavier wagon to catch up. It was getting on toward evening, but the sun was still hot. He took off his hat, wiped the sweat from his face, and dismounted. The women were still lying on the bed in the wagon. Berry slept, her arm curled under her head, one hand on the musket that lay beside her. Rachel's eyes were open and watching as he tied the flap higher to allow the breeze to pass through.

"Are you making out all right?" he asked.

She nodded. "Can I trouble you for a drink of water?"

That woman is hurting something awful, Simon thought as he walked back to the big wagon and the water barrel attached to its side. Her face was covered with a clammy sweat and her hair was glued to her head with it. Fain had told him about the woman. Asa Warfield was a bastard. No doubt about it.

Simon filled his canteen and took it to Rachel. "Take this, ma'am. It won't slosh. The trail won't be so rocky from now on. I'll try..." He stopped speaking and squinted as he looked out the front of the wagon over the ox's back.

Two horsemen had topped the hill and were coming toward them. There was no doubt about who they were. No one rode a horse like Fain. He hated to ride, and sat in the saddle as if he were going to his execution. Lardy was with him, riding ahead. Simon went to stand beside the ox and wait for them.

Fain got stiffly out of the saddle. The horse blew its lips and tossed its head in relief to be rid of the weight on its back. "I thought you'd gone up ta Kaskaskia ta see Pike."

"I did. Light sent word Warfield got himself killed. I came back downriver to town." Simon jerked his head away from the wagons and Fain followed him toward the trees. Simon told him about the killings, about tracking the wagons, and about Rachel. Fain told him about Israel coming to town to find Lardy and Lardy paddling all night and half the morning to fetch him.

"That woman's in a bad way," Simon said with a worried frown. "I never thought I'd be glad to see the day I'd welcome Biedy Cornick's chatter. But she's the only woman I know of that's good at a birthing."

Fain turned away from him. Damn! He didn't want to be anywhere near a birthing! He didn't want to like the woman, didn't want to care about her suffering. But hell... "What're you goin' to do?"

"Well... I thought we could send Lardy for Biedy. Her boys'll bring her downriver. If we get the wagons 'cross the Missouri before dark, we can be at your place before morning."

"It's the best we c'n do. C'n she wait that long?"

"I don't know. She's bleedin'."

"Shitfire!"

"I tell you, Fain, that woman's got spunk. She killed one of them river rats with the rifle. When she fired it, it knocked her down."

"The other'n ain't short on spunk if'n she killed George and sent Linc to the woods." Fain felt a little spurt of something he didn't quite know what to do with when Simon talked about Rachel. Simon wasn't much for getting familiar with womenfolk. Did that mean he fancied her? "Wal . . . we'd better shake our tail. But I ain't a-ridin' on that damn horse. My tail's all buggered up as 'tis. I'll walk with the beast. You go on and get down to the river and get the raft to this side. The ol' Missouri's low fer this time o' year. If'n she gets lower'n she is, we c'n almost ford her."

Berry heard the male voices beside the wagon and woke with a start. Her hand closed around the musket and she sat up. Her mind was drugged with sleep and she looked down at Rachel with sleep-swollen eyes. "Who's out there?"

"Fain."

"Fain? How'n tarnation did he get here?"

"I don't know." Rachel closed her eyes wearily.

Berry placed the musket on the floor and got up on her knees beside Rachel. "Rachel? Are the pains comin'?" Fear knifed through her. Rachel lay on her side, the bulk that was the unborn child resting on the feather tick. The back of her dress was . . . bloody! "Rachel? Oh, Rachel . . . we shoulda stayed in town!"

Rachel opened her eyes. "Don't worry, honey. The pains aren't spaced out yet. Mr. Witcher said he'd get us somewhere. . . ." Her voice trailed away and she sucked her lips between her teeth. Oh,

God, she prayed. Don't let me die and leave Berry out here all alone until she finds a good man to take care of her. "Women have younguns all the time and I ain't no different than anybody else," she said with a sudden brightness in her voice. "Now, stop pullin' that long face. You 'n' me'll have to do this together like we've always done."

Berry jumped out of the wagon, more frightened than she'd been when she faced the men bent on attacking her. Please, God, don't let nothin' happen to Rachel . . . she couldn't help what my pa done to her. . . . "Fain!" she called. Then: "Fain!" Fain stood beside the ox, and Simon was mounting his horse. Berry ran past him to Fain. "We've got to find a place to camp! Rachel's time's near!"

Simon got off the horse and went to the back of the wagon. He climbed inside and knelt beside the woman on the mattress.

Rachel opened her eyes, looked up, and tried to smile at him. "Berry's scared for me," she whispered. "You go on and do what you have to do. I've been watching that cloud bank yonder. It looks like we could have a storm."

"I know. I've been watching it too. We're going to try and get you to Fain's. Do you think you can hold off for a while?" He squeezed the hand she held out to him. "Fain will lead the ox. Berry can ride in here with you. You sing out if you think they ought to stop and boil water or whatever they do at a birthin'."

"I can hold on. But . . . hurry . . ." she whispered, and a tear rolled out of her eye and lost itself in the blond hair at her temple.

Simon climbed out of the wagon and mounted

his horse. "Let's get the wagon rollin'," he said to Fain. Then, to Berry: "You get in there and stay with her." He spoke curtly, angrily.

Simon didn't know why he was angry. He glared down into stormy green eyes that glared back at him. She had ignored him and run to Fain! Fain could have her! Let her work her wiles on him for a change. Damn Asa Warfield for getting himself killed! Why in the hell had he let himself get into this situation in the first place?

With unnecessary force, Simon kicked the horse and rode off up the trail toward the river.

Chapter Seven

Silent heat lightning flashed the promise of a storm.

Not a breath of air circulated beneath the canvas top of the wagon to cool Rachel's sweat-drenched face. She had been lying in the same position, on her side, during the long hours since they had crossed the Missouri and taken the track through the forest toward Fain's homestead. She had cried out once when the wheel of the wagon passed over a rock. The jolt had been painful to Berry's bottom as well. She sat beside Rachel, dread and fear knotted in her stomach. The feeling had been there since she had awakened from the sound sleep and discovered Rachel's time was so near.

A backlash of lightning showed momentarily against the blackness overhead. Berry had always been excited by the spectacle of lightning slicing across the sky, running wild and free. But now she felt utterly detached from the approaching storm, although the bulging clouds were lower and the wind had begun to stir.

A blaze of lightning showed a horse and rider at the end of the wagon. Berry could see only a blurred outline of the man in the hat.

"We're just about to Fain's place. There's a family squatting down the creek a few miles. They've got a couple of womenfolk. One is old. She'll know about birthin'. I'll go and fetch her if she's willing to come. Biedy Cornick won't be here until sometime tomorrow."

"We're obliged," Berry said woodenly, politely. At that instant a dazzling flash lit up the area, followed by utter darkness and a tremendous clap of thunder. Berry shut her eyes; when she opened them, Simon was gone.

When it seemed that they had been moving forever, and the soft moans of pain rose almost continuously from Rachel, the wagon stopped. Berry peered out into the darkness. Fain was talking to a much smaller man who had come out of a small log house beside and back from a larger double cabin. Fain pointed to the second wagon and the man went to the head of the mules. Israel climbed down. He and Fain came to the end of the wagon.

"We got to get her in afore the rain starts." Fain let down the tailgate, reached in, and pulled the feather tick toward him. He gently picked Rachel up in his arms. The almost continuous flashes lighted the sky weirdly as Berry followed Fain to the double cabin with a dogtrot in between. He nudged open a heavy slab door and went inside. The room was so dark that Berry couldn't see her hand in front of her, so she stood beside the door. She could hear

Fain's sure, quick steps and then a small gasp from Rachel as he laid her down.

Fain lit a candle and the flickering light showed a much larger room than Berry had expected. It had bunks attached to the walls on two sides, a washstand, a large wooden trunk, and a magnificent cobblestoned fireplace. In the middle of the room was a heavy square table strewn with gun parts and half-finished gun stocks.

Berry went quickly to Rachel while Fain met Israel at the door. The two men carried the heavy trunk into the room and put it down near the bunk where Rachel lay.

"Fish will take care of the stock," Fain said. "You'd better lash down the wagons."

Israel shuffled out and Berry lifted the lid of the trunk. She pulled out the sheets she and Rachel had prepared for the birthing, a nightdress, towels, and clean rags.

"I'll not be no help to ya," Fain said from behind her. "If'n ya need anythin', anythin' at all..."

"It would help if you got a fire going and lit another candle or two." Berry knelt beside Rachel. "Rachel? We've got to get you out of that dress and get some sheets on the bed. Do you think you can stand up?"

Berry moved the arm Rachel had flung across her face. The color had drained out of it except for the great purple circles under her eyes, and her lips, which were red from continual biting. Her hair, wet with sweat, was drawn back from her forehead. Beads of sweat stood on her temples. Her eyes were closed and her breathing was shallow. Obediently she tried to push herself up from the bed.

Berry glanced over her shoulder to where Fain was kneeling before the fireplace. "Rest a minute more. He'll be leaving." Gently she wiped the sweat from Rachel's pain-chiseled face.

In minutes a fire was crackling in the hearth and Fain was saying, "The kettle's full and there's more candles. I'll set a fresh bucket of water inside the door. Simon'll be comin' soon... with the women-folk." He hurried out the door and crossed the space to the small cabin. He'd get into a card game with Fish. He didn't want to think about the woman or her suffering. He didn't want to hear her screams or see the blood rush out of her. He wanted nothing to do with a birthing! He didn't want to remember....

When the door closed behind Fain, Berry unbuttoned the front of Rachel's dress. "Are you hurtin' pretty good?"

Rachel nodded. Berry put her arm around her to help her sit up. "Ohhh..." The cry was almost a moan that came out with a puff of breath.

Berry brushed the dress from Rachel's shoulders and lifted her to her feet with her hands beneath her arms so the dress could fall to the floor. Rachel leaned on her heavily, as if her legs were about to collapse beneath her. Berry removed the soiled shift and saw the dark purple bruises across Rachel's back.

"Oh, Rachel! Your poor back! You hurt yourself when you fell. Why didn't you tell me?"

"Hurry... I've got to lay down. Oh..." Blood-tinged water gushed from between her legs and formed a puddle around her feet on the floor.

Berry slipped the gown over her head. "Hold it

up above your hips," she urged. "Don't worry about the water. We've got plenty of rags and a oilskin to keep the bed from soppin'. Lean on the wall till I can spread the sheets. There now . . . you can lay down." Berry eased her down on the bunk, being careful not to touch her back. "Simon's gone for a woman. They'll be here soon." She covered Rachel with a sheet and reached into the hump-backed trunk for more rags. She found one of her old shifts and tucked it between Rachel's legs to catch the water.

Berry had the weak trembles. Her mind raced as she mopped the water from the stone floor and lit more candles. Women died in childbirth. It was common! The other two times Rachel had been pregnant she had lost the babies after only a few months. Berry had been to a few birthings with Rachel. The women always walked as long as they could, then kneeled on the floor to give birth. Rachel was hurting too badly to walk. Oh, God, please don't let Rachel die! If someone's got to die, let it be the baby, don't let it be Rachel! Help me to help her. . . .

She laid out the blanket they had prepared to wrap the baby in and took the length of linen string from the trunk and placed it near the foot of the bunk. What to do now?

She knelt beside Rachel. "What do I do now?" she asked desperately.

Rachel opened her eyes. She held out her hand and Berry clasped it in both of hers. She started to speak, then closed her eyes and gritted her teeth as pain rocked her with its intensity. It rolled across her stomach in endless waves. "Please . . ." she pleaded to a silent God. "Oh, please . . ." When it was over, Berry wiped the sweat from her face.

"Not much to do but... wait." Her voice was a mere whisper and the words came out jerkily. "I'm glad to be out of that wagon."

"We should've stayed in town."

"No. This is better." She gripped Berry's hand tightly and tears came to Berry's eyes as she saw the effort Rachel was making not to cry out.

Berry began to talk. "You know what we're goin' to do when this is all over? We'll get Fain to take us to our land 'n' we'll build us a cabin like this one. It won't be as big, but we can add a room a year, till it's as big as we want. We'll make it warm and put us in a fancy fireplace with a cook oven. I got it figured out, Rachel. We can sell the mare and maybe even one of the wagons for cash money. We've got plenty of gunpowder and shot. We've even got that barrel of whiskey we could sell. Israel can fish and we can put us in a garden." Berry stopped talking and sniffed. Rachel opened her eyes. "I ain't bawlin'!" Berry said almost curtly. She sniffed again as she strove to control the quiver in her voice. "It's just... I get so danged mad! Why can't the men have the younguns. They put 'em there!"

A small cry escaped Rachel's lips and she pulled on Berry's hands with all her strength. Her head swung from side to side as she rode out a pain that hurt so much her eyes couldn't focus on the face beside hers.

Distraught, Berry glanced over her shoulder when the door opened. A bent-over old woman came into the room followed by a young girl and Simon. The old woman had a dirty shawl around her shoulders and a cloth bag in her hand.

"I fetched the women to give you a hand," Simon said. Then he stepped out and closed the door.

The girl came to the bedside and looked down at Rachel. She was tall, with wide hips and full breasts. The sleeves of her butternut-colored linsey dress were rolled up to show strong arms. The dress was well worn but clean. Her feet were bare. She had a pretty face and bright brown eyes that moved constantly.

"Granny is good at birthin', but she gets queer when she's called on to heal and don't want no sass." A pain gripped Rachel and she fought to keep from crying out. "It'll git worse'n that afore it's over." The girl smiled cheerfully as if she was enjoying herself. She moved away from the bed and toured the room, looking at everything.

The old woman took off her shawl and let it drop to the floor. She untied her bundle and began to take out herbs, which she laid on a corner of the table. Next she took out a Bible that was old and had pages folded and torn out. These items were arranged in order before she grasped the handle of a sharp knife, looked at it closely, then wiped the blade on the skin of her forearm, cleaning it. Long, crooked fingers then picked up three dried red-pepper pods. She looked at them lovingly before she crushed them in her hands.

Berry sat beside Rachel, waiting. The old woman began to mumble and knelt on the hearth. She poured water from the teakettle into a tankard, sprinkled the crushed peppers into the water, and set it aside to steep. She returned to the table, picked up another of the herbs, cut it with the knife into tiny parts, and mashed it in her palm with the tip of the knife blade. Mumbling, she went to the fireplace once more and dropped the minced herb into the tankard.

The girl continued to wander around the room. She ran her hands over the fur pelts on the walls, fingered the gun parts on the table, caressed the embossed design on the tin top of the trunk, then sat down on one of the bunks, testing its softness.

The old woman opened the Bible and squatted beside the fire. She recited but the words made no sense. She turned the pages, several at a time. As if in a trance she recited and leafed through the pages while Berry watched her.

"What's she doin'?"

"She's prayin' fer 'er sin. She always does it at a birthin'."

"What sin? Rachel needs more help than prayin'."

"Jesus bless 'er!" the old woman shouted. "Pain's God's punishment for fornicatin'... fornicatin'... fornicatin'! She opened 'er legs fer the devil! Forgive 'er!"

Rachel moaned. The old woman nodded, as if that was what she had been waiting for. She laid the open Bible on the table. With trembling hands she tore off the top page, balled it in her hand, touched it with grease from the bowl on the table, held it aloft, and carried it to the fireplace. She knelt down with the tankard in one hand and the ball of paper in the other. She put the ball in the ashes, set the jug down squarely on top of it, and held it there, breathing deeply of the smoke that swirled up around the tankard.

When the smoke stopped, she got to her feet and tasted the brew. Her face wrinkled and her mouth pursed. She mumbled some words, sucked her lips into her toothless mouth, and went to the bed.

"Sit," she commanded.

Berry stood up. "She can't sit up. What're you givin' her?"

She looked around the room for the girl, but she had gone out.

"Sit," the old woman said irritably, ignoring Berry. "It's the Lord's way."

Rachel tried to raise herself and made an effort to focus her eyes on the woman. A spasm grabbed at her stomach, causing blackness to pass over her eyes. She sank back down.

"Get away from her!" Berry tried to wedge herself between the old woman and the bed.

"Berry..." The word faded as Rachel's blue eyes stretched wide with pain and anxiety. Her face seemed to freeze as the pain mounted. Sweat beaded her forehead.

The old woman leaned closer, chanting, "God's comin'! Listen... listen... listen..."

"You crazy old hag! Get away from her!" The old woman's eyes blazed into Berry's and a strong, wiry old hand grasped her shoulder and spun her around. "Simon!" Berry screamed and bolted for the door. "Simon!" She flung open the door and ran out into the yard.

Simon met her and grasped her arm. "What's happened? Berry... what's...?"

"That old woman's crazy!"

"Granny knows what's she's about." The girl was beside them. "She always did the birthin's in Kentuck'."

Rachel screamed. At the sound, Berry and Simon

rushed for the door. They had almost reached it when it was slammed shut and the wooden pole inside was shoved into place. Berry hurled herself at the door and pounded on it with her fist. "Rachel! Rachel!" Inside the room, Rachel screamed again.

"Open this door," Simon shouted. "Goddamned crazy old woman's locked the door!" he said to Fain, who had run from the other cabin.

"I dunno what ye're a-gettin' in a sweat fer." The girl leaned against the cabin wall, her arms folded across her ample breasts. "She's goin' to do a bit of hollerin'. Ain't never seen no one have a youngun without it."

"Why'd she shut the door?" Fain demanded.

"She don't want nobody to get her healin' secret."

"Shitfire!" Fain cursed.

"Rachel!" Berry continued to pound on the door. "Oh, God! She's killin' her!" she sobbed when Rachel let out another piercing scream.

"Damn her!" Simon swore and hit the door with his fist.

"Stand back!" Fain grasped the handle. "Open this door, by gawd, or I'll bust it down!"

"Granny ain't goin' to," the girl said calmly.

Fain put his shoulder to the slab. The door trembled but held. He had made it to withstand almost any blow. Now he kicked it. "I'll kick the goddamn door in, ya old bitch!" Rachel's screams came with almost every breath. Fain threw himself against the door. "Leave her be, ya scrawny old bitch! I'll break ever' bone in your body!"

Simon went to the pile of logs near the stump where they chopped the firewood. He selected a log, pulled it out, and tried to lift it. Israel appeared and lifted one end and they carried it into the dog-trot.

"Move aside, Fain. We'll have to knock it in."

Fain stepped back and grasped the log. The men backed away and ran at the door, ramming it with the end of the log. The door shook but held. They retreated and rammed the log against the door several more times. Finally the door flew open.

Rachel was on her knees on the stone floor and the old woman was kneeling beside her. She had Rachel's face cupped in her bony hands, holding it up so high that Rachel was forced to arch her back. The look on the old face was demonic as she stared into Rachel's eyes. On the floor between them were pages torn from the Bible.

Fain was across the room in two leaps. He seized the old woman, lifted her, and flung her at Simon. "Get 'er outta here!" His voice boomed with anger.

The old woman screamed as she struggled against the arms holding her. She grabbed the end of the bunk and Simon had to pry her hands loose. "Get her plunder," he snapped at the girl, then lifted the old woman off her feet and carried her to the door.

The girl shrugged, then stuffed the herbs, the knife, and the Bible into the cloth bag. "Granny ain't a-goin' to be likin' this," she warned haughtily and snatched the shawl from the floor. "She jist might take a notion to put a spell on 'er. She done it oncet in Kentuck' and..." She let her voice trail off, as if what had occurred was too awful to talk about.

"I'll take them back to their camp," Simon called out to Fain. "Looks like the storm is going around."

"Ain't we goin' to stay the night?" The girl sidled

over to Simon and brushed his arm with her breast.

"No! C'mon out and shut the door." The old woman had gone limp in Simon's arms and his patience was being strained.

The old woman had pulled Rachel out of the bunk and onto the stone floor. Her knees were cut and bleeding, hair streamed down over her face, and her gown was up around her waist. Berry pulled it down over her white buttocks, as Rachel rocked back and forth like a wounded animal.

Fain knelt beside her and lifted the hair from her face. "Ah . . . lass. Birthin's hurtful enough without a ol' hag to torment ya." Rachel moaned and butted her head against his chest as pain took her and she was lost to the world. He waited until the pain rolled away. He doubted she realized he was there. "It's Fain, lass. I'm here to stay with you. I know a mite about birthin' a ewe or a mare. Cain't be a heap of difference. I'm going to get you on the bunk and me 'n' this little gal will help you birth a fine youngun."

Berry was so frightened that she felt as if she were glued to the floor. "Her back is . . . hurt!"

Working slowly and carefully, Fain picked Rachel up in his great arms and eased her onto the bunk. He lifted her gown to free her legs and bent them at the knees so that her feet were flat on the bed. Rachel was beyond knowing or caring who was tending to her. She opened her eyes and stared into Fain's face, not seeing him, but using him as a point on which to focus her mind while her muscles knotted and pulled.

The pain rolled away, leaving her gasping. "Water . . ." The red-pepper brew the old woman had forced down her throat had set her mouth afire. Another pain came and went and then Fain was squeezing cooling water into her mouth from a cloth.

"It's won't be long, lass. Just holler right out 'n' hold on to me and pull. That's a good lass. . . ."

Fain's voice pulled her back time and again from the agony of pain as the powerful contractions shook her and she had no control over her mind or her body.

"Fain! It's comin'!" Berry croaked from the end of the bed. "I can see the top of its head!"

Rachel's eyes opened wide. "Fain!" she screamed.

"I'm here, lass. Pull . . . let it come. Don't hold back from the hurtin'."

An unexpected strength and calmness filled Fain. This was another time, and another sweet lass was hurting. This one wouldn't die if he had to reach inside her and pull the child from her womb. He clamped Rachel's hands around his forearm and felt no pain as her nails dug into his flesh. He placed the palm of his other hand on the hardened mound of her abdomen and waited for another contraction.

The world retreated for Rachel as the crushing pain rolled over her and she knew she was being torn apart.

The head came free and then the shoulders. Berry waited for the final push, then gathered the child to her. She reached for the linen string, tied two heavy knots, and cut between the knots to sever the cord. The baby was covered with birth blood. She grabbed a towel and cleaned the child frantically. The tiny chest was not moving; the eyes were sealed shut.

"Fain!"

Fain scarcely heard her in his relief that the ordeal was over for Rachel. He leaned over and kissed her sweat-slicked face, all the overpowering love he had begun to feel for her showed in his expression.

"Is it dead?" Rachel asked, gasping.

"Fain!" Berry bent over the tiny form on the bed. "It isn't breathing."

Fain grabbed the child by the heels and pulled it to him. He wiped its mouth and nose with the towel and forced a corner into its mouth to clear out the mucus. Then he held the infant upside down and swung it a time or two. Still it did not move. He glanced at Rachel. She was staring at him, her eyes pleading. She'd just gone through hell for another dead child!

In a rush, Fain remembered the time the cow had delivered twin calves and one breathed and one didn't. His pa had plunged it into the cold water in the water tank.

He rushed to the bucket of spring water he had set just inside the door and plunged the infant in up to its neck. He poked his finger into its mouth. "Get air! Get air!" he whispered fervently. He couldn't let Rachel's baby die after all the agony she'd gone through to carry it inside her during the long, torturous journey and then the pain of delivering it.

Suddenly the tiny chest heaved, and the little mouth opened and drew air into the lungs. The baby made a soft mewing sound like a newborn kitten.

"Is it dead?" Rachel's weak voice reached him.

"No, by gawd! It's not dead! It's breathin', lass!"

He crossed the room and placed the tiny bundle of flesh on a towel. He rubbed it briskly, moved the tiny arms and legs, then turned it and rubbed its back until the dead blue that had covered its body moments before turned to bright pink. "Ya got a fine girl, lass!" Fain said happily. He continued to chafe the tiny arms and legs and laughed with delight when the little muscles responded. Tiny hands flayed the air, a cry of protest came from her mouth, and she opened large, beautiful blue eyes. It was a living miracle. Fain's heart leaped with joy and a huge grin split his face. He knelt beside Rachel, holding the wriggling, wailing little body in his hands. "Look-a there, lass! Look-a there at what ya got! It's the purtiest little mess I ever did see!"

"Wrap her up, Fain," Rachel said through her smile.

Berry held a blanket to the fire and warmed it. Fain wrapped the baby and cuddled her against him while he stood with his back to the bed. Berry removed the soiled sheets and slipped a clean one under Rachel. She brought a pan of warm water and washed her face, then cleaned her thighs and covered her. Berry felt drained, hardly believing it was over and Rachel was doing so well. She moved from the bed and made room for Fain. As he knelt beside Rachel and placed the baby in her arms, they looked at each other as if somehow they had created this small miracle between them.

"Has she got . . . ever'thing?" Rachel asked anxiously. Her fingertips stroked the fuzz of blond hair.

"Yep. She's got the right number of ever'thin'. I

counted 'em!" His bright eyes danced from Rachel's face to Berry's. "Now all ya got to do is put a name on 'er."

"She's Berry's sister. She should name her."

Berry was so relieved to see the calm, happy look on Rachel's face that she didn't know whether to cry or to laugh. She marveled that Rachel could even lift her head to look at the child. Color had come back into her face and her eyes had lost the flat, dull look that had been in them for weeks. She looked tired, worn out, but the drawn, haggard look had miraculously disappeared. Berry watched Fain's face as he looked at Rachel and the baby. It was a wholly tender, loving look. Even in her confused state, she grasped the fact Fain was in love with Rachel. A lump thickened her throat.

"Fain should name her. I don't know what we'd've done without him. I didn't know what to do... when she didn't breathe."

Rachel's eyes swung to Fain's. "She's right. You gave her life. You name her. It's something she'll have for the rest of her life."

Fain looked at the baby. Cautiously he ventured to ask, "Are you sure, lass?"

"I'd be obliged and... honored."

"Wal then... if'n it suits you, I'll name her Faith. I was a twin. It was Fain and Faith. My sister was scrawny and weak. I was the big strong one. This one's goin' to make it, lass. Did you hear her a-cryin'?" His chuckle was soft and affectionate.

"'Faith'? I like it. Don't you, Berry?" It was impossible to tell by Rachel's face that half an hour ago she had been almost out of her mind with pain.

"It's a beautiful name. One I'd've liked to have

for my own. I used to wish for a name like Rose-mary, or Caroline."

"Oh, honey. Berry Rose is a pretty name and suits you so well."

"I guess my mama thought so."

Fain stood and stretched. He felt wonderful now that it was all over. "I'm hungry as a bear. How about you, lass?"

Rachel turned away from his inquiring eyes. Sudden awareness of the service he had performed for her turned her face scarlet. "I'm too tired to eat," she murmured and cuddled her daughter to her.

"It'd be better if you sleep. That youngun'll wake hungry and squallin'." He laughed happily. "Well, little gal, shall we take on midwifin'?" he said teasingly to Berry.

"I don't have no bag of herbs and no hot peppers," Berry said saucily.

Fain's laugh was so loud that the baby woke with a startled cry, then promptly went back to sleep.

"There's nothing wrong with her ears," Rachel said with a shy grin.

Fain went to the door and flung it open. Israel and a young man squatted beside the door. "We got a fine girl baby," he announced proudly. "C'mon in 'n' take a look."

A grinning Israel followed a slight-built young man into the room. He looked scarcely older than a boy. His face was smooth, his eyes a clear amber, his hair as fair as the dried grasses in the dead of winter. He was no taller than Berry, and as he approached her their eyes met and held. She nodded and he solemnly returned the greeting.

"Lawdy!" Israel said in awe when Rachel held the

blanket away from the baby's face. Then he backed away, shaking his head.

"Her name is Faith."

The young man moved closer and peered down at the baby. "Congratulations, ma'am. She's beautiful." He spoke in a soft, cultivated voice with a strong English accent. "'Faith' is a commendable name. One she'll live up to, I'm sure."

"She will if she's anything like her sister." Rachel's eyes found Berry at the end of the bed. "I'm Rachel Tompkins, and this is Berry Rose Warfield."

"It's a pleasure, ladies. I'm called Fish." There was nothing pretentious or dandy about the man. He seemed extremely shy.

Berry stirred uncomfortably and tried to smooth the damp ringlets back from her face. In the silence that ensued, her heart throbbed with weariness.

"My stomach's about stuck to my backside. How about servin' up some of that stew you was a-cookin', Fish?" Fain's voice was controlled now. He was speaking softly, and he chuckled. "Wonder how ol' Simon's doin' with the ol' hag and the gal. He's goin' to be madder'n a hornet when he gets back. He's always hated night ridin'. He must-a had his back up or he'd not've struck out with them till daylight."

"The old woman was crying and carrying on and the girl was begging to stay the night. But Simon put the woman in the saddle and the girl up behind her. He rode off leaving a trail of curses." Fish smiled. The smile made him look even younger.

When the men went to the door, Israel stooped to pick up the soiled bedclothes and the rags filled with the afterbirth. "Ah'll put this in a tub o' water till mornin', missy."

"Thank you," Berry murmured. "I'm so tired I'm not sure I've got good sense." She followed the black man to the door. "They're asleep already," she whispered.

"Y'all sit, missy. Ah'll bring ya somethin' Mistah Fish is cookin' up."

Berry looked up into black eyes that were so changed from the hopeless, dull eyes of a few days ago. They were bright, interested eyes, and there seemed to be pride and dignity in the tilt of his head and confidence in his voice.

"Thank you, Israel, for . . . ever'thing you've done to help us. We . . . we couldn't have made it without you. It took courage to go into town and find Mr. Witcher's man. I want you to know I'm sorry for the way my pa treated you."

"Aw . . . missy . . ." Israel stammered. To hear these words from a white woman was far beyond anything he'd ever imagined. He bobbed his head up and down in the familiar gesture.

Berry laughed. "I didn't mean to embarrass you." She sobered. "We've got to get us a shelter built before winter, get us in a garden, and you've got to learn to shoot so you can hunt for us. And . . ." Berry broke off, laughing again. "I'll not worry your mind with all of that now. We'll stay here until Rachel's able."

"Yass'm." Israel shifted from one foot to the other, but his smile broadened as he went out the door.

Berry pushed the door partially shut and blew out all the candles except the one that threw a faint light over Rachel's bed. She sank down in a deep chair. Fatigue washed over her like a heavy wave. There was the distant rumble of thunder from the storm that had swept around them. The night air was cool. Should she build up the fire and keep the room warm for Rachel and the baby? This was Berry's last thought before she fell into a sound, dreamless sleep.

Chapter Eight

The sun was lighting the eastern sky and daylight was seeping through the trees when Simon rode into the yard, dismounted, and unsaddled his tired horse. He too was tired, and irritable and anxious to know what had happened while he was away. He turned the horse into the poled enclosure, measured out a scoop of grain, and poured it into the feedbox. He stood beside the horse for a moment and wondered once again how he had allowed himself to become involved in the affairs of these two women.

There was no activity around the double cabin. The entire homestead was quiet except for the scolding of Fain's pet crow, which sat on the woodchopping stump. Israel and Eben, a black freedman who worked for Fain, were hunkered down before a cookfire at the edge of the clearing where the Warfield wagons were parked.

Simon headed for the small log house set back in the trees. It was a ramshackle affair put there by a settler years before who had decided that frontier life wasn't for him and had given up the land to return East. Simon changed course abruptly, swung on his heel, and went to the big cabin. He would find out for himself how the women had fared.

The door of the cabin was ajar. He pushed it open and went inside. In the dim light he could see Berry asleep in the chair and Rachel on the bed. She was so still that he felt a shiver of dread slice through him. He placed his hat on the table and went closer. A baby was sleeping in the curve of her arm. Her eyelids fluttered open.

"It's all over?" He bent low to whisper.

"Yes." Rachel folded back the blanket so he could see the baby's face. "A girl." Her look was tender and filled with love.

Simon looked down at the baby. She was red and wrinkled and reminded him of a dried persimmon. My God! he thought. She's been through all that pain and agony to get this! He was silent for a moment, trying to find words. Finally he said cautiously, "She's got lots of hair."

"Fain says she's got ever'thin' she's suppose to have. We've named her Faith."

"Biedy'll be fit to be tied when she gets here and finds out she's missed out on all the doings." He smiled and small lines fanned out from the corners of his eyes. He glanced toward the chair where Berry was sleeping.

Rachel caught the look. "She's tired. She's not had much sleep for two nights. She was cross today because she was worn out... and after what happened at the wagon grounds."

"I'll put her on the bunk. There's no reason why she can't sleep the morning away, if you can last awhile without her help."

"I'll get by if you'll lay that stack of cloth over where I can reach it."

Simon knelt in front of Berry, removed her shoes, and held her slender foot in his hand. He noticed her carefully mended stockings and the worn thinness of her dress. His mind flashed to the fine stockings and soft kid slippers in his storehouse in Saint Louis. His eyes searched every feature of her face. He had not had this opportunity to look his fill of her face before. He thought of her laugh tinkling like a wind chime and her eyes flashing brightly. He felt the same unfamiliar feeling, the urge to protect and cherish her, that he had felt the night he kissed her. It was not a purely unselfish emotion that possessed him. He wanted to love her in every way a man could love a woman and to satisfy his own lust as well. What's wrong with that? he questioned his conscience, then tried to put the thought from his mind. It was all happening too fast. Did he want his life, his peace of mind, his future tied up with this slip of a girl?

He scooped her up in his arms as if she weighed no more than a small child. Her head drooped to his shoulder and her breath came warm and moist on his neck. Wisps of her hair clung to his rough cheeks. She smelled like warm sweetened tea, but like hickory smoke, too. Her body was soft and light and he carried her easily to the bunk at the end of the room.

"Simon . . . ?" The word came out on a breath.

Her head fell back on his arm when he lowered her to the bed. She opened drowsy, green eyes. "I'm not asleep."

He remained hunkered down beside the bunk, his arms still around her. "Playin' possum, huh?"

"I'm sorry I called you a . . . mule's ass."

"Well, that's something for a stubborn little mule to admit." He chuckled. "That mouth of yours is going to get you in trouble someday."

"It already has. Simon . . . ? Thanks for coming to find us. I didn't think you would . . . didn't think you wanted to be bothered."

"I came as soon as I heard about your pa." Simon felt trembly on the inside. His arms were still around her and he was terribly conscious of the thinness of her dress between them. He felt the warmth radiating from her and drank it in like a man thirsting for water in the desert. He had tried to ignore the realization earlier, but it kept coming back to him, washing over him like a wave—he was beginning to care for this woman!

"I didn't know what the old woman was like or I'd not have brought her here." He wanted to say something, anything, in order to be with her for a little longer.

"The old woman acted plumb queer. At least I never heard of such as she was doin' to Rachel. The girl was pretty." Berry's eyes were wide open and looking directly into his. She thought she felt his arms tighten but couldn't be sure.

"Uh-huh."

"What's her name?"

"Della. That's what her pa called her."

"Where is their homestead?"

"On down the river. They were just camping by the creek for a while. The old woman's man was sickly. They'll be moving on in a day or two." Simon hoped that what he was saying was making sense because his mind was really on his desire to kiss her moist lips, now slightly parted.

"Do you think their land is anywhere near ours? Rachel will be able to travel by the end of the week. We've got a lot to do before winter."

"Berry..." It was the first time he could remember saying her name aloud. "Forget about taking up land. You couldn't possibly improve on a homestead enough to get title even if the land commissioners would allow it."

"They wouldn't even know about it, if some busybody didn't tell them." Her green eyes turned frosty, and the hand that rested on his chest fell away.

"The gossip would reach them. Every man within a hundred miles would know two young unmarried women were alone on a homestead," he said in flat tones. "How do you think you're going to protect yourself from the likes of Linc Smith back there in the back of nowhere?"

"I'll shoot him!" Berry said staunchly.

"I can find a place for you to stay in Saint Louis. Ernest Wenst, who works for..."

"No!" Berry pushed against his chest to move away from him. His arms held and his hand moved to her chin to hold it in place while he glared at her.

"You stubborn little fool!" Simon raised his voice. In his anger he forgot about Rachel at the other end of the room.

"Don't wake Rachel," Berry hissed through

clenched teeth because his fingers tightened on her chin.

"If you cared so all-fired much about Rachel you wouldn't be so determined to drag her off to a homestead where she'll either starve or be taken by rivermen or Indians." He said the words as if they were curses. "You listen . . . little miss stubborn know-it-all. I'm not running after you again. I've got a business to look after, I've got my land, and I'm going to go upriver with . . ."

"Get your hands off me, you . . . mule's ass! I never asked you to run after me! Get your hands off . . . or I'll hit you in the mouth!"

"You do and I'll pound your butt so hard you won't sit on it for a week! Better yet . . ."

He closed her mouth with his. His face shut out the fury in her green eyes and his arms crushed her to his chest so that there was not a hair's breadth between them. His kiss was long and deep, and slow heat seeped into her body from her mouth to the tip of her toes. The pressure of his lips opened hers and she gave herself up to the shivers of excitement as his tongue slipped inside. She forgot to struggle, forgot Rachel at the end of the room, forgot how angry she was. She remembered only the sweetness of his last kiss and how she had yearned just for this. The fingers that left her chin closed warmly, caressingly over her breast.

Small fires began to build in that private part of her that ached to be fulfilled, and unaccustomed wetness seeped from the apex of her being. His tongue penetrated the sweet hollow of her mouth, exploring, tickling, stroking her lips, teeth, and the roof of her mouth. Berry returned the caresses freely, her inhibitions lost in the wave of longing she felt for him. Her hand moved up his arm to his shoulder and on to press against the back of his neck. Inquisitive, slender fingers combed the soft texture of his hair and circled the curve of his ear. He raised his lips a little away from hers. She opened her eyes to find him looking down at her with a hot intensity that made her heartbeat quicken even more. His eyes were so dark, so close, she could see hers reflected there. She smiled.

Simon gazed long and hard into eyes that shone like shimmering green pools, at a soft red mouth, parted and puffed from the pressure of his. His fingers were moving gently on the nape of his neck, causing feelings of possessive, rueful tenderness to wash over him. He lowered his mouth and placed small, light kisses on her lips, her cheeks, her eyes. His emotions were in an uproar. He wanted to shake her and he wanted to make love to her in a way he had never loved a woman before.

"You bullheaded, stubborn little . . . baggage!" he said through gritted teeth. "You make me so mad I want to shake your teeth out!"

"Why?" Soft giggles blew from her lips.

"You know why," he murmured against her mouth.

She felt the quiver in his arms, the pounding of his heart against her own. Elation that she could cause this great body to tremble sliced through her, and her hand tightened at the back of his neck. She gloried in the warmth of his chest pressed against her breasts.

"I . . . did it again!" It was impossible to have coherent thoughts while he was holding her like this.

"Did what?"

"Called you a mule's ass!"

He grinned, his nose almost touching hers, his eyes brightened by the sparkle in hers. "Sometimes I think you're right about that." He stood when Fain pushed open the door and came into the room.

"I heard ya ride in." Fain's glance took in the fact that Simon had been kneeling beside the bunk where Berry lay.

"I wasn't trying to keep it a secret," Simon said with a tinge of irritation in his voice. He snatched his hat off the table. "I'm hungry. Seems like I haven't eaten since Christmas."

"I'll fix you . . ." Berry swung her feet off the bunk and sat up.

"Stay where you are," he snapped. "I'll rustle up something." He was out the door before Berry could get to her feet.

Fain came across the room chuckling. Something was definitely eating at his friend Simon. Then he forgot everything but the picture before him— Rachel with the baby lying in the crook of her arm. "You 'n' Faith a-makin' out all right?"

Faith had awakened while Simon talked with Berry. Wanting to give them as much privacy as possible, Rachel had turned her back to them and put the baby to her breast. Now she flipped the cover up and over the baby's face.

Fain sat on the edge of the bunk, leaned over, and stroked the baby's fine, silky hair with his fingertips, but his eyes were on Rachel's face. He seemed not to notice the faint pink color that had come up under her skin, making her cheeks seem to glow.

"You're lookin' better, lass."

Rachel could think of nothing to say. Her hand fluttered up to sweep the hair back from her face. "I feel a heap better," she finally managed. She wished he hadn't sat down on the edge of the bed. She wished he would go and she hoped he would stay. What she really wanted was for her stupid heart to settle down so she could think before she made a fool of herself.

"Fish is fixing up some vittles." Fain chuckled. It was beginning to be a familiar sound. "He's cookin' up a mess of eggs and deer meat. He's a good hand at it. Says my cookin' ain't fit for the hogs. You eat all them eggs he brings ya. That'll put some strength back."

"Eggs? I've not had eggs since we left Ohio. I can't just *eat* eggs. You'd better save them for a pie or a puddin'."

"You eat the eggs, lass. There'll be more for puddin', if'n you'll make it. I'd not want to turn Fish loose on a puddin'." His eyes were laughing down into hers and Rachel forgot her embarrassment. "Biedy'll be here late this evenin'. That is, if'n they got a good start. Then the fur will fly! She's the beatin'est woman you ever did see. Beatin'est and talkin'est. Ever'time she comes she scrubs and cleans till thin's is in such a mess I can't find a thing. But she cooks, too. And when she goes we got pies 'n' bread 'n' dumplin's a-comin' out our ears. She'll come loaded, too. Always brings me a crock of butter 'n' sometimes hominy. She knows my fondness for it."

"She sounds like a nice woman."

"She is . . . if'n ya can stand her chatter." From

the laughter in his eyes, Rachel knew he was teasing, and that he would tease only about someone he was fond of.

"Is this your sleeping room?"

"Usually. The other part is the eatin' room. We work on the guns in here some. I'm a gunsmith and part-time farmer 'cause I have to improve on my land. Right now I'm tryin' to teach Fish the gunsmith trade."

"We don't want to misput you. We can move out to the wagons."

"You'll stay right here, lass. I like seein' ya here. You 'n' this little button here." His voice had turned gruff and his hand cupped the baby's small behind through the covers. "Wal... I'd best get on out and see to it Simon don't eat ever'thin' includin' the table."

He stood, and it seemed to Rachel that his presence filled the room. Unaware that she was doing so, her hand reached for his and was engulfed tightly. She gazed at him with soft, caring eyes. "Thank you." The words formed on her lips but couldn't seem to pass the large cotton ball in her throat. He understood. The words hovered between them for a moment, then he dropped her hand and walked quickly from the room.

A sense of elation stayed with Berry throughout the morning.

She was sure that Simon liked her, maybe even loved her. He had liked holding her and kissing her—if not, why had his heart pounded and his mouth drunk from hers as if he couldn't get enough of her? Every word he had said danced through her head. Even when he called her a stubborn little baggage he had grinned afterward. No, she cautioned herself. Don't make too much out of the fact he liked kissing you. He offered to court you once, and nothing came of that.

After breakfast Berry shut and barred the door and washed herself and Rachel. She wanted to wash her hair but had to content herself with a good brisk brushing. She put on a clean shift and dress, then bent over at the waist and worked her fingers through her hair until it hung loosely from the top of her head. She whirled it around in a coil, like a rope, and swirled it around on top of her head and fastened it with two smooth wooden pins.

"I saw a wash pot in the yard. I'll get ever'thin' washed before we move on." Berry rolled the stained cloth from Rachel's bed and the damp padding from the baby in a tight bundle. "I'll put this in the wagon until I can wash it."

Rachel raised herself on her elbow and peered out the open door. "It's a beautiful, sunny day for a washing," she said wistfully. "Fain seems fond of this woman Biedy. It's good of her to come all this way to help us."

"I'll clean before she gets here. We don't want her to think we're slack-handed."

Rachel lay back and sighed. "This is a nice tight cabin. My, my . . . I never expected to see glass windows way out here."

"The room on the other side of the dogtrot is just as big as this one and there's a window in it, too. I wonder why he built the rooms so big."

"He's a big man," Rachel said shyly, and looked down at the baby to keep from looking at Berry.

"The place looks settled. He's got chickens and a smokehouse. He's got a garden in and fruit trees are blooming. It's a sightly place."

"The water is so good. It don't taste like river water."

"That's because there's a spring out back."

"He makes guns." Rachel smiled, and it spread a warm light into her eyes. "I thought that we were a bother, that he would want to work in here, but he says . . . not."

Berry darted a quick look at Rachel and caught the blush on her cheeks. *Was it possible that Rachel liked Fain in . . . that way?* Berry's eyes darted around the cozy room while she tried to get her thoughts together. "Well . . ." she said after a long pause, "it's . . . good of him to say so, but we'll move on soon as we can. We don't want to wear out our welcome."

It was late in the afternoon when a shout came from the direction of the river and an answering halloo issued from the homestead. Berry stepped out to the end of the dogtrot and watched two men in buckskins and a small woman walk up the steep grade toward the cabin. Fain walked out to meet them. One of the men was tall with cotton-white hair; the other was slimmer and smaller, with a drooping mustache curled down at each side of his mouth.

The woman was small and quick. Berry couldn't see her face for the stiff-brimmed bonnet she wore tied in a jaunty bow beneath her chin, but she could hear her voice. It went on and on, interspersed with small trills of musical laughter. The men each carried a pack and a long gun, the woman something wrapped in a cloth. She shoved the bundle into Fain's hands the instant they met.

"My, my, my, Fain! I never thought I'd be a-comin' to a birthin' at your place. Sakes alive! There's somethin' a-happenin' all the time. Silas and the boys woulda brung me, but seein' as how Jeff and Will was a-comin' this way, I just come on with 'em. Lordy mercy! What a ride! I swear they was a-tryin' to drown me. They shoved that boat this-a-way and that-a-way 'n' ever'time I'd holler they'd laugh. Them two is wild! They need a couple good women to settle 'em. I ain't never had me such a wild time a-comin' downriver. Where's that poor woman at? What you a-standin' there that way for, Fain? Birthin's don't wait. Take me to the woman. Silas'll be after me in a day or two. It'll take that long to give that cabin of yourn a good goin'-over."

Biedy Cornick left the men standing in the yard and came toward Berry. She was the plainest woman Berry had ever seen. Her bright blue eyes played up and down and over Berry like a blue flame. Not one of the men had uttered a word, but now Berry heard soft chuckles as they watched the birdlike woman come to the house.

There was absolutely nothing pretty about Biedy Cornick. Her features were sharp, her lips thin, and the hair that framed her face was a fine, brown fuzz. She wore a black apron over a faded butternut dyed homespun dress. She carried herself like a young girl, head up, shoulders back, her feet moving lightly across the ground. It was impossible to tell her age.

When she reached Berry she walked right up to

her and enfolded her in her arms. "Land a goshin'! If'n ya ain't 'bout the purtiest thing I ever set my eyes on." She laughed. Her voice was like a melody, soft and flowing. "Course, ya ain't the one havin' the youngun. I can see that. I'm Biedy Cornick, come to help with the birthin'." She clucked her tongue against the roof of her mouth. "I know what hurtin' goes with birthin'. I had me four boys. They're about grown now. I'd-a give my right arm for a girl—a purty little gal such as you are."

"The baby came last night, Mrs. Cornick."

"It's come? Glory be! Them men coulda said so! Call me Biedy—ever'one does when they ain't a-callin' me chatterbox." The musical laughter came again.

"I'm Berry Rose War—"

"Berry? Oh ... Bring in that berry pie, Fain. If'n it's fit to eat I'll be surprised, what with the way Jeff was a-sloshin' it this-a-way and that-a-way. Bring the butter, too," she called over her shoulder. "Land sakes! Much as that man takes to butter'n thin's, he oughtta keep a cow." She untied her sunbonnet and jerked it from her head. "Wheee ... it's gonna be a scorcher today." She moved past Berry and went into the cabin, tiptoeing and smiling. "There you is. Are ya a-makin' out all right? Are ya wore out? Birthin' ain't easy."

Berry followed Biedy into the room, stood beside the table, and watched her swoop down on Rachel. Her lips curled in a smile when she saw the look on Rachel's face. The woman was like a whirlwind, but like a ray of sunshine, too.

"I'm Biedy," she said to Rachel before she turned the force of her attention on the baby. "It's been a coon's age since I held me a baby." Rachel turned back the cover and the woman needed no other invitation. She lifted Faith and cuddled her in the curve of her arm, clucking and crooning.

"Her name is Faith," Rachel murmured.

"It's a girl baby? Glory be! Faith, ya say? It's a suitable name." Biedy's bright eyes softened and her mouth gentled as she looked at the baby. "You're jist as purty a youngun as I ever did see, lovey." She made dovelike sounds in her throat and rocked from side to side.

Berry exchanged glances and pleased smiles with Rachel and glided out the door.

Simon was bathing at the spring when he heard the shout that told him Jeff Merrick and Will Murdock had arrived with Biedy Cornick. Cleanliness was not a luxury to Simon. It was a necessity that went back to the time he had spent with the Pollard family. There, he and the other children were bathed once a week the year around, whereas their friends were bathed only occasionally in the summer. The habit had stayed with him, and during the warm weather he seldom let two days go by without a dunking in the river or a stream.

He toweled his wet head and dressed quickly. He liked and respected the two Virginians who had come out over a year ago to take up a parcel of land on the Missouri beyond the Cornicks' place. He was almost sure the two were involved in the political intrigue that had flourished in the territory since the land had been purchased by the United States. But their politics were of no concern to him. They were good, reliable men and good company.

It was through them that he had met Lightbody, the French-and-Indian scout they called Light.

The late-afternoon sun shone softly on the leaves and the ground when he left the woods. He sniffed, gratefully identifying the mingling odor of pine, rotting vegetation, and the delicate scent of yellow and purple wildflowers. He loved the forest. Loved it much more than any river. Each month now, new encroachments were made on it as the eastern settlers moved in to establish homesteads. You'll either have to adjust to the population increase or move on, he often told himself.

Cutting around back of the cabin, he unexpectedly came upon Berry. Only minutes ago, while bathing, he had found himself thinking of the arm that had circled his neck and the soft breasts that had pressed against him. He had even found himself looking around for a glimpse of her as he came out of the woods; but now, the sight of her gave him a guilty start. She was standing at the end of the dogtrot, her head tilted back against the rough logs, her eyes closed. She was not aware of his nearness.

"Berry." Her eyes opened. "Are you asleep?"

She stammered for something to say. The smile on his usually solemn brown face and the gleam of the afternoon sun on his dark, wet hair completely wiped all logical thought from her mind.

"I was listening to the sounds." It seemed to her a stupid thing to say even if it was true. He didn't laugh.

"I do that sometimes," he admitted. "The best place to listen is deep in the woods. If you're still enough, you can hear an owl snore in a tree above your head."

The smile on her face was brilliant when she realized he was teasing. He found he could not take his gaze away from her sparkling gray-green eyes and high dark brows, her small nose, and her soft, full mouth. He had an almost irresistible urge to take the pins from her hair and set it free. Anything so beautiful and alive shouldn't be twisted and confined in that harsh knot on the top of her head.

Blast it! What was the matter with him that he stood there staring at her? He'd seen women more beautiful than this one; women who made pleasing a man their life's work.

"Next you'll be telling me you can hear a cloud float overhead."

Her soft voice and the low musical laughter that followed it drew him back to the present and he looked away from her. He felt a tightening in his throat and with it a kind of terror, like that of a child awakening in the dark to find himself half-smothered by a blanket. For one frightening second he imagined himself bound by soft clinging arms, always holding him back.

Berry was very aware that he looked at her strangely. Dark blue eyes bored into hers, eyes bordered by thick, dark lashes. His irises were truly blue, but so dark that they appeared black at this close range. She could see that his eyes had widened, as if he was surprised by something he saw in hers.

"Has Biedy got things under control?"

It wasn't at all what she had expected him to say. She nodded while her mind searched for a logical reply.

Fain's booming laughter shattered the quiet. Simon took a step back, glanced around the corner of the house, nodded to her, and moved out of sight. Berry heard him greet his friends and listened to the voices as they moved away from the cabin. She rested her head against the rough logs, shut her eyes, and recalled the moment when she was held clasped in his arms, his lips on hers. She could feel her body crying to be close to him again, her lips hungering for his kisses. Could he rouse her as he did and feel nothing in return? What could she do? Nothing. It was ever a woman's fate to wait for the man's next move.

Jefferson Merrick was a big man with hair so light that at first it appeared to be gray, but he was a young man. His eyes were dark brown and he had a week's growth of brown whiskers on his cheeks. He wore buckskin pants and shirt much like the French voyageurs wore, but without the fringe and bead decorations. His deerskin moccasins were well worn, as were those of his friend Will. Both men moved with the ease of those who had long used their feet for transportation through the dense forest that lay east of the river.

Jeff squatted with his back to a tree, his long gun in his arms. He handed it over to Fain when the big man reached for it. Fain caressed the carved stock, lifted it to test the balance, and sighted down the long barrel.

"Should hit a pimple on a blue jay's ass at ninety yards," he murmured. "That's if a man knows how to shoot it."

Jeff laughed. "I'll put my shootin' with that rifle up against any in the territory."

"I hadn't oughtta let you hornswoggle me out of it. It's the best I ever made."

"Hornswoggle! Listen to that, Will! I gave the old cuss everything but the skin off my back." He reached for the gun. "Give it back, you old son of a goat. She's my wilderness wife, by gawd!"

Pride in his work was etched in Fain's face. He handed the rifle back to Jeff. There was a proud, wide grin on his face. "Wilderness wife, huh? It'd be a cold comfort to snuggle up to in the wintertime."

"Not if the wolves were a-howlin' at the door or the Indians breathin' down your neck."

"Speaking of Indians," Simon said. "Are you still on good terms with the Osage?"

"So far. They seem to be fascinated by the two black men who live up on the place. They've taken them into the tribe, shared their women. Besides, the Osage and the Delawares are on the warpath and too busy to pay much attention to settlers."

"How's your apprentice a-doin'?" Will asked in the slurry tones of a Virginian.

Fain laughed and glanced at Simon. "Well . . . if he lives to be a hundred he might learn a thin' or two about gunsmithin'. He's a good lad, just ain't handy with borin' tools and the like."

"Did he ever say exactly where he come from?" Jeff asked.

"Back east," Simon said. "I guess he went to Harvard College for a year and to the university at Paris. That's about all we know about him except he was about to be thrown into debtors' prison for family debts and skipped out. He drifted down the Trace and ended up in Saint Louis. He came into the warehouse one day and I told him about Fain being a gunsmith. It was something he wanted to do, he said, so he wandered on up here and made a bargain with Fain."

"He's a better cook than gunsmith, that's certain," Fain added with a chuckle.

"Is he staying around awhile?"

Fain looked at Jeff sharply. It wasn't like the man to ask so many questions. "Dunno. Ain't bothered to ask." He knocked the ashes out of his pipe. "Ya got a notion about Fish?"

"The name Edmund Aston rang a bell when I first heard it, but nothing's cleared in my mind since."

"I'd almost forgot his name." Simon ran his fingers through his still-damp hair. "We've called him Fish since Eben pulled him out of the river. The name stuck. He didn't seem to mind."

Jeff stood. "We've got to be a-pushing on. I'd like to stay and eat some of Biedy's pie, but can't spare the time." The men walked toward the river and the fast skiff they had beached there.

"We're a-headin' for Natchez to see the sights." Will carefully placed his rifle in the boat. "Whoeeeeee... I'm gonna find me a sweet, soft woman 'n' stay abed a week!" His blue eyes twinkled and he jumped in the air and clicked his feet together.

"You'd not last a week," Jeff teased, then said to Simon and Fain, "If Light comes back this way, ask him to check on the homestead. Henry and Jute would be glad for his company."

"We'll do that. Thanks for bringing Biedy." Simon shook hands with the two men.

"It's a shame you can't wait to meet the two purtiest womenfolk to come down the pike," Fain said
when the men stepped into the boat. "Second
thought, seein' your ugly faces mighta scared the
wits outta 'em."

"From what Lardy told us, they don't scare easy.
They sound like gutsy women, my kind of womenfolk." Will smiled his cool, dry smile, but his eyes
teased. "You're lucky I ain't a-stayin' 'round. I'm a-
goin' to let ya get a little head start before I come
a-courtin'."

"Are ya gonna have to listen to that braggin' all
the way to Natchez, Jeff?" Fain called as the boat
pulled away.

"He'll get tired o' talking to himself," Jeff said
cheerfully. Then: "Are the women going back east?"

"We're not sure what they're going to do," Simon
called as the boat pulled away.

They stood on the bank and watched the current
catch the canoe. In a few minutes it was around the
bend and out of sight. They walked back up the
slope toward the house. A burst of feminine laughter came from the open door of the cabin.

"It sounds good a-hearin' womenfolk in the
house," Fain said, and then seemed embarrassed
that he'd voiced his thought.

Simon didn't answer, but silently he agreed.

Chapter Nine

Simon had been gone for four days, and the thought of him was ever in Berry's mind. She thought about his homestead a great deal, too, visualizing a tight, neat cabin and outbuildings, seeing herself there as mistress of it all, loved, cherished beyond all Simon's other possessions. Sometimes in the evenings she would walk out toward the river and give herself up to the recollection of his hands gripping her arms, his mouth against hers, and the lean tautness of his body when he lifted her off her feet to kiss her. At other times she was disgusted with herself for lusting after the tall trader with the quiet, dark face and blue-black eyes.

Berry worked from sunup to sunset each day, enjoying Biedy's cheerful companionship, Rachel's bright, happy face, and the wonder of the baby who slept peacefully most of the time. The double cabin had been scrubbed from top to bottom, the clothes washed and put away, candles made, corn ground for bread and cakes. Fain supplied an abundance of fresh-killed foul for hearty meals, and Berry and Biedy scoured the woods to find salad greens, poke, and fresh green shoots from the wild grapevines to cook with the meat.

Israel had learned to catch the huge catfish that frolicked in the river, and Biedy had taught Berry how to bake them covered with red clay and buried beneath the coals of the outdoor fire.

"I 'spect Silas 'n' the boys will be here tomorry or the next day to fetch me home," Biedy said one evening. She sat in Fain's big chair, her feet barely reaching the floor, and cuddled Faith in her arms. "It's goin' to be plumb miserable leavin' this little lovey. Are ya sure you won't come along home with me, Rachel? You're welcome. You're just as welcome as plum blossoms in the spring. You 'n' Berry both. Why, my land! Two unhitched women in this wild place is rare as a green rooster! There's men all over this territory what'll be flockin' about ya like bears after honey when they hear. Now, if'n my boys was a mite older, I'd steal ya away for 'em."

Rachel moved on swift, merry feet to set the pewter mugs on the shelf. "Thank you, Biedy. It'll be a lucky girl that gets you for a mother-in-law." Rachel had bloomed since the baby was born. Her blue eyes were luminous, her red lips always faintly, lovingly smiling. Overnight she had turned into a beautiful, confident woman who took pride in her appearance. Her hair was shiny clean, pulled up in a pompadour with soft tendrils curling about her face. Her work apron was always turned so the clean side was out when the men came in at mealtime.

From her place beside the door where she was crushing corn into meal on the grinding stone, Berry watched her. Although not a word had been said, she was sure that Rachel had fallen in love with Fain. Berry watched, anxious for a sign that he had a romantic interest in her. Last night the two of them had walked to the edge of the house yard and stood quietly talking. Even Biedy noticed that Fain spent an uncommon amount of time near Rachel and Faith. One time when Fain bent over the baby and chucked her beneath the chin, Biedy winked at Berry, her eyes bright with mischievous delight.

Berry was so deep in thought that when the object of those thoughts came through the dogtrot and stopped at the door, she was startled. Fain stood with an arm along the door frame, his lips pursed, his eyes squinted in thought.

"It's plumb queer how womenfolk can take a perfectly good cabin and smell it all up with soap and flowers and honeycakes." His voice boomed in the thick quiet of the room.

Rachel was suddenly busy straightening the candle holders, her back turned so the blush in her cheeks didn't show.

"Go on wid ya, Fain. Ya ain't never ate such good vittles in all your born days." Biedy was never at a loss for words. Rachel blessed her, then wanted to choke her for what she said next. "If'n you had any gumption at all, you'd not let Rachel 'n' Berry get one step off this here place. You 'n' Simon been floatin' 'round free long enough. It's time ya took a wife, got ya some younguns while ya still can. Ya know what Silas says? He says them what don't, sooner cain't than them what does."

Even Fain was at a loss for words. "Now . . . Biedy. Ah . . . I made somethin' for Faith." He stepped back, reached behind him, and came through the door holding his handy work in front of him.

"Oh..." The gasp came from Rachel. "Oh, Fain! A cradle!"

"It ain't very fancy, but the wood is smooth." He set the cradle on the table and stood back, a shy grin on his face. "It's the best white pine I could find on the place."

"It's beautiful!" Rachel's eyes were shining.

"Well, I do declare! It's sightly, Fain. Plumb sightly! But then I oughtta've knowed ya could do it, 'n' easylike, too. Silas said ya was a great hand with tools." Biedy shoved Faith into his arms. "Here, hold the youngun while we fix up some paddin'."

"There's a feather pillow in the wagon, Rachel. I'll get it." Berry quickly dusted the powdery corn-meal from her hands.

"You'll need a wax cloth to cover," Biedy called. "That youngun's a fierce eater, sleeper, 'n' wetter."

Rachel's eyes drank in the picture of Fain with her child in his arms. Their eyes met and she almost cried at the look on his face. It was a kind of desperate longing! Could it be for her? Her heart told her it was, but her mind said it couldn't be. This man wasn't like any man she had ever met before. And this was a new, wild, wonderful feeling she had for him—and scary, too.

The women made a big to-do about getting the cradle ready. Finally the padding was settled to Biedy's satisfaction and a soft blanket was put in place. Fain had the honor of laying Faith in her new bed for the first time.

"It's perfect!" The smile on Rachel's lips matched the shine in her eyes. "It's just the right height to keep off drafts, and so balanced I only need to give it a little nudge once in a while and it'll keep rocking."

"Wal, I'll swan to goodness!" Biedy exclaimed. "It just keeps on a-rockin'. It's big enough so she can sleep in it till she's scrouged out by another youngun."

Rachel's cheeks flamed and Berry hurried to smooth things for her as she always did.

"If you can make something as fine as this, Fain, how come you've not made a settle chair or a gate-leg table?"

"What for?" His eyes twinkled, knowing she was filling the embarrassing silence that followed Biedy's remark. "All I need is a stout chair 'n' a table to eat 'n' work on."

"Humpt!" Biedy snorted. "I always thought ya was brainier 'n' that! Womenfolk like a thin' to brag on. Somethin' not ever'body's got."

A rumble of laughter broke from Fain. "Do you think you 'n' Berry can take care of things for a while so me 'n' Rachel can walk off down by the river?"

"Well, I reckon! I thought ya wasn't goin' to ask. Get a-goin' 'n' do your courtin'. Silas will be a-comin' fer me. He's a marryin' preacher, ya know. Married up a couple jist last week what come up from Saint Charles 'cause the magistrate was a-lolly-gaggin' around down to Saint Louie."

Rachel looked neither left nor right as she made for the door. Her heart was pounding, her knees were suddenly weak, and she had never felt so warm before in her life. Biedy's words were like blisters on her face. Why, the very idea, for her to think that Fain ... He must be as embarrassed as she was. She'd never be able to look at him now, no matter how wonderful her heart told her he was.

The evening breeze was pleasant against Rachel's hot face, but she was not of a mind to notice. Extremely conscious of the man who walked beside her, she went down the path beneath the towering walnut, cottonwood, and sycamore trees to the sandbar and its miniature forest of willow and poplar seedlings that had sprung up with the coming of spring. Fleets of goslings and ducklings cruised in the backwater and Rachel paused to look and to smile. A whippoorwill swooped overhead, trailing his melodious repeated cry. Evening sounds echoed the peace and contentment of the end of the day with a chorus from the crickets and bullfrogs along the riverbank.

"You're goin' to have to look at me sometime, ya know." Fain put his hand on her arm and pulled her to a halt beneath the overhang of a clay bank. "Are ya lettin' what Biedy said get your goat?" He chuckled. "Biedy's got a runnin' off at the mouth, but she means well."

"I know she does, but sometimes ... she comes out with such personal ... things. ... " She couldn't help but smile when she saw his grin.

"I didn't need no nudgin' from Biedy. All day I've been thinkin' of ways to get ya off to myself."

"I'm afeared we've been a great bother," she said, disbelieving she had heard him correctly. She was stumbling for words, so surprised to find herself alone with him.

"Ya ain't been no bother, lass. You've made me see how much pleasure it is to see a pretty woman ever'day." There was something in the tone of his voice that drew her eyes to his face. She almost forgot to breathe, lost in the beauty and depth of his eyes, which seemed to be reaching out to her. "Do ya like it here, lass?"

"Here?"

"Here. On my land, in my house?"

Rachel took a deep breath, trying to steady her nerves so she could answer. He moved closer to her and put his hands on her shoulders. "It's a lovely place," she whispered.

"It can be your home. Yours and Faith's ... if'n ya c'n take me with it."

"Oh, Fain! You don't have to feel responsible for us. You've already helped..."

"Responsible! Hell, lass, do ya think that's why I'm a-askin' ya to stay?" His arms drew her to him and hers went around his waist. She hid her face in the clean cloth of his shirt. "I don't mind tellin' ya I've been a-fightin' it," he whispered in her hair. "Then it hit me square that you and the babe could be movin' on to Biedy's or someplace else and the love I've got for you and the little button would be a-tearin' me apart."

Rachel felt a thrill catch hold of her and almost wrench her heart out of her breast. "Are you... sure?"

His hand tilted her face toward him. "I've never been so sure 'bout anythin'. I've got to kiss ya, lass. I've been a-wantin' to for so long...."

As she saw his face lowering to hers, she was instantly conscious of how badly she wanted his kiss. He set his lips on hers gently and she kissed him back. Desire spread out across her groin and down her thighs. She pressed her lips fiercely to his. His warmth suffused her and she pressed closer to the wonderful masculine strength of his body and inhaled his pleasing scent. The kiss deepened and was long; she could not bear to have it end. In it was the essence of love between them, the rich, warm, earthy mating of male and female.

He drew his lips from hers at last, and raised his head to look at her, and she smiled at him, then laughed joyously. The laughter rose within her and bubbled up in her throat in sheer delight. *He had been struck with the same jolt that had struck her.* "Is this really happening?"

"If not, it's the best dream I've ever had!"

He caught her hand and drew her toward a grassy spot. He sank down, his arms encircling her skirts. For an instant he buried his face in the bodice of her dress. "Mmm, you smell so good."

Then she was on his lap, swung back in his arms, looking up into his face.

"You'll be mine, darlin' girl," he said in hushed tones. "My woman, in my house. I can come in and look at ya anytime I want." He hugged her to him, and they began to laugh. They laughed like two children sharing a secret.

"Fain," she whispered through his kisses. "Fain!" She clung to him, eyes closed, forgetting—not caring—that he had not yet said he loved her, only that he had a love for her and Faith, conscious only of his warm strong nearness and the darkness that enclosed them. With her arms about his neck, they kissed, soft, loving kisses, while they laughed and whispered.

"Do you love me, lass?"

"Yes, I do, Fain. Yes, I do."

"I love you, too."

"Oh, Fain, I might swoon, I'm so happy."

"Don't do that, lass. I want to kiss you some more."

"I can't believe that you love me. Say it again."

"I love you, love you. I never thought I'd love again, but I do."

"I'm so glad it's me."

"I do love you, lass. Oh, so much. I'll be good to ya, keep ya safe as I know how."

Sometime later, Rachel pulled herself back from his arms to whisper, "Fain, you know Asa never married me. I never was with him . . . willingly. You know that Faith . . ."

"Faith'll have a pa to love her." His fingers worked at the nape of her neck. "I was there to help put life in her. She's mine."

Rachel's heart turned over. She wanted to cry, she wanted to sing. All the years spent without security or love in her life made his words the most beautiful she had ever heard. Yet, more had to be said.

"Berry's almost like my own. I can't leave her till . . ." she choked off the words.

"Ya didn't think I'd turn her out, did ya, lass?" He kissed her hard on the lips. "Her home's with us for as long as she wants." He chuckled and Rachel could feel it against her full breasts. "It won't be for long, I'm a-thinkin'. When Simon comes back and sees the calf eyes Fish makes at her, and after Biedy spreads the word upriver, she'll have suitors aplenty."

Rachel rested in the security of his arms. She had

never felt so safe in her life as she felt here in the wilderness in this man's arms. His fingers flicked gently over her body, touching her lightly through the thin cloth of her dress and tracing over the firm mounds of her breast. His caresses were gentle and loving, strangely devoid of passion. It was a delightful feeling for Rachel, who had known only the rough, cruel touch of a man's hands.

Fain's nose nuzzled her hair and she lifted her mouth and shaped it to his. Her lips clung, soft and sweet and hotly exciting. A husky growl came from his throat and he pulled away from her.

"It won't always be like this, sweet lass," he whispered shakily. "I'm a lusty man, but I'll not hurt ya, or force ya. . . ."

"You'll have to teach me loving," she murmured, and melted once more into his arms.

"I'll not have ya till you're healed and a-wantin' me. I can wait, if'n I can touch ya, hold ya . . . know you're mine." His voice was deep with feeling and she almost cried with the wonder of being loved and wanted.

The time sped by. The moon came up over the river, its light casting one shadow of the two lovers. Fain's hands on her breasts had started the milk to flow. The wetness against his palms sent rivers of desire through him. He could feel his need rising. Painful as it was to leave her, he loosened his arms and lifted her off his lap.

"Whoa now, lass! We got ta stop this while we can. I'll not be fit ta take ya back to the womenfolk," he teased.

Rachel giggled happily. All shyness between them was gone. In its place was an intimacy so precious that she could scarcely contain her bubbling spirit. Her life up to now had been one long time of despair, despite the love and kindness Berry so unselfishly gave her. Still she couldn't believe this wonderful thing had happened to her, and she kept turning her head, trying to make out Fain's features in the darkness. Fain was just as aware of the blending of their spirits as she was, for he held her close in his arms for a long moment, unwilling to let her move as much as a breath away from him.

"It's grand, what's happened to us," he said against her mouth.

"Yes!" she could feel his life pounding against her breast and wondered if he could feel the thud of her heart against his.

"Sweet, sweet Rachel," he murmured and kissed her quickly. With his arm around her, he urged her up the path to the house.

"Berry's heart is set on going to the land her pa signed on," Rachel said quietly.

"Simon said as much. She'll get the notion out of her head and settle down here. It wouldn't do at all for her to go off 'n' try to set up a homestead with only the slave to help 'er. Linc'll be back lookin' for 'er, if'n she didn't kill him. If'n she did, there'll be the Indians and river scum a-lookin' for a woman."

"She's got pride. I'm thinking she won't want to stay for fear she's puttin' us out."

"Don't fret. We'll make her see the right of it."

The steadiness of his voice calmed Rachel's fears. When he pulled her to a stop in the shadows at the corner of the house, her arms went up around his neck and she clung to him.

"Fain ... I got to ask. ... You're sure that ... later on you won't mind about Faith?"

"I'm sure, lass." His eyes met hers and he spoke softly, but there was a firm sincerity in his voice. "I reckon there's more to bein' a pa than startin' the babe. I took her for mine when I helped ya birth her."

Tears glittered in Rachel's eyes and she smiled through them. The smile trembled at the corners of her mouth. "Thank you."

Fain found her trembling lips and kissed her. She responded and pressed body and lips to his. Her arms, tight around him, told him more than her simple word of thanks.

The cabin was dark, but outside, in the forest, the birds were beginning to proclaim daybreak. Berry woke and lay for a moment, listening, trying to understand why her mind refused to rest. And then suddenly it came back to her, that incredible news Rachel had whispered to her in the darkness after she had returned from walking out with Fain. *She and Fain were in love! He wanted to marry her. He wanted Berry, Rachel, and Faith to live with him, here in this cabin. It would be their home.* Berry was wildly happy for Rachel, although a small part of her felt a loss so acute that it was painful. She rolled over on her back and stretched her arms out wide on either side of her, as if to push away the guilt about the naggling shaft of jealousy that pierced her heart. She hadn't dreamed that Rachel would meet a man and fall in love in such a short space of time. Rachel had assured Berry that Fain wanted her to stay with them, but of course that was impossible. Rachel was entitled to a home place of her own. She needn't feel responsible for her; she was a grown woman now. She and Israel and the other Negro, if she could hire him, would go on and build a homestead out in the wilderness.

Biedy was delighted with the wedding plans. "Glory! Fain's got more gumption than I gave him credit for," she exclaimed gleefully as she prepared the morning mush. "Now, if'n we can do us a mite of arm twistin', we jist might get Simon to do some askin', 'n' Berry'd be all settled too."

"Biedy! No! Don't you dare say... anything to him!" The words popped out of Berry's mouth and astonishment froze the lines of her scarlet-red face. "I'm not a-marryin' to find me a home place! Especially Simon Witcher!" She grabbed up the water bucket and fled the cabin. Rachel's troubled eyes followed her.

"Wait up, Miss Berry." Fish came around the corner of the house and she almost plowed into him. "I'll fetch the water."

"There's no need. I can do it."

"Do you mind if I walk along?" He fell in step without waiting for her answer. "Fain says he and Miss Rachel are going to be married." Berry nodded without speaking. "He's going to build a room onto the cabin. Plans to start right away, he said. It shouldn't take over a couple of days with the Cornicks and Simon lending a hand." They came to the narrow path leading to the spring. Fish took the bucket from her hand and stepped aside so she could precede him down the path. "You won't have to be moving on, now. I'm glad, Miss Berry."

"Fain is marrying Rachel, not the whole family," she said tightly. "Of course I'll be going on to my land."

"But Fain said... he wants you to stay."

"It's kind of him, but I'll make out fine."

"I was hoping you'd stay." She turned and looked into pleading eyes on a level with her own. He looked young, boyish, scarcely able to look after himself in this harsh land. "You can't homestead alone, Miss Berry!"

"You don't know that. I don't even know that until I try," she said crossly. "I'm going to have a try at it, Fish. Don't you understand that I can't expect Rachel and Fain to take care of me for the rest of my life. Besides that, I want to amount to something, have things, and I can't do that living off someone else. And—ohhh...!" Her voice broke off in mid-sentence. They had reached the pool that formed beneath the spring and a man was bathing there. His naked back and buttocks were turned toward her. His wet, black hair glistened in the morning sun. Berry turned quickly and started back down the path. Simon! Simon had come back!

"I'll bring the water, miss," Fish called after her.

Berry scarcely heard him for the pounding of her heart. She couldn't seem to move her feet fast enough to get away. Her only thought was to escape back to the house and the safety of Rachel and Biedy's presence.

Simon's wilderness-trained ears had heard the voices coming down the path toward the pool before he had glimpsed the slender body and dark hair. He turned quickly, presenting his back to her, knowing it was impossible to leave the pool. All his senses were focused on the woman who had been constantly in his mind. What is she thinking, he thought, when she looks at me with eyes the color of young willow leaves in the spring? Suddenly he felt a sickness in his stomach. A sickness he had felt once before. He'd stepped into quicksand and was sinking. He'd thought surely he would die. Only Fain's quick thinking and strong arms had saved him. He was scared like that now. This woman could take his heart and more of his soul than a man was prepared to give. What had gone wrong with his life? He'd thought he'd planned it well. He'd take a woman when the time was right, when he was ready to settle down, when he'd seen all the country he wanted to see. He hadn't planned on meeting a woman who would become his joy, the all-consuming factor in his life. His thoughts were an unwielding jumble in his mind.

The last five days had been long and full of tempestuous thoughts. He had forced himself to stay away from Fain's homestead, forced himself to work on his own until he was so weary each evening that he slept as if drugged. Last night he had gotten out of bed at midnight and sat on the door stone looking out over the moonlit river. The loneliness of his life had seemed to press down on him.

At first light he had pulled his canoe up onto the riverbank below Fain's place. His eyes had searched the landscape, a habit of almost a lifetime, before he had walked up the slope to the house.

Simon had finished bathing and was dressing when Fain walked down to the pool. "Mornin'. Fish said I had a critter in my pond."

"Mornin'." Simon put his hat on his wet head and

picked up his rifle. "News travels fast. This place is getting plumb crowded."

"You'll have to watch yourself 'bout jumpin' bare-assed in my pond now that there'll be womenfolk on the homestead." Fain's grin widened.

"Permanent?" Simon jerked his head around to ask the question.

"I'm takin' a wife." Fain narrowed his eyes as he watched his friend's face.

"A wife?" Simon echoed.

"Rachel. I asked her last night. Silas can tie the knot when he comes for Biedy. It's just as bindin' as if that drunken magistrate from Saint Charles did it."

"Isn't this kinda sudden?"

"I reckon it is. But I been a-thinkin' 'bout it for a time, but didn't reckon I had a chance. She's a woman that's not had it easy, Simon. I reckon to change that."

"I'm right pleased for you, Fain. I reckon she'll make you a good wife."

Fain looked pleased with the world. "I plan to add on a room. Ya got any plans for the next few days?"

"None that can't be put off." Simon smiled back at his friend. "I plan on using that muscle of yours one of these days." He stuck out his hand.

Fain bellowed with laughter, grabbed Simon's hand, and tried to jerk him off his feet. Simon was prepared and braced himself. It was a friendly tug of war the two men played every time they had a chance and ended when Fain gave in and dropped his hand.

"Not every man gets two women to do for him when he takes a wife." Simon bent and retrieved his rifle.

The smile left Fain's face. "Rachel's worried some about the girl. She's got it in her head to homestead."

"Hasn't she got over that notion? That's the most hairbrained thing I ever heard of! Good Lord, Fain! What's she thinkin' she's gonna do for a cabin? She can't live in that wagon come winter. And... every no-good in the territory would be a-beatin' a path to her door... and the Osage'd love to get their hands on a young white woman even if she does have black hair. Them green eyes of hers would be enough. She don't have the brains of a flea if she thinks she'd last a month out there. She's not going! That's final! I'll see to it."

Fain clapped him on the shoulder. "You do that, Simon. You just go right ahead and do that." He grinned at the sight of the stiff back stalking ahead of him up the path toward the house.

Simon's eyes met Berry's the instant he walked into the eating room. They stared at each other for a moment that was so still it seemed as if time had stopped moving. He looked at her searchingly and nodded in greeting, but he didn't speak.

Fain came in behind him. "Morning!" His voice boomed happily and his twinkling eyes honed in on Rachel's face. Her slightly flushed cheeks made her blue eyes seem all the brighter.

"Mornin'," she murmured.

Fain went to her, put his arms around her, and kissed her on the lips. He was announcing to all that this was his woman. "Mornin'," he whispered just to her. The intimate greeting was so sweet it made her blush.

"Well, Fain! If'n ya ain't the beatin'est man. I do declare!" Biedy turned the meat in the spider skillet. "I swan to goodness if'n you ain't got that girl to blushin' somethin' awful. Now, if'n it was me ya was a-kissin', I'd just stand there bare-faced 'n' let ya." She cackled with laughter that turned to shrieks when Fain came toward her. "Ya behave yourself, Fain. I was a-funnin'! Mind me, now. I got this hot grease and I'm liable ta spill it. Word might get back to Silas. . . . Fain! Simon, make him behave." She dodged a peck on the cheek.

"I'm afraid I can't do that, Biedy. He's bigger than I am."

"Rachel . . . you goin' to let your man go 'round kissin' women? If'n ya do, they'll be lined up from here to the river."

"Then I won't lack for company, will I?" There was light, happy laughter in Rachel's voice. She stepped over to the fireplace oven and pulled out a pan of bread. Fain roared with laughter and patted her affectionately on the shoulder.

Simon shuffled his feet, his dark eyes watching the horseplay. "I'm right pleased that you and Fain will be wed. He don't amount to much, but maybe you can make something out of him."

Rachel glanced at him and was surprised to see his usually somber face creased with smiles. "I'll surely try."

Berry had never seen Rachel act so young and carefree. Her eyes followed her light steps from the hearth to the table, and she vowed silently that she would do nothing, say nothing, about not making her home here until after the wedding. But, law! It would be hard to leave here without Rachel. It had been just the two of them for so long.

The morning was spent making huckleberry pies and cleaning and picking the pinfeathers from a giant tom turkey Simon had brought to the kitchen an hour after breakfast. As they worked the women made plans for the wedding that would be held when Silas came to take Biedy home. They decided to decorate the room with honeysuckle and plum blossoms, and Rachel's good dress would have to be washed and ironed. Biedy wished she could get word to Silas to bring their eldest son, Isaac, and his fiddle. There was a fair chance, she said, that he would do it knowing a birthing was always a cause for a celebration.

Rachel and Fain spent considerable time outside the cabin marking off where the new room would be built. They decided that the kitchen side of the cabin would be more suitable because the stone fireplace could also be used to heat the room. Impatient to start, Fain bellowed to Simon, Fish, and the two Negroes. They shouldered their axes and went into the dense woods to fell trees.

The emptiness that had lain heavy as a stone on Berry's heart since she had first learned that Rachel would be staying here with Fain gradually lifted. It was wonderful to see Rachel happy and to know her dearest friend was loved and would be taken care of by a good man.

Biedy talked nonstop.

"Land sakes! But it's goin' to be a grand day for a weddin'. We'll have to pick us a fine mess of dandelion greens. Pshaw! If'n I'd-a knowed, I'd-a brought mincemeat for a cake. I do love a weddin', or a buryin', or a cabin raisin'. It's them times when standoffish folks ain't so standoffish." She paused for a breath. "Lordy, what I wouldn't give for that crock o' honey I got in the cellar. We could make us up some honeycakes."

"Sounds like we'll have food aplenty," Rachel said when she got the chance.

"There's them folk camped down by the runoff. Course, I'd just as soon they come off without that crazy ol' woman what don't know straight up about birthin'. It'd be plumb enjoyable ta have us a big bunch here for the weddin'."

Berry's eyes met Rachel's across the room. They exchanged smiles. The smiling, gentle Rachel in no way resembled the pale, frightened woman who for years had lived with the terrible acceptance of a woman used and scorned.

"I got to slip off and see 'bout that baby what's almost mine. My, my, my, she's a little darlin'. Not at all colicky." Biedy skipped out the door as light on her feet as a young girl.

Berry went to Rachel and put her arms around her. "I couldn't be happier for you. You deserve this and much, much more."

Tears spurted in Rachel's eyes and she sucked her lips between her teeth to still her trembling. "I was afraid you'd be disappointed... that I was goin' to stay here. He's so good and gentle, Berry. He wants a home place with a woman in it to cook and clean... and have his... babes. He..."

Berry shook her gently. "You don't have to tell me what *he* wants. Do you love him?"

"I don't know love, except for you ... and now Faith." Tears rolled down her cheeks. "It's all new to me. I've lived for so long in ... despair. I feel safe with him. I know he'll not hurt me."

"It's enough," Berry said gently. "I liked him right away. And after he helped with the birthin', I knew he was a good man."

Rachel wiped her eyes on the end of her apron. "I'm glad you like him. It's all turned out so much better than I ever dreamed it would. Sometimes I think I'm dreaming and this isn't happening at all."

"It was just meant to be, Rachel. It was just meant to be that you'd find him. I'm so glad you did."

Chapter 10

Silas Cornick, his hair water-slicked, his beard neatly trimmed, produced his book and leafed through it to find his place. He cleared his throat. "You jist stand right over there, Fain. Take her hand."

Rachel looked up at Fain shyly. Her long, slim fingers trembled and he gripped them tightly. Biedy and Berry had arranged her blond hair neatly atop her head with sprigs of honeysuckle blossoms surrounding the knot. Her good dress was faded from many washings and was ill fitted due to her recent loss of weight, but it was free of wrinkles. Berry's shoes pinched her toes, but the warm admiration in Fain's eyes made her forget that discomfort. She felt beautiful, so she smiled and held herself proudly.

Berry had never heard the marriage ceremony before, and she listened closely to the solemn words that Silas spoke. When he asked Fain if he would take this woman, Fain's answer was firm. He said he certainly would, and would cherish and protect her the best he knew how. Rachel's answers were low and trembly, as if she wanted to cry.

During the ceremony Biedy stood beside her son Isaac, with her head slightly lowered, but her eyes never ceased their traveling from face to face of the group gathered attentively around the bridal couple. Fish stood beside them. Berry stood alone; just beyond her and a little to the side was Simon. His eyes never left Berry's face.

Rachel and Fain were turning toward each other in the last minutes of the ceremony when Berry raised her eyes. She looked straight into the mirrored depths of Simon's eyes and was caught there. The impact was as vivid as if he had reached across and touched her. A bead of sweat appeared on Berry's upper lip. After a moment she swallowed, and with an effort she drew her eyes away and refused to look at him again.

The wedding was over in minutes. To Berry it seemed awfully short to bind a man and woman together for the rest of their lives. Then Fain was kissing Rachel. Biedy was chortling happily at Rachel's confusion, while Fish, Simon, and Isaac were slapping Fain on the back. Rachel's eyes were shining and Berry's were misty as they hugged each other. Then everyone moved out into the yard where the wedding feast was spread out on a plank table set in the shade of the walls of the new room.

The men crowded in, drinking a toast to the happiness of the bride and groom from a clay jug set on one end of the table. Biedy and Berry moved about uncovering dishes of food, slicing the baked turkey, and cutting slabs of cornbread and suet cake.

Israel and Eben hung back until Fain urged them forward. He filled their mugs with whiskey and Biedy filled their plates with food.

Simon stood by quietly, but Berry knew that nothing escaped his eyes. When she saw him move away from the others and come toward her, she tried in vain to still the frenzied beating of her heart. She moved quickly to the table and wedged herself between Biedy and Rachel.

Later she stood in an agony of embarrassment when Isaac got out his fiddle and struck up a tune, and Silas and Biedy began a mad gallop about the yard. She had never danced in her life and this was only the second time she had seen it done. She hoped desperately that no one expected her to do it! She started guiltily when someone touched her arm, but relief flooded through her when she saw it was Fish.

"Will you dance with me, Miss Berry?"

"No! Oh, no! I . . . don't know how."

"You don't have to know how," he said teasingly. "All you do is hop to the music. Come. I'll show you." He took her hand and turned her to face him. "Put your hand on my shoulder," he said and grasped her waist. "Now . . . first on one foot and then the other. I'll propel us around. All you have to do is follow."

Berry had the hang of it in a matter of minutes. Laughter, sweeter than the sound of the fiddle, broke from her lips. "What's the name of the song, Fish?"

"It's called 'Yankee Doodle.' It's been around since the war for independence."

"Do you know the words?"

"There are many verses. Some people make up their own:

> "Oh, Yankee Doodle is the tune
>   A-mer-i-cans de-light in;
> 'Twill do to whis-tle, sing or play,
>   and just the thing for fight-in'."

He finished singing the verse and whirled her around until the skirt of her weathered dress billowed out behind her.

The dancing fascinated Berry. She bounced lightly with Fish across the dirt yard. "Sing another verse," she urged.

"All right . . . let me see. . . ." He slowed their steps.

> "A-mer-i-ca's a dandy place,
>   the people are all brothers;
> And when one's got a pumpkin pie,
>   he shares it with the others."

Berry laughed delightedly. The sound reached the tall man leaning against the side of the house. Simon couldn't keep his eyes away from her. He'd not had a chance to speak to her alone for the entire two days he had been here working on the new room. It galled him to see her laughing with Fish. The young squirt wasn't even dry behind the ears yet! He didn't understand why Berry had been avoiding him, but it was clear as day that she had been doing just that. She had stuck so close to Rachel and Biedy you'd've thought she was glued to them, he thought with irritation.

When the dancing couple passed close to him, Simon was tempted to reach out and snatch her to him. Her head was thrown back, her red mouth open as she gasped for breath. Never had he seen a woman so beautiful, so alive. He wondered for the hundredth time why her skin was so clear and white, why her hair was so shiny, and why the sound of her laughter was like the joyous ringing of a bell.

"Sing 'Sally Goodin,'" Fain called out to Isaac when he lowered the fiddle to take a break. He was dancing with Rachel, holding her as if she were a precious piece of fine glass, moving with slow, sure steps, being careful not to tire her out.

Isaac played a few bars of a fast tune, then lowered the fiddle to sing:

"I had a piece of pie, 'n' I had a piece of puddin',
I gave it all away to hug Sally Goodin."

He played the fiddle between the verses, stomping his booted foot on the ground in time with the music.

"My Isaac c'n sing and clog as good as anybody," Biedy shouted as Berry and Fish whirled past. "All my boys c'n cut the pigeon wing and ride a short loper with the best." She and Silas had stopped dancing and were clapping their hands to the music.

Silas moved up beside his son and his singing voice carried into every corner of the homestead.

"How old are you, my pretty little miss?
How old are you, my honey?
She answered him with a 'He, he he.
I'll be sixteen next Sunday.'"

When one song was done, Isaac started another, the dancing continuing all the while. Rachel stopped and leaned against Fain. He fanned her flushed face with a turkey wing that Biedy had left on the bench.

"No more dancin' for you, Miz MacCartney. You get in there 'n' rest yourself while ya tend to Faith. I'm a-goin' to dance with Berry."

The dance was long and exhausting; as Isaac stopped fiddling, the dancers flopped to the benches, and the black men, who had been shuffling their feet, flopped to the ground.

Simon sat on the woodchopping stump, Fain's pet crow on his shoulder. He fed the bird bits of turkey meat. The brim of his hat was pulled low over his eyes, but Berry knew they rested on her often. What was he thinking? Did he think she was making a fool of herself carrying on like that? Did he think dancing was frivolous? He hadn't danced with Rachel or Biedy and certainly not with her. She jumped up to help Biedy clear the table, and Fain moved over to hunker down beside Simon.

"Ya can't beat the Cornicks for gettin' up a shindig. I'm plumb glad. I wanted Rachel to have a grand weddin' day."

"It appears like you wore her out." Simon nodded toward the doorstone, where Rachel sat holding Faith to her shoulder. She had removed her shoes and her bare toes wiggled and dug into the cool grass.

Fain gazed intently at his new wife for a long moment before he spoke. "She needs some fixings for herself. I'd be obliged if you'd send up a parcel from your storehouse."

"Send Fish or Eben down and get what you want."

"I'd trip in with ya myself, but I want to get back to work on my guns."

"No need of it, if you tell me what you want." Simon drew his gaze away from Berry and saw the excitement in Fain's eyes. "You getting close to working the bugs out of that new piece?"

There was exhilaration in Fain's voice when he answered. "I've about got it worked out in my mind how I c'n insert the bullet at the breech. But I gotta figure out a device stout enough to hold the powder explosion. If'n it'll work, I c'n load in half the time, even if the barrel is fouled from previous firings. Think on what that would mean, Simon!" He struck his palm with his fist. "My gun would be favored over them German short barrels and that flat-faced hammer French rifle."

"If you're on to something you'd better keep it to yourself," Simon said quietly.

"I've been thinkin' on that, too. I don't want this to get out to no other gunsmith till I can get my stamp on it. You're the only one that knows what I'm working on besides Fish. The kid's a good shot. He c'n hit a man-sized target at a hundred yards seven times out of ten, but he'll not make no gunsmith. He's not got the hands or the 'stick to' for it."

"Has he mentioned anything about moving on?"

"You wantin' him gone?"

"It makes no never mind to me if he goes or stays, but there's something queer about a feller with his background a-hangin' around a place like this. You'd think he'd be a-tryin' to better himself." Simon looked steadily into Fain's twinkling eyes.

Fain chuckled, picked up a twig from the ground, and stuck it into the corner of his mouth. "I'd say he's a-workin' on somethin', or ain't ya noticed?"

"I noticed! I'm not blind! He'd be about as much use to her as tits on a boar!"

"Maybe he ain't plannin' on settlin' on a homestead. He might be plannin' on goin' back to the East and a-takin' her with him. She'd be a beauty all dressed in fancy clothes." Fain goaded his friend while watching him closely.

Simon swung his head around so his eyes could follow Berry. "I can't see a strong-willed woman like her getting took up with a slack-handed kid."

"He mightn't be slack-handed if'n he found his niche." Fain shook his head. "Ya never know about women. Maybe ya don't have nothin' to worry about."

"Who's worrying?" Simon snapped.

Fain let the remark pass. "Maybe it ain't marryin' he's got on his mind. Maybe he's just a-bidin' his time. He talked some 'bout joinin' up with Pike."

"Bullshit!" Simon snorted. "Pike'd not take on a kid like him. He'd not last through the first portage."

"Pike's got a lot at stake. It's said he's takin' Wilkinson's son on this trip upriver."

"I can tell you, Fain, but it's not to be let out. Wilkinson's ordered Pike to make a journey of exploration into the country to the south and west. It's the route Manuel Lisa's planning to take. You can bet your bottom dollar Lisa'll not stand aside and let someone else open up that trade. He fights dirty."

"Is he still after you to invest in the venture?"

"He don't give up easy. It don't set with him or Chouteau that I'm doing a little fur business. Course, what I do is nothing compared to Lisa or the Chouteau family operations."

"Watch Lisa. He ain't above doin' a little arm twistin'."

"I trust him about as far as Wilkinson. He's got his feelers out for a profit. I'd trust neither one as far as I can throw a mule by the tail."

"It'd be like him to have his spies out a-checkin' on Pike. Have ya run into anythin'?"

Simon was silent for a long moment. "You could say so." He dropped the news and waited for Fain's reaction. A puzzled frown crossed his face. "I was sitting on my doorstone a few nights back and saw something on the river. I got out my glass and could see a canoe plain as day in the moonlight. I went down to the river to get a better look and saw another canoe pulled up on the bank a ways downriver. I cut through the woods to see what they was up to. When they pulled to shore, a man came out of the timber and talked to them. I couldn't get close enough to see who he was and could catch just a few words they said, but I did hear one say something about 'by any means you can.' After a while one canoe went back downriver and the other one crossed over."

Fain chewed on the twig for a while before speaking. "What do you make of it?"

"I don't know. I don't care what Manuel Lisa or Pike do to each other as long as they leave me out of it. I'll not invest in Lisa's expedition. What I'd really like to do is get out of the trading business and start building up my farm. I'm going down to talk with Ernest. We got a share of the business to outfit Pike and I don't think Lisa was happy about it."

Fain chuckled. "What can he do?"

Simon grinned. "He could burn me out, but that would be too obvious."

"We'll keep an eye out . . . huh?"

Simon wasn't listening. His eyes went past Fain when Berry's laughter drifted across the yard. It was in response to something Fish had said to her, and she dodged around him and dashed into the cabin, only to come out minutes later with the laughter still on her lips. She threw a pan of dishwater out into the yard dangerously close to where Fish was standing. When he jumped back, musical, girlish laughter rang from her lips again before she darted back inside. Simon watched the play and listened to the happy sound. As always, the sound of her laughter gave him a surge of pleasure, and his eyes lingered on the empty doorway.

It was deepening dusk when Berry came out of the cabin and crossed the yard to her wagons. It would be strange, she thought, to sleep in the wagon without Rachel. It was something she would have to get used to doing. It had been a long time since she had been alone, and the emptiness of it pressed down upon her. Don't look back, she cautioned herself, lest you stumble for naught. She couldn't remember when she had first heard the familiar old saying. Perhaps it was something Rachel had said to her.

Fain and Rachel had gone into the big, new room. Fain had promised to put in a plank floor and build a big double bed. In the meanwhile they would

sleep on pallets on the smooth dirt floor. When they
had gone inside and dropped the hide flap that
covered the door, it was like the final parting for
Berry. Not that she wasn't happy for Rachel, but
... oh ... there was a sick, empty feeling in the pit
of her stomach.

Berry sat down on the trunk and looked around
her at the things she had known all her life: the
pine chest, the spinning wheel, the barrel churn,
and the tin chamber pot. She had come here to gain
comfort from being among these familiar things.

"I want to talk to you, Berry."

Simon! His voice was an impassioned whisper in
her ears. The constant awareness of him was fire in
her veins and energy in her fingers. All day she had
worked furiously, danced furiously, to keep him
from consuming her every thought. She saw his
outline at the end of the wagon and stood slowly,
feeling puzzled and self-conscious. She looked into
his face but could not speak.

"Come on down," he said and reached for her.
His head was bare and his hair looked wet, as if he
had been in the pool again. His hands circled her
waist and lifted her down. "Let's walk out a ways."
It wasn't a request, it was just simply—"let's walk
out a ways." She felt dwarfed as she moved along
beside him.

"We'll walk down by the river. Soon the mosquitoes will take over and it'll be misery to be near
the river when there's no breeze."

Berry drew a deep breath and tried to calm the
unease that had been fermenting in her breast. There
was something sweetly fascinating in being beside
him in the near darkness. Down the faint slope lay

the shimmering river with its unbroken border of trees. The night sounds had commenced around them: the low swish of the river, the faint hoot of an owl, the scrappy twit of a bird.

He drew her to a downed tree trunk and they sat down. *What did he bring her here to say?* She turned away from him, letting her glance move over the great river with its acrid, muddy smell of decay, over the little islands that seem to float on the river, tapestried in the pale green of budding cottonwoods. Berry drew a long satisfied breath, consciously permitting herself to enjoy the view.

She must speak, she told herself sternly. She must speak casually, trying to deny with her tone how shaken she was. "It's . . . pleasant here."

"Beats a town all hollow, doesn't it?"

At something in his tone she looked at him. He was not smiling, but there was a wicked mischief in his eyes; she could tell by the tiny creases that fanned out at the corners. She dropped her eyelids and focused on the loosely fitted white shirt that covered his broad shoulders and chest. *I wonder who washes his clothes.* It was her last coherent thought as a strange feeling swamped her, as if she lacked breath and could not speak, as if she were sad to the point of tears; and yet through it, like a rainbow through clouds, the promise of excitement and joy appeared.

He put his fist under her chin and lifted her face. "Are you unhappy that Rachel married? Is that what makes you look so sad?"

"I'm glad for Rachel. She deserves the best."

"She's got it. Fain's the best man I know. He'll take good care of her and the babe."

"I know that."

"Fain said you've got it into your head to go on out to the land your pa filed on. I can tell you, now, that land will never be under a plow, will not grow anything but willows and swamp grass."

"How do you know? You don't even know where it is!" She cast him a challenging glance.

"Rachel showed me the map. It's low and swampy."

"How do you know?" she repeated softly, although she wanted to shout at him.

"I've been there. I've been twenty, thirty miles back all along the river, and the land your pa filed on isn't good for anything but water moccasins. Even the Osage stay clear of it."

"You're just saying that. Papa wouldn't take swampy land."

"He didn't see it before he filed. He only knew what the land man told him, and he hadn't seen it either."

"I don't believe a word you're saying! I'll go and see for myself." She stood. Simon grasped her hand to keep her from moving away. "I'll not ask you to take me there, if that's what's worryin' you," she said scathingly.

"I'm not worried about it at all. I wouldn't do it," he said matter-of-factly, his voice deep and low, a smile hovering at the edges of his wide mouth. His very attitude of quiet self-confidence jarred her taut nerves.

"Fish will take me," she said abruptly.

"Hellfire!" He snorted. "You'd more'n likely have to take care of him."

"I don't need anybody," she said recklessly. "I'll go alone and take Israel."

"No, you won't. I won't permit it."

"You . . . won't . . . what?"

"You heard me, Berry. You may be a spitfire and need some strong handling, but you're not stupid. I'll not allow my *wife* to go traipsing off in the woods like an Indian squaw when she's got her own work to do on our place upriver." He pulled on her hand. She was so stunned by his words that she sat down before she realized it. She tried to get back to her feet, but he held her.

"Your . . . wife? You mean . . . ? You mean . . . me?" The air around her seemed to vibrate first with her astonishment and then with her anger. "You . . . you . . . Damn you to hell! You're tellin', not askin'! I'll not wed you to get a . . . place for myself. What do you think I am?" The words burst from her in bitter rage. She was shaking all over and felt as if something inside her was giving way.

"I think you're a woman with warm, red lips, white arms, and hair as black and shiny as a blackbird's wing. A woman with stormy green eyes that flash like lightning, a woman that can drive a man mad with wanting her."

And then he was kissing her, one arm locked around her shoulders, the other at her waist pulling her hard against him. His mouth was hard against hers, and the skin around it and on his chin was rough with new beard. He kissed her until her lips burned, and until the strength dissolved from her body.

Simon raised his head to stare down at the shadowed face and closed eyes when he felt her go limp against him. He had long ago admitted to himself the overwhelming attraction he felt for her. She had touched his heart and entered his mind even as he willed it otherwise. He knew she was willful, headstrong, exasperating, and foolish. He had spent the day wavering between a desire to make love to her and an urge to bend her over his knee for the sound beating she needed for even thinking of leaving the security of this place. Yet there was another side to her. She was spunky and brave. She had fought like a little wildcat to protect herself and Rachel from the river scum who had come to their camp. She was uplifting, fun, and endearing. She made him forget to be so serious about life, made his heart laugh, and he didn't want that feeling to stop.

He felt a strong desire to force her to want him— to see in her eyes a need and a longing for him. Calmly, he made a vow that he would make that happen, make her want to be with him for the rest of her life, make her depend on him to keep her safe. His eyes roamed her quiet face, her youthful, rounded breasts and trim waist, and her silky black hair. The intensity of his gaze caused her to open her eyes and regain her senses.

"I don't like to be kissed," she declared imperiously. She could see his face if she tilted her head back onto his crooked arm.

"Yes, you do," he said with matter-of-fact confidence.

"I don't! And you're no gentleman to say it!"

He laughed softly. "You're right. I'm no gentleman. But you're no lady, either."

"I am," she declared. "I was taught by my mother, who was a lady! I'm not a . . . tart!"

His laugh was low and rumbling and came from deep inside him. He blew warm, moist breath on her face when he laughed. His lips touched her forehead briefly before his cheek pressed against hers.

"I don't know what you are," he admitted in a rough whisper. "I'm afraid to scratch the surface. No telling what I'd find."

Suddenly the laughter bubbled up out of her. The absurdity of their banter had reached her senses and her sense of humor took over. Her laughter turned to giggles she couldn't stop. The enchantment that floated about her enfolded Simon in its aura so that he laughed with her.

The mood changed without either of them being aware of it. Berry melted against him, allowing his hands to mold and shape her to his hard form as he wished. His mouth moved over hers, as if he sought to draw her heart out through her lips. For the first time she touched him with her hands, stroking his back and shoulders, then tangled her fingers in the soft hair at the nape of his neck. Simon responded to the touch of her hands and to the movement of her lips with urgent, seeking hands. He drew an uneven breath and his deep voice vibrated with feeling.

"I've never seen anyone like you. You're like finding a soft, beautiful pelt among a pack of mangy hides. I want to stroke you . . . feel you. . . ."

Berry felt a spurt of surprise on hearing those words, but then his mouth closed over hers, parting her lips, blotting out all rational thought. His kiss was tender and probing . . . deep and disturbing. She felt his tongue pushing against the inner pads of her lips, intruding with gentle insistence until she tingled with the unfamiliar sensations he awak-

ened. He lifted his mouth and tucked her face into
the curve of his neck. His breath came in gasps and
she could feel the pounding of his heart against her
breast. Her breast! His hand was on her other one.
How long had it been there? He shouldn't... She
shouldn't let him. She tilted her head and opened
her eyes to find his inches from hers.

"What's the matter?" he asked softly.

"Nothing. I..."

"Then relax."

"You shouldn't..." She grasped the wrist of the
hand covering her breast and tried, in vain, to push
it away. "I think we should go back now."

"I don't." He rubbed his palm gently over her
breast, liking the feel of the soft globe in his hand.
He covered her mouth with his again and molded
her so tightly to him that she wondered if the imprint of his body would remain on hers when they
parted. His kiss was a dark, sweet eternity of firm
lips and warm breath. She felt a small fire kindling
deep within her.

When he drew back he traced a finger softly across
her kiss-puffed lips. "You like what I do. You like
being in my arms."

"No..."

"Yes. No man has kissed you but me. No man
has touched your soft breast, nibbled on the skin
below your ear, held your bottom in his hand." The
words were spoken with deliberate possessiveness
before his lips moved back to hers. This time hers
opened magically beneath his.

Berry felt her defenses begin to crumble away
from the longing that had grown inside her. She
became aware of a new warmth spreading over her,

and with surprise she discovered his hand beneath her skirt stroking her thighs. She knew this was forbidden and dangerous, but what he was doing was so pleasant, so gentle, that she didn't want him to stop.

The desire Simon felt for the exquisite form he clasped so tightly to his own was a deep pain gnawing his vitals. Her fierce pride was an intense irritation to him, yet it touched his heart and commanded respect. Stubborn little baggage! No other woman had ever come close to making him feel like this woman did. Someday he would tell her that. His laugh was low and tender when he wasn't kissing her sweet-smelling mouth.

Why couldn't she think? What was this leading to? His hand beneath her skirt moved up to cup her bare buttocks. A bold, searching mouth was nipping at the corner of hers, tracing a path to her eyes and then back to close over her mouth as if his lips couldn't stay away. His tongue was insistent, demanding that she meet it with hers. She responded hesitantly at first, then with welcome, and finally with blatant craving. She clung to him, her hands sliding over him, feeling the strength of his muscles, the smoothness of his shoulders and back. A small warning crept into the back of her mind. She knew she should be pushing him away, but every part of her being was responding to his touch. It was wildly exciting. This is foolish, her sanity argued. But she didn't want it to end. Not yet!

Berry felt as if she were drifting on a sea of soft, white clouds. Tomorrow she would hate herself for what she was doing and allowing him to do, but that was tomorrow. Right now she felt a wondrous warmth and rightness at what was happening. His mouth was persistent, snatching away her breath as well as her ability to think. There was also a rightness to the feel of his hands on her body beneath her skirt and her arms entwined around his neck.

"Damn! Damn!" Simon groaned in frustrated agony and buried his mouth in the hair behind her ear. "You don't know what this is leading up to, do you? Soon I'll not be able to stop! I'll have all of you right here in the grass. Damnation! You deserve more than that. You deserve long, sweet loving ... and coaxing ... and gentling. ..."

"Simon ..." she protested softly.

His arms dropped from around her and he slid to the grass and leaned back against the tree trunk on which they had been sitting. He pulled her down on his lap and wrapped her in his arms. She cuddled contentedly against him.

"Berry ... girl ..." The sound of his deep voice caressing her name made her tilt her head so she could nuzzle his jaw with her nose. "I can't let you go back to the house ... just yet."

His hand caressed her cheek and moved down over her shoulder. While he kissed the hollow of her throat, his fingers worked on the buttons on her dress, then he brushed aside the garment and gently cupped her exposed flesh. He worked the nipple with his callused palm, teasing it to hardness.

"Someday your breasts will be filled with mother's milk," he murmured half to himself. "But now ... they are only for me." He moved the fabric farther back and bent his head. Softly he kissed her breast, and then, to her wide-eyed surprise, his lips surrounded her nipple and he suckled her gently. The roughness of his tongue and the pull of his whiskers on her skin caused a warm rush of sensation to surge through her and she felt lightheaded. The feeling was so acute that she arched her back and with her arm around his neck held his head to her breast. The tormenting touch of his mouth brought her to an ardent, fevered frenzy. She made no protest when his hand moved beneath her skirt to wedge itself between her thighs.

"Berry...girl..." He whispered the words in a strangely broken voice. He was almost dizzy with desire. He wanted to bury himself in her, suckle her soft breasts, kiss her warm, wet mouth, and satisfy the hunger that gnawed at him. But, young and innocent as she was, it wasn't fair to her! She shouldn't be taken fully clothed on the damp grass. She should be able to taste the full pleasure of it. He forcibly held himself back, withdrew his hands from her body, pulled down her skirts, and covered her breasts. He cuddled her in his arms. She could not guess the depth of torture it put him through to stem the tide of his passion.

"When the time is right I'll make it long and sweet for you and you'll have no regrets."

For a long moment he simply held her. Reason dissolved the hunger that tormented him. He stroked the hair back from her face as if she were a child and kissed her forehead, her nose, and her eyelids. She would be his—the small, firm body, the beautiful green eyes, the dark curling hair, breasts, lips—all his. He would be able to touch her, possess her, whenever he wanted to.... The thought sent a quiver of desire through him. He lifted her face with a finger beneath her chin. Their eyes locked, hers moist and faintly confused, his tender and searching.

"I shouldn't have let you. . . . It was wrong." Her eyes wavered beneath the intensity of his. She was suddenly a small girl trying to account for her actions. She summoned all her determination to speak, but her voice still came out thin and weak. "I don't know what possessed me to let you. . . ." Her lower lip quivered and she ducked her head.

"The urge is as old as time," he whispered.

"Yes, but without . . . without . . ."

He lifted her off his lap, stood, and pulled her up beside him. His fingers worked at the front closing of her dress and she stood like an obedient child. He put his fist beneath her chin and lifted her face. "Smile for me."

"You treat me like a child."

"You are a child." He pressed his hands briefly to her shoulders. "Come. We'd better be getting back."

"What did you mean about a . . . wife?" She refused to move when he took her arm.

"Just what I said. We'll wed and I'll take you up to my place. The cabin isn't much, but we'll build something else later on."

"You've not said that you love me."

"Love?" His eyes laughed at her. "What's love? You need a husband more than love."

"But I don't want a husband unless there's love, too."

"Foolish fancies." He shrugged. "But then you're only a child."

"Stop saying that! I'm eighteen."

"That old? A woman of eighteen should be old enough to know she can't get along in this country without a man. If she finds a decent one she ought to take him without expecting love to be part of the deal."

His eyes were still wrinkled at the corners, his lips still twitching. She couldn't tell if he was teasing. She wanted him to be serious. She had to say it, had to let him know what she had to have before she would wed. She peered up at him. "I want . . . to . . . love my husband." She spaced the words to give them emphasis, to be sure he understood.

"Then love him." His voice was light, as if he was laughing inside. "There's no law that I know of that says you can't love him."

"I want to be sure that he loves me," she said stubbornly.

He laughed so uninhibitedly that she drew back, her green eyes flashing up at him with insolent appraisal. Setting a hand on each rounded hip, she cocked her head in challenge. "Don't you laugh at me, Simon Witcher!"

"The first thing you've got to learn about men in this country is that they can spin a wild yarn that'll curl your hair, and woo a woman with soft words if that's what she wants to hear. Never believe a man's soft words of love, Berry. Pay a mind to what he does."

"I like soft words," she said angrily.

He laughed again and she wanted to hit him. She balled her fist and prepared to swing. Before she could move, he was kissing her with a violence that stunned her. She stiffened her body, but his tight clasp bent that stiffness to the curve of his body.

He crushed her lips so hard with his that she couldn't tell whether he was kissing her or trying to hurt her. After an instant his lips softened and her resistance vanished, leaving nothing but the awareness of him, awareness that rose like a hot fountain from the core of her being. It rose to consume her with the force of its heat. She closed her eyes. Her lips surrendered to the searing heat of his.

They drew apart slowly. "You may like soft words, but you like hard kisses better," he said with a deep chuckle in his voice and ignored the needling glance she threw at him.

Berry choked down the quick denial that his words provoked. She couldn't summon the bitchiness needed to end this night on an ugly note.

They walked silently up the path to the house. Simon left her at the cabin door with only a brief touch of his fingers on her cheek. She watched him cross the yard and disappear in the shadows before she slipped into the house.

She crossed to the bunk and sat down, immeasurably glad to be alone in the room. She undressed in the dark and slipped her night rail over her head. *Simon Witcher, you make me so damn mad!* Her mind was boiling with emotions. Among her turbulent thoughts one stood out above all the others: *she would make him love her and she would make him say it!*

Chapter 11

Berry woke from a sound sleep.

"Is the blackberries ready for pickin'?" Biedy was trying to speak softly, but her voice rang like a bell in the close confines of the room. "Did ya put the cream in the spring for coolin' till I can get to the churnin'? And 'bout my hens—did ya pen 'em and caution the boys to be on the lookout for weasels?"

It was Silas's voice, patient and gruff, that answered her.

"I done it all, Biedy, jist like ye knowed I would. Now, get on with the vittles so's we can be gone."

Berry blinked and looked away from the light the glowing candle made in the dark room. Excitement zigzagged through her like lightning as memory returned and each and every moment, every detail of the hours she had spent with Simon, came clearly to mind. *He wanted to marry her! Spend his life with her!* She could hardly wait to see him again.

She reached for her dress and slipped it over her head while she was still beneath the sheet, fastened the front buttons, then swung her feet to the floor. Silas was bending over the cookfire and Biedy was smiling and nodding to her. Berry stood and smoothed her dress down over her night rail.

"Mornin'."

"Mornin'. It's a mite early, but Silas is strainin' to be goin'. He's the beatin'est man! If'n it's startin' or stoppin', he's bound to get it done right away. I'll declare, Silas, I got to have me more fire'n that if'n ya want meat 'n' gravy for breakfast."

"Hold your taters, hon'. It's a-comin'."

Berry went to the wash dish, scooped water into her hands, and splashed her face. After drying it on the soft, clean towel that hung on a nail beside the washstand, she tidied her hair and pinned the braid to the top of her head.

"Mornin', Miz MacCartney." Silas spoke from beside the fireplace.

"Mornin'." Rachel paused in the doorway and then hurried to help with breakfast. "My, my! How misput of me to let guests cook their own vittles! You made no noise at all or I'd-a been up."

"I heard Faith a-frettin' in the night. Is she all right?" Biedy lifted the big spider skillet onto the grate.

"She's a glutton, is what she is. She was hungry," Rachel replied with a laugh. "Morning, Berry."

There was no way Rachel could contain her happiness. It shone in her eyes, tilted her lips, and quickened her steps. She had a wonderfully considerate husband who had held her tenderly in his arms all night long and whispered that when the time came that she was well and strong, he'd not allow her a wink of sleep. She felt loved and wanted for the first time in her life. She had a home and a man to take care of her, and at last she was able to do something for Berry. These thoughts and many more danced about in her mind while she set the table for the first time in what was truly her home.

Rachel took her place at the end of the table opposite Fain when they sat down to breakfast. Silas and Biedy sat on one side, Berry and Isaac on the other. Biedy ceased her chatter long enough for Silas to say grace. Isaac nodded silently when Fain inquired if he had tied onto their mounts the sack of shot and the small keg of gunpowder he had set out for them to take, along with the candle mold and beeswax for Biedy.

"I just feel plumb bad 'bout takin' that mold. Course, I don't feel bad enough to give it back," Biedy said with her musical titter. "My, my! Just imagine! I'll be havin' my own mold. I got me plenty of milkweed floss I've been a-savin' for wicks. But mercy, Rachel, it was plumb kind of ya..."

Fain interrupted. "You just go ahead and enjoy the mold. Rachel'll have another one soon's I can send down to Simon's storehouse." He smiled into his bride's blue eyes and slightly flushed face. "When you come again, she'll more'n likely have curtains on the winders 'n' a cloth on the table 'n' you'll not be findin' a place to set for all the knickknacks. I'll have to run Fish outta that shack so I'll have me someplace to go to get out from underfoot," he teased.

"Fain..." Rachel protested. "I'll not..."

"I can always go up to Simon's if'n there gets to be so many knickknacks I can't walk through my own cabin."

"Fain..."

He laughed with delight at Rachel's reddened face, covered her hand with his, and gripped it tightly.

"Don't start off lettin' him get your goat, Rachel. Silas tried a-doin' that with me 'n' I set him down good, didn't I, Silas?" Biedy didn't wait for her husband to answer. "What ya got to do is get a hold 'n' take charge of things. This'n's been carefree too long and it'll take some doin' to get him in line, but think on it and you'll know what to do. Ya just be so tired nights for a good long while and sleep on the cot by yourself. In a while he'll knuckle under!" Her bright blue eyes flicked knowingly toward her husband.

Fain roared with laughter, and Rachel's and Berry's faces flamed. Biedy's family didn't seem to notice her outspoken words.

Berry sat quietly, scarcely hearing anything except the last part of the conversation, for she was quivering inwardly in anticipation of Simon's coming into the room. *Surely he had heard Isaac getting the horses out of the barn lot.*

"Simon said to tell ya that he'd be seein' ya on his next trip downriver. He had to get on down to Saint Louis and I think he's goin' on down to see Pike. He's hell-bent on makin' that trip up north. Hairbrained, if'n ya ask me, Pike a-goin' up there. More'n likely he'll have to winter there." Fain spoke between sips of hot black coffee.

Berry heard only the first part of what he said. Simon was gone! The information was like a blow to Berry's stomach. All the energy was suddenly driven from her. A chill settled over her with the knowledge that she meant so little to him that he'd left the homestead without a word to her. All he'd said last night was for naught! He'd been playing with her! The thought was like a dagger twisting in her heart.

Berry came back to the present to hear Biedy protesting that she should help with the clean-up before they left and Rachel assuring her that she and Berry would make short work of it. Berry followed them out into the dogtrot, stumbling over the doorstone when she left the candlelit room. The stars were still blinking in the sky and a cool breeze fanned her hot face. *Damn you, Simon Witcher!*

Silas mounted the horse and Biedy sprang up behind him, as agile as a young girl. "'Bye, Rachel. 'Bye, Berry. Y'all come, now. You're welcome anytime. Come 'n' bring that sweet little darlin'. Fain, I'm glad ya had the gumption to marry up with Rachel. Ya take care of them, now. Rachel, if'n Faith gets colic, ya just get some goldenrod 'n' take the leaves and tops off 'n' boil 'em up good. Give her a few sips. And if'n there's a time her bowels don't move, you give 'er a little buckthorn bark. Boil it up the same way. Now... if'n she gets the runnin'-offs, ya can use meadow sweet root. And ... My land! I forgot to tell ya about coltsfoot...."

Silas broke in. "'Bye, Fain. Biedy's had a week to say all she wanted to. Don't seem like she's goin' to run down, so we'd better get." Silas put the horse in motion. "We'll come a-runnin' if'n we're needed." He waved his hand.

"'Bye, Rachel. 'Bye, Berry." Biedy grabbed Silas around the waist and tossed a bright glance back over her shoulder. "Ya make me so mad, Silas Cornick! Ya never let me finish. I was goin' to tell her 'bout wormwood, henbane, 'n' fennel seed. If'n that little love gets a fever 'n' Rachel don't know 'bout sage, you're just goin' to have to bring me back! It'd just serve ya right! 'Cause I wanted to tell her 'bout..."

Distance and darkness swallowed the Cornicks. Fain laughed and put his arm across Rachel's shoulders. "Did you ever know of a woman what talked so much?"

"I liked her. I liked her more than any woman I ever knew except Berry. I hope they come back soon."

"But not too soon, darlin'. I'm wantin' to have my family all to myself for a while." He put his other arm around Berry's shoulder, and they moved back into the house.

Berry's mind moved like wheels through mud. Simon was gone. She would erase last night from her mind as if it hadn't happened. There was only one thing to do now: take Israel, the stock, and the wagons and leave here as soon as possible, or there wouldn't be time to get set up on the homestead before winter. She hoped she'd never see Simon Witcher again! But she prayed that if she did, she would be already married to a big, handsome man who would punch him in the mouth if he even glanced her way!

A week passed and then two. Rachel would have seen supremely happy if not for worrying over the change in Berry. She seldom laughed, and when she did, it was the forced laughter that Rachel recognized from the times on the trail from Ohio when she was trying to keep Rachel's spirits up. Berry worked from dawn until dark. If she wasn't helping with the meals, she was tending to Faith, working in the garden, or doing any one of the countless things to be done on the homestead.

A fur trapper dropped off a bundle from Simon's storehouse. Berry and Rachel went through the pack and exclaimed delightedly over the dress goods, hairpins, stockings, slippers, ribbons, and sweet-smelling soap. There was even a glass mirror in the bundle, and candy wrapped in oiled paper. It was the same rum-flavored sweet Simon had given Berry in Saint Louis. There were two of everything, but to Rachel's disappointment Berry would have no part of it. Fain smiled at Rachel's excitement and went back to work on his guns. Rachel carefully laid aside half of the finery, biding her time until Berry was in a more favorable frame of mind.

Early in the second week, Berry began to ride out on the sorrel mare that had been her pa's. Soon it was her greatest pleasure and each day she rode farther and farther from the cabin. She studied the land, the river, and the map that marked the location of *her* land.

A plan began to form in her mind. She mulled it over for several days before she made up her mind what she would do. She would go see for herself if her land was swampy and unfit for farming. She knew Fain would never allow her to leave the homestead—if he knew she was going. She would have to be careful and appear to be settled. In order to do that, she took several items from her wagon and set them up in Fain's house. She spent several evenings spinning wool they had carded before they'd left Ohio.

After giving her plan much thought, Berry decided to confide in Fish. Every minute the young man had to spare was spent dogging her tracks. She knew he liked her, liked her a lot, although she hadn't given him any encouragement toward a personal relationship. He seemed satisfied with friendship and she was grateful and flattered—she had never had a male friend before.

One hot afternoon Fish came out to the garden where Berry was picking potato bugs off the plants. She moved out of the patch and into the shade and drank thirstily from the water jar he had brought to her. Fish hunkered down beside her. His fair hair was plastered to his head with sweat, and rivulets of it trickled down his smooth face. He looked at her adoringly with his wide amber eyes.

"This is the map the land man gave my pa," she said, drawing the folded paper from her apron pocket. "I want to go there, but don't tell Fain and Rachel." Her green eyes beseeched him.

Fish took a trembling breath. "You know I won't tell, Miss Berry, if you ask me not to. But why in the world do you want to go there? You can't take up a land contract without a man to help you." His eyes searched her face; he had known the answer to his question before he asked it. "Would you let me . . . ?"

"No, Fish," she said quickly. "I just want to see what it's like. I know I can't improve on it enough to get clear title," she fibbed. "I just want to see it. After all, I came all the way from Ohio and . . . it's not fair that I don't even get to see where my new home would have been if my . . . pa had lived." She put just the right amount of quiver in her voice and allowed her lower lip to tremble slightly.

"Ahhh . . . Miss Berry. You've got a home here. Fain wouldn't hear of you not being here with Miz MacCartney. In the months I've been here I've not seen him so happy."

"He's been wonderful to me," Berry admitted. "But . . . do you know the location of this section?" She pointed to the marked spot on the map.

"It's about twenty miles, I'd say." Fish studied the map. "It wouldn't be hard to find. It seems to me it's the land beyond this creek or dry gulch— whichever it is."

"Are we here?" Berry pointed to a spot on the map with a small twig. When Fish nodded, she poked a small hole to mark the place. "Then it would be best to go north and then west?"

"I'd say so. Go north until you run into a creek and follow it until it runs out. Then a few miles on west would be the place your pa filed on. It says the boundary is marked by ax marks on the trees." He sank down beside her and took her hand. His wasn't much larger than her own. "I don't want you going off by yourself, Berry. I'll go with you."

"It's sweet of you, Fish. I've not even decided for sure if I'm going. Fain will be angry and Rachel will worry. I'll have to think about it for a while. You won't tell anyone I'm thinking about it?"

"Of course I won't." He squeezed her hand and got to his feet. "Don't stay out here in the sun too long," he cautioned, and Berry felt a surge of affection for him.

"I won't," she promised, and watched his slight figure walk away, head bent, shoulders slumped dejectedly.

Twenty miles! Berry was elated. She could make that distance in one day on the mare. Plans crowded into her mind. She would take a good look around, decide the best way to bring the wagons in, and return the next day. She was sorry for the worry it would cause Rachel, but there was no help for it. She would go alone. Fish would be nothing but company for her, and she didn't need that. She would take the rifle or the musket—that would be all the protection she would need. She toyed with the idea of taking Israel, thinking it would ease Rachel's mind to know she wasn't alone, but she dismissed the idea—Israel on a mule would just slow her down.

Berry didn't allow herself to think about Simon and prided herself on not taking one taste of the treat he had sent. Fain teased about the candy and talked on and on about Simon's taking his trade goods down to Pike's camp. *The devil take Simon!* He was the one who had said that a woman should pay no attention to a man's soft words, but should judge him by his actions. He'd gone off without a word to her. His actions told her what he thought of her. She would not take a husband who thought no more of her feelings than that. Mr. Simon Witcher had better understand that right now!

The sky was still dark but showing faint signs of light in the east when Berry slipped out to the barnyard and saddled the mare. She had a blanket and a two-day supply of food wrapped in a cloth. A musket was tucked into the waistband of her skirt, and the powder and shot hung from a bag thrown over her shoulder. With a pounding heart, expecting Fain or Fish to come running after her any minute, she led the horse into the woods.

Only Israel, from his pallet beneath the wagon, saw her go. He rose on his elbow, watched, and lay back down. The missy was taking an early ride.

She had done it! It had been amazingly easy. Berry took a moment to soothe and praise the mare before leading her to a stump and mounting her. Once away from the homestead, she laughed with relief. The note she had left telling Rachel she had gone to the chokecherry patch to pick while it was cool would give her a few hours before they realized she was gone.

"I'm sorry to cause you worry, Rachel," she murmured, and the sound of her voice in the quiet of the forest was a comfort. "I won't sit and wait for Simon or any man to come along and take care of me. I've served my time knuckling under to a man's wishes, just as you have."

Saying the words seemed to lift her spirits. She saw in her mind's eye the map she had tucked in her pocket and turned the mare to the edge of the woods and followed the line of trees. She had ridden out this way several times before and judged she wouldn't reach unfamiliar territory until almost daylight.

In spite of all she could do to prevent it, her thoughts continually drifted to Simon. She envisioned him vividly. He was a handsome man when he didn't have that damned hat on his head! Things would have been different between them, she mused, if he'd done some asking instead of telling her he would marry her as if it were something he had to do. Damn him! This was the first time in her life she had some say in what she would or wouldn't do. She was going to make the most of it, and if she discovered that the land was swampy, as he had said, she would cross that bridge when she came to it.

The sky lighted with dawn. Berry crossed a meadow and the pale light was enough to help her see the countryside and give wide berth to a marsh that would have slowed down the mare. She rode on. She was already hungry, but she would have to wait until mid-morning when she stopped to rest the mare. The woods ahead looked thick and dark. Berry stood in the stirrups and tried to see the river, but could see only more brush and trees. The mare stopped of her own volition and Berry pulled the map from her pocket.

She sat the horse for a long moment and studied the terrain before and behind her. The creek would lead her west. It should be ahead. She pointed the mare to the north and urged her forward. Taking her time, Berry worked her way through the trees. A wild turkey gobbled and scurried into the under-brush, then the woods were silent, except for the sound of the mare's hooves and an occasional twitter from a bird in the branches overhead.

It seemed an eternity before she reached the creek and pulled the horse to a stop. She slid from the saddle and led the mare to the water. Berry found a place where she could kneel down to drink. The bright, hot sun beat down on her. She untied the strings of the stiff-brimmed calico bonnet that rode on her back and fanned her face with the brim before she put the bonnet on her head. She didn't like to wear it, because it made her feel as if she were seeing the world through a tunnel, but it was the only headgear she owned. She pushed it as far back on her head as she could so that she could see on each side of her as well as in front. When she mounted the mare, she had to kick her several times before she would leave the lush grass that grew beside the stream.

"You can have more later on," she promised.

Berry soon discovered that the going had been easier before she reached the creek and turned west. Here the grass came up to the mare's belly and at times came up to drag on her feet in the stirrups. It was hard walking for the mare. As soon as she found a place where she could cross the stream she did so and followed an animal path that ran parallel to the creek. The mare blew bubbles from her lips in appreciation and Berry patted her neck in understanding.

Noon came and the creek showed no sign of diminishing as indicated on the map. If anything, it was wider and deeper. Berry paused long enough to eat a couple of biscuits and to let the mare rest, then pushed on. At times she had to move into the woods, out of sight of the creek, when the underbrush became too thick to pass through. By mid-afternoon she didn't have even an animal trail to follow. Tired and disappointed, she let the mare amble on at her own pace.

When next she came out of the woods she stopped in surprise. The sun hung just over the treetops to the west. The day had passed swiftly. She was tired.

The insides of her thighs were galled from being wet with sweat and rubbing against the saddle leather. She had never before ridden for so long, and her back and bottom ached. She urged the mare down to the creek and onto a sandy bank. Looking ahead, the creek was wide and filled with flowing water as far as she could see. Berry was sure she had traveled more than twenty miles. She had been riding for ten hours, or close to it by her reckoning, which meant that she had to be at least forty miles from Fain's farm. The thought alarmed her. For the first time she doubted her wisdom in coming. The only bright spot in her thinking was the fact that she hadn't come through swampy land, except for the tract with the tall grass, and that was shortly after she had turned west to follow the creek. That couldn't be *her* land. The map showed *her* land north of the creek.

Should she start back? She gave a deep, disappointed sigh and slid from the mare's back. She went to stand at the mare's head and rub her nose.

"You're tired, too. Let's rest here for a while and we'll have to start back. Oh, damn! How I hate to give up." She took off her bonnet and let the breeze cool her face. "Phew! It's hot."

Berry let the horse graze until the sun disappeared behind the treetops before she mounted and turned back. She wanted to get through the thick stand of trees and into the open before she stopped for the night.

She wasn't sure when she felt the first prickle of fear. It may have been with her for hours; it had surfaced gradually. The mare's ears had twitched and swiveled back even before they stopped on the sandbar. Now everything was so quiet. She no longer heard the twittering of birds or the chatter of squirrels. But of course, she and the mare would be enough to scare them away, she thought with her customary logic. She hung her bonnet on the saddle horn and scolded herself for letting her imagination run away with her. The weight of the musket in her skirt band was a comfort. What is there to be afraid of? she asked herself. A panther or a wildcat would be just as afraid of me as I am of it. They only attack when they're hungry, and there's plenty of small game here. She had seen deer, rabbits, and turkey.

The Indians in this area are Osage, she reasoned, and they have a government agreement to supply beaver pelts to Manuel Lisa, an important trader in Saint Louis. They wouldn't jeopardize that agreement by harming a white girl.

But then again . . . there's the Shawnee and the Delaware. They were pushed out of their homeland and across the river by Mad Anthony Wayne. They could take her, wander on west, and she would never be heard from again. Oh, damn! Why did she have to think of that?

Her thoughts were so busy that she came through the woods and out into the clearing before she realized it. She was tempted to push on, but she couldn't remember another place to stop as suitable as this one. The mare had to rest. Her sides were heaving and the saddle blanket was soaked with sweat. Berry stopped the horse and got stiffly down. She held tightly to the reins and looked back toward the woods, glad to be through them. Night was coming on fast. In a short time it would be dark.

Berry led the mare to the creek to drink, then

tied her to a downed tree trunk where she could reach the grass. She pulled the heavy saddle from the horse's back and hung the wet blanket over a branch to dry, then carried her own blanket and food pack to the base of a large cottonwood. Just as she was about to drop her blanket she heard the warning sound of a rattlesnake. She jumped back. Not five feet away, coiled and ready to strike, was the largest snake she had ever seen. Cautiously she backed away while keeping her eyes on the snake. After a while it slowly uncoiled and slithered into the underbrush.

The snake's departure didn't ease Berry's fright in the least. What to do now? She found a branch and beat the ground around the tree before she dropped her blanket and sat down. It wasn't just the snake that caused her uneasiness. It was more than that. Every so often the mare would raise her head sharply, twitch her ears restlessly, and look back into the dense forest in the direction from which they had come. The wind had gone down and flies and mosquitoes swarmed around the sweat-covered mare. She stamped her feet and swished her tail in an effort to be rid of them.

Berry ate a jam-filled biscuit and tried to justify in her own mind her reason for being here. She wished with all her heart that she had let Fish come with her. He was the one who had said it couldn't be over twenty miles to her land. He was the one who had said to follow the creek until it ran out. Darn you, Fish, she thought, you didn't know any more about the map than I did!

The sky darkened rapidly. Feeling lonely and afraid, Berry watched the mare and listened to her crop the grass. She fought back her fear with logic. One girl and one horse in all this vast land was like one pebble on the riverbed, one tree among the millions of trees, one star in the heavens. Who or what could find her here on this small spot of earth? She tried to reassure herself with the thought but had little success. Her fingers clung to the one real thing in all this frightening wilderness—the musket.

There was not a footfall to warn her.

Suddenly, as if they materialized out of her imagination, two Indians, whose austere features were streaked with yellow and white paint, loomed over her. One let out a bloodcurdling whoop and grabbed the hair at the top of her head. Berry was momentarily struck numb and didn't have time to raise the musket before a moccasined foot lashed out and kicked it from her hand. She looked into the face of her assailant. What she saw caused the blood to freeze in her veins. She gasped with horror at the most terrifying vision she had ever beheld. The Indian who held her by the hair was naked except for a loincloth. His dark, wiry body was covered with grease. His eyes were deep set and hollow; they looked like the two dark eye sockets of a skull. White feathers, tied to strands of thick straight hair, hung down on each side of his face.

Berry recovered from the initial shock of the attack and began to struggle. She struck out at the Indian's brown chest with all her might and clawed at his face with her nails. A blow landed on the side of her head and she found herself knocked flat to the ground. Breath left her, but when she finally was able to draw air into her lungs she came up fighting. She reached for the Indian's face, intent on scratching out his eyes. Her feet kicked out high and wild. Untamed rage boiled up inside her and gave her strength. *She would go down fighting!* Kicking and thrashing, she continued her attack, heedless of the blows to the side of her head and the smelly body that pressed her to the ground. Determined to fight to the end against the overwhelming odds, Berry saw an opportunity and took it. She sank her teeth into the Indian's arm and held on.

The hand in her hair jerked so hard that she thought the top of her head would come off. The pain was excruciating! Her jaws opened. She screamed. The Indian hauled her to her feet and she stood swaying. The blood in her mouth ran down her chin. Her stomach heaved and she threw up. The iron grip on her hair kept her head erect and the vomit spewed out and down over her breast.

Reason returned and she realized that the other Indian was laughing. He laughed and shouted taunts at her attacker. Older, but not as repulsive-looking as the one who held her, he continued to laugh, showing stubs of yellow teeth. He pointed to his companion's loincloth and spraddled his legs. His gesture clearly indicated that he was calling him a woman for letting a weak white woman inflict injury.

The attacker scowled and shoved Berry facedown to the ground. She gasped from the pain and tears sprang to her eyes. Too numb with fear to move, she lay where he had flung her, shaking uncontrollably. She clenched her jaws to keep from crying out when her tormentor placed a foot on her hips and trod on her in a sign of contempt when he went to retrieve the musket.

Berry had never considered the possibility of being taken prisoner by Indians. The Indians they had met on the trail from Ohio had been a hungry, ragtag bunch looking for handouts. It was believed that the Osage across the river were more civilized than most, and this was their territory. What would they do with her? Would they kill her? Would the young one keep her for his squaw? The second thought was the one that filled her with dread. She wept inside for what might have been. *Simon . . . Simon . . . Now I'll never know what it was we didn't do that night. You'll never make it long and sweet for me, like you promised.*

Berry lay still, hoping, praying that they would take the horse and leave. She could hear them talking and moved her head ever so slightly so she could peer beneath her outflung arm. The old Indian was building a fire, and the young one was eating the dried meat from her food pack. They were ignoring her! Maybe she could crawl into the underbrush and get away. She dug her elbows into the ground and pushed herself forward, stopped to see if the Indians had noticed, then pushed herself forward again. The old Indian had his back to her as he fed small sticks into the fire. The young one sat cross-legged on the ground, eating the food from her food pack as if he was starved. Berry inched her way to the bushes and rolled under them. She waited and listened. The only sounds were the crackling of the fire and the pounding of her heart.

Slowly, carefully, she moved out from under the tangled brush and got to her feet. The first thing she saw were moccasin feet and dirty leggings. The young Indian stood before her, hands on his hips. Almost before she could blink, his hand lashed out, collided with her jaw, and sent her stumbling back into the prickly brush.

"You ... savage!" she screamed. "You ... ugly, dirty, stinking savage!"

Her captor barked an order and gestured toward the fire. Berry turned her back on him and buried her face in her hands. He wrapped his hand in the thick dark hair that trailed down her back and gave a tug. There was nothing for her to do but to go where he indicated. She was a white woman, a captive of savages whose cruelty she did not even begin to know.

Fear constricted her stomach into a hard knot and she bowed her head, weeping wildly.

Chapter 12

Simon sat his horse on the crest of the hill and watched the mules pull the heavily laden freight wagon up the steep grade. The two milk cows, tied on behind a lighter wagon that followed, walked placidly along, swishing their tails at the pesky flies. The crate of chickens tied to the side of the wagon were not so patient. They clucked and squawked angrily and, for lack of anything else to do, pecked at each other.

Simon took off his hat and wiped his forehead on the sleeve of his shirt. It had been seventeen days since he had left Fain's homestead. He felt a deep satisfaction at all he had accomplished in that short time. First and foremost, he had turned his trading business over to Ernest after taking the goods he wanted from the storehouse. The stock in the warehouse had been inventoried and the purchase price agreed upon. Ernest would pay an amount yearly in gold coin. Simon felt free for the first time in years.

He had also traveled to Kaskaskia for a long talk with Zebulon Pike. He would have to make a decision within the next couple of weeks whether to go up the Mississippi with the expedition. Pike planned to leave in the middle of August. This trip, requested by James Wilkinson, governor of the Louisiana Territory, was a forerunner of an expedition into the country to the southwest. Pike talked enthusiastically about this journey and the fact that Manuel Lisa, a prominent Saint Louis merchant, also had ambitions for such a trip to establish a trade route. Pike was sure that Lisa would do everything in his power to sabotage his expedition.

Simon had listened to all this innuendo with only half an ear. He had been surprised at his disinterest. He was there only to deliver the last of the supplies Pike had ordered and to find out when the territorial government would come through with payment. Soon, Pike had promised.

Now that the wagons had reached the top of the hill, Simon gave himself up to the luxury of thinking about Berry. He wasn't sure that what he felt for her was love. He told himself that this strange emotion stirring beneath his breast was nothing more than the age-old desire to procreate, to leave something of yourself behind to show you had spent time on earth. He admitted to himself that what he had felt when he held her in his arms and kissed her was a sensation he had never felt before. She had seemed so vulnerable at that moment, not at all like the proud girl he had seen standing up to her pa and fighting off the attentions of Linc Smith.

He thought of her almost constantly—pictured her standing in Fain's house yard waiting for him.

He felt a thrill of excitement knowing that by sundown he would see her again. He chuckled aloud. What would she think of all the fixings he had brought for their home? She would spend only one winter in that small cabin, but she would be comfortable. His wife would have things to do with, he thought with satisfaction. Early next spring the materials and the craftsmen would arrive to build a fine new house on the bluff overlooking the river.

Simon had always intended to do this sometime in his life. He supposed that seeing Fain happily married, knowing he had a woman in his cabin doing for him, waiting for him, a woman he could turn to in the night for warmth and comfort, had spurred him into the decision to marry Berry. He laughed aloud—a strange sound amid the jingle of harnesses and the clip-clop of horses' hooves.

Berry wanted love. What was love, anyway? He had never loved anyone and no one had ever loved him. He'd had good companions and friends. Wasn't it enough that he liked to be with her, liked to look at her, and that the sound of her laughter made him want to laugh, too? He supposed he would love a child if he ever had one. The grin on his face was continuous. He could picture it in his mind—Berry walking about, holding her beautiful head high, as if she were royalty, with her stomach swollen with his son. Then the smile faded when he recalled the agony Rachel had gone through giving birth.

Simon supervised the crossing of the Missouri, and when the second wagon and the cows pulled up onto the bank from the ferry, he rode to the freight wagon and told Lardy he would ride on ahead to Fain's place. One of the cows was a wedding gift for Fain and Rachel, the other for him and Berry. He wanted to be there to see Berry's face when she saw the cow, the chickens, the cast-iron oven, and the rocking chair.

Suddenly conscious of the silly grin on his face, he gave himself a mental shake, disgusted with himself for acting like a callow youth. In spite of this stern self-discipline, excitement put his heels to the stallion and urged him into a gallop.

Rachel was standing beside the entrance to the dogtrot when he rode up the trail and into the yard. His eyes quickly scanned the clearing for signs of Berry, then turned back to Rachel. *Something was wrong!* Rachel stood quietly, Fain's long gun cradled in her arms. He tried to stifle the feeling of dread that shot through him and swung from the saddle. Rachel ran to him and burst into tears.

"What's happened?" he asked anxiously and took the heavy gun from her hands.

"Berry..." she choked.

"Berry? What's happened to Berry?" Simon felt as if all the air had left his lungs and he would never be able to fill them again.

"Berry's... gone! She went to pick chokecherries yesterday morning... but Israel says she went north and..."

"She's been gone since yesterday morning? Where's Fain?"

"Looking for her. Israel told us he saw her ride out on the sorrel mare before daylight. She had a blanket and the musket and he thought he saw a bag of food."

"Did Fish ride out to look for her?"

"He left yesterday morning before we knew Berry

was ... gone. We thought she was in the choke-cherry patch."

Simon swore viciously. The stupid little chit had gone looking for the land her pa had filed on. He tried to recall the details of the map Rachel had shown him. More than likely she had gone north and then followed the creek west.

"Why didn't Fain go after her?" he asked sharply. "Eben is reliable. He'd've looked after the place until he got back."

Rachel wiped her eyes on the hem of her skirt, straightened up, and tried to steady her voice when she spoke. "Israel found Eben ... dead. His throat was cut." Her face crumbled again and hot tears ran down her cheeks. "Simon ... I'm so afraid something terrible has happened to Berry!"

Rachel's desperate words sent a pain through Simon's heart that was almost unbearable. His arm went out and drew the sobbing woman to him for a brief, sympathetic hug, then he held her away from him. Bitter lines formed around his mouth.

"When was Eben killed?"

"Sometime yesterday. Israel and Eben were down by the river when Fish left. Fish told them he was going to Saint Louis and didn't know when he would be back. Eben went back to work on his fishnets and Israel went to the garden. When Berry wasn't back by noon, I got worried and told Fain. He went to the patch and she wasn't there. Later, Fain sent Israel down to get Eben to come up here and stay while he looked for her. Israel came back and told us Eben was in his shack and that he was ... dead." Rachel glanced toward the house when she heard Faith begin to cry. "We buried Eben last night, and this morning Fain went out to look for Berry. Israel is around somewhere, but he's so scared he's almost out of his mind. I told him to keep out of sight and call out if he saw anyone coming." Rachel's voice was trembly with the fear that gripped her. "Please find her, Simon. Fain don't want to leave me and Faith here alone for long. He don't understand why anyone would kill Eben, unless it was for the gold he got for his furs this spring."

Unreasoning rage was a bitter taste in Simon's throat. Damn fool girl! He'd thought they had an understanding. He'd told her he would wed her! She'd not said no, so why couldn't she have waited here for him? If this was an example of what it would be like if he had a woman, he didn't know if he wanted one! He'd been gone only seventeen days. She'll get herself killed! Killed or worse! The thought sent a spiral of fear down his spine. He pushed it from his mind so he could think clearly. He felt sick and empty inside. Then his feelings swung to anger.

Damn her!

Fain returned at about the same time the freight wagons pulled to a stop beside the pole corral. Israel appeared and took charge of the cows and the chickens. Fain went immediately to the house to see Rachel, then returned to report that a meal would be ready shortly. After the mules were unhitched, watered, and fed, the men squatted down beside the wagons.

"I trailed her to the first creek," Fain said. "She turned west and I came on back. Hellfire, Simon! I couldn't risk leaving Rachel here alone after what happened to Eben." Irritation made his voice gruff. "I can't for the life of me understand why she went off like she did. I thought somebody took 'er after we found Eben, but the mare's tracks are plain as day and there ain't no others."

"Then you don't think there's a connection between her leaving and Eben's death?"

"None that I can think of. 'Pears Berry was gone from here before somebody got to Eben. That's queer, too. It ain't natural Eben'd get his throat cut. He was strong as a bull 'n' knowed how to take care of hisself. He's been on the river three, four years." Fain shook his shaggy head. "I hate what happened. I purely do. It's a pity when a man has to die for a few coin."

"Eben had no coin," Simon said slowly and thoughtfully. "He always took credit for his furs."

"That's worse yet. The bastard killed him fer nothin'."

Simon didn't comment. Presently, after he removed his hat and ran his fingers through his hair, he got to his feet. "I'll eat a bite and be off. Fain, you and Olson better stay with Rachel." He nodded toward the quiet, bearded freighter he had hired to drive the light wagon. "If Rachel will draw a map, the best she can remember, Lardy can take it and go upriver to Saint Charles. He might run into Light. If anyone can find Berry, it'd be Light."

"Did ya hear anythin' of Linc Smith when ya was in town? If'n he lived, he'll try 'n' even the score with the girl for shootin' him."

"Nary a word. The riverfront bunch was het up a bit about the shooting at the campgrounds, but nothing will come of it. Linc and George had spread word the women were whores and visits were welcome. Ernest is putting out the straight of it."

"Goddamn bastards!" Fain swore. "Goddamn sonofabitches! I oughtta've nailed their balls to a stump!"

Rachel came to the end of the dogtrot and waved her apron.

"How come Fish took off? Did he decide he wasn't no gunsmith after all?" Simon asked on the way to the house.

"I think he give up on gunsmithin'. He'd been hangin' 'round 'cause of Berry. Guess he figured he didn't have no chance o' courtin' her. It's pure queer, him a-goin' off, Eben gettin' hisself killed, and Berry a-doin' the fool thin' she done, all in a day. I've got no notion at all about one havin' a thin' to do with the other."

When Simon was ready to leave, Rachel brought out a food pouch. Her trembling hand caught and held back the wisp of blond hair that the breeze had torn loose from its knotted roll. She looked toward the north, her eyes anxious. Shaking her head, she muttered, "Oh, Berry, why did you go?" Then, to Simon: "Please find her."

Darkness was approaching when Simon rode the stallion into the thick forest of tall oak, cottonwood, and elm trees. Soaring willows, their thin branches hanging to the ground, grew along the backwater of the river, making a solid curtain to the east. The need to hurry pressed heavily on Simon as he made his way over the familiar trail. Had Berry met with an accident? Had she been taken by rivermen? Linc Smith? Indians? Or was she merely camping out, roaming the wilderness looking for her pa's contract land? If that was the case, by God, she'd get the shaking and the tongue-lashing of her life! Stubborn, mule-headed little baggage! He whipped up his anger to dull the edge of worry that plagued him and listened to the soft sounds made by the stallion's hooves as he moved over the needle-strewn ground.

The first night was dreadful. Berry sat on the ground, her arms around a small sapling, her wrists bound together with a thin strip of rawhide. Moonlight filtered through the trees in ghostly patches, feeding her imagination. She could not sleep and periodically she shivered violently. Her teeth chattered, intensifying the pain in her jaw, which the Indian had struck when he knocked her to the ground. The whole side of her face ached and at first she had feared her jaw was broken.

Ugly was the only word to describe the younger of the two Indians. It seemed to Berry that the bone structure of his face had gone askew. His eyes were scarcely an inch apart. The rest of his face was broad, with a small lump for a nose. His mouth was wide and flat. However, he had a magnificent physique and was well aware of it. He strutted and preened when he saw her watching him. Once he went a few yards from her and let water. He laughed when she hid her face against the rough bark of the tree.

The older Indian paid little attention to her. She thought of him simply as "Old." She didn't think he had looked at her since he had teased his companion about his difficulty in subduing her.

Berry was afraid; more than afraid—she was terrified. She was also tired after the long ride from Fain's homestead. Weariness and despair began to crawl through her veins. Enveloped in hopelessness, her shoulders slumped. She leaned her forehead against the tree as silent sobs wrenched her body. She fought the tears. The other time she had cried, Ugly had curled his lips in contempt and spat on her as if he despised her.

I'll never see Rachel or . . . Simon again! *Simon . . . Simon* . . . She felt the warm, thick flood of tears rising to her eyes, and she was helpless against them.

After a while she quieted and went to sleep.

Berry awoke when it was just turning daylight. Heavy eyelids opened instantly. She was stricken with terror! A dark face loomed close to hers. She stared wildly, jumped, and tried to pull herself backward. Fear, like a great dark shadow, moved down over her, and she screamed. Once she started, she couldn't stop. The sound of her screams breaking into the silence was so frightening that she tried to get to her feet so she could get away from it. Her legs wouldn't hold her and she fell to her knees.

Reason returned and she realized that the old man had untied her hands and was holding out a strip of dried meat. He had a puzzled look on his face. Berry looked beyond him and saw Ugly loping through the clearing toward them. With an exclamation and a movement so unexpected that she had no time to shield her face, he hit her with the flat of his hand. Unmistakable insults and threats spewed from his lips. Berry cried out and braced herself for more blows, but they didn't come. With aching arms she pushed herself up. Her hair hung like a curtain over her face. She felt sick and dizzy. She licked her lips and tasted salt. Her senses were now too numbed for her to feel the pain.

It was sometime later in the day that Berry's tired mind began to wonder why she and the older Indian were riding her mare and the ugly one was walking up ahead. He had flung her up behind the old man and tied her hands in front of him. Her skirts came up to her knees, but the Indians seemed not to notice. Now her back and buttocks ached and she was tempted to rest her head against the Indian's thick back, but she resisted and held herself erect.

Ugly coveted the mare. Berry could tell by the way his small eyes roamed over the horse. He was notably zealous in the care he took of the animal. *Then why was he walking and not riding?* The old man must have a higher rank in the tribe, she decided.

"I'm thirsty," she said to the back of Old's head.

He gave no sign he heard.

After a while she said, "I'm thirsty and hungry. And . . . I'll kill you the first chance I get!"

Still he ignored her.

They followed no trail that she could see. They left the creek and went down a ravine and into a forest so thick with trees that the sun came through only in small, isolated patches. The scrub and underbrush were thick and scratched her bare legs, now almost numb from hanging over the sides of the horse. They crossed a stream and climbed a rough, steep hillside. It would be impossible for anyone to follow, Berry thought with a sinking heart.

Hours passed and by evening she was lulled into drowsiness by the rhythmic rocking of the seemingly tireless mare. She was truly weary now, with an increasing ache and soreness throughout her body. They stopped, but she was scarcely aware of it until the thong was removed from her wrists. Her arms fell to her sides. She couldn't suppress a moan as pain shot through her shoulders. The old man helped her down. She stood for a moment, then her knees collapsed and she fell.

Every muscle in her body quaked with weakness and she wondered if she would have the strength to ride away if an opportunity did present itself. Soon she realized that she would have no opportunity. Her hands were retied and she was led like a dog on a leash to a spring where she was allowed to kneel and drink. As soon as the old man had had enough water, he jerked on the leash and she stumbled after him to a sapling that stood like a stake in the earth. He tied her to it.

Ugly took charge of the mare. He wiped her down with grass, led her to water, and hobbled her before he drank.

Berry didn't even think now, because she was incapable of anything but sleep. She took the food the old Indian brought her and before she could finish eating it she fell asleep.

She was awakened almost at once—or so it seemed. It was dark. She realized with a shock that they were preparing to move again. Ugly lifted her up behind the old man and tied her wrists as he had done before. The Indians seemed able to see in the darkness, for they traveled at the same pace as before.

They need not fear pursuit, Berry thought, and tears gathered on her lashes. Simon had said he wasn't going to come chasing after her again. She should dread to face him, fear his wrath, despise him for leading her on to think they would wed and then deserting her. But she couldn't—not now. She would get down on her knees to him if only he would ride up and rescue her from these savages!

Berry had long since lost all sense of direction. They went up hills, down hills, through briar patches and thickets. It seemed to her that Ugly was making it as hard as possible for rescuers to follow. It occurred to her that if he'd been alone, he would have killed her, because he didn't want the burden of a captive. He wanted only the horse. But the old man wanted her. The young Indian ignored her most of the time, although he would stand and stare at her during the humiliating times when she was forced to relieve herself in full view of the two men.

They traveled all night and Berry lost all sense of time, too. Several times during the night she would jerk her head erect after finding she had let it rest against the Indian's back. The pace Ugly set never seemed to slacken. When the going was exceptionally rough, he moved back to the mare's head and led the animal.

The darkness overhead had begun to pale when they finally stopped at the end of a steep climb. Berry had feared she would slide off the rear of the horse and drag the old man with her. The blanket they were sitting on was wet and her legs and thighs were raw from gripping the sweating horse's sides.

When her wrists were untied she was pulled off the mare and fell in a heap on a thick mat of dead leaves. A great longing swept over her to simply lie there and sleep. She felt weak in every bone in her body and thought it would be simpler if she went to sleep never to awaken. At that moment she felt the hopelessness of her situation more than at any other time since she had first looked into Ugly's face. Surely she must wake from this nightmare!

Berry struggled to raise her head, to lift her leaden eyelids. It was turning daylight. She lay where she had fallen, weak and exhausted. Pains stabbed her back and buttocks. The old man was laying a fire and paying no attention to her. The need to relieve herself forced her to get to her feet. She backed slowly toward a bush. The old man looked up and nodded. She felt a surge of relief before other thoughts crowded her mind. He knows there's nowhere for me to go, and if there was, I'd be too weak to make the effort. The thought brought her will to survive into her full consciousness like the pounding of a hammer on an anvil.

She had to start using her mind—to think, to take better care of herself, to eat and drink when she could. When the time came for her to make a break, she would have the strength to do it. She went back to the old man, straightened her back proudly, and looked him in the eye.

"I want a drink of water."

He looked at her with piercing black eyes, and it occurred to her that he wasn't as old as she had at first thought he was. The desire she saw in his eyes made her skin crawl, but she was determined to not cower before him even if he killed her. She put her hands on her hips. Resentment and anger flared in her eyes.

"I said I was thirsty, you old . . . coot!" she shouted. The stoic face broke into smiles. Then loud cackles of laughter came from his almost toothless mouth. He laughed and slapped his hands against his dirty buckskin leggings. He jabbed her with his forefinger. "Coot...coot..."

"Not me! You, you dirty old buzzard!" She jabbed him with her finger.

He continued to laugh, stomping his foot on the ground and waving his arms.

Angry and frustrated, Berry walked to the edge of the clearing. She saw a small stream of water oozing out of the rocks to form a small puddle before it went on down the rocky slope they had climbed in the dark. She fell to her knees and drank, scooping up the water in her hands. It was cool and delicious. After she drank, she splashed her face and pushed back the tight curls that framed it. She tore a strip from the hem of her dress and tied her hair at the nape of her neck. She longed to remove her shoes and cool her feet in the water, but she saw the ugly one coming up the slope. Just the sight of him made a chill slither down her spine. She stood, not wanting him to tower over her.

He threw two rabbits at her feet and then stared at her contemptuously. Berry looked at the rabbits and then at his face. His flat lips were curled in a sneer.

"You think I can't clean and cook a rabbit!" she said. "You'd like an excuse to kill me." Her green eyes flashed a confidence she didn't feel. "You ugly, disgusting, stinking polecat! What do you think I'll clean them with? My teeth?"

To her surprise, he reached for the knife in his belt. With a flick of his wrist he sent it into the ground at her feet. She had heard somewhere that most Indians knew a little English. She wondered just how much these two knew.

Berry dressed and washed the rabbits and took them back to the fire. The Indians were sitting cross-legged on the ground—arguing. The young one was angry. The sounds he made were clear and distinct. The old one mumbled, but Berry got the impression that he was having the last word. Their talk exasperated her. Instinctively she knew they were arguing about her. Damn them! She would do some talking herself and see how much English they knew.

"When Simon Witcher comes to get me, he'll cut off your heads and feed them to the wolves. Simon Witcher..." She said the name slowly and distinctly. "He'll bring Fain MacCartney, Zebulon Pike, Manuel Lisa, and soldiers." She kept her back turned to the now-quiet Indians and searched her memory for names of prominent people. "The people in Saint Louis will be looking for me. I'm the daughter of Auguste Chouteau. The scout called Light will send his knife into your backs." She heard a small grunt but didn't look around. She bent her head over the rabbits and repeated, "The scout called Light... will come for me."

The hand on her shoulder spun her around and slammed her to the ground. The ugly Indian, his face twisted in anger, wrapped the thong about her wrist and tied her to a tree. What had she said that made him so angry? Which of the men she had named did he fear? He knew at least a few English words—she was sure of that now.

The meat on the spit was done, and the smell of it caused Berry's stomach to rumble and her mouth to water. She watched angrily and resentfully as the two men ate. Finally, when they finished, the old one came to her with a hind leg and a piece of the back that was crusted and blackened from being so close to the blaze. Berry took it gratefully and her sharp teeth tore into the meat.

The young Indian stamped out the fire, muttering angrily at the old one, who sat and watched impassively, the calm expression on his face never changing. Berry also watched, amazed at how completely he erased all trace of the fire. He doused the coals with water, carried the blackened pieces of wood away from the camp, and buried them under a thick layer of leaves. Then he covered the place where the fire had been with dirt, raked it, and laid leaves over it until it was impossible to tell that a fire had ever been built in that place. He also removed all traces at the site where she had cleaned the rabbits. Berry now wished she hadn't been so neat. She could have splashed so much blood over the rocks that it would have been impossible for him to remove it.

Ugly stood over the old man, glowering, arguing, and pointing toward the distant hills. The old man folded his hands over his stomach and belched. Ugly grew more insistent, raising his voice. Berry watched in terror as he drew the knife from his belt and brandished it with swift, unmistakable motions. *He wanted to kill her!* A thousand tiny hammers pounded in her head while she waited to see what the old man would do.

Finally he got slowly to his feet and folded his arms over his chest. He straightened himself proudly and shook his head. The word he spat out was the harshest she had heard him utter. He shook his head and pointed to his chest.

Ugly stared at him and walked away. Berry realized that a crisis had been averted. When the old man came for her, she got to her feet and walked behind him down the rocky slope. The mare was chomping on the grass at the bottom of the hill and Ugly stood waiting.

They traveled all day. They waded upstream in a creek that stopped abruptly when they came to a spring. The country is full of springs, Berry thought absently. They pushed through green meadows. Bees hummed thickly in the air. Elk and deer suddenly bounded from the shadows as Berry and the Indians passed through wooded valleys, but she was too miserable to see the beauty.

After three days and nights of riding, the pain that would have been unbearable was somewhat dulled by the curious blanking of mind that nature provides to carry one through suffering. Days and nights, trees, hills, and streams—food she determinedly swallowed. Snatches of sleep. They rode on and on. The whole world seemed contained in the movement of the mare, the slap of the brush against her legs, the sound of the hooves—the Indians. Her head hung forward and she didn't have the strength to straighten her neck.

Hours after she had passed the desperate need to lie down that had plagued her for these past days and nights—when she thought she would go on and on forever like this, and that there would be no end—they stopped. She was powerless to move. Strong hands pulled her from the horse. She lay crumbled and dazed. A curious cone-shaped shelter danced before her eyes, but its meaning eluded the grasp of her mind.

Her eyes closed. She drifted into darkness.

Chapter 13

Simon passed through the country with eyes as bleak as Berry's had been when she passed through it. The only difference was that his eyes searched for signs of her passing. He thanked God for the time he had spent with Light and for all Light had taught him about the wilderness. Unerringly he followed the trail the Indians had taken, guided by a broken branch, a scuff mark on a stone, or the strands of silky black hair left caught on a brush or a low limb. He made his way rapidly through the forest by day, pausing only when darkness came.

It had not taken much wilderness training to read the sign the morning he found Berry's camp. Two Indians, more than likely renegade Shawnee, had surprised her as she prepared to camp for the night. It was plain that there had been a struggle and that she had been knocked to the ground. She had crawled under a bush, and when she stood, she had been knocked to the ground again. Simon found where she had been tied to a tree; found her discarded grub bag and saddle. The Indians had made no attempt to erase the signs of the abduction. *They must have been sure they wouldn't be followed.*

Simon was no longer able to whip up his anger to crowd the heavy worry and dread from his mind. He knew his only hope of finding her alive was to stay on the trail and pray that he caught up with her and her abductors before they caught up with the rest of their party.

At night, while attempting to rest, he relived every minute of the time he'd spent with her. It haunted him now, the way she had returned his kisses and pushed her trusting young body against his. Beset with loneliness, his thoughts turned inward. He thought back to the evening he first saw Berry bending over the cookfire. He felt once again her difference from all other woman—her boundless pride, the stubbornness of her will, and her deep-rooted integrity. There is much more to Berry Warfield than her startling beauty, he decided solemnly.

Simon was not naive enough to believe in love at first sight. He was not even sure he knew what this thing called love was all about. He'd only heard about it. But it was reasonable to believe it could not flower until the seed had been fertilized with understanding and nurtured by acceptance. It seemed that Berry had neither understood nor accepted him, or she would have been waiting for his return.

Did he love her? He felt a strong animal hunger when he was near her, but he didn't regard that physical urge as a sign of love. He'd had that feeling before. But right from the start he'd felt a need to help Berry. He thought about that fact very carefully; that, and the happiness he felt when he was with her. She made him laugh, made his heart sing.

God, what a fool he'd been to think he wanted her merely as a nucleus around which to build a family. It was torture now to think he had laughed when she had said she wanted love. At last he realized the truth about his feelings for her, and it was a truth that was both frightening and exhilarating. His feeling for her was deep and eternal, and it bound him forever to this girl who had first touched his heart.

"Goddammit!" he hissed under his breath. "Why was I such a fool? Why didn't I just marry her when Fain married Rachel?"

He dozed and his dreams were filled with haunting memories of silky black curls spilling down on snowy-white shoulders, clinging arms, and firm young breasts. Strange, pleading green eyes looked out of the darkness and begged him to hurry.

At daylight he saddled his horse. When I find her, he vowed silently, I'll keep her with me always.

At noon he found traces of a bivouac of the preceding night and knew he was closing the gap. This time care had been taken to remove the sign. Wilted leaves on an overhanging branch were evidence that a fire had been built beneath them. A careful search revealed rabbit hair at a spot beside the spring where the grass was trampled down, and where a knife had stabbed the earth. Droppings from the mare indicated the direction in which they had gone.

The heat became blistering. Swarms of gnats, flies, and mosquitoes plagued him. He paced himself and conserved his strength and that of his horse as he followed the trail of the Shawnee braves and Berry.

As he traveled deeper into the wilderness Simon was quick to note that the braves were becoming increasingly careless again and made no attempt to cover their trail. Finally Simon surmised that they were traveling at night. Their haste made Simon uneasy. He was almost sure they were hurrying to meet a larger party.

At dusk one evening he detected the odor of a wood fire. He slowed his horse to a cautious walk. Taking care to make no noise, he glided through the trees, his rifle cocked and ready for instant use. When he heard the sounds of shouting and raucous laughter in the distance, he dismounted, tied his horse, and crept toward the edge of the woods. The noise became louder, and soon he saw that a clearing lay beyond the trees and brush. He crept closer, moving at a snail's pace. A bright glow told him that a cookfire was burning.

He crouched behind the trunk of a giant oak. The first thing he saw was Berry. The sight of her was both startling and sickening. Her thick black hair hung in a tangle down her back. She wore nothing at all except her thin shift. Her hands were tied behind her back with a thong, and she looked as if she was about to drop in her tracks. Her captors had doused her with water so that her shift clung to her young body like a second skin, revealing rosy-tipped breasts and the dark patch between her thighs. Her captors were forcing her to dance around the campfire.

Shouting and leaping, two braves danced in and out of the firelight and around Berry as she was forced to keep pace with them. Another Indian and two squaws sat cross-legged on the ground. Although the language was impossible for Simon to understand, he knew they were heaping insults on her. However, verbal abuse was the least of her torments.

One of the braves, one with the ugliest face Simon had ever seen, reached with both hands for her breasts. When she jerked away from him and tried to kick him, the other brave wrapped his hand with her hair, forcing her to stand and endure the rough fondling. When the dancing resumed, a fat squaw lashed at her legs with a makeshift whip of supple vine. She cried out in anguish and the entire party became still more excited and howled with laughter.

Simon shielded his eyes from the glare of the fire. Attempting to close his mind to the pain Berry was forced to endure, he made a careful assessment of the camp. In addition to the two braves who were dancing, a third was sitting quietly beside the fire, and another lay in the grass beside the ragged, ill-kept tepee.

The two squaws, both fairly young, rose to their feet. One was wearing Berry's dress, the other her shoes and stiff-brimmed bonnet. The one in the shoes fell and lay in the grass giggling. She reached for a bag and squirted some of its contents into her mouth.

They were drinking fermented berry juice! The two squaws and the old Indian beside the fire were drunk. Simon didn't know about the one lying in the grass or the two who danced beside the fire. He was sure the two dancing braves were working themselves into a frenzy and that he'd have to act soon.

He steeled himself to the sound of Berry's cries as the squaws continued to lash her. The situation was discouraging. He had one shot and the knife. He'd not have a chance to reload before they were on him unless he could take them by surprise and take out at least two of them. Berry's sobs increased his sense of helpless frenzy while he tried to form a plan of action. He had little fear of the squaws, but four braves were more than he could handle at the moment, and he couldn't stand by and wait for them to tire of their play and bed down.

Thunder rumbled in the distance. A few spatters of rain fell. The wind picked up and sent sparks from the fire flying off into the night. Simon backed off, circled the camp, and came up behind the te-pee. Carefully he cut the leather lacing until the skins were hanging on the poles. On his hands and knees he crawled to where the brave lay sleeping in the grass. In one quick, dispassionate movement, he drew his knife across the brave's throat, stopping his drunken snores.

A crack of thunder sounded and a flash of lightning illuminated the sky. The storm was moving swiftly, and a strong wind, hot and humid, suddenly sprang up, making the loose skins flap on the poles. It's too much to hope the wind will blow the skins toward the fire and cause a diversion, Simon thought. The Indians seemed indifferent to the approaching storm.

Simon circled the camp again and came as close to Berry as possible. She lay prostrate on the ground, the women capering around her. He dropped to his knee and chose his target. The ugly Indian seemed to be the most dangerous. Just as more thunder shook the heavens he squeezed off a shot. The Indian clutched his chest and dropped to his knees, then stretched out in the grass. Simon waited for the confusion he was sure would follow. He could scarcely believe his good fortune when he realized that none of the others were aware of what had happened. Simon's shot had been lost in the boom of thunder. He quickly opened his powder bag and prepared to reload. At that moment the earth shook as a crack of thunder split the sky. A deluge of rain drenched the entire area. He grabbed for the bag. Too late! His powder would be too wet to use for many hours. The downpour reduced the fire to a few faint embers, then darkness.

Simon had no opportunity to develop a plan of assault. He was barely able to see. He knew the two braves were similarly hampered. Shouting at the top of his lungs, he sprang into the clearing.

"Ye...ooo! Run, Berry! For God's sake, run!"

He reversed his hold on his rifle and, grasping it by the barrel, swung the butt in a vicious arc, gambling that the braves would be unable to discharge their weapons. He was wrong. A bullet sang past his ear, but his initial gamble paid off as the butt of his rifle connected with the side of the brave's head. The man doubled over.

The wind came howling through the trees, sending the skins from the tepee into the fray, swishing and swirling. Simon ran to Berry and with a single slash of his knife cut the bonds that held her wrists.

At that instant one of the squaws landed on Simon's back and sent him sprawling in the mud. He rolled over in an attempt to shake off the determined woman. She was biting and kicking and her hands wound in his hair. He didn't want to kill her, but he had to get rid of her! He grabbed her hair, pulled her face around, and hit her with all his strength. She loosened her hold and fell limply to the ground.

The lightning came again, followed by thunder and more lightning. He saw Berry on her feet. The wind catapulted her toward him. He grabbed her arm and together they stumbled back to where he had dropped his rifle when the squaw attacked him. The rain was coming down so hard that it was impossible to see more than a few feet. He half-dragged, half-led the dazed girl toward the forest.

"Can you run?" he shouted.

It had all happened so fast that Berry hadn't until now realized who had rescued her. Recognition, combined with her fear of the Indians, galvanized her into action. She ran far faster than she had ever believed herself capable of. Several times she stumbled and fell, but Simon hauled her to her feet and they ran on. The rain continued, making the night so black that it took Simon some time to find his horse. But at last they found him in a grove of maples, indifferent to the downpour.

Simon climbed into the saddle and pulled Berry up behind him. Her arms encircled his waist and she pressed her face to his back. Flash followed flash of lightning and the thunder crashed continuously. The wind tore at her hair and the icy rain poured over her. She leaned gratefully against Simon, her breasts pressed tightly to his back and her face buried in his sodden shirt. He moved the horse recklessly through the dense forest. Berry didn't know how he had found her or where they were going. All that mattered to her was that he was here. This was her man. He had come for her!

It seemed like hours had passed and still the rain came down. Simon kept the big stallion moving at a steady pace. Then the storm was moving away, the thunder and lightning came less frequently, but the rain continued to fall. Grayness crept into the forest as daylight struggled to establish itself. Simon turned the horse, urged him up a rocky incline, and moved in under the overhang of a bluff. He stopped.

Berry was shivering almost uncontrollably and he had to pull apart her clasped hands so that he could dismount. He lifted her down and held her close to his side while he led the horse through a narrow opening in the side of the rocky bluff. They entered a shallow cave, out of the wind and rain.

"I'm sure they won't follow us while it rains. It'll give me time to dry my powder." He pulled a blanket from his pack and wrapped it around her. Then he wrapped her in his arms, holding her tightly against him. "I don't know whether to kiss you or beat you." His big hands wiped the rain from her face and wrung the water from her streaming hair. "I've got to tend the horse and get a fire going."

Berry's body ached with cold, her feet and legs almost numb, but the glowing warmth inside her and the wonder of the words whispered hoarsely in her ear—if in fact she'd heard them correctly— were too precious to allow the misery in her body to overshadow the moment.

Simon pulled the saddle from the horse and with his hands rubbed the water from his slick coat. The animal moved obediently when Simon pushed him to stand with his rear to the entrance of the cave. In the gloomy light Berry watched as Simon raked up dry leaves that had drifted into the enclosure. He heaped them in a pile along with some small twigs, then struck a spark with his flint, and soon a small blaze appeared.

"I'll find some wood. Keep it goin'."

Shivering, and keeping her jaws clenched to keep her teeth from chattering, Berry knelt by the small flame and fed it with the twigs the wind had blown against the stone wall. When Simon returned, she backed away and watched him strip the wet bark from the dead branches he'd brought in. He didn't look at her or even acknowledge her presence until the fire was blazing steadily and he had rolled a large flat stone up close to the flame.

"When the stone gets warm, I'll move it out and lay my powder sack on it. I've got to dry the powder so we can defend ourselves if the Indians follow us. I don't think we have anything to worry about as long as it continues to rain, and maybe not even then. It looks like it's set in to rain all day. I hope so. It will give us a chance to dry out."

Simon stood, and for the first time Berry saw him clearly. His thick black hair, which hung almost to his shoulders, was dripping wet. His deep-set eyes looked black as night, but she knew they were dark blue, just as she knew his skin was sun-coppered beneath the black beard that shadowed his cheeks.

"Simon..."

"We've got to get you dry and warm or you might come down with a roaring case of the ague." He reached for the blanket and pulled it away from her trembling body. "Pull off that wet thing and I'll wrap you up again."

"But..."

"No arguing, Berry. Take it off."

Berry complied, reluctantly.

He enfolded her in the blanket the instant her wet garment left her body. He wrung the water from the shift and hung it on a branch he had dragged in to burn. Then he pulled off his shirt and spread it out to dry.

Berry stood beside the fire feeling awkward and shy. She heard the rain splashing against the boulder at the entrance of the cave. When Simon pulled her down onto the blanket he had spread on the sandy floor, her knees buckled and she almost fell.

"Simon, I've got to say... I'm sorry." Her jaws shook when she spoke.

As if realizing how chilled she was, he knelt beside her and gathered her in his arms. The heaven of being held close, her face in the warmth of his neck, was too much. Tears spurted and she tried desperately to control them. All the pain and the humiliation she had suffered, and the rescue by Simon when she had despaired of living through the night, flooded her in a backwash of emotion. She cried, with her mouth against his neck.

"Hush. Hush, darlin'," he crooned and rocked her gently in his arms. "Shhh... You've got to tell me about them so I'll know what to expect." His warm mouth moved over her wet face. "Ahhh... sweet girl, my whiskers will scratch your sweet face."

Berry's arm crept out of the blanket and around his neck. Delightful sensations ran through the whole of her being, bringing joy—a consummation of all the yearning dreams she had ever dreamed.

"I don't care about the whiskers. I don't care. Kiss me, Simon...."

His lips moved from her cheek, and she knew they were coming to meet hers even before she felt their touch. Slowly, deliberately, his mouth covered hers, pressing gently at first while he slowly sank down onto the blanket and pulled her onto his lap. His kiss deepened and she leaned into it, floating in a sea of sensuality where in a dreamlike state she hovered against his masculine strength. His lips were seeking, and she automatically parted hers in invitation. The touch of his tongue at the corner of her mouth was persuasive rather than demanding, and she gave herself up to the waves of emotion crashing over her.

The soft utterance that came from her throat was a purr of pure pleasure when he expanded the kiss with a pressure that sought deeper satisfaction. The fever of her passion excited him and he tried to meet it with restrained response.

Berry felt her mind whirl and her nerves become acutely sensitized with the almost overwhelming need to melt into him and ease the ache of her aroused body. Caught in the throes of desire, she pressed against him, her arm winding around his neck with surprising strength.

Resisting the pressure around his neck, Simon lifted his head and looked down at her. The face beneath his was pale and beautiful, still and waiting. Her breath came quickly and was cool on his lips, made wet by her kiss.

"Berry, you're the damnedest woman ever created, and the ... sweetest," he said in a raspy whisper. His hand moved to the nape of her neck and his fingers lifted her wet hair.

"Does that mean you're not . . . angry with me?"

"No, it doesn't mean that at all. I'm so mad at you that I want to beat you! But . . . I want to kiss you, too."

"I said I was sorry," she said, trying to collect her scattered senses.

"Being sorry wouldn't matter, Berry, if we were dead." He pulled slightly away, yet she was still in his arms, her head still resting on his shoulder. He was speaking smoothly, reasonably, with no censure in his voice. "You and I are going to have to come to an understanding, Berry. I'll not tolerate your headstrong behavior. You'll listen to what I say and you'll act accordingly. It was a miracle I found you when I did. It was a miracle the storm struck and I was able to get you out of that camp. You would've been raped before the night was over." Now his voice became sharper, more anxious. "Now I want you to tell me everything, starting at the time you left Fain's."

Tears filled Berry's eyes—the result of nerves strung taut by her ordeal and his onslaught on her senses. She was disappointed by his obvious refusal to accept her apology after they had shared the sweetness of the kiss.

"What do you want to know?" she asked, stalling for time while she composed herself. She tried to move away from him, but he tightened his arms, forcing her to remain where she was.

"Everything," he replied candidly.

"I left Fain's early. Fish said it was only twenty miles, and I thought I could get there and back in one day, or stay over the night and come back. I couldn't find . . . my land, and I was on my way back when they . . . took me." She despised the tears that flowed onto her cheeks, but was rather proud that she was able to steady her voice as she told how the Indians had pounced on her and taken her gun and horse. "One of them wanted to kill me. He was the ugliest man I ever saw. The old man wanted me. When we met the others, the braves tried to trade the old man something for me. The squaws were the worst. They . . . pulled off my . . . clothes and hit me with the switches and . . ." She stopped, her voice choked off.

"And what?" he urged.

"They . . . spread their legs for the men, right there in front of everyone." A sob tore from her throat. "I didn't know Indians were like that. I hate them! They're dirt! Filth!"

"Hold on," Simon said firmly. "All Indians are not the same, just as all white men are not the same. I figure the ones who took you are castoffs. They were cast out of their tribe for some reason or the other. How many horses did they have?"

"I saw only one, besides my mare."

"I killed two of them, so that means there's a mount for each of the braves." He was silent for a moment. "I don't think they'll come after us."

"The ugly one will. He hated me!"

"I killed him," Simon said simply. "I had one sure shot and I figured he was the more dangerous one." He lifted her off his lap and moved over to add more fuel to the small fire. He raked the rock away from the blaze with a stick and tested the heat by holding his hand near it. Satisfied that it was warm but not too hot, he pulled the rock farther from the fire and set his open leather powder bag on it. He turned her shift and his shirt, then went to the mouth of the cave to look out.

"The sky is heavy with rain clouds. It'll be a while before it lets up," he commented. He came back, sat down, pulled off his knee-high moccasins, and set them close to the fire.

Berry huddled in the blanket and wondered how he could stand the chill of his wet buckskin breeches. "Where's your hat?" she asked.

Simon turned and looked at the enormous green eyes staring at him out of her white face. He couldn't speak for a moment. She looked so small, so vulnerable, but he knew she was tougher than she appeared. He grinned at her and reached out a hand to cup her cheek.

"I lost it when the squaw jumped on my back. She's probably wearing it now."

In spite of her fatigue, Berry laughed. "One in your hat, the other in my bonnet. They'll be a sight."

Warmth spread through her chilled body at last. She loosened the blanket from around her neck and let it slip to her shoulders. Her eyes searched his face. She didn't dare lie down and fall asleep... not yet. Not without making her peace with Simon. Her eyes burned, and she had to open them wide to keep them from closing.

"Go to sleep," he said, and gently pushed her down and pulled the blanket up over her shoulders. "You don't have to be afraid. I'll be watching." He held out his hand, and without hesitation she pressed her palm to his. His fingers entwined with hers.

"Are you still... mad?"

"Not too mad to kiss you again." His lips skimmed her cheek. "You're a spunky woman. Life with you will never be dull. I may want to beat you, but I'll want to kiss you, too."

She clutched his hand, smiled contentedly, and drifted off to sleep.

Berry was astride a great white horse. Her arms were locked around the bronzed body of the man in front of her. Her laughter rang out as he urged the beast to greater speed until it seemed to fly over the short green turf. Soundless words came drifting back to her as they floated up and down with the movements of the horse. She pressed her cheek to the muscled back before trailing kisses from his shoulder blade to where the dark hair grew at the nape of his neck. She arched her back and laughed. The man turned. His eye sockets were empty, and there was no flesh on his face; she knew it was the ugly Indian.

An agonized cry tore from her throat and she was instantly awake. Simon's face was close to hers. She clutched at him, thinking he would vanish.

"Shhh . . . You're all right. You were having a bad dream."

With a soft, welcoming cry, she reached for him and wrapped her arms around his neck. "Oh, Simon! Don't go! Don't leave me again."

"Is there room for me under that blanket, love?"

She lifted the edge in invitation. He slid in beside her and gathered her in his arms. Warm gladness welled in her heart and flooded her body, and her arms encircled him as she gloried in the feel of his hard warmth.

He curled his arm beneath her, while his other

hand caressed down along her spine to pull her hips closer to his. He was as naked as she, and it seemed natural and right.

"I wanted to wake you," he whispered before finding her parted lips with his, moving them slowly and touching them with his tongue. "I've been watching you, wanting to hold you, but I know how tired you are."

"Your skin is so smooth," she whispered, breathing against his lips. "I didn't know you'd feel like this ... so solid and warm." Her head was spinning helplessly from the torrent of her churning desires. She moved her body so that her breast rubbed against the rough hair on his chest. "Your heart is beating so fast!" The uneven rhythm of her breathing was making speech difficult, but that didn't stop her from expressing her thoughts. "Does it always beat like this, or is it because you're as excited as I am?"

A growl of laughter broke from his lips and he placed light kisses on her face. "Only when I have a pretty girl in my arms and I want to love her ... in every way there is...."

"Are we going to do what we didn't do the other night?"

"I'll die if we don't...."

"I want to! Oh, Simon, I want to do it all! I thought about it while I was with the Indians. You said you'd make it long and sweet and I'd have no regrets. Even if you don't, and if you don't love me like I want you to, I'll have no regrets."

"Ahhh ... sweetheart..." His mouth moved over hers with warm urgency. His tongue caressed her lips, sought entrance, and found warm welcome.

Instinctively she moved closer, grinding her pelvis into his masculine hardness. Stirred by an incredible arousal, she met his passion with intimate sensuousness and glided the tip of her tongue across the edge of his teeth before she pulled away, her deep-rooted curiosity taking over.

"Do married people do this every night?"

"Some of them."

"Does the man always make it long and sweet, or does he just jump on like a stallion?"

"For God's sake, Berry!" He groaned. "Not all men are like that!" he added patiently.

"Does it hurt you when it's hard like this?" Her hand wriggled down between them, and her touch caused a jolt to pass through his body.

"Yes!" he said gratingly between clenched teeth. "You're the talkin'est woman!" He tried to shut her mouth with his, but she evaded his lips.

"How'll I know things if I don't ask? I couldn't ask any other man."

His head jerked back and he glared down at her even as his arms tightened so that she could scarcely breathe. "You'll not get a chance to ask another man! If I hear of you talkin' like this to another man, I'll beat you within an inch of your life! This man . . . this body, is all you're goin' to know about!"

His anger pleased her and she laughed. The musical sound rang in his ears and caused a wave of tenderness to well up in him. He pressed his face into the curve of her neck.

"What else do you want to know, sweet, sassy brat?"

"Do you plan to put that whole thing . . . inside

me?" she whispered huskily and moved her hips against him in instinctive invitation.

His head jerked up again as if he had been grabbed by the hair. "Yes, by God, I do!"

There was laughter, love, and teasing in the sparkling eyes that met his. "Then you'd better get on with it. The rain's about to stop."

"Oh, Berry! Oh, darlin' girl . . ."

They laughed together and rolled, their arms and legs entwined. Berry could feel the happiness in him and longed to look into his face and see love and laughter there, but he was kissing her, loving her with his hands.

"Are you happy, Simon? Are you glad you met me?"

"Glad? If you don't hush talkin' I'll . . ." His words melted on her lips.

Their mouths met and were no longer gentle. They kissed deeply, hungrily. His hand moved down her spine, found her taut buttocks, and pressed hard. Her arousal was evident in her rock-hard nipples pressed to his chest and the moistness between her thighs when he touched her there. The stinging welts made by the switch, the soreness in her buttocks and back, and the growling of her empty stomach were all forgotten as she gave herself up to the sweet abandonment he was urging upon her. His fingers stroked her breasts before moving down over her stomach to toy with soft curls. She welcomed his gentle touch with parted thighs and an urgency that incited him to lift his mouth from hers and whisper hoarsely in her ear.

"Now, darlin'? I can't wait!"

He slid smoothly over her body, seeking entrance while she waited in rapt and arching anguish. Everything he did felt so good, so right, that she was caught up in an overpowering desire and need for physical release.

He moved between her legs and pressed into her tightness. He stayed there, gulping air into his lungs, feeling for the first time the touch of his rigid maleness against the membrane guarding her virginity. He waited, savoring the wondrous moment. Then his hips made a jerking motion, paused, and he lifted himself almost out of her.

At the moment of their union, Berry felt a sharp stab of pain. But it was not agonizing pain. It seemed a mere discomfort compared to the other, all-encompassing pain that cried out to be eased. The pain-pleasure of their joining would forever be imprinted in her memory. She was part of him, he was her world, her universe, and she vibrated with all the love she had to give to him.

He lifted her to undreamed-of sensual heights. She no longer wanted him to be gentle and let her hips move in unison with his, slowly at first, then more and more frantically until her body moved with untamed urgency beneath him. Sensation after sensation rushed through her, causing her flesh to quiver, her muscles to contract. She was only vaguely aware of the sharp, powerful contractions of the body locked with hers. She felt her own body sweeping toward some great height that would release her from this sweet torment. At the crest there was a burst of exquisite sensation and she seemed to float out of herself.

They came out of the clouds together and exchanged soft, moaning kisses, their bodies welded together in the aftermath of heated sensation. Simon raised his head, his dark, fathomless eyes searching her passion-clouded ones. He felt himself still fully extended inside her, for all the violent completeness of the act just accomplished.

Berry reached up and ran her fingers through the dense mass of dark hair over his temples. Her lips spread in a dreamy, sweet smile. "This is the real Simon," she murmured softly. "Sweet 'n' warm way down deep. You only wear that serious face so folks won't know how sweet 'n' lovin' you are. You won't be able to hide it from me now. You're the dream I've held on to for so long."

He flexed his hips, implanting himself more deeply. "I'm only a man," he said, his voice raspy with emotion.

"My man?"

"If you'll have me."

Her laugh was warm and moist against his mouth. Again he flexed his hips, and she tensed briefly against her soreness, but soon her discomfort was forgotten. His mouth found hers, sending tendrils of flame and desire through her once again. Her hands slid around his waist and gripped hard, and they were locked together in a straining embrace. She moved with him, timing her actions with instinctive precision. Then the climax seized them; she cried out, and he let the flood pour out of him with a violence that rendered him dazed and spent.

Berry struggled up from languor and stirred in Simon's arms. She leaned her elbows on his chest, her nose just inches from his. Her eyes were green, shining pools of pure happiness. In her newfound freedom to touch and love him she gloried in running her lips over his face, nipping the skin on his neck, and wriggling the tip of her tongue between his lips.

"I warn you, Simon," she murmured between kisses. "When we're wed you've got to do this every night!"

"Oh, Lord!"

She felt the laughter in his body before it burst from his mouth. She pressed her palms against his cheeks, her fingers tugging at his ears.

"What's so funny?"

"You, darlin'. I didn't know there was anyone in the world like you!"

Chapter 14

The dark clouds overhead were rolling away. A few stars appeared in the evening sky. Fully dressed in his dry clothes, Simon stepped around his horse's rump and viewed the scene of dripping trees and rain-washed hills and valleys. He looked back. Berry was sleeping soundly. Her smooth skin glistened in the soft gloom. Once more, pleasurable sensations started to build. She looked so desirable that he turned away quickly so as not to be tempted to lie down beside her and take her in his arms. There were a few things he needed to know before he could settle down for the night.

Taking his rifle, ammunition, and powder bag, he started toward a hill about a hundred yards away to survey the area. He doubted that the two braves would come after them. They each had a horse, he reasoned with calm logic. It wasn't likely they would risk death to get a mount for their squaws.

He stood for a long while studying the landscape. To the west, a river of water was running through a wash that had been dry when they crossed over it. Water stood in the low spots, and all around the ground was littered with twigs and leaves torn from the trees by the wind. He silently thanked God that the rain had not come a day sooner. If it had, he would never have been able to trail Berry and the Indians, and she would have been lost to him forever.

Satisfied that they were in no immediate danger, Simon went back to the cave, lay down beside Berry, and pulled her into his arms.

All day they rode through the rain-soaked wilderness, skirting the flooded lowlands. The course they followed was rugged with fallen trees and choked with underbrush. Simon walked most of the time. Berry, wearing his shirt and riding the horse, tried to shield her bare legs and feet from the sting of the brush they passed. The soreness between her legs was uncomfortable, but she never complained; she was far too happy to complain about anything. Simon, her man, strode confidently ahead, leading the horse with one hand, the rifle held firmly in the other.

The sky was blue gray; the sun, unobscured by floating clouds, poured down its heat. Small animals scattered as Simon and Berry approached, and birds which had been singing merrily took to the wing. Deep forest surrounded them and Berry wondered how Simon knew which way to go.

They reached the riverbank just after sunset. Simon lifted her down from the horse and kissed her lustily before setting her away from him.

"I've wanted to do that all day."

"There's no reason that I know of why you couldn't've," she replied saucily. "Is lovin' only for nighttime?"

He whacked her on the backside. He was more jolly, more exuberant than Berry had ever imagined he could be. His dark hair was wet with sweat and his chest and shoulders gleamed with it. His dark eyes were warm and amiable, his wide, full mouth smiling. There was a boyish charm about him now that seemed entirely out of keeping with the serious, silent man she first met.

"Hungry?"

"How can you ask? My stomach has been slapping the heck out of my backbone all day."

"How about fish for supper?"

"Fish? How'll you catch it? Do we dare risk a fire?"

"I figure it's safe enough if we keep it small." He unsaddled the horse and led him to water before he staked him in a grassy patch near their campsite. "Star will let us know if anyone is about," he said while he sharpened one end of a branch he'd cut from a small tree. "He hears every sound. He can see and hear better than a man, and being mountain bred he's got a strong instinct to survive. That makes him naturally spooky." He finished whittling and held out the crude spear. "Let's go see if it works."

Berry stood on the bank while Simon took off his moccasins and rolled up the legs of his buckskins. He stepped carefully into the water and moved upstream holding the spear aloft. He edged close to the bank, waited, then brought down the spear with a powerful motion. There was a mighty splash, followed by Simon's triumphant whoop. He held aloft a large, silvery fish impaled on the spear. He flung spear and fish up onto the bank and came out of the water.

"That bugger must weigh ten pounds!" He was as happy and excited as a small boy. "I learned that trick from Light. It works every time," he explained happily.

Berry let out a burst of joyous laughter. "Oh, Simon! I like your face when you laugh!"

His eyes twinkled at her. "I'm glad. It's the only face I have."

She laughed again and whirled around, her arms above her head. Simon thought she looked like a picture he'd seen of a wood nymph. Her hair was kinky-curly from the damp air. Her lips and cheeks were pink. His shirt came to the middle of her thighs, and the white shift she wore beneath it came to slightly below her knees. Her feet were bare and dirty, but she was lovely—and she was his.

It seemed hours before the fish was cooked, then cooled enough so they could eat it. The meat was juicy and succulent. They agreed that it was quite the best they'd ever eaten. Being so hungry had something to do with it, they admitted laughingly. They put aside a portion of the fish for morning and went down to the river. Standing in the shallows, they washed their hands, splashed their faces, and smiled at each other.

Simon spread a blanket on the grass beneath the boughs of a tree. Berry sat down and tried to comb some of the tangles from her hair with her fingers.

"I thought the Mississippi flowed north and south.

I'm sure we traveled west. How can this be the river when we're still so far from home?"

Simon lay propped on one elbow and watched her. The fire had long since gone out. Through the branches of the trees the stars glittered brightly. Berry's face was a white blur, but he knew every feature, every line. There's never been a woman like her, he thought with quickening pride; she's beautiful and spunky beyond all reason. He couldn't stop looking at her and could just barely concentrate on what she was saying. She was his to care for, to keep safe. It would be hard now to consider a future without her.

"Simon?"

"Sorry, sweet girl. I was daydreaming. You asked about the river? Just beyond the point where the Missouri flows into the Mississippi it makes a deep bend and curves toward the northwest. A few miles farther it makes another bend going south and then northwest again. I've never been that far west, so I headed northeast, knowing sooner or later we would reach the river and could follow it home. We reached it a little sooner than I thought we would."

"If we had a raft we could float down the river."

Simon chuckled softly at her logic. "It's not as simple as that. That river has a mind of its own. We'd have no way to steer a raft. Besides, Star wouldn't stand for it. He hates to even cross on the ferry."

"How long will it take us to get home?"

"Three, maybe four days. It depends on how often we stop—how much dallyin' we do...." His hand reached out to caress her ankle and calf. A teasing grin played on his wide mouth, and wild, sweet enchantment rippled through her veins.

"I like being with you, Simon. I'd rather be with you than anyone in the world." She moved closer to him and drew his head down onto her lap. Her fingers combed his hair, then trailed down the side of his face. "I thought I'd never see you again." Her voice was strained, as though she was trying not to cry. "The ugly one wanted to kill me! It seems so strange that they found me when the rest of their party was so far west."

"They could've come down the Missouri to sell some furs. It's hard to tell about roving renegades."

Berry felt compelled to talk about the time she had spent with the Indians. "I suspected they could understand English, so one night I named everyone I could think of. I said, 'Simon Witcher will come for me.' I mentioned Fain, Mr. Pike, Mr. Lisa, and I even told them I was the daughter of Mr. Chouteau. They didn't seem to pay much attention until I mentioned the scout called Light. Then the ugly one hit me and tied me up."

"Every Indian in the territory along the rivers knows about Light. He's friend to some tribes and a deadly enemy to others. Oh, Lord, sweetheart! There's so many *ifs* I don't want to think about them. *If* it had rained a day sooner. *If* I hadn't come back to Fain's when I did. *If* I'd not found you..." His hand gripped hers so tightly that it was painful.

"Why did you leave Fain's that morning... without a word?" she asked quietly after a heavy silence.

"What do you mean 'without a word'? We talked for hours the night before. I told you then that we'd wed and I'd take you to my homestead. There were things I had to do in Saint Louis. It only took me seventeen days."

"Only seventeen days!" she sputtered. "And I suppose you thought I'd be right there waiting when you decided to come back to get me."

"You're damn right I did! I was madder than hell when you wasn't."

"Only mad?" she asked, her voice tight.

"Mad and scared! So scared I thought I'd lose my supper. Don't ever pull a stunt like that again. When I tell you to stay put, you stay put!"

"Then you care for me after all. You've never said so."

"I don't go to Saint Louis to fetch home a cow, chickens, goods to make curtains and dresses, and a bake oven for every woman that crosses the river," he said with exaggerated patience.

"You went to get those things for me . . . for us?"

"For us, you mule-headed little baggage!" He moved over and drew her down beside him. His arms snatched her up against him and pillowed her head on his shoulder.

"I haven't called you a mule's ass lately," she said between giggles and snuggled her face against his rough-haired chest.

"True," he said and chuckled. "Do you suppose you're learnin' some manners?"

"I got enough manners. What I need is a bath."

"We'll find a stream tomorrow and we'll both bathe. It's too dangerous to bathe in the river—too many sinkholes."

He lifted her face and covered her mouth with his. It was a long, leisurely kiss, exquisitely tender and full of sweetness. He leaned over her, his lips savoring hers while his hand moved inside the neck of the shirt and gently massaged her breast beneath her thin shift. Then he raised his head and looked into her eyes. His soft chuckles fanned warm breath on her wet lips.

"It might take us a week to get home," he threatened.

"Home to your place or Fain's?"

"Mine. We reach it before we get to Fain's. I figure we can stay overnight, then go on down and let Rachel know you're safe. We'll get our cow and a few other things I hauled up from the warehouse." He paused to kiss her. "I shoulda had Silas marry us when he wed Fain and Rachel. I thought about it, but didn't know how it would set with you. You seemed mighty stuck on Fish."

"Stuck on Fish?" she repeated. Then a little devil with horns prodded her to say, "He *is* handsome, and he's got such good manners. I just never thought about him being stuck on me," she lied. "Do you suppose that's why he danced with me and taught me the words to 'Yankee Doodle'?"

"He's not the man for you," Simon said, his tone a growl, mentally kicking himself for mentioning the man's name.

"Why not? He told me about his home back east. He said I'd be a belle...."

"I'll tell you *why not!*" Roughly his hands gripped her arms and pulled them up to encircle his neck. His face was inches from hers. She could hear the click of his teeth when he snapped his jaws shut. "Because you belong to me, by God! Even if you didn't, a weak-kneed sissy britches like him wouldn't be able to handle you. You'd be leading him around by the nose in no time at all. You need a man who'll make you toe the line."

"Make me . . . toe the line?" She tried to pull her arms from around his neck and push him away from her, but he held them and forced her to stay still. "I'll not be any man's slave, Simon Witcher! My pa was like that: *Do this, do that!* I hated him! I thought we'd share things . . . be like Fain and Rachel."

"And we will, as long as you don't go running off on another wild goose chase. When it comes to the matter of taking sensible precautions, you'll listen to me. Is that clear?"

"I only wanted to find my pa's land," Berry said stubbornly.

"Don't mention that goddamn land again!" He was almost shouting.

"Are you going to hold this against me for the rest of my life?"

"No, darlin' girl." His voice softened. "I can't go through the hell again of not knowing if you're dead or alive, or . . . what's happening to you."

"Ahhh . . . Simon, love . . ." Her mood changed instantly. She pulled his face down and covered his chin with kisses. "You do care for me! Why can't you say it?"

"Are the words so important?"

"To me they are. I thought you didn't care for me. When you went away and left me, I thought you had been just talkin' . . . funnin', like men do. I had no words to cling to."

"All right. I care for you. I've never cared for anyone before, except for the woman who took care of me when I was young. I have to get used to that feeling. So don't be throwing up Fish's fancy manners to me. I'm not a man to be teased." He rolled onto his side and drew her to him. "Now hush up talkin'."

"There's only one way to stop me," she whispered happily.

They kissed until they both were moist with urgency. Berry tingled and came alight when his hands moved up under her shift. She pulled away from him, shrugged out of his heavy shirt, then nestled against him. Wherever he put his hands on her, that place grew warm. His hands on her thigh made her body ache with pleasure, familiar pleasure, calling for more.

She knew how to kiss him now. Her lips were soft and moist, her tongue reaching for his. His hand beneath her shift found her quick and wet to his fingers. He unfastened his buckskins, slipped them down, and slid over her. She opened to receive him, flesh sliding hot and sweet along his extended masculinity. Her pubic hair was silky as he entered, penetrating her carefully, conscious of the soreness she must feel from their previous couplings.

"Oh, Simon . . . you don't have to be gentle," she begged and pressed on his buttocks. He had entered her only partially and the ache of pleasure was farther inside. She felt him hot and throbbing, as she was. She arched frantically, urging him on. A fierce life burst within her, the strong hard prodding of his body setting off a clamor of vibrating waves. They kissed and moved together, joined in hungry flesh. She felt him hard and deep inside her body. He shuddered, and the hot splash of his seed awakened a soft explosion from her own body. They lay entwined, flesh glued together by the sweat of their loving.

"Did I hurt you?" Simon's breath came in ragged gasps and he moved away, but only a little.

"No! Oh, no. I like doin' this, Simon. I like lovin' with you." She was still adrift in a hazy world of pleasure.

"I was afraid you might be too sore... after last night, and riding all day," he said and lifted himself out of her.

"It's wonderful how we fit together. Don't you think God did a good job when he thought this up?"

Simon chuckled. She was a constant delight. "Settle down and get some sleep," he murmured.

Berry turned over and insinuated herself into the curve of his body, tucking herself snugly so that her bottom pressed against his lower abdomen. Simon wrapped her in his arms and smiled into the darkness. He held a world of treasure in his arms.

On the evening of the fourth day they came out of the forest and onto land that had been cleared for planting. They were home—this was Simon's land.

During the journey they had not seen another human being. They had crossed over swiftly moving streams that poured into the great river and traversed trails that writhed like snakes beneath giant trees like sentinels that threatened to block out the sky. They had carefully skirted a she-bear and her cubs and shivered at the sound of a cougar's scream.

They had not gone hungry on the trip, due to Simon's proficiency with his makeshift spear and to the wild berries, plums, and pears that grew jungle-like along the riverbank. While she was with Simon, there was never a time when Berry was afraid. He guided them surely and confidently through terrain that took them at times far from the river, as he chose the path through the tangle of trees, vines, and brush. Berry never questioned his ability to get them home safely. She obeyed his every order. He taught her to be watchful while in the forest and more so when traveling through open terrain.

In the evenings they bathed when possible, ate their meal, and made love. It seemed to Berry that she was living in paradise—that they were the only two people on the face of the earth. Now that it was over, she didn't know if she was sorry or glad.

Simon led her up the course of a little stream that cascaded sparkling from the crest of a bluff. They came out on an open prairie that extended across a wide plateau overlooking the river. The rich prairie rolled gently away to the edge of the forest. The carpet of waving grass parted to frame the clear blue of the stream that meandered pleasantly across the meadow before plunging over the escarpment to disappear into the bottomland. Nestled against the backdrop of tall cedars was the homestead. Simon's home site was doubly blessed with the gracious fertility of valley land and a hilltop view.

Simon had built his cabin on a bluff overlooking the river. It wasn't a high bluff, but high enough, he explained, that they wouldn't need to worry about the river flooding and washing them away. The cabin was small—about half the size of Fain's double cabin. There was a lean-to shed and a split-rail enclosure for the animals. That was all. Berry tried not to be disappointed.

"I haven't spent much time here," Simon explained and lifted her off the horse. "Lardy and I made just enough improvements so I could hold the land. I plan to build a house to the left there among the oaks. I want to put up a barn large enough to hold a winter's supply of hay, and a smokehouse, and build a landing down on the river."

Berry stood with her bare toes nestled in the loose dirt and looked at the forlorn cabin. "Who stays here while you're gone?"

"Lardy is here some of the time. If we both leave, we nail the door shut. Indians come by every so often and steal food, but that's to be expected. They don't figure it's stealing."

Simon led Star toward the lean-to and Berry went around to the cabin door. She was surprised to see that it was standing open, hanging crazily from one iron-forged hinge. She was puzzled and disappointed. She hadn't expected the cabin to be as well cared for as Fain's, but she hadn't expected it to be so dilapidated, either. The door moved easily when she pushed on it.

She stood in the doorway because she couldn't go farther into the cabin for the debris that littered the floor. The place looked like a pigsty! Berry's nose twitched with distaste as repugnant odors wafted from the room. A hunk of raw, spoiled meat, covered with buzzing flies, lay on the table. Cooking and eating utensils were scattered on the floor along with the contents of a wardrobe that stood beside the window, its doors hanging open, the inside looking like empty, gaping cavities. The straw-filled mattress lay half-on, half-off the bunk.

"What the hell!" Simon crowded past her and stood among his scattered possessions. He cursed again. Everything in the cabin bespoke savage destruction. Battered utensils lay near the fireplace, the mantel wiped clean of candles and books. Simon's coal-oil reading lamp lay shattered on the floor.

"Do Indians always make such a mess when they come to steal food?"

Simon picked up a knife, plunged it into the rotten meat, carried it out into the yard, and flung it away from the house. He came back with a bucket of water. "This isn't the work of Indians," he said gratingly, and pulled the table out into the yard and splashed water over the top. "This is the work of a goddamn river rat! An Indian wouldn't leave meat. He'd cook it and take it with him."

Berry found a pair of Simon's boots and stepped into them so that she could walk in the room without fear of cutting her feet on the glass. From amid the debris she dragged an iron pot, filled it with water, and set it over a blaze to heat. Then she picked up the clothes and piled them on the bunk, and salvaged what she could from the wreckage on the floor before she swept it clean with the remnant of a broom she'd found in the corner.

Berry and Simon labored with water, lye soap, and mop until the room fairly gleamed with cleanliness. They proudly surveyed the results of their labor and admitted, smiling at each other, that they were ravenously hungry.

"What's there to eat?" Simon wiped the sweat

from his face and neck on a shirt he had taken from the pile to be washed.

"The only thing that wasn't spoiled was the cornmeal. I can make us some mush." She gave him an auspicious smile.

"I've got a jug of sorghum and a few other things hid away in the shed." His eyes caught hers and held them with conspiratorial laughter.

Berry had removed Simon's shirt while she'd worked. She stood in her shift. It stuck to her wet young body, revealing uptilting breasts and a flat, firm belly. Her feet were bare, and loose strands of hair stuck to her wet cheeks. She was still so beautiful and desirable that, just from looking at her, Simon felt a stirring of his maleness.

"How about a bath?" he said, and from the tone of his voice she knew what was on his mind.

"And after that . . . ?" Her eyes twinkled into his after they lifted from the evidence of his arousal.

"We'll eat." His eyes teased and his wide mouth stretched into a grin. He whacked her lustily on the backside.

Berry's merry laughter rang out. This was the man she had dreamed about, the man she would spend her life with. They would laugh and love . . . tease and play. He was roughhewn and capable, yet considerate and tender. During the last few days he had shed much of the serious, protective coating he had worn like a shield to hide his lonely inner self. *She loved him so much!* Surely he loved her! He had to love her!

She snatched a shirt from the bunk and darted out the door. "Last one in is a . . . mule's ass!" she shouted over her shoulder.

Simon caught up with her by the time she reached the stream and they went splashing into the water together, naked as the day they were born. He gave her a shove and she toppled back into the water, and like children they wrestled and splashed each other. She wrapped her arms around his knees, and he lost his footing and fell, then came up sputtering and coughing. With shrieks of protest she tried to evade his reaching arms. Roaring with the first uninhibited laughter she had heard from him, he grabbed her and ducked her under the water. Then he was kissing her furiously, as if he could never have his fill of her. They fell, but his lips continued to cover hers. He rose to his feet with her in his arms and carried her to the grassy bank.

When they made love it was unlike anything they had experienced before. It was a passionate, furious, explosive loving. They wrestled in sensuous abandonment until their agonizing spasms climaxed on a note of sheer incredulity, endured endlessly, then slowly eased. He held her tenderly, kissing her neck, her shoulders, and her nipples while minutes passed. Then he made love to her again— slowly, gently, giving himself to her with incredible tenderness.

This has to be love, Berry thought with a sense of desperation. This isn't the animal coupling of male and female. She caressed his back, his shoulders, his buttocks. She rose to meet him, held him, and with every touch tried desperately to convey all the love she had for him.

They bathed again, dried each other's bodies, and dressed. Darkness was beginning to fall as they walked arm in arm back to the cabin.

"Will we go to Fain's tomorrow?"

"I think we should. Rachel was worried about you."

"I'm sorry about that. I didn't mean for her to worry."

They reached the door of the darkened cabin and Berry stepped up on the doorstone, turned, and put her arms around his neck. Their faces were on a level and she kissed his nose before setting her lips against his.

"Rachel was the only person I ever loved or even cared about after my mother died. Then I met you. I love you, Simon."

"You do, huh?" His arms tightened around her.

"Yes, I do!" she said stoutly. "You love me, too. Someday you'll shout it! It'll just come boiling out of you!"

He lifted her and swung her around before he set her back down on the doorstone. "You'd better fix that mush," he said with a trace of huskiness. "I've got to keep up my strength if I'm going to be doin' all this lovin'."

"Simon! You're a... horny toad!" She giggled helplessly, bit his neck, and danced away.

Chapter 15

Worry and dread had lain like a rock in the pit of Rachel's stomach since the morning they discovered Berry had left the homestead and Eben had been brutally murdered in his shack by the river. It had sapped her strength and controlled her thoughts, yet it had given energy to her hands. She had chinked the walls of the new room from ceiling to floor with river mud, made the hominy Fain was so fond of, ground corn, and made soap. In spite of protest from Fain, she chopped enough kindling to last for weeks.

She managed to stumble through the days, filling them with hard labor, trying to keep from her mind the nagging fear that she might never see Berry again. After a week, the shock of Berry's leaving had worn off to some extent. Rachel now feared that Simon would come riding in without her. As long as he was away, there was hope. Thank God for Simon and Fain.

"Faith's sleepin'." Fain's voice jarred into her thoughts.

She pushed her hair from her face with the back of her hand. It had become a nightly routine for him to rock the baby while she cleaned up after the evening meal. The sight of him holding her child always made her heart lurch. What made some men so full of goodness, she wondered, and others so rotten?

"I'll put her to bed."

"I'll do it."

Rachel smoothed the sheet over the mattress in the cradle and Fain laid the baby down, turned her over on her stomach, and drew a light cover over her. His big hand gently stroked the head of the sleeping child. Tears started in Rachel's eyes and she turned away.

Fain carried the cradle to the sleeping room and Rachel followed with the candle. She sat it on the table beside the bed and pulled the pins from her hair.

"Let me do that." Fain was behind her, his hands gently pushing hers away so that he could complete the task. His fingers combed through the heavy strands until they hung like a curtain to her waist. Then he pulled her back against him and placed loving kisses along the side of her face.

In an agony of need, she turned and flung her arms around him, blindly seeking comfort. Strong arms wrapped around her, and her face found refuge in the hollow beneath his chin. A fountain of tears erupted and she cried with the pathetic urgency of a small child.

He held her snuggled against him, rocking her

in his arms and stroking her hair. "There, there, darlin'. It's been a tryin' time. It purely has. But Simon'll find her. Shhhh ... Don't carry on so...."

Fain sat on the edge of the new double bed he'd made this past week in order to be near her. He had strung the frame with heavy rope, and he and Olson, the freighter Simon had left behind, had cut fresh, sweet grass to lay over them. He had promised Rachel that before the snow fell they would have enough hides to make a mattress and enough feathers to fill it.

When it seemed she had cried herself dry, Rachel found herself cuddled on his lap. She felt weak, as if her tears had washed away her strength.

"I don't know what got into me." She almost choked on the words.

"You're just 'bout wore out, that's what." Fain's lips were against her ear. "You're not strong, ya cain't be doin' all this hard work 'n' hold up. Ya got to slow down or ya'll get sick."

"I'm sorry for cryin'." She reached for the hem of her skirt so she could wipe her eyes and nose.

Fain pressed her head back down onto his shoulder and held it there. "Ya've put up with more'n a woman ought to, darlin'. Ya don't have to be a bit sorry for cryin', 'n' ya don't have to put up with nothin' by yourself no more. Ya got me now." The words were muffled in her hair. His hand traveled down her back, soothing, caressing. A strange, relaxing warmth spread through her.

"Ahhh ... Fain! I never dreamed there were men like you." She burrowed deeper in his arms. "I can stand all the trouble in the world as long as you're with me."

Fain's gaze wandered over her upturned face, then he found her eyes and held them. They were teary bright, but full of love for him. His arms tightened and he slowly lowered his lips to hers. He kissed her mouth and her wet cheeks. His hand stroked her in a comforting gesture. The softness of her body, the warm flush of her skin, and the soft sweetness of her mouth caused his maleness to stir against the soft hips on his lap. This woman and her child had made an enormous difference in his life. They had made this spot in the wilderness a home. He loved her with every breath and would spend his life keeping her safe and happy.

Rachel closed her eyes and lifted trembling lips to meet his suddenly greedy ones. He kissed her face, her ears, her throat, his lips and tongue making her mouth his own. She heard his harsh breathing in her ear and the hoarsely whispered words of love.

"Darlin' lass. Sweet, darlin' lass, I'd take away the hurt 'n' worry 'n' ya'd never shed another tear, if'n I could. I'd go look for Berry, but I can't leave ya here with only Olson and Israel to protect ya." Muttered words of love fell from his lips as he pressed feverish kisses along the soft skin of her throat.

"I know you can't go. I keep thinking Lardy will come back and tell us that he's found Light."

"And he might. He might come in the mornin'." He pushed the damp hair back from her face and his heart swelled. He had not dared to hope, to dream, that he might find a woman like this. "Get outta that dress 'n' get in bed," he whispered. "I'll take a look 'round 'n' be back for some of our special lovin'." He lifted her off his lap and stood up. Their eyes locked. Slowly he pulled her to him and his mouth possessed hers with insistent pressure.

Rachel undressed and slipped into bed. She left her hair loose, because Fain liked it that way. Every day she looked forward to this special time they spent together before falling asleep. She had been shy with him at first, but now she felt free to caress and love him in any way that pleased her. He had made her realize it was natural and right.

Fain came back into the room and stooped over the cradle to drop a kiss on the infant's head. He was bare chested, and Rachel knew he had been to the wash basin for his nightly wash. He pinched out the candle, finished undressing, and slipped into bed beside her. They both sighed and reached for each other. Rachel's hand slid around to the corded muscles of his back, trying to pull him closer. Even after sleeping with him for several weeks, she was still shattered by the sheer pleasure of lying naked beside him. Free of her fumbling uncertainty, she reached out to explore and caress his warm, hard body, letting her fingertips find his masculine nipples and follow the line of fine gold hair down to his taut, flat stomach and beyond. She felt the tremor that always shook him when her hand boldly sought and found the rock-hard organ that he pressed against her. Her hands on his body were like a torch being added to his already flaming desire.

"Ah, sweet lass. Ah . . . sweet, soft woman of mine! I love ya. Truly I do. You're the sweetness of my life. I'm glad I found ya." His voice was husky and rawly disturbed.

Rachel loved the words of love he whispered during their most intimate moments. She placed her lips to his ear. "So am I, my darlin'. Oh, so am I!"

He kissed her long and leisurely before moving his lips to her ear. "You're workin' too hard, darlin'." He caressed her from shoulder to knee. "I can feel the sharp edge of your hip bone," he chided lovingly. "I don't want ya to work yourself down to a nubbin. Save yourself for me." His tone was anxious.

"Fain, my love, you'll always come first with me. Faith takes my time now while she's a babe, but someday she'll be grown up and will leave us. You and I will be together for as long as we live."

She wound her fingers in his hair and gave a slow tug, pulling his head to her parted lips. His mouth was on hers, open and caressing, and hers answered it. Her hands were on him, eager and possessive. She thought she was going to die of wanting when his hand moved up between her thighs in a gentle stroking motion, causing her to flinch.

"Ya want me now, my love? You're so warm, so wet. I don't wanta take ya till you're ready, my sweet lass..." he whispered and held himself rigidly over her.

"Yes, yes..." She gasped and arched herself against him. Her body opened to him, needing him above all other things, welcoming the solid length of his maleness as if it were a part of her.

Rachel was made to know all the power and need of this big, gentle man she had come to love so passionately. His hands closed over her buttocks and held them while he pressed into her. She felt the thunderous beat of his heart against her naked breast and heard his hoarse, ragged breathing in her ear. He moved slowly at first, as if she were a delicate, precious flower he feared to crush. Then as wild, flooding pleasure shot through her and she became more persistent, he moved faster and faster.

Rachel yielded to pure feeling, blocking out everything but this. She whispered his name, her fingers biting into his skin, her hips arching to meet his thrusts and take him deep, frenziedly seeking the release she knew was coming.

"My darlin', my darlin', my sweetness, my love..." He whispered the love words. The hammering urge to release his passion was acute, but he waited, holding back until he felt the first tremor deep inside her. Then he was free to plunge, to rise, to let go. And he did.

An explosion of ecstasy swept them away from the physical world.

An eternity later, he raised his head to kiss her lips, her nose, her neck, to lick her cheeks with joyous frenzy. He leaned on his forearms to take some of his weight off her body, yet he remained buried deep inside her.

"My purty girl..." He burrowed his face in her hair and waited for his galloping heart to slow to its regular beat. "I'm too heavy for ya," he whispered worriedly. He lifted himself out of her and rolled onto his side. The strong ropes beneath them squeaked in protest as he turned into the grass mattress that cradled them. He put his hand on her hair, feeling its soft, silky texture. It enshrouded his face, caressed his shoulders. "Oh, sweet lass... I couldn't live without ya now."

He lay holding her, arms wrapped around her.

She fit so perfectly in the nest made by his arms and muscular thighs. She lay warm and soft and infinitely dear against him. Thoughts swarmed his mind. Someday he hoped to make her understand how she had wrapped her sweetness into the very core of his being. She had penetrated his heart with her gentle ways as not even his first love had done. It frightened him. What if he should lose her? She could be killed as Eben had been killed... she could die in childbirth... even now his seed could have found her fertile valley and she could be growing his child.

Rachel gave a tired little sigh and closed her eyes in sweet exhaustion. "Tomorrow I'll do the washin' if it don't rain," she murmured and fell into deep sleep.

The sky was alight with a new day when Fain carried the last bucket of water from the spring and poured it into the big iron pot he had hung from a stout pole. Israel had built a fire beneath it and was now bringing the wooden washtub from the shed. A bench, newly made, stood against the wall of the cabin. Rachel had been amazed when she first saw the huge wooden tub. She had expected to lift the clothes from the boiling water, lay them on a smooth half-log, and beat them clean with a paddle as she had always done. Fain had explained that Simon had transported the tub all the way up from New Orleans so that they would be able to bathe in the wintertime. Now it would serve a double purpose.

By the time Faith had been fed and put back to sleep, the breakfast things had been put away, and the meat with cabbage and onions for the noon meal had begun to simmer, the water boiling in the iron pot. Fain carried Faith and the cradle out into the yard. He placed the baby in the shade near where Rachel was working.

Israel came over and hunkered down to look at the babe. A huge smile split his face. Fain lingered beside the cradle, gently stroking the tiny blond head with his fingertips.

"She's a-growin', Mistah Fain. She sho is."

"She's a beaut—that's what she is," Fain said with affection. "She knows her pa, too. She c'n be a-whinin' 'n' frettin' 'n' if I pick her up she hushes up 'n' goes to sleep."

"Babes know somethin' like that when they's so little?" Israel asked.

"This one does," Fain said proudly. "Look a-there at her hands. Rachel had to cut her fingernails already 'cause she was scratchin' her face."

"They's mighty little."

Rachel turned her back and punched the clothes down into the boiling water so that Fain and Israel wouldn't see her smile. Love for her husband flooded her heart. She pressed her face to his shirt before dropping it into the suds.

Olson came across the yard, his rifle in his hand. He gave her a friendly wave and walked toward the river. Rachel sensed that the men were more concerned about Eben's murder than they let on to her.

"Me 'n' Israel are goin' to dig us a cellar. Where'd'ya want it?" Fain came up behind her and nuzzled her neck.

"Oh ... you scared me, Fain!" She lifted her shoulder, giving his face a brief hug between it and her cheek. "A cellar? Goodness! Are you sure you want to work on it now? I thought you were anxious to work on your guns."

"I got all winter to work on the guns. If'n my woman wants a cellar—I'll dig her one."

"You'll not get it done this summer if you don't quit huggin' me, and I'll not get the washin' done either," she chided, but turned her face for his kiss, not knowing or caring if Israel was watching. "You're a-spoilin' me," she cautioned.

"Whatta ya think about next to the house there?" He turned her so that she could see where he was pointing. "It'd be handy. We could get into it from the outside, and we c'n put a trap door in our sleepin' room. We could get in if a cyclone come."

"I can't think of a better place. We can keep the milk and garden stuff down there where it's cool."

"It's settled, then?"

"It's settled. Now, Fain..." He was nuzzling her neck again. "I've got to get the washin' done before Faith wakes up," she protested lovingly.

"I cain't get enough of ya. I think I'll carry ya off to the woods," he teased, and his fingers worked at the front of her dress while his eyes twinkled at her. He waited until she smiled. "That's what I wanted—a big smile on my woman's face." He patted her on the backside and left her.

When the washing was done and spread out on the bushes in the full sun, Rachel took her suds into the eating room and scrubbed the floor and everything in it, including the thick fireplace mantel, the work shelf, and the big trestle table. When she finished, the room was soap-smelling clean. She poured out the water well away from the cabin so that the men wouldn't track mud onto her clean floor. It was still an hour before noon, so she sat in the rocker with her knitting needles and the wool she'd unraveled from an old shawl. Fain had gaping holes in his socks and she had vowed to knit him a pair as soon as possible.

Fain heaved himself up and out of the hole he and Israel were digging. It was hot, hard work, but he welcomed it. It gave him a chance to think of other things while putting his foot on the spade and sinking it into the ground.

It had been a week since Simon had left to look for Berry. Lardy should have been back days ago, if only to report that Light was not in the area. Fain was puzzled about not hearing from him. He was worried about Berry and about Simon, who should have been back by now unless he was trailing Berry deep into the wilderness. He'd heard of roving bands of Indians who stole women for slaves; the women had disappeared, never to be heard from again. How would Rachel bear the uncertainty of not knowing if Berry was dead or alive? He tried to push the thought aside and concentrate on the problem at hand.

"Pound out that broken handle on the shovel, Israel. I've got another in the shed. I'll fetch it. I always used ash for helves, but Simon told me hickory had more stayin' power. I made up some last winter when I had time on my hands. We'll give 'em a try."

Fain watched Israel walk toward the shed. He knew that the slave had been mighty shaken up about Eben's murder. The two men had become friends, not only because of their color but because of Eben's compassionate nature. He had taken Israel in tow, and in just a few short weeks Fain had seen a world of difference in the man: he became more confident and lost much of his hangdog look. But in the past week he'd reverted to his former cowed, frightened attitude. The words he had spoken this morning when he stood over the cradle and looked at Faith were the first he had volunteered in a week.

Fain stepped around the corner of the house and headed for the shed. He stopped short. Two men were coming into the house yard from the south. They were less than a hundred feet away. His first thought was that he'd left his rifle leaning against the cabin wall. His second thought was—why hadn't Olson warned him of the strangers' approach?

One of the men walked slightly ahead of the other. He was dressed in a white silk shirt with flowing sleeves cuffed at the wrist. His tan breeches were fashionably tight, and the legs were tucked into shiny black boots. He wore a broad blue ascot looped beneath his chin and a feathered, three-cornered hat. The musket in his belt looked to be silver plated. Fain instinctively noted the gun. It was second nature for him to notice firearms.

The other man wore the loose breeches and heavy boots of a riverman. A knife hung from his belt and he carried a long gun.

These observations took only a few seconds; then recognition, followed by relief so great that he let loose with a bellow of welcome.

"Fish! Damned if I didn't think the governor'd

come to call!" He strode forward and held out his hand.

"Hello, Fain. I take it you're surprised to see me."

"Surprised to see ya so all gussied up, boy. How be ya?"

"I couldn't be better. Is Simon around?"

"No, lad. We've had a heap of trouble since ya left. Berry took off to try 'n' find the land her pa filed on the same mornin' ya took off down the river. Simon's gone a-lookin' for her. He's been gone more'n a week. I'm afeared the girl's come to grief."

"It's possible he found her and they're spending some time upriver at his homestead." Fish didn't seem surprised or concerned about Berry, but that fact didn't register with Fain until later.

"Could be they did that," Fain agreed. "But it's not like the girl to not c'mon back and set Rachel's mind to rest."

Fain's eyes honed in on the man who stood behind and to the side of Fish. His feet were spread, he held a rifle up and under his arm, and his eyes roamed. He was a big man, almost as big as Fain. The two of them dwarfed Fish. "Who's your friend?"

"Emil Harrison," Fish said without looking at the man, pointedly refusing to introduce him. "Have you got the kinks worked out of the breechloader yet?"

"I've not worked on it since ya left."

"You made some progress on it before I left."

His tone caused Fain's eyes to narrow and gave him a stab of irritation. "Nothin' much come of it," he said and shrugged. Then, wanting to change the subject, he said, "Ya look fine, boy. Ya look quality."

"I *am* quality."

Hearing the hardness in the voice, Fain jerked his eyes to meet the cold blue ones of the man who had enjoyed his hospitality for the past several months. There was an aloof look of superiority on Fish's face that made Fain angry, then a quiver of apprehension traveled the length of his spine. However, he allowed none of it to show in his face, and was about to make a laughing apology, but Fish cut him off.

"Is Berry's nigger here?"

"He's over back of the cabin. We're diggin' a cellar." Something in Fish's face and the other man's attitude prompted Fain to add, "One of Simon's freighters is here, and I'm a-lookin' for Lardy anytime." There was a frozen moment of silence. Fain broke it by saying, "C'mon and see Rachel, Fish. She'll be glad to see ya."

"My name is Edmund Aston Carwild."

Fain's eyes flicked from Fish's suddenly flushed face to the other man. *When had the rifle barrel tilted in his direction?* He looked back at Fish, searching for some glimmer of the lad whom Eben had fished out of the river and who had stayed on wanting to learn gunsmithing. The face was not the same. It no longer looked boyish. The face of this man was etched in uncompromising lines. The body was the same, but it was held stiffly, arrogantly. Fain's mind was in an uproar. *Something was going to happen, and he was powerless to stop it.*

"I knowed about the Edmund Aston part. Ya never let on the other name riled ya."

"It did and it does," Fish said flatly. "But a man learns to swallow his pride...when necessary."

"Is that right?" Fain said sarcastically. He made no pretense now of being amicable. He felt a tightening in his chest. There was something deadly here. There was no doubt that Fish was going to turn aside every effort to be friendly. It would be best to get it all out in the open, so that Fain would know what he was facing. His eyes shifted to the man with the rifle. He'd seen his type roaming the river: a man who would slit his own mother's throat for a gold coin. "It's plain you're not friendly, *Mister Carwild*. Spit it out. What's eatin' atcha?"

"You've got something I want, *Mister MacCartney*—the breechloader."

"The hell you do!" Now Fain looked like a different person. The amiable man was replaced by a deadly sober one with a tight mouth and hard, fierce eyes. Anger was stamped on his face and in every line of his body.

Fish raised his brows into a haughty, contemptuous line. "Why do you think I hung around here these past few months? It certainly wasn't because I enjoyed living in a hovel. It wasn't because I was stimulated by your brilliant conversation, and it wasn't because I wanted to earn a miserly living as a gunsmith. Think, Fain. Your little secret found its way all the way downriver to Natchez."

"Ya'll get that breechloader over my dead body!" Fain roared.

"If that's what it takes, Fain. I'll get it, and over your wife's, too." He tipped his head toward the cabin.

Fain's eyes followed the gesture. A thin, rangy man with a black beard and black hair stood in the doorway. He was armed with a rifle and a musket. Fain froze as fear gripped him, but his rage came boiling out.

"Ya stinkin' low-lifed fop! Ya cowardly sonofabitch! If'n a one of ya lays a hand on my wife I'll snuff ya out like ya was a chicken!" His huge fist clenched and unclenched. The rifle that nudged his belly was the only thing that kept him from grabbing Fish by the throat.

"Calm yourself. You're one against three, soon to be four. Don't do anything foolish. You and the nigger can't stand against us."

"You're forgettin' Olson and Lardy!"

"Don't count on Olson and Lardy."

Fain opened his mouth, then snapped it shut when the import of the words sank into the turmoil in his mind.

"God Almighty! Ya murderin' sonofabitch!"

"Don't think to rile me by calling my mother a bitch. She was one. Now, are you going to cooperate, or will I have to send Jackson in there to have a little sport with Rachel?"

Somehow Fain managed to fill his lungs with air. "Ya can have the goddamn rifle, but I warn ya, Fish..."

"*Mister Carwild*. Don't insult me by calling me that name again."

"Ya killed Eben!" The words burst from Fain's lips as the thought invaded his mind. "The man saved your miserable life!"

Fish laughed. "He thought he did. I swim like a

. . . fish. He was useful for a while, but he was only a nigger. Eben was sly. He did a lot of snooping. I shouldn't have been so quick. I should have taught him a lesson before I killed him."

Fain was speechless. He shook his head numbly. "I just wouldn't-a thought it of ya."

Fish laughed again. "I'm a good actor. I should be, I've had the best training London has to offer," he added dryly.

Fain examined the smirking face with its belligerent blue eyes. "Jesus Christ! I admit I was fooled. Take the gun and go."

"Thank you, but I'll wait until you finish it. I'll give you two days. Meanwhile, one of my men will keep Rachel company in the cabin."

Fain started forward but was stopped by the hard probe of the rifle barrel in his stomach. "If'n you scum touch 'er, I'll. . ."

"That'll depend on you. Oh, Israel," Fish called. "Come here, boy."

Israel hadn't heard what the white men were talking about, but he saw the rifle barrel against Fain's stomach. Something was wrong, he knew, and Fish was part of it.

"Yassuh." Israel hid his fear behind the mask of a simpleton.

"My men and I will be here for a few days. I'll need you to stay close in case I need you. Do you think you can do that?"

"Yassuh."

"Do you know what will happen to you if you disobey me?"

"Nawsuh."

"You must have helped Fain bury Eben. I cut his throat from ear to ear." Fish whipped out a small dirk and held it against Israel's windpipe.

"Ah...ah...." He rolled his eyes helplessly toward Fain.

"I know," Fish said as if talking to a child. He removed the dirk. "You'll mind me, won't you? Now go tell Rachel she can serve the noon meal."

"I wanta talk to my wife." Fain angrily thrust the rifle away from him.

"Of course. We'll both talk to her." Fish walked beside him toward the cabin, and the man with the rifle fell in behind.

Rachel stood silently waiting in the doorway, her face white, her hands clenched together in front of her. Israel passed her without looking at her and disappeared around the corner of the house. She backed away from the doorway as the men approached.

"Stand over the kid, Jackson. If either of them makes a bad move, bash its head with your rifle butt."

"Nooooo...!" Rachel screamed and ran toward the cradle. Emil grabbed her arm and jerked her to a halt.

"Get your hands off her!" Fain roared and lunged forward.

Moving swiftly, Jackson stepped between them and clubbed Fain on the side of the head with his rifle barrel. Fain staggered but didn't fall. He swore viciously and shook his head like a maddened bull, spattering blood from his wound over the rest of his face.

"Rachel," Fish said evenly, "unless you want me

to hurt Fain or the baby, do as I say. We will be here until Fain gives me the breechloader. One of my men will stay here with you, just to make sure Fain works swiftly and diligently. And, Fain, if you had worked steadily on that rifle and completed it, I'd have taken it off your hands and none of this would be happening. Tut ... tut ..." He shook his head in mock dismay. "You've developed some sloppy work habits since you took a wife."

"I don't understand you," Rachel said. "You were always such a ... gentleman."

"I *am* a gentleman, Rachel." Fish grinned, picked up a cloth that lay on the work counter, and tossed it to her. "Bind up Fain's head. I don't want him to bleed to death. Then put the meal on the table and we'll sit down and eat like civilized folk."

Rachel poured water into the washbasin and wet the cloth. Her frightened heart was throbbing so violently that she was having a hard time breathing. She passed the cradle on her way to Fain and glanced down at the sleeping child. Jackson swung a chair over beside the cradle and sat down. He placed his rifle across his knees, the barrel pointed at Fain. Rachel looked into his hard black eyes and saw no mercy there.

She knew that the wound on Fain's forehead should be stitched, and she told him so. He shook his head numbly, his eyes holding hers, trying to tell her how sorry he was that he had allowed them to get into this fix. Rachel didn't speak. She stopped the bleeding with wet compresses and bound a strip of cloth around his head to hold them in place. Before she left him she pressed his shoulder reassuringly. Her features were composed, her hands steady. *She'd not shame him by breaking down*. She walked calmly to the door and threw the bloody water out into the yard.

Swiftly and efficiently she dished up the meat and cabbage from the kettle and took corn pone from the griddle. Not a word was spoken until she looked at her husband and nodded.

Fain made no move toward the table.

"You'd better eat, Fain," Fish said. "You'll be working until that gun is finished." He carefully removed his hat and hung it on the peg beside the door, then smoothed his blond hair and straightened his ascot.

"I wanta talk to my wife."

"That's a reasonable request—but eat first." Fish seemed to delight in having the upper hand.

Fain sat in his customary place at the head of the table. Fish and Emil sat on the same side. Rachel stood beside the fireplace and spooned more corn pone onto the griddle. Jackson remained sitting beside the cradle. To add to Rachel's irritation, he spat on her clean floor.

Emil filled his bowl and slurped noisily. When he pounded his mug against the table to demand more, Rachel grabbed it angrily out of his hand. Fain scarcely touched his meal, and Fish ate his daintily.

"I take my tea with milk, Rachel," he said as if speaking to a serving girl.

Always before it had been *Miss* Rachel or *Mrs*. MacCartney. Rachel prayed that Fain wouldn't notice the lack of respect and make a fuss. Fish looked at her now as if he despised her. Why? It was as if he had never eaten at her table, laughed, visited, and politely offered to fetch water or firewood. But she didn't have time to ponder this. Fain pushed back his chair and rose to his feet.

"I'll speak to my wife... *now!*"

"Go ahead," Fish said pleasantly. "We'll not wake the child. Stay in the dogtrot where I can see you. Remember"—his voice hardened—"it wouldn't bother me at all to bust the little bastard's head."

Chapter 16

Fain took Rachel's hand and they went out the door. On the far side of the dogtrot, he turned his back to the watching eyes and pulled her in front of him.

"What's happened to him? What does he want?" Rachel whispered urgently.

"The bastard wants my breechloader. Jesus Christ! I was blind to him. Now that I think of it, Jeff and Will had a queer feelin' about him—they said as much." His big hands gripped her shoulders. "I ain't sure what he'll do if'n I give the breechloader to him. I gotta stall, darlin'. I gotta stall 'n' hope somethin' happens to give me a edge."

"Lardy should be comin' anytime," Rachel said hopefully. Then, as if suddenly remembering: "I'll send Israel with some dinner for Mr. Olson."

Fain hesitated. "He ain't around. He might've took to the woods. He might've gone for help, but we can't count on it."

"Fain! Look at me. They killed him! Merciful heaven!"

Fain didn't deny it. "If ya get a chance, get a musket out of the chest and hide it in your apron. Don't use it less'n they're a-forcin' ya. Understand?"

Rachel nodded. "I'm afraid for you. Don't lose your temper... please...."

"Hold Faith as much as ya can. Pinch her to make her cry, if'n ya have to." He put his lips to her ear and spoke rapidly. "Lordy, what I wouldn't give to see Will and Jeff and Light. But there's not much chance. Will and Jeff are in Natchez, 'n' no tellin' where Light is." He bent and kissed her trembling mouth.

"You think they'll kill us after you give them the gun, don't you?"

"Nooo... There'd be no reason...."

"Don't try to keep it from me, love." She placed her fingers on his lips. Fain refused to meet her eyes. He closed his and kissed her hard. "I don't understand why he'd do this for one gun," Rachel whispered and pressed her forehead to his chin.

"He'll take it back east, register it in his name like it was his. Then he'll get a gunsmith to make up a batch. Loadin' c'n be done in half the time. Think what that would mean durin' a war."

"Fain!" Fish said sharply from the doorway. "There's only one musket and two rifles in here." A helpless groan escaped Fain's throat. "Did Berry take one of the muskets?" When neither Fain nor Rachel answered him, Fish shrugged and crossed to the other room. He came out minutes later with two more rifles. He handed them to Emil, who looked them over with a greedy gleam in his eye.

"Now 'ere's a gun, guv'nor," he said, revealing a cockney accent. He lifted one of the guns and sighted down the barrel. His rough hands caressed the smooth stock.

Fish laughed. "There's a dozen more in there just like it."

"Ya bloody well hit the mark, guv'l"

"My friend Fain is cagey, Emil. They're all without firing pins."

"My gawd!"

"We'll take care of that before we leave. I'm sure Fain can be . . . persuaded to give us the missing part."

"'At ain't all we'll take care of, guv'l" His bloodshot, watery eyes roamed over Rachel. "She's a foine-bodied wench. I've 'ad me aplenty, but I ain't 'ad me one like 'er."

"Ya goddamn English bastard! Ya lay a hand on my woman 'n' I'll strip the goddamn flesh off'n your mangy bones!" Fain almost exploded with anger.

"Give me the breechloader, Fain, and you've got nothing to worry about. I'll keep my men under control." Fish stuck his head through the doorway and called to Jackson, "I'm going out to the shack where Fain works. Emil will keep watch. You know what to do if there's trouble."

Rachel heard Faith crying. Reluctant to leave Fain, her eyes clung to his. Her heart almost broke at the helpless look she saw in their depths.

"Try not to worry. We'll be all right," she said, forcing her voice to be steady although her insides were a mishmash of tangled nerves and her heart was beating altogether too fast. She placed a soft kiss on Fain's lips and left him.

Faith was crying lustily, her arms and legs waving and kicking. Jackson sat with his chair tilted back against the wall. As soon as Rachel entered the room, his black eyes squinted and he stared at her without blinking. She snatched the baby up and retreated to the far side of the room. With her back to him, she unbuttoned her dress and put the baby to her breast. Faith whimpered until her hungry little mouth found Rachel's nipple.

"Turn 'round."

Rachel froze on hearing the softly spoken command. She looked over her shoulder as the two front legs of the chair struck the floor.

"Sit." He indicated the rocking chair that was scarcely three feet from where he sat. Rachel stayed where she was, hugging the small, warm body close to her. "Ain't goin' ta tell ya agin."

Fear caused her legs to tremble. She snatched a cloth from the workbench and draped it over her breast and the baby's face. With every ounce of courage she could muster, she lifted her head proudly, moved to the rocker, and sat down. A big, rough hand grabbed the cloth and jerked it away. Her face flamed, but she refused to look at him. She could feel his eyes as acutely as if they were stroking her flesh.

"I likes ta look at titties."

The blunt words caused a crimson tide to flood her face. She lifted the baby higher, trying to shield her breast from his eyes. He reached out with the rifle barrel and prodded her arm down. She looked up in alarm. He was grinning at her. He had two front teeth missing. While she watched, he spat between the gaps. The spittle hit the floor with a splash. Rachel shivered with disgust—he was sickening!

"I nussed a squaw's titties a few winters back when I come down with the ague. Ever since I get me a cravin' for nussin'."

The horror of what he was implying caused hot rage to bubble up out of Rachel. He was an animal! At that moment she decided there were things worse than death.

"You're a filthy excuse for a man! I'll die before I let you touch me! I'll kill myself and my child. Then how will you force my husband to finish the gun?"

"Shee-it! I ain't carin' if'n that sissy little fop gets *that* gun. What's here is more'n enough for me. I'll nuss ya when the time's right. Ya'll not make no fuss, neither—if'n I hang that youngun up by its heels."

Rachel looked into the dark abyss of his eyes, searching for some spark of human compassion. There was only animal lust and cold indifference. She opened her mouth to fling condemning words at him, then closed it. Nothing she could say would penetrate the hard shell of his conscience.

He laughed when he saw the despair written on her face, then he spat again. Her despair changed to revulsion, but she forced herself to speak with some semblence of control.

"If you're going to eat, do it. I must clear away the nooning and start the supper meal."

"Ya can bring it ta me. I ain't had a sightly woman dishin' up my vittles for a spell."

When the baby's small stomach was full she went back to sleep. Rachel slipped her nipple from the baby's mouth and closed her dress almost in the same motion. The child was wet, but she couldn't bring herself to bend over the cradle to change her with Jackson sitting so close. She had decided she would scream as loud as she could if he grabbed her. She was almost sure that Fish would come if he heard her. He wanted Fain to stay calm so that he could work on the gun.

Rachel almost breathed a sigh of relief when Fish came into the room. "If I remember right, there's another rifle around here. Where is it?"

"I don't know," she replied curtly. "I've never concerned myself with Fain's guns. I know nothing about them."

"You know enough to kill a man with one—or was it two?" His eyes flicked over her arrogantly.

Rachel returned his look contemptuously. He's a little man trying to act big, she thought. I wonder if he resents his size? She almost voiced the question, then she said, "We were defending ourselves, as you know."

He ignored what she said. "There's another rifle around here. Where is it?"

"Simon may have taken it when he went to look for Berry, or it may be the one Fain sold." Rachel dished up a bowl of meat and cabbage from the pot, stuck a spoon into it, and handed it to Jackson, who managed to touch her hand when he took it.

"Who'd he sell it to?"

"I don't know. I just heard him say he sold one to someone passing on the river. I don't know if it was before or after you left."

"Fain said he sold it to a trapper."

"He don't bring riffraff to the house, as you well

know." Rachel tried not to let the relief show in her voice. How lucky that both of them had hit upon the same reason for a gun to be missing!

"An old friend of yours will be here sometime this evening. You remember Linc Smith? You or Berry killed his partner and Berry shot him in the face. He's not a pretty sight to look at these days."

Rachel felt the color drain from her face. She seemed to go numb. She closed her eyes in an effort to control the darkness that threatened to close in on her. Thank God her back was to him and he wouldn't get the satisfaction of knowing his words were like a blow to her midsection. Her mind registered the sound of Jackson wolfing down his food. By the time she turned to face Fish, she was in control once again.

"He was never a pretty sight to look at."

"He's worse now. He lives to get his hands on Berry. Do you think he'd be satisfied if I deliver you up to him?"

"Men such as you and Linc Smith are never satisfied."

"Maybe." He strutted around the room, looked out the window, then spun around on his heels as if he were performing on the stage. "I'm a whole lot smarter than you give me credit for, Rachel. I got Berry out of the way. She couldn't see me as poor Fish, but she'll change her tune when she meets Edmund Aston Carwild in Saint Charles in a few days."

"You've . . . got Berry?" At that moment Rachel could have killed him with her bare hands.

He laughed at the shocked expression on her face. "She wanted to find her pa's miserable land.

I pointed it out to her on the map and then made arrangements for a couple of Indians I know to meet her there. Those two will do anything for horses. They'll bring her to me, if they want the fifty head of horses I've promised them." He paused dramatically. "It's better than Linc Smith getting his hands on her. Don't you agree it was a smart move?"

"Fifty head? Shee-it!" Jackson said. "Thar ain't that many horses in one bunch this side of the river!"

"I know it and you know it, but the Shawnee don't know it," Fish stated sternly, angered by Jackson's input into the conversation. He hooked his thumbs in the waistband of his breeches and spread his legs. "Berry will be a sensation in London and Paris dressed as the wife of Edmund Carwild should be dressed."

Rachel could hardly stand to look at him. He reminded her of a bantam rooster they had on the farm in Ohio. All he could do was strut and crow!

"Simon will find Berry. Fain says there's not a better tracker in the territory than Light, and he taught Simon."

Fish shrugged. "I told them to expect Simon to catch up. They'll know what to do. Linc made a trip up to his place to see if he had doubled back. Light went downriver with a bunch of Osage, and Will and Jeff are in Natchez, so we'll not be troubled by them."

"More!" Jackson pounded the floor with his bowl. Faith woke, let out a whimper, and went back to sleep.

"Get it yourself!" Rachel hissed and turned back to the work bench. There was silence; she waited breathlessly. Then she heard the clang of the dipper being dipped into the iron pot. *Filthy animals! Varmints! Linc Smith coming here! Oh, my God! And I thought Asa Warfield the lowest of all humans!*

"Where's the nigger?" Fish asked, then went to the door and yelled, "Israel!"

"Yassuh?" Israel appeared almost instantly.

"What are you doing?"

"Diggin' the cellar."

"Get a bucket of water."

"Yassuh." Israel sidled into the kitchen and picked up the bucket.

"See if there are any eggs," Fish said. "And kill a chicken—"

"No!" Rachel said firmly. "We've got meat in the smokehouse."

"Kill a chicken, Israel. A fat hen." Fish followed him to the door. "I want chicken and dumplings tonight, Rachel. You made it once before with prairie chicken. It'll be better with a nice fat hen."

The snort that came from Jackson irritated her and she turned on him. "You ... shut up!"

When Israel brought the plucked, gutted chicken, Rachel tightened her lips and took it from his hand. What did it matter? They'd be killed as soon as Fish had the gun. She felt so helpless, and so sorry for Faith. At least she and Fain had lived and loved. Faith's life had just begun. There was no danger that the child could tell what had happened here. They couldn't be *that* cruel! Rachel felt tears sting her eyes and blinked them away.

Almost as soon as Rachel began to pick the pinfeathers from the tough skin of the chicken, she realized that Israel had killed the crippled old rooster that had lost his harem of hens to the spry young rooster Simon had brought. She almost smiled. Israel knew how she treasured those hens! She wondered if he had thought to clean the chicken away from the house so that Fish wouldn't notice the red feathers. Her hens were fluffy white. She hurried with cleaning, cut the meat and covered it with water, and swung the pot over the flame.

The silent man who watched her made her flesh crawl. She went to the cradle and picked up the baby. Faith was sopping wet, as Rachel had known she would be. Ignoring the eyes that followed her every move, she took cloth and a dry gown from the chest and changed the baby's clothes on the kitchen table. When she finished, she held the child upright against her shoulder and walked out the door.

She heard the front legs of the chair hit the floor, then felt a heavy hand on her shoulder. Jackson moved fast for a big man—she would remember that.

"Where're you goin'?"

"To get my dry wash." She shrugged away from his hand.

"Leave the youngun."

"I'll not do it," she said harshly. "You've got a gun. Are you such a poor shot you're scared a woman carryin' a babe'll get away from you?" she taunted.

"I c'n hit a jaybird in the arse at eighty yards."

"My husband can knock a gnat off a jaybird at a hundred yards and not ruffle a feather," she retorted. She turned her back and looked around. She knew that Fain and Fish would be in the old cabin where Fish had stayed when he lived here and where Fain now worked on his guns. Israel was nowhere to be seen, so she called his name. He appeared, like a shadow, from around the corner of the freight wagons.

Rachel went toward him and said, "Help me get my wash off the bushes." She walked past him and he followed. Holding Faith to her with one arm, she carefully lifted the clothes from the thorny bushes with the other and piled them in Israel's arms. Jackson stood in the yard and watched. She was facing him, so she didn't dare speak to Israel. Even if Jackson couldn't hear what she was saying, he would see her lips move.

"Hide the gun for mastah in cellar dirt..." The words were the merest whisper.

Rachel's startled eyes sought the black man's and she blinked to let him know she understood. When she placed Fain's shirt on the pile in his arms, she managed to press his hand. Jackson edged closer and there wasn't a chance for her to tell Israel to try to get the word to Fain. But somehow she knew that he would. She was so grateful that she wanted to cry.

Fain came in for the evening meal with Fish and Emil. He went straight to Rachel and took her in his arms.

"You all right?"

"Yes. How's your head?" Her fingers adjusted the bandage.

"It's all right." He kissed her forehead, then went to the cradle to look down and stroke the baby's head with his fingertips. He looked long and hard into the face of the man who sat beside the cradle before he took his seat at the table.

Jackson went outside to stand guard while Emil

ate his meal. He gulped from the bowl and threw chicken bones into the fireplace. Fish ignored him. There was almost dead silence during the meal. Rachel took the opportunity to nurse the baby. She sat in the rocker with a cloth over her breast. By the time the men had finished eating, it was dark.

Voices in the dogtrot caused her to jerk her nipple from the mouth of her sleeping child and quickly fasten her dress. Her heart began its frightened flutter, and her eyes sought Fain's. She continued to look at him. Everything seemed to go slightly out of focus. It seemed to her that she was standing a long way off, watching a scene unfold that had nothing to do with her. Things in the room were hazy, blurred. She shook her head and saw Fain coming toward her....

"Are ya all right, love?"

"I'd like a drink of water."

Fain glanced at Fish as if daring him to interfere, then brought the dipper and held it to her lips. She drank. Fish went to the door, and Rachel held up her lips to be kissed.

"Gun's under cellar dirt," she whispered.

"And I love you, too, darlin'." Fain's voice was loud enough to reach Fish.

He took the dipper and moved aside. Nothing could have prepared Rachel for the sight of the man who stood in the doorway beside Fish.

He looked to be more an animal than a man. His hair was long and shaggy. Beard covered one side of his face. The other side was sunken, twisted, scarred from the corner of his mouth up and over what had once been a cheekbone and into an empty eye socket. The near side of his face was completely

devoid of hair. The healing of the skin had pulled
his mouth to one side and down, so that spittle
dripped continuously. His buckskin pants were stiff
with grease and dirt. The cloth shirt that hung on
his scrawny frame was filthy beyond recognition and
hung in tatters. About him was the odor of sweat
and of animal blood and fat.

Fish backed away from him and stood against the
wall.

"Put the child down, Rachel, and dish up some
food for my friend."

Rachel stood immediately. She was afraid that
Fain would lunge at the man and be killed. Keeping
her eyes averted, she lay Faith in the cradle and
filled a bowl with food. She set it on the table and
moved away.

"Get back to work, Fain. You've worked at night
before."

Fain watched Linc creep to the table like a stalking animal. He hadn't taken his one eye off Rachel's
slim figure.

"I'll not move a step till I know my wife 'n' child
are safe."

"They'll not be harmed as long as you work. I'll
see to that."

"Your tellin' me ain't enough. I want 'em behind
barred doors," Fain said firmly. "I can't think of
what I'm doin' for worryin' about them."

"All right. Rachel can sleep in the other room
and she can bar the door. But I'll have a man outside
to blast a hole in that door if you make a wrong
move."

"No! I'll not have Linc Smith in this cabin with
only a plank door 'tween him 'n' my wife."

"Linc will stay outside."

"Ya ain't a-tellin' me where I'll stay. Ya said the other'n'd be here. Emil says she ain't." Linc stood and faced Fish, broth dripping down his chin.

"She'll be here just like I promised. Now finish eating and go down to the landing and make sure no one comes in on us."

"I ain't goin' ta be stuck off down there," Linc said, growling, and took a step toward Fish.

Fish stood his ground. "You'll do as I say. You made a deal. You help me get what I want, and I help you get what you want."

Rachel's mind was spinning dizzily: Fish is bluffing Linc. He's planning to leave the country with Berry, and Linc thinks she's coming here. I wonder what would happen if I told him.

"I'll be all right, Fain. If one of them touches me, I'll scream so loud you'll hear me."

Fain turned on Fish angrily. "If'n that happens, ya might as well kill me, 'cause I'll not put a hand to that gun."

"Goddammit! I'm tired of you telling me what you'll do and not do. You've got tonight and to-morrow to get it in shape so you can test it. You know what's got to be done. You've told me a hundred times. You've even got the bands made to go around the stock and barrel."

"I've got to make a part stout enough to hold the charge," Fain's voice boomed. His frustration and anger turned his face a dark red.

"I know what you've got to do. You brought back a dozen designs from that smithy in Louisville, along with enough forged barrels, locks, and hammers to outfit an expedition." Fish cocked his head and grinned. "Do you think I don't know you plan to furnish Pike firearms for his trip west? You thought to assemble them this winter while he's up north."

"So you're working for Manuel Lisa," Fain said, sneering. "I thought him too smart to send a boy to do a man's job."

"Be as insulting as you want, Fain. It'll all be the same in the end." Jackson came into the room then and Fish spoke to him. "Let the woman and the kid go in there." He jerked his head toward the sleeping room.

Fain picked up the cradle and Rachel followed him with a candle. He placed the cradle beside the bed, and as he bent to kiss the infant's forehead he slipped a small dirk under the blanket. His eyes sought Rachel's to be sure she had seen the movement. She smiled, set the candle on the table, and went into his arms.

"The past month has been the most wonderful of my life," she whispered. "I love you."

"I love you, lass. Don't ya be givin' up," he murmured in her ear. "Bar the door. I'll see ya in the mornin'." He left her and pushed past Fish, who stood in the doorway.

Rachel shut the flimsy plank door that had been built only for privacy and hooked the leather strap over the peg. One push with a heavy boot was all it would take to gain entrance. She looked around for something to prop against the door and remembered the planks Fain had bought from a keelboat captain to use as flooring. As quietly as she could, she pulled the heavy slabs of wood from beneath the bed and wedged them against the door. At least it would require more than one blow to break it down, and she wouldn't be taken by surprise.

She blew out the candle and felt her way along the wall to the tin chamber pot. It would be such a blessed relief to empty her bladder! A series of scenes passed before her mind's eye as she sat on the cool rim: Berry flinging the pot at Linc Smith, and the whip raised in Asa's hand and the knife that came out of the darkness to pin his arm to the wagon bed. She thought of the riverman trying to claw his way into the wagon and the shot she had fired that slammed her against the trunk. Then—Fain picking her up off the stone floor where the crazy old crone had dragged her. Tears filled her eyes and rolled down her cheeks. She and Berry had been through so much. Now this. Berry would never know what had happened to her and Fain and Faith. Fain would never know the joy of birthing his own child.

Rachel sat on the edge of the bed and pressed her fingers to her eyes as if to hold back the weight of tears that strived for release against a barrier of despair. It seemed to her as if hours passed. The light from the other room no longer came through the cracks in the door. Rachel thought of the table full of soiled dishes and the unclean workbench. Just this morning she had scrubbed it with the suds left from the wash. This morning seemed a million years away. She wished fervently for Fain. This might be the last night of their lives, and they couldn't even spend it together. She cried silently, inwardly, the dry tears of hopelessness.

Faith woke and she put her to her breast. She

took comfort in the small body and held her lovingly.

At first she thought the small scratching sounds she heard came from the ropes on the bed when she shifted her weight. She listened. She heard the faintest sound. It was coming from the other side of the wall—the side where Fain and Israel were digging the cellar. She got down on her knees and crawled to the wall. She put her ear to it. Someone was digging! It had to be Israel! Was he trying to dig under the wall and pass her the rifle?

Rachel felt her way to the cradle, fumbled for the dirk Fain had slipped beneath the cover, and laid Faith on her back. The baby began to cry.

"I'm sorry, darlin'," she whispered. "I know you hate lying on your back." She went back to the wall, listened for a moment, then began to dig frantically with the dirk. The baby's wails covered the scraping sounds. The child's cries became more insistent and Rachel began to croon as if she were rocking and cuddling her. "It's all right, darlin'. Mama's got you. Go to sleep."

Faith was angry. Not only was she lying on her back, she hadn't finished her meal. She protested in the only way she knew how.

"Bye-o, my baby. Bye-o, my baby. Mama's got to tend the fire, while Papa's gone a-huntin'." Rachel sang softly as she dug and pulled the dirt away with her hands.

To let Israel know she was digging from the inside, she tapped lightly on the wall with the handle of the dirk. He answered with a like signal. Rachel's heart pounded furiously. Panic was almost choking her. Israel was taking such a chance! Oh, why hadn't they taken the time to teach him to fire the gun? Fish and his men would kill him without a second thought if they caught him. Rachel dug faster and continued to croon to Faith in a breathless voice, thanking God that her daughter had powerful lungs.

Finally they broke through the wall that separated them and she touched Israel's hand. A few minutes later she felt the butt of the rifle. She was trying to pull it through the opening when a pounding on the door caused her heart to drop to her toes.

"Hush up that youngun!"

"I'm tryin' to," she called. "She's got colic."

"Well, nuss 'er, less'n ya wants to nuss me." There was a low, vulgar chuckle.

Rachel pulled the rifle free and shoved it under the bed. She snatched her daughter up in her arms and opened her dress. The hungry, seeking little mouth found the nipple and with a gurgle of contentment sucked the milk into her mouth. The silence beat in Rachel's ears like a drum. Then heavy footsteps moved away from the door and tears of relief rolled down Rachel's face.

Faith fell into an exhausted sleep. Rachel kissed her tiny face and laid her on her stomach. "You done good, little love. I hope I get the chance to tell your papa how you helped."

Moving slowly and deliberately, Rachel drew the rifle from under the bed. She felt in the barrel to see if it was free of dirt, then carefully lifted the end of the grass pad that covered the ropes and hid it within easy reach. She raked the loose dirt back into the hole. Israel had blocked it from the other side. It filled quickly. Feeling her way carefully, she took a hide from the pile she was saving to stitch into a mattress for the feather bed and placed it over the fresh dirt. Then she set the chamber pot on top of it.

Satisfied that she had done all she could do, she found a cloth under the pillow in the cradle and tied the dirk to her thigh.

Somehow, I'll kill Fish, she promised herself. She lay down on the side of the bed Fain slept on and buried her face in his pillow.

Chapter 17

The trail along the riverbank was white with blossoming wild plums and dogwood trees. Frogs peeped in the marshy places, crows cawed. A flock of birds suddenly erupted into screaming flight. Berry laughed with delight, tilted her head against Simon's shoulder, and watched the flock assemble, break apart, and reassemble overhead. Simon pulled Star to a halt. They shaded their eyes with their hands to peer up into the bright morning sunlight. The metallic green plumage and red-feathered heads of the flock gleamed like fire as they soared, dipped, and spiraled upward before disappearing over the tops of the towering trees.

"They're so pretty!" Berry said quietly, awestruck by the spectacular scene.

"They're parakeets," Simon explained. "In the winter they roost in great flocks. I've seen so many in one tree it looked as if the tree was lit by a thousand candles."

Star danced in place, eager to be moving. Simon

eased up on the reins. The horse moved slowly, not due to the added weight of the girl on his back, but because it was hot and for once his master was not in a hurry.

Sitting astride in front of Simon, his arms around her, Berry wiggled her firm buttocks against his groin, threw her arms wide, and laughed, a bubbling free laugh.

"I'm so happy, Simon, my love. We'll be together every day, every night, for the rest of our lives. I can hardly wait to tell Rachel. How long before we get there?"

"Stop your wiggling or we'll not get there at all," he cautioned teasingly. "It's not more than a couple of miles."

"I like wearing your pants." Happy laughter gurgled up. She held out her legs, her bare feet protruding from the rolled-up buckskin breeches. "I might make myself a pair."

"Ah . . . no! I like feeling up under your skirt." His hand slid down her thigh. "Nope . . . I'll not have my wife in pants."

Berry, hearing his chuckle, turned and, looking deeply into his warm dark eyes, held her lips up for a kiss. So this was how it was going to be from now on. Just the two of them, able to run, laugh, play, and make love when and where they wanted. Little flickers of anticipation shivered through her. Her urgent mouth found his, yet he kept his lips firmly closed from the onslaught of her determined little tongue.

"Behave yourself, you little witch," he said with a growl. "If we stop we won't get to Fain's till suppertime."

"You know you want to stop and roll in the grass with me," she said in an exaggerated, seductive whisper. Her fingers worked their way up and down his hard thigh. "You've already introduced me to the pleasures of the flesh, made me a fallen woman, ruined me." Her laughing green eyes probed his smiling dark ones.

"You're a tempting little baggage!" His arms tightened and she nestled against his chest. "Now sit still, or . . . I'll swat that little butt that keeps wigglin' against me." His voice in her ear was warm, loving, teasing.

"All right. But don't blame me when Rachel sees that great lump in your pants." She turned and pressed her back to his chest. He felt the tremors of giggles she was trying to suppress.

Simon tenderly swept the ebony hair back from her neck and placed his lips there. He moved his hand from her rib cage to her breast and felt her heart beating rapidly. An exquisite pang of aching tenderness shot through him when he thought of all this small woman had endured. She turned to look at him. Her green eyes gleamed with mischief, then closed when he pressed her lips with his in a hard kiss. Her face found refuge beneath his chin. The brim of his hat shaded her cheeks from the noon sun. He nourished her in his arms, and they were silent in their contentment.

It was early afternoon when Berry and Simon arrived at Fain's homestead. Simon had put his heels to the stallion a quarter of a mile back and they galloped into the clearing between the barn and the house. Berry's laughter had preceded them. Conscious only of each other, they were unaware of the hostile eyes that watched them. Berry glanced around quickly, disappointed that Rachel wasn't there to meet her.

"Rachel! Rachel!" she shouted as Simon pulled Star to a halt. She threw her leg up and over the horse's broad neck, grasped Simon's hand, and dropped to her feet. She ran toward the house, her black hair flying. "C'mon, slow poke," she called over her shoulder.

A man in a feathered, three-cornered hat stepped from the dogtrot and her running feet stopped abruptly. His sudden appearance startled her. The fact that he was so richly dressed was almost as startling. Her green eyes blinked, rounded, then sparkled.

"Fish? Oh, Fish, you look so grand, I didn't know you."

"Hello, Berry. I see Simon brought you back."

"Yes, he found me. I'm anxious to see Rachel." She moved to go around him. He moved with her and blocked the entrance. She looked at him questioningly, tilted her head, and grinned. "I didn't find my pa's land. It was a wild goose chase, Fish. I should never have gone. Oh, here's Rachel...."

Rachel came through the doorway, her face white and haggard. Berry rushed to her and threw her arms around her.

"Berry... oh, Berry..." Rachel sobbed.

"I'm sorry. Truly I am. I swear to goodness, Rachel. I don't know what made me do such a dumb thing."

"It's not only that...." Rachel grasped her shoulders and turned her around to face the yard. "Something terrible is happening here. Look..."

Simon stood beside his horse, a man on each side

of him. One of them held the barrel of a long gun against his side. Berry blinked, stared, then took a step forward. Rachel grabbed her arm and held her back.

"What... ? Is that..." she stammered, her eyes on the man in the tattered shirt. Beard covered one side of his face, the other was horribly mutilated.

"Linc Smith," Rachel whispered hoarsely.

"Linc Smith?" Berry jerked away from Rachel and spun around frantically, looking for a weapon. She came up against Fish. She grasped his arms, her green eyes looking into his imploringly. "Oh, Fish! He's a terrible man, a beast! Do something!"

Fish stood impassive, his arms folded across his chest.

"He'll not help, Berry. He's with them. He brought them here," Rachel said scathingly. She couldn't resist letting him see her deep-seated contempt.

Berry stood for a dozen heartbeats as if she had turned to stone. Then, as if jerked by invisible strings, she whirled, her eyes wild, her hair flying. Rage blinded her. All she could see was Simon with the rope Linc Smith had looped around his neck. With a scream of rage, she charged from the dog-trot.

Fish caught her and flung her against the rough logs as she tried to dart around him. She screamed curses and clawed at his face. Her nails raked his smooth cheek. She felt the crack of his hand against her face, but still she fought, disoriented, half-crazed. Her knee came up between his legs to render him helpless, but he blocked it and they fell to the ground. Berry kicked, bit, and screamed like a wild thing. Her flying fists connected, but she felt no pain as her knuckles split on his sharp teeth. Blow followed blow as he struck her face in an effort to subdue her. Strengthened by her crazed fear for Simon, she fought until a final blow drew a curtain of darkness over her.

Berry awakened to a throbbing headache. Every beat of her heart felt like a hammer pounding on her head. She tried to press her temples with her fingers. Something was wrong. Her eyes flew open, and in spite of the blinding light she saw that her wrists were bound together. Her ankles also were tied.

"Simon..." she croaked through swollen lips. She tasted blood in her mouth. "Simon..." she cried in anguish as near hysteria closed in on her.

"Shhh..." Rachel knelt beside her. The wet cloth on Berry's face soothed her flesh, but not her troubled thoughts.

"Where's Simon?" Berry whispered. "What's goin' on?" Her eyes were frantic in their search of the room. She managed to get an elbow under her and raised her head and shoulders. Rachel, with a dipper of water, blocked her view.

"Drink this. Please, Berry... don't make a fuss. Simon's tied up outside."

Berry drank the water, then swung her bound feet over the edge of the bunk and sat up. Now she saw a man with a bushy black beard sitting beside the cradle, his chair tipped back against the wall.

"God Almighty!" she murmured and shook her head as if to rid it of the puzzling thoughts that filled it.

"Talk so I c'n hear ya," Jackson demanded.

Rachel talked. She left out nothing. "Fish killed Eben the morning you left. He bragged that he had gotten you out of the way and how you would be returned to him by the Indians who took you." Rachel spoke dispassionately. She told of the cold-blooded killing of Olson and said that she suspected they had killed Lardy too. "Fish wants the breech-loader Fain is working on. He wants to sell it for a large amount of money. He's given him today and tonight to finish it."

"What's he watchin' us for? What does he think we can do?" Berry swung resentful, hate-filled eyes to the man in the chair.

"If Fain don't do what Fish says, he'll...kill us...." Rachel broke down and sobs long held in check broke from her throat. She hid her face in her hands until she could choke off her cries.

"I just never dreamed that Fish was like this," Berry said, still looking across the room at the bearded woodsman who leaned so carelessly against the wall.

"Fish's rotten clear through. He'd have to be to kill a man who had saved his life," Rachel said venomously. "All the time he was here, he was play-acting. He bragged about it. He'd heard about the gun and came here with the excuse that he wanted to be a gunsmith. Fain is so good, so trusting. He took him at his word."

"But how'd he get tied up with Linc Smith?"

"He's using him, just as he's using those other two stupid fools that came with him. They're like big, dumb ox. They've not got brains enough to know they'll get nothin' from the gun." Rachel raised her voice and looked pointedly at Jackson. "Does she have to stay tied up? Are you afraid she'll overpower you and take your gun?" she taunted.

"Ya c'n take 'em off her feet. Her hands stay."

Rachel knelt and worked at the strip of rawhide. Berry looked over her head to the man in the chair. His eyes were as dark and intent as the ugly Indian's had been and she felt chilled to the bone. Rachel stood, pulled Berry to her feet, and turned to the man whose presence was like a deadly gloom hanging over them.

"You may be part human after all, Mr. Jackson," she said with a proud lift to her chin.

Jackson said nothing, but pinpoints of light glittered in his dark eyes and his head moved in the briefest of nods.

"They'll kill Simon." The dreaded words burst from Berry. She felt as if she were about to tumble into the pit of darkness again. "Can't we do something?"

Rachel put her arm around her and led her to the window. Silhouetted against the red wash of the evening sky, Simon hung, shirtless, his bound hands pulled up and tied to a branch. His head hung between his arms, and his legs sagged. He was making an effort to stiffen his legs to take the pressure off his arms. Berry couldn't see his face, but she could see the red, bleeding cuts on his back made by a whip.

"God in heaven!" Berry whispered in a stricken voice. "They'll kill him!"

"He's not dead yet," Rachel hissed. "Buck up, for God's sake. We can't do a thing if we fall to pieces."

"What can we do?" Berry's lips barely moved. Huge tears blurred the figure of her lover.

Rachel put her arms around her, pressed her cheek to hers, and whispered, "A rifle under my mattress. We've got to bide our time." She moved back and with her fingertips wiped the tears from Berry's cheeks. "These men had all merciful feeling crushed out of them a long time ago. They have few human qualities. They've lived as vultures and scavengers so long they don't know how to live like decent folks. I doubt that Mr. Jackson ever lived in a house. He spits on the floor!"

Berry vaguely heard Rachel's words through the fog of her emotional turbulence. She glanced at the man beside the cradle. His eyes were on Rachel, and it seemed to Berry that they had not moved from Rachel's face since she had first looked at him.

"Well...I see you've recovered from your swoon."

Fish came through the door from the dogtrot. He removed his hat and carefully smoothed his hair with his palms. His boots struck dull echoes on the plank flooring, and Berry turned to look at him as if seeing him for the first time. The long, red scratches down his cheek and his puffed lips gave her a breath of pleasure that was instantly smothered as fury tore through her, shutting off her breath. She started to speak, choked, and gulped down spittle and air.

"You...pukey little weasel! You lyin', wishy-washy bastard!" Berry shouted, blindly searching for some word that would convey her complete disgust. "You pissant! You addle-brained fool! You got no feelings at all!" She fought her rage in a shaking voice. "You're worse than a savage, worse than Linc Smith."

"Watch your mouth, Berry," Fish said curtly. "If I'm more of a savage than Linc, perhaps you'd like to join him. I tried to keep you out of this. I'm sure Rachel has lost no time telling you about that. I'll not take you with me now. The picture has changed. Meanwhile, I'll use you and Simon as a lever to keep Fain working. I've already told him that Simon gets five lashes with the black snake for every hour he delays. We'll soon find out how much of a man your lover is. He'll be begging for death before long."

"Damn you to hell! I'll cut your heart out!" She was close to losing control. She took a long, slow breath to steady herself. "You'll die for this."

For an endless moment Fish stood staring at the cold-eyed girl. He was not surprised by the lethal hatred he saw in her face. He expected it. She was the type of woman who loved with all her heart and hated passionately.

"You're not using good judgment spewing your hatred, Berry. I can see now that it would have been a mistake to take an uncivilized woman like you back east to mix with genteel womenfolk, regardless of your beauty." His eyes were flat and still, his voice as void of resonance as a drum struck with the palm of the hand. "If you're so anxious to see killing done, perhaps we can start with Rachel." He paused to see the effect of his words. "But then, I've half-promised her to Emil."

The legs of Jackson's chair hit the floor. "Emil ain't havin' 'er."

"So you fancy her too, Jackson? Things may get interesting before this is over," Fish said, grimly amused. "That leaves Berry, the kid, and the nigger." He spoke to Jackson as if the women were not in the room. "Fain would know I mean business if we hang the kid up out there where he can see it."

A scream of acute agony came from Rachel. She sprang forward, snatched the baby up in her arms, and backed toward the sleeping room, her eyes wild in her white face.

Jackson, within easy reach of her, sat stoically. He didn't move a muscle to stop her.

Fish rocked forward and brought both hands crashing down on the table with a violence that jarred the crockery. "What the hell game are you playing, Jackson?" His face was suffused with crimson. "You getting soft? You'll back my hand, or else you're out!" He straightened his bearing, his blue eyes hard in a face that looked young but wasn't. "I should have had Emil in here with the women."

Rachel was crying silently, helplessly, her eyes shifting from one man to the other.

"I never dreamed that men could be such beasts!" Berry said in a shaking voice.

Fish ignored her. "Are you so smitten with the woman you'll not carry out my orders, Jackson?"

Jackson spat on the floor. "Time ain't right."

"You're giving orders now?"

"Killin' the kid'd rattle the man. I'm a-wantin' him to get the job done so I c'n be gone." Jackson's unblinking eyes never left Fish's face.

Silence closed in so completely that Rachel's ragged breathing was all that was heard. Fish swiveled his head around to look at her, then back to Jackson.

"You may be right," he said thoughtfully. "We'll string up the nigger."

Berry felt as if she had been hit in the stomach. The air left her lungs. Her bound hands flew to her mouth. It was no idle threat. They would kill gentle, faithful Israel as if he were no more important than a dog.

"Please ... please don't hurt Israel. He's simpleminded. He'd not hurt a fly."

"Are you begging, Berry?"

"If that's what it takes, yes. Please, don't do this awful thing to Israel."

"Where is he, Rachel?" Fish set his hat carefully on his head. "I haven't seen him for a while."

"I don't know. He's so scared he might've run off in the woods. He'll come if you call him."

"You'd better hope he does." He looked pointedly at the child in her arms. "The hour is almost up. It's time to give Simon another taste of the lash."

"Fish, don't!" Berry cried. "Please ... don't! I'll do anything you want—anything at all!"

"Are you offering to sleep with me?" He threw back his head and loosed a whoop of derisive laughter. "Do you think I'd take you to bed after you've been in the woods with a couple of filthy Indians and a backwoods buck like Simon Witcher? That's what he is, Berry, in spite of the little trading business he runs. You've nothing to offer me now. I've screwed the highest-paid whores in Europe. Save yourself for Linc." His mouth twisted sarcastically. "He's looking forward to showing you a few new tricks. He's half-crazed since you made an animal out of him. He deserves some . . . consoling."

Silence fell over the room when he left it, a strange unwanted silence. Rachel, her chin resting on her collarbone, rocked the child in her arms. This silent agony was harder for Berry to endure than moaning and wailing. She put her bound hands to her mouth in an effort to hold back the screams that were demanding release. *Think*, she told herself sternly, and forced her mind out of its crazy spin and into a calmer channel.

"Please . . . help us," she said to the silent man in a harsh croak. "We've done nothing to you. If it's money, Simon will give you some."

Jackson's eyes slid to her for only an instant, then back to Rachel. He tilted the back of his chair against the wall and with dark, unfathomable eyes watched the blond woman and the child.

Rachel lifted her head and looked at him. Her white face was contorted, and her full lips quivered. There was a soundless outpouring of grief from her blue eyes. She opened her mouth to speak, but the words didn't come. She shook her head, her eyes still holding his. Finally she said in a hoarse whisper, "Thank you."

The fire that blazed across Simon's back hauled him up from the depth of darkness. He grunted under the searing pain. He heard the swish of the leaded whip as it came down across his back like a white flame. He sagged, the rawhide bonds tearing into the flesh of his wrists. He spun on his toes and exposed his chest to the white-hot agony of the next blow, which brought his voice tearing up and out of him. He lifted his head to the sky.

"Ber...ry...I love you! I love you!" he bellowed.

Pinpoints of light danced crazily around behind his unseeing eyes as the whip sent flames of pain writhing across his back, shoulders, and arms. The enveloping heat engulfed him until his flesh could no longer send the message of torture and terror to his brain. He hung limply, accepting the blows. I'm dying, he thought. I wanted to tell Berry I love her. I wish I had time....

From somewhere far away he heard a voice say, "That's enough, Linc. You'll kill him too soon."

"Sonofabitch ain't had half enough."

"Cut him down! I got the goddamn gun ready to test." Fain's bellow penetrated into Simon's consciousness.

Simon opened his eyes and saw the tree dancing, swaying, then whirling faster and faster. The serpent fire was surrounding his back and shoulders, his chest and stomach. The hot, leaded tongue was seeking the symbol of his manhood and he was helpless to protect it. He tried to spin away, to pivot, but couldn't control his ponderous weight. I can't bear much more of this, he thought dully.

"Put the whip down, ya fucker, or I'll blow your goddamn head off!"

"Careful, Fain. I'll handle this. Give me the whip, Linc." He took the whip from the hand of the slobbering riverman. "Calm down. Mr. MacCartney is about to demonstrate his wonderful new invention. If it works, we'll be leaving here tonight." He looked steadily at Fain, who held the rifle centered on him.

"I suggest you be very careful that Jackson doesn't get the idea that you've got the upper hand."

"I said cut him down. I got a feelin' I ain't got nothin' to lose. There's a bullet in the breech 'n' another in my pocket."

"Jackson or Emil could pick you off easily."

"Maybe. But my finger on this here trigger won't do you no good." He threw a look of pure hatred at the riverman. "Shootin' a man's one thing, beatin' him to death is another."

"You say the gun is ready to test?"

"That's what I said, but don't get any idea ya don't need me to show ya how it works. Cut Simon down. I'll not have 'im hangin' there like a side of meat for the crows to pick at."

For the space of a dozen heartbeats the riverman hesitated. Then he pulled his knife from his belt and held the hilt in his hand. Fain watched his muscles bunch.

"Don't even nick 'im," Fain said softly. "I c'n kill ya 'n' reload in five seconds."

The knife sliced the leather between Simon's palms. His wrists came free and he fell helplessly to the ground. Even from the darkness into which he sank, he felt the agony as the boot connected with his ribs, and a haunting cry tore from his throat.

"Get that fucker outta here. I can't stand to look at 'im. Tell 'im to leave the knife. I ain't a-wantin' to worry 'bout it gettin' in my back while we're a-testin'."

"Give me the knife, Linc," Fish said sternly. "Don't worry. You'll get all I promised, and more."

The riverman handed over his knife like an obedient child. "Ya said I could—"

"I know what I said, and you shall," Fish said patiently. "Go to Emil and tell him we're going to test the gun."

"I wantta see 'er. I ain't seen her yet," he said stubbornly.

"All right. Go to the cabin, but don't cause a ruckus. Wait there for me." He watched the man lumber away, then said to Fain, "Don't forget that Jackson is with the women." He pulled his musket, cocked it, and leveled it on him. "You can carry the rifle, but keep the barrel pointed to the ground."

"I ain't a fool, Fish, even if I did swallow your cock-'n'-bull story." He walked ahead of him toward the target set up in the woods.

Rachel walked the floor with the baby in her arms. It was as if her mind had become unhinged. She stared at Berry with dull eyes and passed her as if she were a stranger. Berry sat tensely on the edge of the bunk, straining her ears. She heard Fish calling to Israel and listened for the black man to answer, but she heard nothing. The full terrible horror of what was happening swept in on her. She found herself as a small child again needing her only friend to give her comfort. But Rachel had retreated within herself, and Berry was alone with the awful truth—*they were all going to die*. She would never again know the joy of being held in Simon's arms. She would never hear him say that he loved her.

"No!" Berry said vehemently. She jumped to her feet and crossed the room to Jackson. "I can't sit here doing nothing." She held out her bound hands. "Take off the rope so I can make coffee."

His eyes roamed over her, from her cut, bruised

face and tangled ebony hair to the huge cloth shirt and buckskin breeches that failed to hide her slender form. Then his eyes swept up to meet her steady green ones. Without a change of expression he whipped out a thin-bladed knife and sliced the rope between her wrists. The rope fell to the floor and Berry turned away.

She rekindled the fire, filled the teakettle from the oaken bucket that sat on the shelf beside the door, and swung it over the blaze. At the workbench she opened a small wooden cask, peered in, and closed it. She uncorked a crock. It contained salt.

"Where's the coffee, Rachel?" She spoke louder than usual, not sure that Rachel would hear her or answer if she did.

To her surprise, Rachel shifted the sleeping child to her shoulder and came up close beside her. With her free hand she reached for the small bag on the second shelf and set it on the workbench. As she did so, she flipped back a cloth, exposing a small dirk, then covered it and walked away.

Berry scooped the coffee from the bag and poured the coarse grounds into the boiling water. Thank God! Rachel still had her wits after all! *How could she get the dirk off the workbench and on her person?*

A moaning cry from Rachel brought the front legs of Jackson's chair crashing to the floor and a fresh stab of terror to Berry's heart. She ran to the window and went up on her toes so that she could see over Rachel's shoulder. Her mouth dropped and a wave of nausea rolled up into her throat. "Oh, Lordy! Oh, sweet Jesus!" The feeling of hate and terror clamped down around her.

Linc pulled back the whip and applied it to Simon's back with all his strength. Simon's body jerked and the skin split. A stream of blood blossomed and crisscrossed other streams of blood. The second strike wrapped the thin cruel leather around his body. A scream of rage tore from Berry's throat. She turned and sped to the door. An arm as hard as steel closed around her and lifted her off the floor.

"Ber...ry! I love you! I love you!"

Simon's agonized cry tore through her heart like a knife. She fell into a fit of helpless sobbing. The words she had spoken to him came back to haunt her cruelly. *Someday you'll shout it,* she'd said. *It'll just come boilin' up out of you!*

"Simon...Simon..." Berry went limp and the arm holding her let go. She dropped to the floor, lay there, then slowly got to her hands and knees and crawled to Rachel. She wrapped her arms around Rachel's legs and buried her face in her skirts. She cried as she had not done since her mother died and left her so long ago.

Rachel pulled on her arm and said, "Stand up and look, Berry."

Linc had cut Simon down from the tree and he lay face down in the dirt. They couldn't hear what Fain and Fish were saying, but they saw that Fain had a rifle and was angry. Then Berry saw Linc coming toward the cabin. The silent approach of this evil man gave the whole scene an air of unreality that came to her like a numbing coldness rising from the ground and working its way through her. She was cold, yet her insides quivered hotly.

She sidled toward the workbench and the dirk hidden under the cloth. More than anything in the world she wanted to go to Simon, but first she would kill Linc Smith.

Fain led the way to the shooting range he had set up the year before to test his guns. He had marked the distances of sixty yards, eighty yards, and one hundred yards from the target with stakes driven into the ground. The target was a heavy-skinned log propped against the crotch of a tree. A piece of tin, showing many bullet holes, was nailed to the log.

Fain stopped beside the stake marking one hundred yards from the target. His hands caressed the rifle. He'd spent a year working on the gun and he considered it his masterpiece. His blue eyes bored into those of the man who had worked beside him as a friend, but who now stood beside him as a bitter enemy, a murderer. He knew better than to ask what would happen after the rifle was tested. There was no way Fish would allow any of them to live after he had stolen the gun and passed it off as his.

"Let's see what it will do," Fish said impatiently.

Fain backed several steps from the stake, raised the gun to his shoulder, sighted carefully down the long barrel, and fired. The bullet smashed directly into the center of the target.

"By the Lord Henry! Good God Almighty!" Fish proclaimed loudly. "It works! This gun can win wars. It can change the course of history!" He reached for it.

"I'll show ya how it's loaded." Sweat rolled from Fain's face as if he had dunked his head into a bucket of water. He took the second bullet from his pocket.

Fish watched closely. Fain could feel the prod of Fish's silver-plated musket in his back and was careful how he handled the gun. In five seconds the rifle was reloaded and he shoved it into Fish's hands. His own hands were trembling like leaves in a light breeze.

"Ya can't best my shot," he said in a wintry voice that betrayed none of the agonizing suspense he had just endured.

"Move back." Fish gestured with the musket and Fain moved to the side. "Over there." He pointed to a tree some distance away. Fain backed until he was against a huge oak. Fish tucked the musket into his belt. His face was flushed with excitement.

Fain watched Fish handle the gun. He lifted it for balance and sighted down the long barrel. It was the longest moment of Fain's life. The cocky, deceitful little sonofabitch might turn the gun on him, using him for a target. He started to speak, to goad him about his marksmanship, but didn't want to draw attention to himself unless he had no other choice.

"It galled you that I could outshoot you, didn't it, Fain?" Fish shot him a smiling, superior glance.

"Ya'll have to hit dead center to beat me, and if'n ya wait much longer, your excuse'll be it was too dark ta see." All of Fain's muscles were bunched. He had never been so afraid in his life. This could be the last few seconds he'd spend on earth.

Fish spread his feet in the stance of a military rifleman and raised the gun to his shoulder. He moved the barrel up and down and swung it in a wide arc before he leveled it on the target. He sighted carefully down the long barrel. It seemed to Fain he stood there for an eternity before he pulled the trigger.

The explosion was deafening. The metal plate fragmented and flew off the side of the rifle as Fain had suspected it would. The flying metal took part of Fish's head with it. He was thrown to the side like a sack of grain, his feathered hat tossed high. Bits of flesh and bone, blood, and tufts of blond hair were all that remained atop his body.

The echo of the blast was still resounding in Fain's head as he leaped forward to get the musket from Fish's body. There was a flash of color, a shot, and a bullet went whizzing past his head. Emil came running toward him, pulling his musket out of his belt, his rifle still in his hand. Fain wheeled. *He had thought the man was at the landing on the river!* If not for the musket, he could reach Fish before the riverman could reload. But now...

Fain's stout legs carried him into the woods. He'd played the only card he had. He could hear Emil crashing through the brush after him. He ran on, praying he'd not sealed the fate of the others at the cabin.

Chapter 18

Berry stood with her back to the workbench, her eyes on the door. The instant Linc entered the room and Jackson's eyes swung to him, she snatched the dirk from beneath the cloth and held it behind her.

The man's small, watery eye, under the bushy brow and thinning hair, leveled on her. A minute passed—or was it an hour? The eye stabbed into her. Terror took hold and shook her. Fear gnawed at the very core of her being, and she hit back in the only way she knew—verbally, abusively.

"I shoulda made sure you died! I shoulda followed you and cut your rotten heart out!" Her voice started out weak but quickly gained strength. "You're no more human than a belly-crawlin' snake. You knifed my pa, took his money, then you and that bastard you hung out with thought you'd get me and Rachel," she yelled at the top of her voice. Faith began to cry. "You're all that's left of the scum that come for us, and damn you, I'll see you dead!"

A strained growl came from Linc's throat. "Ya goddamn bitch! Ya ruint me!" he shouted.

"You filthy, disgustin', stinkin' animal!" Her fury burst forth in a strangled shout, her enraged voice overriding his. Suddenly she realized she was close to losing control. She ceased her strident outburst and stood in the wavering light of the guttering fire, loathing washing over her like a sizzling gush from a hot spring. She forgot Rachel, forgot the black-bearded man watching. She only vaguely heard the baby's cries.

Linc's fuddled brain saw in the girl confronting him the essence of all that had gone wrong in his life. He wanted to choke the life from her with his bare hands! He opened his mouth as if being strangled, clenched his fists, and reached for his knife, which wasn't there. He started around the table for her. The sound of a shot stopped him. He glanced at Jackson, who sat up in the chair.

"They's testin' the gun." The guttural sounds came from Linc's slanted mouth, and spittle fell onto his shirt, still wet with Simon's blood.

Jackson leaned back in the chair. Rachel walked back and forth in front of the bedroom door with Faith in her arms. Berry didn't take her eyes off Linc. The sound of the shot had distracted him, but now his eye shifted between her, Rachel, and Jackson.

Boom! The sound of the explosion reverberated in the room like a clap of thunder. Linc wheeled, and Jackson jumped to his feet. The sharp crack of a rifle, and then a shout, reached them.

Berry's mind was locked in on one thing—killing Linc. She leaped toward him, the dirk raised to strike. He turned and the blade struck his shoulder blade. The surprise attack caught him off balance and he fell to his knees. Berry jumped onto his back and jabbed viciously with the short blade. Her mind had gone blank. She was in a frenzy to kill him. He roared with anger and pain. Suddenly she was plucked from Linc's sweating body and slammed against the wall. Her head cracked against a hard object and the room whirled, then straightened.

Linc crawled out the door, bleeding from the cuts, roaring curses at the top of his voice.

Jackson scowled down at the small, plucky girl he'd jerked off Linc. Abruptly, as if sensing danger, he wheeled around. Rachel stood in the sleeping-room doorway holding the rifle. She fired. The sound of the shot was deafening. The bullet struck him in the right shoulder and spun him around. He grabbed the door frame to keep from falling. Rachel lowered the rifle and waited for him to kill her. She had missed her one chance. His face showed surprise, the first readable emotion she had seen there.

"What'd you do that for? I'd-a took ya with me." There was a note of disappointment in his voice. He backed from the door.

Rachel had been sure that he was going to kill her. She stood, suspended in stunned silence, for a long moment. Then terror moved her to action. She rushed to the door, slammed it, and dropped the bar. She was seized with panic and quickly dropped the solid wood shutter down over the window, her body working independently of her mind. The room was almost dark without the light from the window and the door.

"Berry! Get up!"

Berry got to her feet and held on to Rachel until the floor stopped moving. "I'm all right. Did you kill him?"

"No, but I hurt him... bad. He could've shot me, but he didn't."

"Linc?"

"You hurt him. He was bleedin', but I don't think it was bad. He was crawling for the door when I got the gun." Faith was bawling lustily. Rachel went to her, returned, and opened her dress. She put the child to her breast and instantly the loud cries ceased. Rachel wiped the dampness from the baby's head. "Poor little thing," she crooned. "Poor, helpless, little babe."

Berry unhooked the shutter covering the window and lifted it so that she could look out. The sky was darkening. Already a few twinkling stars dotted the sky. There was no one within the range of her vision. She could faintly see the outline of Simon's body lying in the dirt beneath the tree. The birds came to roost in the branches over his head. She heard their tittering and saw one after another silhouetted against the sky as they gathered for the night.

"I'm going to Simon." Berry closed the shutter and locked it. "I'm going out to get him, Rachel. If I'm going to die, I'll die out there with him."

"He's unconscious. You can't lift him. Please... wait..." Rachel began to cry. Sobs shook her shoulders. "Fain is dead! I know he is...."

"We don't know that."

"He told me many times he didn't have a metal strong enough to hold the explosion. He had some that he thought would hold one time, but not twice.

Fish made him fire it, and it killed him!" She bent over and pounded her forehead against the wall. "I can't bear... not knowing!" she wailed.

"Stop it! Fain wouldn't want you to act like this. If the gun had blown up, Fish would be back here by now. Something else has happened, and I'm going to get Simon before they come back."

"You can't! They'll kill you, or... take you off!" Rachel grabbed Berry's arm and clung to her. "But I understand. Let me put Faith down and I'll go with you."

"No. It's best if one of us stays here. If both of us should die out there, what would become of Faith?" Berry kissed the woman who had been both mother and friend to her. "Finish feeding that youngun so you can open the door when you see me coming with Simon." She dropped a kiss on the baby's head.

Berry tied a cloth around her waist and tucked the dirk inside. "Is there powder and shot in the other room?" she asked hopefully, looking longingly at the rifle Rachel had dropped when she went to bar the door.

"Fish took everything except Fain's stock of guns, and they don't have the firing pins."

Berry swore. "That bastard! Sweet Jesus, it's hot in here. Keep a fire under that water. You can throw it on them if they try to bust down the door." Berry opened the door a crack. There was no sound, no movement.

"Wait a minute," Rachel whispered. She went to the window, raised it a crack, looked out, then looked back at Berry and nodded.

Berry slipped out the door and closed it behind

her. She leaned against it while her eyes adjusted to the darkness before she looked around. After a minute she heard the bar slide into place and knew Rachel was at the window. She edged along the wall until she reached the end of the dogtrot. Cautiously she peered around the corner. She saw nothing. Still she waited, her heart pounding, her eyes on the still figure lying on the ground. After what seemed an eternity of waiting she sped across the intervening space. She reached Simon and fell to her knees.

"Simon . . . darlin'!" She touched his face, his neck. Her hands came away sticky. She let out a shuddering cry. "Oh, my God! Your back is cut to ribbons." She forced herself to think calmly. "Simon, can you hear me?" she whispered urgently.

His reply was a faint murmur.

Berry put her hands beneath his arms to lift him. She succeeded in raising him an inch or two. He mumbled and grunted with pain. Determined to get him to his feet, she straddled his body in an effort to lift him to a sitting position. She pulled with all her strength . . . and realized, with growing panic, that she was incapable of lifting him.

"Help me, darlin', please . . . help me." Then: "Damn you, Simon! Help me. I can't lift you." Sobbing, she let him sink back down. "Goddammit! I'm going to get you to the house if I have to drag you!" She positioned herself between his feet, grabbed one in each hand, and pulled. She dug her bare feet into the ground and strained. She pulled him a few inches and paused. Pulled again and paused. She clenched her teeth and strained. Simon's body twitched and he groaned.

During one of her brief pauses she glanced over her shoulder toward the house. Such a long way to go. She sobbed her frustration and dug into the great wealth of swear words she'd learned from her father.

She heard Rachel's muted cry from the window at the same instant as she saw the lumbering figure bearing down on her. She grabbed the dirk, turned, and straddled Simon's body. Linc reached for her and she slashed his arm. A hoarse sound came from his throat and he sprang back. Berry crouched, thinking to push the blade upward. This is it, she thought. Simon and I will die, but before I do, I'll rip into Linc's guts! She jabbed the blade into his thigh when he grabbed her hair. He let out a bellow of rage and flung her to the ground. Berry saw his foot lift to stomp her, then a sound like no other she'd ever heard split the silence.

"*Zaah ... aawa ... haaa!*" The primitive war cry of Israel's ancestors tore from his throat as his gleaming black body shot from the shadows. With his huge hands he grabbed Linc and lifted him high over his head. He whirled him around faster and faster to gain momentum. A howl of pure terror erupted from Linc seconds before he was slammed against the trunk of the tree with maddening, brute force. There was a sickening sound as his body struck. He lay broken, twisted and lifeless.

Berry jumped to her feet. "Help me!" she cried.

Israel bent over Simon. His shirtless black body gleamed with sweat. He lifted him gently and pulled him up and over his shoulder. They ran to the house. The door opened. They never broke stride until they were inside the cabin, which seemed unusually bright from the firelight and the single candle.

Rachel slammed the door shut and dropped the bar. "Over here," she directed, and Israel eased Simon off his shoulder and onto the bunk.

"Oh, my God!" Berry whispered in a stricken voice. She could see the blood glistening wetly on Simon's back, and his pants were wet with it. His face was beaten beyond recognition; blood came from his nose and mouth. She felt her stomach heave, and she shut her eyes, fighting down a surge of nausea. Behind her she heard Rachel suck in her breath at the sight of the mutilation.

"I'm glad Israel killed the brute!" Rachel turned to the black man. He seemed to have taken on a new dignity. His head was high and his eyes as he looked back at her were alert and knowing.

"Thank you, Israel." Berry went to him and grasped his hand. "You're a good man. You saw what had to be done and did it. We've been through a lot together since we left Ohio. Somehow we'll get through this, too. I'm so glad you're here with us."

"Yass'm, missy."

"Did you see Fain, Israel?" Rachel choked on the words.

"Yass'm. The gun kill Mistah Fish. Mistah Fain is a-hidin' in the woods."

"Oh, thank God!" Rachel's face crumbled and tears poured down her cheeks.

"Ah was a-lookin' fo' him when I saw missy."

"The gun exploded and killed Fish! I'm glad!" Berry said stoutly. "Maybe the other two will leave."

"They's lookin' fo' Mistah Fain."

"He'll try to get to the cabin," Rachel said. "I

know he will. What can he do against two armed men?"

"He'll not have to worry so much about us now. He'll see that Simon is gone and know Israel is the only one who could have carried him away." Berry dipped water into a pan and set it on the floor beside Simon. He lay on his stomach, his face turned toward her. She sponged his face with a wet cloth and kissed his cheek. "Oh, your poor back! I don't know if I can do it, darlin'. I don't know what to do!"

"Let me do it, Berry. Israel, help me get his breeches off." Rachel dipped a towel into the warm water, then placed it, still dripping, on Simon's back. "Get clean sheet and some cloth for bandages, Berry."

Berry fought down the hopelessness that threatened to overcome her when she saw the dirt embedded in the bloody welter of Simon's back. She washed the blood from his hips and covered them with the sheet. Don't think, she scolded herself sternly. Do what you have to do.

Rachel continued to lay dripping towels on Simon's shredded flesh. Each time she removed one it was coated with dirt. Israel took away the bloody water and returned with clean. After each trip he lifted the shutter and looked out the window.

Berry knelt at Simon's head and smoothed his dark hair back from his still face. It seemed so strange to see him so still. She had never seen him sleeping. He looked young and helpless, and a great outpouring of protectiveness flooded her heart. She caressed his head with her fingertips, kissed his face, and murmured that she loved him. When the tips of her fingers slid to the nape of his neck and up, she felt a large sticky lump and let out a cry of alarm.

"I knew it was there," Rachel said softly. "There had to be a reason for him to be unconscious all this time. I want to do as much as I can to his back before he comes to, because the pain will be terrible."

"Will he . . . die?"

"All we can do is pray that infection doesn't set in. There . . . I think I've got it clean. We'll cover it with bear oil and a clean cloth. I'm afraid to move him so I can see what's on the other side. I'm quite sure he has some broken ribs." Rachel gathered up the basin and the towels and moved away.

Berry stayed on her knees beside the bunk. She noticed how slowly Simon breathed. Occasionally his brow wrinkled with a frown. He was encased in pain. It penetrated into the fragments of his consciousness. She suffered with him, crying silently.

Despite her overpowering concern for Simon, Berry was acutely aware of the danger that lurked outside. She listened to the low murmur of Rachel's and Israel's voices, knowing that they kept watch at the window for a sign of Fain.

"I shot one of them with the rifle you passed to me, Israel. I missed my shot and got him in the shoulder. I wish I'd killed him—then there would have been only one left out there."

"Yass'm. Ah went ta the river way down yonder 'n' saw Lardy dead. The buzzards done picked out his eyes. Ah took 'im to where the ferry come 'n' left 'im there on the boards."

"You found Lardy and you came back to help us. Why didn't you go on and save yourself?"

"I's yours 'n' missy's slave, Miz Rachel. I a big, dumb nigga, but I stay with my missy."

"You're far from dumb, Israel. Don't ever think that. You were smart enough to fool Fish into thinking you're dumb." There was a long silence, then Rachel sighed tiredly. "I want Fain to come and I don't want him to. I want him with us, but I'm afraid that's what they expect him to do and will be waiting for him."

Hours passed. It was suffocatingly hot in the cabin. The baby fussed. Rachel nursed her and walked the floor. Israel prowled, stopping every so often to put his ear to the outside wall and listen. Berry sat beside Simon, bathed his face, and watched Israel. He moved soundlessly on his huge bare feet; it seemed impossible that he, so big and gentle, had screamed that primitive war cry and charged Linc Smith with such fury.

Simon groaned, his eyelashes fluttered, and he opened his eyes. Berry tilted her head and leaned toward him so that her face was level with his.

"Simon? Darlin', are you awake?"

"Berry . . . What's wrong? Where am I?" he whispered through his puffed lips.

"You're in the cabin, love. Israel carried you. He killed Linc, the brute that did this to you. Fish is dead too." She kissed his bruised cheek. "You must lie still. Don't try to roll over on your back."

Simon closed his eyes. "I couldn't move if I wanted to," he said weakly. "Where's Fain?"

"He'll be along soon. Go back to sleep. You'll feel better in the morning."

"I didn't think I'd make it. . . . I love you." His hand tightened on hers.

"And I love you."

"I'm glad it's over. I wouldn't be no use to you. I couldn't . . . help. . . ." She felt his hand relax and knew he was asleep.

Berry sat beside him, watching his face, listening to his breathing. Not even sleep could wholly free him from the pain. Every so often there was a catch in his breath, followed by a faint moan. It was a steady, hurtful sound. She found herself waiting tensely for the slow breath to catch and hold. His lips moved, but she couldn't catch what he was saying. She leaned down. He ran his tongue over dry lips and mumbled.

"I can't hear you," she whispered.

"I . . . like to hear her laugh. It sounds . . . like bells and makes me feel good."

"Oh, Simon!" Her tears fell on his face.

Rachel came to lay her hand on his forehead. "Sleep is what he needs now," she said quietly.

Berry walked with her to the other side of the room. "He thinks it's over. I told him that Fain would be coming soon. I couldn't tell him, Rachel. He's so helpless."

"You did right to ease his mind. There's nothing he can do."

"Missy! They out there." Israel moved from the window so that the women could look out.

The tall, gaunt figure of Jackson, his rifle tucked under his right arm, and the heavier figure of Emil stood beside Linc's body. They looked toward the house, then Jackson gestured with his rifle and vanished in the dark shadows. Emil lolled against the tree, his booted foot callously propped on Linc's body.

"Mistah Fain!" Israel's urgent whisper and his hand on Rachel's back startled her and she let out a small cry. Her body began to shake and she clutched his arm. He urged her toward the door. On the way he pinched out the flame of the candle, plunging the room into darkness.

Rachel pressed her ear to the door. All she could hear was the pounding of her own heart. Israel gently pushed her aside and lifted the bar. He pulled up on the handle, the door opened silently, and Fain slipped into the room. Just as silently the door closed behind him.

"Fain!" Rachel reached for him and his arms closed around her. Her tear-wet lips searched for his, found them, and kissed hungrily. "Oh, love . . . are you all right?"

"Fine. And you, lass?" His arms strained her to him, his whisper hoarse and urgent.

"We're all right. Simon is here."

Israel lit the candle and in the soft glow Fain's eyes searched the room. He held out his hand to Berry and she went to him. He put his other arm around her and hugged her to him.

"The bastard was tryin' to beat him to death! How is he?"

Rachel answered. "He's sleeping. We did all we could do."

"What happened to Linc? That *is* him out there under the tree . . . ?"

"Israel killed him. He slammed him against the tree trunk. He would've killed me and Simon." Berry sniffed, holding back sudden tears.

"You're all wet," Rachel exclaimed, suddenly noticing Fain's dripping clothes and the smell of the river.

"I've been looking ever'where for the guns. I waded to a boat anchored out from the bank, but they're not there. They musta stashed 'em off in the woods. They think I've gone down toward the Missouri. They'll do whatever they're goin' to do soon, 'cause they've got to skeedaddle 'n case I come with help."

"We heard the explosion and I was so afraid... I was just sure that..." Rachel hugged him tightly. The sheer heaven of having him back with her made her feel as weak as a kitten.

Fain chuckled. "I lived me ten years in a minute or two, lass. I kinda thought the plate I put on would hold for one shot, but I knew it'd not hold for two. I thought if'n Fish was dead, the other'ns would take what they wanted 'n' go. But they ain't a-goin' to." He looked at Israel and held out his hand. "I thanky, man. I was a-countin' on ya, 'n' ya come through just fine."

Israel looked at the hand extended toward him and backed up. Never had he thought to shake the hand of a white man. Berry realized his confusion and gently took his hand and put it in Fain's.

"I don't know what we'd've done without him. I didn't even hear you at the door." Rachel clung to Fain's arm as if afraid he'd vanish if she let go of it.

Fain gripped Israel's hand hard and said again, "I thanky, man." He went to look down at Simon. He lifted the cloth from his back and swore viciously. "I wish there was a way to get ya out," he said tiredly. "I'm afeared they'll set fire to the house. That Jackson wants ya, lass. He wants ya bad." He looked straight at Rachel, wanting to know the worst.

"I shot him."

"Ain't that. He wants ya for his woman. You a-shootin' him made him want ya all the more. I heard 'em a-talkin'. He said ya was a woman to winter with. He's the one we got to look out for. He's got no more feelin' in 'im than a wild dog. He's been in the woods so long he don't know nothin' except take what he wants. The other'n just wants plunder."

"I'm glad you told me," Rachel said quietly.

"There ain't never gonna be no secrets a'tween us, lass."

"What'll we do?"

"I dunno. Israel 'n' I could slip out 'n' try to get the jump on 'em. But without a gun or knife . . . I'm a-thinkin' to bargain, to stall. . . ."

"Mistah Fain, they's a-lightin' a fire."

Fain pinched out the candle and went to the window. Emil had dragged dry brush to the wood-chopping stump in the center of the yard, piled on woodchips, and set it ablaze. He threw on an armload of the kindling Rachel had chopped and the fire caught, flared, and lighted the area. A fog rising from the river added a demonic glitter to the figure moving around in the glare of the flames.

Fain lowered the shutter to a mere crack as the flames shot higher and the light extended to the cabin. Rachel and Israel stood nervously behind him. Berry crouched beside the bunk where Simon lay.

Fain began to swear under his breath, and Rachel crowded in under his arm so that she could see what had caused his sudden fury. He allowed her a brief look, then closed the shutter.

"They're a-rollin' a barrel of gunpowder down against the wall. Ya know what that means."

Rachel gripped Fain's forearms. "I'd go out to him if I thought it would save you. But it wouldn't! They won't leave anyone alive to tell what happened. Tell us what to do, Fain."

"Take Berry and the babe and go," Fain said roughly. "Israel can slip out. There's no way we can get Simon out of here. Him 'n' me'll stay."

"No!" Berry and Rachel said sharply at the same moment.

Rachel flung back the shutter. "Jackson!" she yelled. The bearded woodsman stepped out of the darkness and into the light of the fire. "Do you want me to come with you?"

He hesitated, as if the question surprised him. "I'll take ya for my woman." He paused, then said as if reminding her, "I coulda killed ya."

"I know that. If I come with you, can I bring my baby?"

Berry jerked on her arm. "Rachel!" she hissed. "You can't..."

"Ya can bring it."

"Give me a minute." Rachel turned from the window, leaned against the wall, and held her hands to her stomach.

"Go, lass. Take the babe. It's better than dyin'." Fain took her in his arms and kissed her.

"I'm stayin'!" Berry ran sobbing to Simon.

Rachel broke free of Fain and turned to the window. "Jackson," she called, her voice trembling. "I'm afraid to come out. I'm afraid you'll fire my house."

"It'll make no never mind about no house when you're gone from it." There was anger in his tone.

"But I'm afraid . . . of Emil."

"Emil won't bother."

"But he will. I'm afraid. Fish said he wanted me."

The woodsman turned and looked across the fire at the English sailor. Without hesitation, he lifted his rifle and fired. The sound of the shot echoed through the foggy clearing from the river to the curtain of tall trees to the west. Emil took one long, sudden step backward, tripped on nothing, and dropped limply to the ground. The hair was gone from the top of his head. Blood and brains poured out into the dirt.

In the aftermath, Rachel stared, stunned. Her face was frozen with shock, as were those of the others behind her.

"Emil won't bother," Jackson said again. He dropped the empty rifle and picked up another. "I got horses. C'mon."

"I . . . have to gather up some things." Rachel almost choked on the words. She turned and closed the shutter. "He killed him! I was just stalling for time, and he killed him!" She buried her face in Fain's shirt.

"Ya got rid of one of 'em, love. Get your things together 'n' go." His words were calm, but there was raw emotion in his shaky voice.

"Oh, Fain! Did you think I'd leave you? Faith

and I will die right here with you. I'll never leave you! I love you . . . so much!" She wound her arms around his waist.

"I want ya to live," he protested huskily.

"Not without you!"

"Woman!" Jackson yelled.

Fain looked through the crack. Jackson, his feet spread, his rifle under his arm, stood in the same place. He could see both the door and the window. "The sonofabitch's takin' no chances," Fain said. "He's got four shots before he's got to reload."

"Are ya comin', woman? If'n ya ain't, I'm a-puttin' a shot in the powder barrel."

"I'm comin'," Rachel called.

She went to the cradle, picked up her daughter, and returned to Fain. He put his arms around the two of them, took them to the far side of the room, and turned his back to the window.

Berry hovered over the sleeping Simon and kissed his face. "I love you, darlin'. I love you." Israel came to stand beside her. She reached up and took his hand and felt it close tightly around her small one. He'll not die standing off by himself, she thought with calm reasoning. She pulled on his hand and he knelt beside her.

"Woman!" Jackson's dreaded voice broke a wordless run of time. He was angry, impatient. "I ain't a-standin' here a-bleedin' 'n' waitin' on ya no more! C'mon out or I'll blow ya up with 'em."

There was deadly silence in the room. Berry's mind went blank. She didn't feel Israel trembling beside her or hear the faint groans coming from Simon when her lips found the cut on the side of his mouth and pressed hard. Time went on and on, and still they waited. Faith whimpered, Rachel shushed her, and then there was silence again.

The rap on the door came so suddenly it startled them all. Seconds later there was another rap and a voice called, "Fain? Are you in there?"

"Good God Almighty!"

"Fain? Don't shoot. It's Jeff."

"Lordy!" Fain was across the room in one bound. He flung open the door. "Jeff! Good God, man..."

"What's going on around here? That bastard was going to blow you to splinters with that powder. Light took care of him with a toss of his pig sticker. Will carried the powder back away from the house in case of shootin'. Whew...it's hot in here. This place is like a bake oven!"

Rachel began to sob wildly.

"Is it over?" Berry asked anxiously.

"It's over," Fain said wearily. "Light a candle, Israel."

Chapter 19

Berry fanned Simon with the stiff brim of her sunbonnet as she listened to the talk of the men who sat at the table drinking coffee. Israel had thought to slink out of the room, but Fain had stopped him, and he now sat awkwardly on the chair that Jackson had occupied for the last two days. He had been praised by these white men. His hand had been shaken. He was a little dazed by it all, but proud, too.

Jeff and Will had returned early from their trip to Natchez. They had met with Light and a group of his Osage relatives downriver and had come on north. They had found Lardy's body on the ferry landing. It was evident to them that the body had been carried there and left as a signal. Israel's big, bare footprints had been easily recognizable to Light and his men, and they had lost no time in getting to Fain's homestead.

"We heard a shot about the time we reached the

edge of the timber," Will said in his lazy drawl. "We come on in 'n' it didn't take much figurin' to see who'd shot him and what he was a-goin' to shoot at next. Light wormed his way around the freight wagons 'n' dropped the sucker with his knife. Course, we was all set to shoot the bastard, but our rifles ain't what you'd call downright turkey-shootin' rifles, bein's how they was made by a slack-handed gunsmith that we know of."

The good-natured teasing went on, easing the tension. Every detail of the past two days was discussed. Rachel told how Israel had dug under the wall to pass her the rifle and how he had charged Linc Smith and saved Berry and Simon. She even told how he had fooled Fish and killed the crippled old rooster instead of one of her fat hens. Israel hung his head and grinned shyly.

Rachel apologized for the untidy eating room. She made more coffee. Her hand lingered on Fain's shoulder each time she passed him.

"We found out some purely interesting facts about Edmund Aston Carwild when we stopped to talk to Zeb Pike at Kaskaskia," Jeff said. "He's got spies out all over now that he and Manuel Lisa are in a race to blaze a trail to the Southwest. Zeb says that Fish, as we know him, is a shirttail relation to James Wilkinson."

"I ain't a-thinkin' that'd be much to be proud of," Will said dryly.

"You know our Governor Wilkinson is a fine, upstanding man, Will," Jeff teased.

"Humph! Damned if he ain't! He's got his fingers in ever' shady thing he can get 'em in," Will said heatedly.

"It seems that Wilkinson sent Fish up here on a mission," Jeff explained. "At first, I thought he'd sent him away to get him out of his hair. Now we know. . . . You're famous, Fain! You're known all the way to New Orleans."

"I don't think Fish was plannin' on sharin' with Wilkinson. He was goin' to skeedaddle to Europe 'n' sell to the highest bidder," Fain said; then with a bit of amazement in his voice he added, "You mean that bastard Wilkinson wanted my gun?"

"It would seem so," Jeff said with a chuckle.

"I'm a long way from makin' it safe."

"It shore enough blew the top off Fish's head," Will commented dryly.

Fain laughed nervously. "I didn't know if'n the plate I put on would hold once." His eyes sought Rachel's. "I sure as hell knew it'd not hold a second time. I was sweatin' it out, I tell you."

Light sat at the end of the table. He spoke seldom, but his dark eyes traveled from one face to the other and he listened carefully to everything that was said. Berry's eyes turned to him often. He seemed so lonely. She wanted to say something to him, to thank him for what he'd done for them at the camp ground in Saint Louis and for helping them tonight, but he seemed unapproachable.

Several days passed before Berry got the opportunity to thank Light, and by that time she had another reason to be grateful to the half-breed scout.

Morning came.

Berry woke feeling as if she had been physically mauled. She shook her head to clear it, and winced as pinpricks of pain lanced down her neck and along her right side. She had been asleep for some time, sitting on the floor beside Simon's bed. She tried to rise, only to discover that her right leg was useless. Grasping the edge of the bunk, she dragged herself to her knees and gritted her teeth while she waited for the blood to resume its flow to her legs.

She moved stiffly to the wash shelf, picked up the water bucket, and crossed the dogtrot to the other room. On her way she noticed that the sun had traveled one-quarter of the way across the sky. I've slept half the morning away! she thought. She continued on to the other room, stripped off Simon's shirt and breeches, and washed herself. She scooped water onto her face, still bruised and swollen from the blows Fish had inflicted with his fists. At length, feeling somewhat revived, she pulled on a clean dress over her head and tied an apron around her waist. She set about trying to put her hair in order. It was such a tangled mess that the task seemed hopeless, and in the end she tied the rebellious mass at the base of her neck with one of the ribbons Simon had sent up from Saint Louis, which she had refused to accept.

Berry returned to Simon, bent to kiss his cheek, and noticed his breathing was heavier and faster. Heat radiated from his body. He moved his arms and legs continually and turned his head from side to side. He opened his eyes, made impatient, muttering noises, and closed them again.

"How do you feel, darlin'?"

There was no answer. He rolled his head away from her and continued to move his limbs spasmodically. "He's worse, much worse!" Berry said the words aloud, although there was no one to hear them. The knowledge that he might die brought her to her feet. She held on to the end of the bunk, trying with all her strength to regain control of her nerves. When she felt quite steady on her feet, she went out into the bright sunlight to look for Rachel.

"Is Simon awake yet?" Fain called. He and Light were loading the bodies of the dead men onto a wagon bed.

"He's worse! He's burning with fever!" Berry's voice carried a note of hysteria. "We've got to do something. He'll die!"

"There now, lass. It cain't be so bad. Let's don't borrow no trouble," Fain said calmly. "We'll come take a look."

"He's out of his head," Berry cried. She wanted to get control of herself, but she felt as if she would melt and run all over the floor. "Isn't there something we can do?"

"He's hot all right," Fain said when he felt Simon's forehead. "What do you think, Light?"

The scout knelt beside the bed, felt Simon's head and body, and lifted his eyelids. "He burn up soon. Get cold water from the spring and wet him down. Get some water in his mouth. I go for Nowatha. Be back three, maybe four hours." Light turned on his heels and trotted from the room.

Berry hovered over Simon, her mind blank.

"Get a hold of yourself, lass. Your man needs ya." Fain poured water into the washbowl and set it on a chair beside the bed. "Get to wettin' him down like Light said. I'll get a bucket of cold spring water for ya, then I got to drive the wagon out to where Jeff and Will are diggin' the graves. I'll send Rachel to ya."

Berry sat beside Simon throughout the long afternoon, bathing his face, his chest, and his arms. Rachel kept her supplied with water from the buckets Fain brought from the spring. Will and Jeff examined Simon's ribs, decided they were badly bruised, possibly cracked, but not broken. They lifted him onto his side so that Berry could get water into his mouth.

"Is Light bringing a doctor?"

"Nowatha's better'n a doctor." Will squatted beside her. "She's Light's aunt. They'll be here soon. If'n Light said three or four hours, that's what it'll be. Ya can count on it."

Simon almost reared up in bed, opened his eyes, and said, "Don't you touch her, you sonofabitch. She's mine." Then he lay back down. "I love you . . . I love . . . you. . . ." The words were almost inaudible, his breathing heavy.

During the afternoon he called for his mother, cursed a drunken riverman, and hallucinated his fight with the Indians during the rainstorm. Over and over he pleaded for time to tell Berry that he loved her.

The minutes piled slowly one on top of the other until an hour passed, then dissolved and started the process all over again. All the while Simon's breathing remained ragged and uneven, from heavy labored breathing to breathing so light that Berry was afraid he wasn't breathing at all.

"What if he gets worse?" she asked Will, who had taken over the chore of bringing water from the spring. "He can't take much more of this."

"I wouldn't worry overly much. He's tough."

"You sound very sure."

"He ain't goin' to die. But you're goin' to worry yourself crazy a-thinkin' he is."

Berry thought Will might be right. Her bones ached. She had no appetite; and thoughts born of this lonely waiting began to drift through her mind. She thought lingeringly of Simon's words: *What's love? Foolish fancies, but then you're only a child. If a woman finds a decent man she should take him without expecting love to be part of the deal.* Then she thought of the words that had come boiling up out of his torment: *Berry . . . I love you. I love you.* He had shouted them as if to put up a barrier between himself and the agony of the whip. Silent and serious, he hid his loneliness behind the closed-in look that pulled all feeling out of his face.

"Poor, lonely little boy," she whispered over the lump in her throat. "You've got me now. I'll love you, make you laugh, make you feel good. We've been through too much together for me to lose you now."

She leaned down, intending to kiss him on the cheek, but he rolled his head so that her lips found his mouth instead. The gesture, which was meant to be a fleeting caress, became something entirely different. His hand found the back of her head and pulled her lips firmly to his. Berry gave a little gasp and drew back. His eyes were open but glazed and unseeing. As she watched, his eyelids fluttered and closed and his hand fell limply to the bed.

The waiting and the silence ran on, with Berry sinking deeper and deeper into her misery. She slumped forward and put her hands over her face, refusing the comfort of tears lest he should wake and see them.

The sounds of voices roused her. She looked up to see Rachel going out the door. She shook her head to clear it, got shakily to her feet, and followed Rachel. Two horses were trotting into the yard: Light, on Simon's stallion, and an Indian woman on a spotted pony.

Berry grabbed Rachel's arm. "She's an Indian!"

"She's Light's aunt."

"Rachel! I'll not have her shaking a rattle over Simon or . . . wrapping a snake skin around his neck! He needs a doctor, not some Indian witchcraft!"

"Shhh . . . Don't be rude!" Rachel started forward. Berry refused to release her arm.

"Rachel, please . . . I didn't know she'd be an *Indian!*"

"Berry, for crying out loud! Straighten up! She's all the help we've got. Light knows what he's doing." She shook off Berry's hand and went to meet the woman.

Berry had to admit that the woman who slid off the pony was an arresting figure. Her jet-black hair was worn in two braids that hung down over her breasts. She was a tall, handsome, full-bodied woman, dressed in a colorful long shirt and buckskin leggings. A red, beaded sash was belted tightly around her waist. Her strong features were curiously expressionless. It was the same mask that Light had worn last night while he listened to Will, Jeff, and Fain.

"We're grateful to you for coming," Rachel said slowly, spacing her words. She waited for some response, but the woman merely stared back at her. Rachel's face flooded with embarrassment. She looked around uncertainly, not knowing what to do next. Light led the horses away. The Indian woman picked up a twig basket that Light had been carrying and stood silently looking Rachel over and then Berry.

"Howdy, Nowatha." Will came from the shed. He was obviously pleased to see her. "How're ya doin'?"

"Why you say this to me, Will?"

"'Cause it riles ya, I guess. How's your daughter?"

"She big with papoose again, damn her."

Will laughed. "How many does that make?"

"Eight girls. Five live. She don't know how to make a boy," she said without amusement, then turned back to Rachel. "Where this man? Light say I come help."

Rachel led the way into the house. "He's been unconscious since about this time yesterday. This morning the fever struck."

Nowatha, oblivious to Berry, who stood protectively close to Simon at the head of the bunk, bent and lifted the oiled bandage from Simon's back. She studied the swollen lacerations, then leaned close and sniffed. She felt the lump at the base of his skull, then ran her hand down over his body. She rocked back on her heels and continued to study the deeply scored back.

It seemed to Berry that Nowatha was never going to speak. Then she uttered a short, grunting sound and looked directly at her. "Hurt bad."

"I know he's hurt bad," Berry retorted. "He needs a *doctor*."

"Me doctor. Me fix."

"What're you goin' to do?" Berry demanded. She

looked up to see Will standing behind Nowatha and laughing soundlessly. He reached for Berry's arm and urged her across the room and out the door. "I'm not leavin' him with *her!*" she protested. But he drew her around the corner of the house and pushed her down on the wash bench.

"Sit 'n' tell me 'bout where ya come from."

"You're just tryin' to keep me out of there. I can't sit here and gossip when Simon's in there with that ...witch doctor."

"Don't worry. She'll not boil a toad or smear him with chicken dung." His eyes mirrored his amusement.

"Be serious. Please!"

"You're just upset 'cause she could say more than 'ugh'!"

"I'm not! I thought she was Light's aunt from the other side of his family."

Will laughed. "Berry, girl, Simon's goin' to have a time with you. I wish I'd-a seen ya first! C'mon. I gotta set your mind to rest." He put his hand beneath her elbow and lifted her to her feet. "We'll watch and see that she don't scalp him."

"Will, you're a... pissant!" She flashed him a quick grin in spite of herself.

When they returned to the room they found Nowatha pulverizing some dried leaves, which she then added to a pan of steaming water. This was not the first ingredient to have gone into the pan, Berry knew, because already a pungent, spicy odor wafted across the room. Nowatha stirred the concoction, bent to sniff it, added more powdered leaves, and continued to stir, completely indifferent to her surroundings.

When she was satisfied with the brew, she lifted the pan from the flames and dropped a square of cloth from the pile on the table into the liquid. She turned her attention to her basket, selected more dried leaves, and crumbled them into a cup she'd taken from the shelf. She poured water from the teakettle into the cup, swirled it around, tasted it, and looked over at Will.

"Lift man, damn you. We pour this down."

Will obediently went to the bunk and lifted Simon into a half-sitting position. Nowatha forced his mouth open and poured the liquid down his throat. He spat and sputtered, but she doggedly persisted until the cup was empty.

Berry spent the next couple of hours sitting in a chair, her head resting against the wall, watching the Indian woman take the bandages from the brew in the pan and place them on Simon's back. She repeated the process over and over, all the while keeping cold wet cloths on his head and legs. She and Will poured cup after cup of liquid down his throat. Finally, Nowatha dried his naked body, laid one last bandage across his back, and left him alone.

"He better now."

"Are you sure?" Berry asked hopefully.

"I say it, damn you," Nowatha said coolly, as if she was unaccustomed to having her word questioned.

Evening came. Fain roasted a turkey over a fire that Israel built in the yard. After they ate, the men came, one at a time, to stand beside the bed and speak to Berry in low tones, then move on. Rachel took care of the evening chores and put Faith to bed. Nowatha came periodically to dampen the bandage on Simon's back. Berry sat beside the bed and watched the big man who meant everything to her. He seemed to be sleeping peacefully. There was a different rhythm to his breathing. Berry slipped to her knees, rested her cheek against Simon's hand, and went to sleep.

On the second morning Simon drifted up from the black, bottomless pit and saw a pale-faced girl with raven hair, curly and unruly, slouched in the chair by his bed. Her elbow was propped on her knee and her chin rested in her palm. Dazed green eyes were looking directly into his.

"You look tired, Berry."

Startled by the suddenness of his voice, Berry's head jerked away from her palm and she peered intently down at him. His lips were cracked and peeling, there were deep caverns under his cheekbones, and his cheeks and chin were rough with whiskers, but his eyes were clear.

"Simon! Darlin', are you awake?"

"I think so," he said weakly.

Berry touched his head, his cheeks, his arms, as if she was unable to believe that the fever was gone. "How do you feel?"

"Like I've been kicked by a mule. I'm weak, but my back doesn't hurt so much." He made a weak attempt to lift himself onto his elbow.

"Are you hungry?"

"Hungry? Lordy! I could eat a buffalo."

"I'll cook you one!" she laughed joyously.

"Ahhh ... that's what I wanted to hear. I want to hear you laugh every day for the rest of my life. I love you. I was so afraid I'd not get to tell you."

"And I love you." She fell to her knees beside the bed and kissed his chin, his cheeks, and his dry lips. "I've got lots to tell you, but it can wait. Darlin', I've got to tell everybody. We've all been so worried."

Berry ran to the door and called out happily, "He's awake. The fever's gone! He's goin' to be all right."

Nowatha came and lifted the bandage from Simon's back. She grunted with satisfaction and moved aside so that Berry could see. "I say I make well," she said coolly, with a proud lift of her brows.

"I don't believe it!" Berry exclaimed. "Oh, Simon! The cuts are closed and the swelling is down. You'll be all healed in no time at all."

"I make well more than that." Nowatha flicked her fingers at Simon's back indifferently. "You think me dumb Indian, damn you."

"No! I didn't think that...."

"When time come to drop papoose, send Light. I come and make water on you so you get boy." She lifted her head arrogantly, her proud body stiff with disdain.

Berry saw an instant flicker of amusement in the woman's obsidian-colored eyes. Her happy laughter rang through the room like a silver bell.

"You're teasing! Nowatha, what a treasure you are! Oh, thank you, thank you!" She threw her arms around the tall, domineering woman and hugged her fiercely.

"Ahhh... God the damn hell!" Nowatha disengaged herself from Berry's arms. "I go home now." She picked up her basket, gave Berry and Simon a steady look, then turned away.

"Isn't she wonderful?" Berry got down on her knees beside Simon's bed.

"Not as wonderful as you. Give me a kiss, sweetheart, then get me something to eat. I've got to get my strength back."

Berry kissed him, giggled, and leaned away from him so that she could look into his dark, love-filled eyes. Her own eyes glinted with mischief.

"You'd better eat a lot and get strong quick. I've got lots of lovin' saved up for you."

Epilogue

The story of the siege at the MacCartney homestead and Berry's heroic effort to save her lover from Linc Smith, the mad riverman, spread up and down the Mississippi and Missouri rivers like petals in the wind. The pioneers had a heroine, and on her wedding day they came to wish her well.

Silas and Biedy and three of their four boys arrived two days before the appointed day so that Biedy could help prepare the wedding feast. Jeff, Light, and Will followed soon after, with an antelope and a half-dozen turkeys. They had helped to pass the word to the settlers, and shortly after daybreak the local families began to arrive. The women came to the house to introduce themselves and to leave contributions to the wedding feast.

The men, under Fain's supervision, set up long tables in the yard. The women gathered wild flowers to make a bower for the couple to stand under during the ceremony. Ernest Wenst and his family arrived from Saint Louis, as did Della, the girl who had come to the homestead with her granny the night Faith was born. She rode in on horseback with her pa and little brother. Rachel made all her guests feel welcome.

The homestead buzzed with activity. Children played, running beneath the table, and were scolded by their mothers. The men gathered in front of the shed and drank whiskey from the keg placed conveniently on the wash bench. It was a time to get acquainted, exchange gossip, and argue politics.

Shortly before the ceremony was to begin, a blast from a riverboat was heard. A young boy came running to the homestead with the exciting news that Zebulon Pike had arrived for the wedding. The flamboyant Pike led a detail of six men up the trail from the river. He doffed his feathered hat, dipped into the whiskey barrel, and entered into the festivities.

Berry and Rachel came out of the house at straight-up noon. Berry made a picture that the assembled guests would long remember. She was attired in a beautiful white dress Simon had had made for her in Saint Louis and Ernest Wenst had delivered this morning. Her raven hair was piled atop her small head and entwined with white blooms from the dogwood tree. She wore soft kid slippers, and pinned to a white ribbon encircling her neck was a delicate gold brooch, Simon's gift to his bride.

She was unbelievably beautiful. Her whole being glowed with a happiness that seemed to surround her like an aura. Simon went forward to take her arm, and her green eyes glinted up at him, causing him to pause and to stare. Admiring grins crinkled the burly faces of his friends as they surrounded the couple, ushering them toward the bower.

For this most important event in his life Simon had dressed for the occasion in a white silk shirt and dark blue coat and breeches. Berry had never seen him dressed so elegantly, but that wasn't what drew her eyes to him again and again. It was the pure pleasure she saw written in every line of his face, in the smile on his lips, and in his eyes. The dark seriousness was gone. Happiness radiated from his dark eyes.

Silas performed the ceremony before a gathering of almost a half a hundred people, with only the wilderness sounds to break the silence. When it was over, the hushed crowed erupted in shouts of traditional well-wishing and advice as they surged around the bride and groom.

The dancing began as soon as the wedding feast was over. Isaac Cornick got out his fiddle and the clearing rang with music and merrymaking. Berry danced with Simon and then with those men who were able to dance after their numerous trips to the whiskey barrel. Simon danced with all the ladies but kept his eyes on the vision in the white dress who clogged and whirled and clapped her hands with obvious enjoyment.

It seemed like hours before the bride and groom were free of other partners. Simon caught her hand and ran with her into the woods. They ran between the trees, laughing, dodging, and shouting. Berry gathered her skirts in her hands and raced away from him. He pursued, and when they were deep in the woods he caught her from behind, wrapped his arms around her, lifted her up, and twirled her around. She shrieked with joyous laughter. It stopped only when she slid down his body and he turned her in his arms to cover her mouth with his.

The kiss was long and sweet and dedicated to the love they shared. He lifted his head and looked down at her, his face open, his eyes adoring.

"Everything about you is so beautiful. I love you so much."

She clung to him tightly. She felt safe, loved, and, for the first time in her life, wanted. "I wanted to love my husband," she said softly, with just a touch of happy tears in her voice. "Remember when I said that?"

"I remember." He kissed her with tender concern.

"I do love him. I love him so much I think I'll burst from it."

He smiled down at her, loving every expression that flitted across her face. "I also remember you saying you liked soft words."

"I did say that . . . and you'd better remember it for the next forty years, Simon Witcher!" Mischief glinted in her green eyes. She rose on tiptoes so that her lips could reach his ear. "And you know what else I like!"